Bailey Dunn
BAILEY DUNN & CO. DUET

A.M. MCCOY

COPYRIGHT

Copyright © 2022 by A.M. McCoy

All rights reserved.

No part of this book may be reproduced in any form or by any electronic or mechanical means, including information storage and retrieval systems, without written permission from the author, except for the use of brief quotations in a book review.

This is a work of fiction. The names, characters, incidents, and places are products of the author's imagination and are not to be construed as real except where noted and authorized. Any resemblance to persons, living or dead, or actual events are entirely coincidental. Any trademarks, service marks, product names, or names featured are assumed to be the property of their respective owners and are used only for reference. There is no implied endorsement if any of these terms are used.

The author acknowledges the trademarked status and trademark owners of various products referenced in this work, which have been used without permission. The publication/use of these trademarks is not authorized, associated with, or sponsored by the trademark owners.

This book is intended for mature audiences.

Contents

1. Chapter 1 — 1
2. Chapter 1- Bailey — 2
3. Chapter 2- Finn — 10
4. Chapter 3- Bailey — 12
5. Chapter 4- Finn — 15
6. Chapter 5- Bailey — 24
7. Chapter 6- Walker — 28
8. Chapter 7- Bailey — 35
9. Chapter 8 –Finn — 38
10. Chapter 9- Bailey — 44
11. Chapter 10 – Walker — 56
12. Chapter 11- Finn — 63
13. Chapter 12 – Bailey — 69
14. Chapter 13- Walker — 82
15. Chapter 14- Bailey — 92
16. Chapter 15- Finn — 97
17. Chapter 16- Bailey — 106

18. Chapter 17- Walker 119
19. Chapter 18- Bailey 136
20. Chapter 19- Finn 155
21. Chapter 20- Bailey 168
22. Chapter 21- Walker 192
23. Chapter 22– Bailey 202
24. Chapter 23- Finn 218
25. Chapter 24- Bailey 231
26. Chapter 25- Walker 253
27. Chapter 26- Bailey 257
28. Chapter 27- Walker 268
29. Chapter 28- Bailey 275
30. Chapter 29- Finn 284
31. Chapter 30- Walker 297
32. Epilogue – Bailey 304

To my amazing husband, for supporting my dreams and jumping into this world headfirst with me.

Chapter 1 – Bailey

Mayfield, Montana, was everything I thought it would be. It was small, rustic, and charming. Every single person I came in contact with so far had been polite and kind, which was a far cry from my last home in Nevada. Living right outside of Las Vegas made me grow up way faster than I should have, and I knew on the eve of my twenty-sixth birthday that I had overstayed my welcome in Sin City.

Mostly it was because my apartment building had burned to the ground that day, leaving me few other options. The official report claimed it was faulty wiring and my neighbors and I weren't shocked, considering the place should have been condemned in the eighties, but affordable housing was in low supply there, so we'd had to make do.

The fire had cost me everything. Other than a small bag of clothing I had with me from staying at a friend's house that night, I had nothing left: no pictures, keepsakes, or anything to remind me of the better years of my childhood. I essentially had a forced clean slate and instead of wallowing in what I'd lost, I took the chance to gain from it. Thankfully, I'd listened to my mom and had renter's insurance or I would have been screwed.

That was a year ago now; I moved in with my mom in California last year and saved every penny I made for my fresh start. My mom begged me not to move here—she was a hippie and loved old Hollywood to her core and wanted me to stay with her there—but it was just like Las Vegas for me. It was busy and congested and I wanted to wake up every day and taste fresh air, not the stale cigarettes of my downstairs neighbor who chain-smoked on his balcony directly below mine.

After living with my mom for a month, I opened an old atlas she had in her office, laid it out on the wall, closed my eyes, and literally threw a dart at it. Lo and behold, Mayfield, Montana, was where it had landed, so it was where I landed.

Finding an apartment and commercial space for a shop in a town I had never stepped foot into was surprisingly easier than I had thought it would be. I hired a realtor and told her what I was looking for and what I could afford, and within a week, she had a page of listings in my email and I essentially had my fresh start.

Two days ago, I arrived in town for the first time and moved into my apartment right away. It was a cute little carriage house off the side of a larger ranch on the outskirts of town. The older couple that owned the house had renovated it for the wife's mother in the nineties when she lived with them, and she had passed away a couple of years ago so they had finally gotten around to renting it. It was a third of what I paid for a studio apartment in Vegas, and it was a million times nicer.

The kitchen was painted a sunny yellow, and it had a cozy little reading nook in the living room. I instantly felt at peace walking in and knew I was home, which helped settled the nerves in my gut that had been fluttering since leaving Hollywood.

I spent two days setting up my new home, and after many trips back and forth to the department store, I had almost everything I needed to be comfortable. I was having a couch and a new bed delivered next week, but for now, I was sleeping on an air mattress in the living room.

Today, I was going to my new shop space. It was the first time I was getting to see it in person. The excitement had kept me up all night as I watched the clock, waiting for dawn to come. The owner of the building on Main Street had been renovating it and asked what color scheme I was thinking of using for décor and managed to paint the walls to match.

You didn't find that kindness in cities very often. But apparently, it was plentiful in Mayfield.

I parked my car on Main Street, right outside of my new space, and let my eyes travel around the surroundings as I stepped up onto the sidewalk. There was a florist next door with beautiful arraignments in the storefront and a diner across the street. A bank and a hardware store sat down the way a bit, and a few other little shops filled in the gaps along the quaint avenue.

My new front door glowed in the sunrise as I slid my shiny new key in and turned. I pushed the bright, freshly painted glass door open and stepped into my space with a deep breath of excitement.

It was magical!

The mahogany hardwood floors shined with a fresh coat of stain, and the walls were painted a soft gray with white trim. The space already had an industrial look to it, with black steel fixtures and exposed brick, and it matched the theme of my shop perfectly.

Bailey Dunn & Co. had been a dream of mine since I graduated high school, and to be standing here in the middle of it turned into reality was so surreal, I almost wanted to pinch myself to make sure I wasn't dreaming. When the realtor had asked me what I was planning on using the commercial space for, I knew she was skeptical, but it would just make it sweeter when I succeeded here and made a name for myself.

I was a twenty-seven-year-old female and the owner of a brand-new barber shop in a small western Montana town. I had loved the art of barbering after learning from my dad, who had been one in the Navy when he was younger before honing his craft as he got older and passing it all down to me.

Mayfield didn't have a barber shop and surprisingly, the closest one was two towns over, leaving most residents with a thirty-minute drive one way for a haircut and shave not given inside a beauty salon. I was hoping to tap into that clientele. Barbering had lost its art a few decades ago, but in the last few years, it was coming back and now was a very elite business, even for a young female. I had worked at a distinguished shop in Vegas and another one in Hollywood last year, and I learned so much every single day. I knew I was ready to branch out on my own.

My new space had enough room for another three or four barbers and I was hoping to add some to the shop eventually and make it a bustling business, but for now, it was just me.

The brand-new equipment I bought for the multiple stations was delivered yesterday, and it all sat wrapped up in the center of the space. My hands itched to unwrap the new chairs and set up the shop, to make it look worthy of the trust I was putting into this new future.

With a grin, I walked up to the huge front windows and started tearing off the brown paper that covered the panes during renovations. Beautiful Montana sunshine brightly lit up the space with each inch of glass revealed. As I pulled the paper down, a few people walking by waved and tipped their hats to me in greeting, warming that spot in my soul that had always felt so lonely in the busy city where no one spoke to strangers on the street.

The warmth of the day was already burning off the morning dew, so I rolled up my shorts to keep them in place and got to work. The bandana I wore to keep my hair off my face hardly worked, thanks to my obnoxious mess of blonde curls, but it was better than nothing.

I worked right through the morning, putting away tools and products that had been delivered while simultaneously trying to plan the layout for the stations. Before I knew it, lunch had come and gone, and I was ravenous.

I stopped to check my appearance in one of the new mirrors and shook my head when I saw how much dirt and grime covered my face and arms from my work. I tried to wash up in the hair sink as best as I could, but I knew it was mostly a lost cause. I was too hungry to let the smudges on my face keep me from getting some food, though, so I walked across the street to the cute little diner as I was.

Logically, I knew it was going to happen, the theatrical stares and the way conversations paused when the new girl walked into the small-town diner, a stranger amongst regulars. It was true small-town living at its best, but it still made me a bit uneasy. I wasn't good at being the center of attention.

Nonetheless, I smiled at everyone as I passed by on my way to the counter and took a seat. I wanted to seem approachable and friendly as a new business owner, so I was going to need to keep appearances polite and welcoming. The waitress was a middle-aged woman with a kind smile, and she walked over right away with a tall glass of water and a menu.

"Good afternoon. My name's Thea." She set both down in front of me, and I smiled and nodded.

"Nice to meet you, Thea. I'm Bailey." I put my hand out to shake and she took it happily.

"You just moved here, right?"

I smirked; it took no time at all to spot the new girl. "Yes, I did. I got in a couple of days ago. I'm opening a shop up across the street, so that's why I look so haggard. I do apologize and hope I don't scare off your customers."

She chuckled and leaned her hip against the counter. "Honey, if they don't go running when Old Man Al comes in for dinner every night smelling like a porta-john, they won't run when a pretty thing like you comes in with a bit of dirt on her face."

"Old Man Al, huh?" I asked with a quirk of my lips.

She chuckled and nodded her head. "Where you from?"

"All over really. Vegas and Hollywood most recently."

"Vegas? What the heck would bring you from Vegas to Mayfield?" she asked as she grabbed a coffee pot and filled a cup for a man a couple of seats down. He nodded his head to me as I watched and I smiled back.

Everyone was so damn polite. People didn't even look at each other in Vegas.

"The truth?" I asked when she came back over as I leaned back on my stool.

"Nothing less." She raised an eyebrow at me, as if she dared me to lie.

"I threw a dart at a map on the wall and it landed here. It was fate, if you ask me, because there were no barber shops here and that's what I do. So I packed up and moved here."

"Just like that, huh?" she asked, shaking her head and leaning her hip back on the counter. "I never would have pegged you for a barber just from looking at you."

"Why not?" I asked, genuinely curious about what it looked like I should do for a living.

"Pretty little blonde thing no bigger than a minute like yourself would fit in better at the beauty salon maybe. The only barbers we've had around here for decades have been crotchety old men." She shrugged and smirked. "I guess it's my own idea of what a barber should look like that's a bit warped."

"Maybe it's time you all had a change of pace around here then," I said, leaning forward on my elbows, looking around. There were so many cowboy hats and weathered stares in the place, I had doubts about me fitting in around here, but I wouldn't let any of them know that or they would doubt me too.

She nodded her head and smiled at me with wise eyes, "I think you're just what this little town needs, Bailey. I can't wait to see what you do here."

I beamed a full smile at her and opened the menu as happiness coursed through me at the bit of confidence she'd boosted me with from her warm welcome to town. She went about the diner, filling coffee mugs and clearing plates. It wasn't overly busy, given that the lunch rush had passed already, but there was still quite a bit of traffic in and out.

Google told me it was the only eatery besides a couple of pizza joints and a bowling alley, so that made sense.

I ordered a club sandwich and fries and waited patiently for my meal as I rested my tired muscles.

The bell on the front door rang as it opened, and I watched from the corner of my eye as a man walked in, came up to the counter a few places down from me, and took a seat. I looked over at him and smiled hello as he did a double take at me, no doubt noticing I was new.

He was around my age, maybe early thirties, and had dirty blond hair that hung a bit long over his ears and bright eyes. He wore a T-shirt with grease stains on it and a pair of Dickie work pants and boots.

Thea came over with my sandwich and set it down in front of me with a wink as she walked over to him, and I listened to their banter.

"You here for your usual, Clay?" she asked him.

I dunked a fry in some ketchup and waited to hear his response, but he didn't say anything. I glanced over at him and was surprised to see him staring at me and not paying attention to Thea.

When our eyes met, he quickly whipped back to the waitress, her hands on her hips and an unimpressed look on her face from catching him staring.

"Uh, yeah, sorry. Yes, please," he stammered, and I tilted my head down and let my hair cover my face and the laugh that pulled at my lips.

I chanced a glance at Thea from my seat and she was still glaring at him before looking over at me again. I tried to look innocent and not at all nosey.

"You leave her to her meal and don't bother her, Clay," she warned as she walked away, and it didn't sound like a request. It was more direct than that.

I looked over again, now that she had brought me into the conversation, and the man was staring back with a sheepish schoolboy look on his face at being chided by the woman.

I gave him a small smirk and took a drink of my water, trying to focus on the meal that I had been starved for just a moment ago.

"Uh—" he stammered, drawing my attention again as he leaned over one of the two stools between us. "I'm Clay." He held his hand out, and I wiped mine on my napkin and then leaned over to shake it.

It was warm and rough with permanent grease stains in the cracks, but it wasn't at all a turn-off for me. He also wasn't my normal type. I was usually more attracted to men who were burly, tall, dark, and handsome.

"Bailey," I said in response as he shook my hand and held on to it a second longer than polite. When he let go, I leaned back over onto my stool.

I had no idea how to flirt with small-town boys. The guys that I had given any attention to back home were rough and tough assholes, for lack of a better word, and there was hardly ever any flirting involved as they usually made their intent known from the start.

"I've never seen you around here before, and I haven't heard any of the small-town buzz about a newbie being around yet," he said, pulling my attention back to him.

He had an easy smile with a bit of a bad-boy smirk mixed in.

I nodded. "I just moved here. I guess the small-town buzz is a bit behind."

"I guess so," he said as his eyes traveled down my bare arms and back up to my face. "You're quite the mess. You doing some gardening or something?"

I turned my arm over and saw the streaks of dirt up it that I missed when I'd cleaned up and shrugged. "No, unpacking and moving furniture around." I nodded my head to the side towards the street. "I'm opening up a shop across the street. I'm just taking a lunch break before getting back to it."

He looked to the open storefront and then back to me as he raised his eyebrows. "What kind of shop?"

"Barbershop."

I watched as the shock lit his eyes up the same way it had Thea's when I said it.

"Hmm," he replied as his food was delivered by a younger waitress. She was pretty, with dark-brown hair and eyes, and she lingered as she laid his food down on the counter. Clay only looked up at her for a second before nodding his head and looking back over at me. She looked at me and I smiled at her kindly, but she didn't return it as she walked away, leaving an awkward silence in her wake.

"I think you hurt her feelings," I guessed as I looked at him from the corner of my eye and took a bite of my sandwich.

"Who?" he asked as he took a bite of his meal.

I chuckled and scoffed at him, "The girl who just brought your food."

He looked at me and then back the way the girl had gone. "Who, Julie?" I nodded in accord to him. "Oh, she's just a girl from around here."

I raised my eyebrows at him but just went back to my meal and shook my head.

"Can you blame me?" he asked after a minute.

"For?"

"Not noticing her when I was captivated by you."

I choked on a fry, coughing a few times gracelessly.

He had the decency to look apologetic as I caught my breath. "Too much?" he asked while I took a drink and regained my composure.

"Perhaps," I agreed and bobbed my head at his absurdity.

I was just about done with my sandwich and felt the need to move on back to my own space and away from Clay's penetrating stare, so I took some cash out of my pocket and grabbed Thea's attention.

She knew exactly what was happening and was quick to come over with a box and my check. I paid her and thanked her graciously for her hospitality.

"Have a good day," I said to Clay as I stood up and walked out the front door before practically running across the street to my shop. I felt his eyes on me the whole way.

I let the mountain of work waiting for me distract me from the entire bizarre interaction as I dove back in. I wanted to open as soon as possible and start building my business, so I put all of my energy into that and none into the bachelor options of the small town.

It was dark when I finally forced myself to lock up and leave for the night. As I turned off the lights and locked the door behind me, I stood on the street for a couple of seconds and admired the storefront in awe.

It was all mine. And tomorrow, my sign would be hung over the front door and it would be real.

I screeched with joy and tried to click my heels together as I skipped to my car. I, of course, failed miserably and nearly face-planted, but I was too elated to be embarrassed.

It was all coming together.

Chapter 2 – Finn

I sat in my cruiser, parked on the side of Main Street, and ate my cold sandwich as I read through my reports. I was dragging ass and my shift had just begun. Luckily, in a few hours, I could head on out of town and patrol the county, which had more going for it in terms of mischief and riffraff.

Because good old Mayfield was calm and quiet on this late summer night, leaving me utterly bored.

A flash of gold caught my eye up the street, and I looked up the deserted lane. A woman walked out of a storefront and stood back, looking back up at the front of the building, smiling madly. She was petite in height but had curves for miles under her T-shirt and cutoffs. She had a red bandana holding back a mass of blonde curls, and dirt streaked every inch of her honeyed skin.

She turned and practically skipped down the sidewalk, stopping to jump in the air and click her heels together. The move was uncoordinated and clumsy, nearly making her hit the deck before she caught herself on a lamppost.

She tilted her head back and laughed up at the stars as she spun around a few times with her arms out wide before opening the door of an SUV, getting in, and driving off.

I had never seen a more striking woman in my life. And I had no clue who she was.

It was a very foreign concept for me because not only had I lived in Mayfield my entire life, but I was also a county deputy and a coach for the high school varsity football team.

I knew every single person in town from one of those three roles, but I still didn't know her.

I put my sandwich to the side and stepped out of my cruiser, walking across the street and down the sidewalk she had just danced on.

When I got to the storefront she walked out of, I looked in the window. A couple of barber chairs sat in the middle of the floor with other hair-cutting equipment scattered across the space.

Tom Hanson owned this building, and I knew it had recently been vacant and that he was renovating it, but I hadn't realized he had rented it out already.

No sign hung on the front of the building yet and nothing I could see inside told me anything more about the mysterious woman, but I felt myself smirk as I thought about how she danced and skipped in joy down the sidewalk.

I was going to have to see what I could find out about her as soon as possible. Any man within twenty miles would be chasing after her when word got out about how beautiful the new girl in town was. I wanted to make sure I was at the front of that race.

Chapter 3 – Bailey

I pulled on the heavy desk, begging it to move more than an inch at a time, but to my dismay, it barely budged.

"Oh, come on!" I huffed and walked to the other side, shoving my hip into it. All that I achieved was sliding my feet across the floor as the desk stayed still. "You pain in the ass."

"Hello?" The deep timber came from a voice that called from the open doorway.

I looked up from my unflattering position crouched between the desk and the wall and squeaked in embarrassment from being caught swearing and grunting.

I stood up, catching my toe on the foot of the desk, and lurched forward, only catching myself milliseconds before I crashed into the floor.

"Hi." I gasped as I pushed my hair back out of my face for the millionth time this afternoon and looked at my visitor.

A man stood in the doorway with the edges of a smirk on his face as he watched me make a fool of myself. He was hands down the sexiest man on the planet. He was tall—well over six feet—his chest was wide, and his arms were the size of my thighs. Up one of those arms were intricate black and gray tattoos. He had dark-brown hair and a short beard with light-brown eyes that glowed against his tanned face. To put the cherry on top of the orgasmic ice cream sundae standing in front of me . . . he was wearing a cop uniform.

And he was wearing it damn well.

"You alright?" he asked, making my eyes snap back up to his from where they sat pinpointed on the gun belt that hung deliciously off his narrow hips.

"Uh-huh." I hummed and nodded my head quickly, not trusting myself to not drool if I opened my mouth to let more words out.

He smirked again, half of his mouth turning up. "I heard you struggling from the street and thought maybe I could give you a hand." He gestured to the desk at my hip.

"I was that loud, huh?" I asked, finally able to control my tone and breathing. I pushed a curl out of my face again and wiped my hands on my shirt nervously.

"Well, I may or may not have been looking in the window at the same time."

"Ah," I said and stepped to the side. "Thank you, but it's okay. I can get it." I nodded towards the desk as I grabbed my water and took a drink.

He walked farther into my shop, suddenly making the space feel much smaller than it had before. "I'll tell you what," he started. "I can help you now and move it where you need it, or I can come back in an hour or two and help you move it to where you need it from the few inches farther you'll have gotten it in the time that I'm gone."

His eyes were warm and affectionate as he smiled at me fully, crossing his arms across his giant chest.

I blushed and bowed my head in defeat. "Well, when you put it that way." I looked back up at him. "Thank you." I walked over to the side of the desk I had been shoving from originally, ready to help. He stepped forward with his long legs, crossing the space quickly, and put his hand on my arm, stopping me.

"I can handle it," he said and winked down at me as he slid himself between me and the offensive piece of wood and metal. "Where are we going with it?" he asked as he laid his big hands on the edge and leaned forward.

My brain fried looking at the man. Every single thing he did was sexy.

"Uh," I mumbled, rubbing my forehead with my hand and then pointing over by the door. "Over there, it's a reception desk."

He pushed the desk across the floor effortlessly to where I said and watched for me to tell him when to stop with it, and then he stood up.

"You made that look way too easy." I sighed, jealous of his impressive strength. "It took three delivery guys to get it off the truck this morning."

He chuckled and adjusted his gun belt, once again drawing my eyes down to that area of him, before he shrugged and said, "All in a day's work."

I got closer to him and held my hand out. "I bet. I'm Bailey."

He took my hand in his, and my skin sizzled where his rough callouses rubbed against my soft palm as he shook it strongly.

"Finn Camden," he offered. Being this close to him, I had to keep my head leaning way back to look into his eyes directly. "Is this your shop?" he asked, reluctantly letting go of my hand and looking around. My brand-new sign leaned against the wall, waiting to be hung on the front of the building in the afternoon, and it caught his eye. "Bailey Dunn & Co.," he read and looked over at me with his eyebrow raised.

"Yeah, I'm hoping to open in the next few days."

"Barbering?" he asked as he looked around more.

"Uh-huh," I said, watching him pass judgement on my space. For some reason, standing there as he innocently looked at the shop made me feel vulnerable and intimidated.

"I wouldn't have taken you for a barber," he said, turning back and watching me closely after letting his eyes travel from my toes to my curls.

A flush followed his eyes up my body, as if he had physically touched me.

"You're not the first one to say that since I got here," I answered, holding his gaze in challenge of his appraisal of me.

"I guess I'll have to stop in when you open and see what you've got," he said as he reached up to rub his hand along the beard on his chin, and then he winked at me.

"I'll be happy to show you whenever you want, on the house for your help with the desk," I replied. I was being way bolder than I normally would be, and his pupils dilated and his nostrils flared as he took in a deep breath.

The radio on his shoulder chose that moment to break the tension between us, as someone on the other end squawked out terms I didn't understand. He waited until it went silent before responding to it, all while keeping his eyes on me.

"49-02 responding."

With that, he took a few steps back towards the door before once again looking around the shop and smiling. "Until next time, Bailey Dunn."

"Can't wait, Finn Camden," I replied as he turned and walked out the front door and then down the sidewalk towards his police cruiser parked down the street.

When he was out of sight, I collapsed into one of the barber chairs and fanned myself.

"Holy crap," I muttered. I wasn't sure how I stood on my own two feet while also talking through the entire interaction because now that he was gone and I could breathe freely again, I was nothing more than a puddle on the floor.

Chapter 4 – Finn

Four days ago, I had lucked my way into the presence of the sunshine that was Bailey Dunn. I had been walking by her shop for no less than the tenth time since seeing her the night before on the sidewalk. As I passed her door that last time, I heard her struggling inside and I walked in, throwing myself into offering her my assistance.

While I may have appeared chivalrous and helpful, my intentions had been far less pure. I wanted to meet her, talk to her, see the color of her eyes, and hear the laugh in her voice.

She was all I had thought about since then too. She'd been crouched down when I walked in and looked up at me through her big green doe eyes, and carnal thoughts instantly flashed through my brain. I imagined her looking up at me on her knees like that for far more sensual reasons, and I had nearly made a fool of myself in front of her because of it.

She was even more gorgeous up close than I realized the night before from a distance. She had freckles across her nose and cheeks and her lips were lush and pillowy and the color of burgundy wine. Dark lashes framed those sage-green eyes that made me fall into a trance if I dared to look into them for too long.

I had been right about her body though. She had curves in all the right places. She was even more divine than I'd thought because when I was in her space, I was in her scent too.

And damn it if she didn't smell like heaven and sin wrapped in one.

She opened up her shop two days ago and from the chatter I overheard around town, she had a steady stream of men waiting in line out her front door since the morning that she flipped the sign to open. I'd be lying if I didn't admit to seeing more than one good old boy suddenly sporting a trendy and dapper new hairstyle with a bit more of a pep in his step too.

Turned out the men of Mayfield enjoyed the way she made them feel and look.

I parked my truck on Main Street, outside of the diner, and looked over through the big windows in the front of her shop. I could see her working her hands on some lucky cuss's hair as she chatted with him. Everything inside of me wanted to walk over and see her, talk to her, and see her beautiful smile, even for just a few minutes, but I was trying to exercise restraint to prove to myself that I wasn't some junkie trying to get his fix. So I stayed on the opposite side of the street.

I got off of work earlier and went home to shower because I was due to be at the football field in a while to run practice, but I was planning on getting a bite to eat while I watched Bailey from afar before I went.

Dinner and show, if you will.

I sat down at the counter, facing the street, and the matriarch of the diner herself walked over to me and handed me a menu.

"Evening, Ms. Thea," I said in greeting, flashing a smile at her.

"Good evening, honey. You off to practice tonight?" She nodded to my shirt with the team logo on the chest as she set a coffee cup down in front of me and filled it up.

"Yes, ma'am," I said, taking a sip of the hot caffeine. "Busy tonight, huh?" I asked, noticing how every booth was filled and most of the seats at the counter were taken.

She looked around and chuckled and tsked at me. "Must be something in the air this evening has got everyone feeling social," she joked, but she looked over her shoulder and across the street to Bailey's shop as she said it.

She turned back to me and caught me still gazing out the window behind her. "You could stand to give Ms. Bailey a visit yourself, boy," she said as she reached up and pushed my shaggy hair off my forehead.

I shrugged her off and gave her a pointed look. I was a pretty intimidating man, from my size and my tattoos to my occupation, and most people chose to keep a bit of distance from me, but not Thea. She had been friends with my mama for decades and thought that gave her the right to always treat me like the six-year-old boy who needed to be paid a visit from a switch in the front yard and have a licked thumb wiped across my face at any given time.

"Actually I think you should pay Ms. Bailey a visit regardless if it's to get your hair cut or not," she said, lowering her voice so the others didn't hear.

"Why is that?" I asked, leaning forward on my elbows.

She looked me square in the eye. "I think the attention she's gotten the last few days has been a bit overwhelming and not all good," she replied with a seriousness to her tone. "Might ease her mind a bit knowing a good man or *two* is watching out for her."

"What happened?" I interrogated her as she poked the protector inside of me, putting me on alert.

She looked around again and bent forward, resting her elbows on the counter. "Mikey was over there this morning waiting on a cut. He came back here afterward pretty upset. He wouldn't say exactly what happened, but I'm thinking someone stepped out of line with her."

Mikey was Thea's nephew and a good kid. He had Down syndrome and sometimes wasn't able to communicate the way he wanted to and that flustered him, so he would give up without trying every so often.

I nodded to her, making my mind up that after my meal, I'd go over there and talk to her about it. My selfish interests aside, I wanted to make sure she wasn't being hassled or harassed.

When Thea stepped away, I saw Clay Mathews sitting across the counter from me, looking out of the window and across the street like I had been. He had paid a visit to Bailey; his hair and shave were fresh, and it made him look decent. For some reason, knowing he had had the joy of having her hands on him made me green with envy.

"Looking sharp, Clay," I said. The asshole in me just loved to mock him. We went to school together and he had been the worst kind of bully. I guessed that added to my discontent about Bailey doing his hair.

He turned around and looked at me, wondering what my game was before nodding his head at me in response. Thea walked back over and watched the exchange.

"She's quite talented," she added. "I have to admit, I couldn't imagine her as a barber when she first told me, but apparently, looks can be deceiving. She has made some of the roughest-looking men look presentable." She winked at me and then looked over at Clay. "And that's no easy deed."

"Doesn't hurt that she's the most beautiful girl in the county either," Clay said with a lewd grin, and a couple of his friends down the counter chuckled and nodded in agreement.

"I told you to leave her be, Clay. The last thing that girl needs is to get mixed up with the likes of you," Thea chided as she poured more coffee into his cup.

"What's so wrong with me?" he asked as he sat up straight and pulled his shoulders back.

She just raised her eyebrows and pursed her lips.

He was a fucking creep, that was what. But I decided to keep my mouth shut and drink my coffee.

"I'm taking her out on a date next week," he said to his buddies, and my fingers tightened around my mug as I looked over at him.

He was leering and making innuendos about what kind of date they were going on, and I was getting ready to stand up and walk the fuck out.

The alternative was to smash my fist into his ugly face for talking disrespectfully about her.

As I was about to tell Thea I'd take my meal to go, a mess of blonde curls walked in the front door of the diner and I stopped cold.

Bailey looked around when she walked in, saw all the booths full, and headed towards the counter. She spotted Clay and her steps faltered before she stopped walking altogether. His back was to her so he hadn't seen her yet, and she looked like she was going to turn around and walk back out.

Then, as if she felt me staring, she looked to her left and locked eyes with me where I sat. I raised an eyebrow at her and looked from her to Clay and back.

She bit her bottom lip, and I thought perhaps there was a bit of fear on her face. Clay saw her out of his peripheral and turned towards her, pulling her attention to him as she realized she'd been spotted.

"Hey, B." B? Fucking hell. "Come on over and have a seat," he said as he nudged one of his friends over, opening up a seat between them.

Bailey stood still for a second and then started moving again, but not towards Clay.

She headed toward me and slid onto the stool next to me with a small smile on her face.

"Maybe another time, Clay," she said as she grabbed the menu from the counter and buried her face in it like it was the most interesting thing in the world.

He looked at me with a snide glare for a second and then put a smile on his face. "Sure, no problem." But I knew he meant anything but.

And so did Bailey.

She took a deep breath and flexed her fingers behind the menu.

"Sorry," she said softly, not looking up.

I set my coffee cup down and turned towards her on my stool until my knees brushed against her leg, waiting for her to look up at me.

"For what?"

"That whole awkwardness and assuming you'd be okay with me sitting by you. I can move down to another seat if you're waiting for someone."

"Don't ever apologize for sitting by me. And I assure you, there's no one for me to wait for," I added, plainly telling her I wasn't involved with anyone.

"Oh," she said, her big green eyes staring back at me intently.

"You want to tell me about that?" I asked, tipping my head across the counter toward Clay, who I could see, out of the corner of my eye, was watching us closely.

She took a trembling breath and looked back down at her menu. "Not particularly." And then, after a second, she added, "Not here and now, at least." She looked up from under her lashes and saw Clay staring at her, and a flush crept up to the apples of her cheeks.

"Then after we eat." I settled it and turned back toward the counter.

She glanced up at me again and sat a bit taller on her stool, like she felt a little more confident in her situation now.

Good.

Thea came over and set a cup of hot tea in front of her and took her order. I didn't miss the affectionate smile Thea gave her and then the pointed glance at me before she walked away.

Man, that woman loved to meddle. Silence fell upon us as Bailey played with the spoon from her tea.

"You look nice," I said after a while. She was wearing a sunflower-yellow sundress with little black flowers on it and a pair of wedge sandals. Her hair was pulled into an updo, but a few errant curls broke free at her temples and neck.

She looked up at me and her lips parted for a second. "Me?" she asked.

I chuckled and turned toward her more, "Well, I wasn't talking about Old Man Al down past you," I said and nodded toward the half-asleep farmer a few seats down.

She giggled, covered her mouth, and elbowed me lightly to reprimand me.

"Thank you," she said and gave me a look over. I noticed how she lingered on the tattoos on my arm before snapping back up to my eyes. "So do you."

Thea set down our meals and winked at us before taking off to help someone else.

Clay got up from where he sat and tossed some cash down on the counter, paying for his meal before nodding to Bailey and saying, "See you later B."

She didn't say anything back to him, just nodded her head once. I noticed how multiple other people turned to look from Clay to her and back, wondering what was going on between them considering she was sitting next to me.

It wasn't like the whole town didn't know I had a shit-ass reputation where women were concerned.

It probably looked like she'd traded one predator for another to all of them.

"Be careful with him," I said and watched as her brows knitted in the center.

"What do you mean?"

"Your date. You need to be smart about spending time with him. He doesn't have the best history of treating women right."

"Date?" She wiped her mouth aggressively with her napkin and turned to face me. This time, her bare knees brushed my thigh, and I let my eyes wander down to that bare skin before bringing them back to hers. They were glowing with an intensity that surprised me.

"I'm not going on a date with Clay." She shook her head madly and her curls bounced around her face like they were adding emphasis to her mood.

"He told the whole diner you were," I replied, trying to gauge her reaction.

Red crawled up her neck and cheeks as she looked around the diner and caught more than a few glances, but I realized too late that it wasn't a blush coloring her skin.

I watched as an array of emotions crossed Bailey's face, from anger to frustration and then to what looked like hurt. She looked down at her hands in her lap and turned back around, but something caught my attention.

"Hey," I said, but she refused to look back up at me as she pushed her salad away half-eaten. "Bailey," I said again with more authority, and while she paused, she still looked away. I put my fingers under her chin and turned her head to face me. Surprise filled her eyes, but it didn't hide the unshed tears in them. "Are you done with your salad?" I asked, letting go of her chin.

"Yes," she answered softly.

"Then let's go."

She watched with uncertainty as I stood up from my stool and pulled out money, laying it down on the counter. "For hers too," I said to Thea as she came over and grabbed it.

Bailey started to protest but I just took her small hand in mine and pulled her to her feet and then walked out of the restaurant with our hands still joined.

That should send a message to everyone.

I was laying my claim.

That same electricity that burned the other day with her touch came back even more intense. She didn't protest, instead lacing her fingers through mine, anchoring herself to me as I moved us across the street to where her car was parked outside of her shop.

I didn't tell her how I knew which one was hers, and she didn't ask.

I kept her hand in mine as I turned on the sidewalk and faced her. "You can either get in your car and go home and relax for the rest of the night—which you've earned after how this town has run you ragged the last few days—or we can go to your shop and talk about what Clay or anyone else has done to upset you and I can take care of it for you."

Her chest rose and fell deeply as she contemplated her answer, but she kept those gorgeous green eyes locked on mine. "Why would you want to take care of anything for me? You don't even know me."

I smiled at her and looked off to the side, scratching my beard. "Perhaps I'm trying to change that." I ran my thumb back and forth over her knuckles as I said it to show her I was serious, even if I made it sound like I wasn't.

"Oh. Okay," she whispered, turning back toward her shop, and I followed after.

I chuckled and she looked up at me from under those dark lashes again, and it did things to me deep inside of my soul.

She unlocked the door and we walked into the quiet space. She flipped the switch and a soft light glowed overhead. She had put curtains up over the giant windows and they were closed now, leaving us completely alone.

She sighed and lifted herself onto the counter next to a washing station and swung her feet back and forth. I tried hard not to get distracted by the way her dress slid up and exposed more of her smooth thighs to my eyes with the motion, but it was hard.

"Tell me what happened with Clay," I said, sitting down in her barber chair and turning it to face her.

She looked to the ceiling and then reached back and undid the clip holding her curls up, letting them tumble down around her face. I doubted she meant to do anything by letting them fall. However, I soon found it hard to breathe from just watching her as she ran her fingers through the roots of her hair, massaging her scalp.

"I met him the first day I was here at the diner, and he threw a few over-the-top pick-up lines at me that I dodged hard. Then, he came in here this morning and kept it up, telling me things like I owed it to myself to go out with him because he could show me what it's like to be with a country man." She rolled her eyes. "I politely told him I wasn't interested and gave him a whole list of reasons why, but he just kept going."

She shook her head and clenched her jaw. "He kept reaching out and touching me like it was his right to do so. I finally told him I was going to have to ask him to leave if he touched me again, and I swear, he acted like I was just playing hard to get because it just spurred him on harder. So I finished his cut and sent him out the door. I only had one other customer in here at the time, but I think it made him upset." She smiled sadly, thinking back to Mikey. "He was so sweet and nice; he said his name was Mikey."

My jaw ticked from how hard I was clenching my teeth while listening to her. I wanted so badly to go down to JJ's bar, where Clay would be holed up for the rest of the evening, and break every bone in his face.

"How did he touch you?" I asked and leaned forward with my elbows on my knees, leveling her with a stare.

She tried to shrug it off. "Just stupid, little things, nothing crazy."

"I don't believe you."

She looked at me and chewed on her bottom lip. It drew my attention to her mouth, and I saw when she noticed me looking because she let her juicy lip out from between her teeth and it popped free.

I nearly groaned. She flushed again, and I watched as the color rose to her temples. Something passed between us, but I was here trying to find out how another man had stepped out of line with her, and I wasn't going to, in turn, do it myself.

"Tell me the truth."

She jumped off the counter and started picking things up, keeping her hands busy. "I don't know, like touching my hair or my arm. One time, he—" She paused and avoided my eyes. "He ran his hand up the back of my thigh while he was sitting in the chair. That's when I told him he needed to leave if he did it again."

She finally looked over at me again and watched as I processed the emotions running through my body.

"I can't tell what you're thinking," she said softly and walked closer to me. I leaned back into the chair and looked at her as she stopped directly in front of me. "I don't want you to do anything that's going to make this worse. I just plan on refusing him service in the future and avoiding him in public until he gets tired of it and moves on to someone else."

"I won't do anything that will fall back on you, Bailey. I promise you that."

She twisted her lips and paused, thinking about it. "Okay."

"Okay." I nodded, repeating it.

"Thank you."

"For what?" I asked, grinning.

"For making me feel like someone is watching out for me here."

Thea's words replayed in my head. *Might ease her mind a bit knowing a good man or two is watching out for her.*

Yeah, little did she know, she was more than likely going to have two very alpha, dominating men watching out for her before long.

Hoped she was ready.

Chapter 5 – Bailey

He was sitting in my chair and had just helped me out of a sticky situation without asking for anything in return.

I wasn't used to that, so I decided to give him a bit of repayment for his help—twice now.

I walked over and grabbed the cape and neckcloth from the side of my station and walked back toward him as he watched me pensively.

"What do you say? Ready to find out if I'm good with a razor and scissors?" I asked, and he looked down at my hands and back up.

"You worked all day; I'm not going to let you do that now when you should be relaxing," he said, but he turned toward me anyway.

"Can I tell you a secret?" I asked, walking around to stand behind him, looking at him in the mirror.

"Hmm." He groaned, keeping his eyes locked on mine.

"There's one person I've wanted to walk through my door the last two days, but he just never did." He kept my gaze in the mirror, but his neck muscles twitched and his Adam's apple bobbed as he swallowed. "Until now." I grinned at him, but he still hadn't moved.

The mood shifted from angry and frustrated, while we were talking about Clay and his bad manners, to something sizzling in the air around us. I knew he felt it too. I just hoped he felt it as strongly as I did.

He spread his arms wide, and I watched his bicep muscles roll under his skin. "Do your worst then." He smiled at me with a playful grin that could only be described as "panty melting."

Damn.

I put the cape and neckcloth on and went about gathering what supplies I needed.

"How do you usually get it done?" I asked, running my fingers through the hair at the back of his head and trying not to notice how his eyes slowly fell shut as I did.

Doing a man's hair that I found attractive or was interested in was an aphrodisiac for me. It was part of my love language, which was why I genuinely enjoyed the art of barbering.

"Well, I don't go get it done professionally very often, but usually a taper and an Ivy League on top."

"And your beard? Do you keep the lines where they are now?"

"Yeah, but the length a bit shorter."

"Okay." I couldn't help the cheeky smile pulling my lips back as I turned on my clippers and dove in.

He watched me intently in the mirror as I worked, and I soon lost myself in the process and the sensation of it being him.

"You enjoy doing this, don't you?" he asked when I realized I was still smiling.

"Some days more than others," I said truthfully.

What I wanted to say was some clients more than others, but I didn't want to put *this* in the box of a client and barber relationship because if I was honest, I was hoping for more than that at some point.

I did his hair and sharpened up all of the edges and lines, leaving him looking even more edible than he had before.

Which was going to be a problem for my panties.

I tried to keep myself focused and laid the seat back and reveled in the hooded gaze from his deep eyes as he looked up at me cautiously.

I chuckled. "Have you ever had a hot towel shave?"

"I don't even know what that is, so no."

"Hmm." I hummed. "You'll forever be a changed man when you leave."

As I turned and walked over to the hot towels, he murmured from behind me, "I will be regardless of the shave."

I looked over my shoulder where he lay back in the chair with his head turned toward me, and naughty thoughts rushed through my brain. How easy would it be to go over and climb up onto his lap and ride him right there? I could imagine how his big hands would rove over my body as I took pleasure from him and gave him his.

Whew, hot flash.

I grabbed the towel and shook it off as I walked back.

"Close your eyes," I said, my voice low and husky, and I felt a shiver run down my body. When I laid the towel on his face, he sucked in a deep breath and his entire body relaxed as it started to work its magic.

I selfishly took the opportunity to gaze over his incredible body while his eyes were closed under the towel. The black T-shirt he wore had the school logo on it and was tucked into his light-wash jeans and belt. Maybe it was because in high school, I was a loner and went unnoticed in a sea of thousands or something, but the nerd in me loved that he was all jock and he bothered to pay me even the least bit of attention.

Maybe it was just who he was that excited me. Who knew?

After the towel had done its work, I got to shave him. He kept his eyes closed and I used my fingers to keep his skin taut and focused on the job at hand. When I was done, I set my tools down and turned back to him and his eyes were still closed.

"Are you asleep?"

"Hmm." He hummed but still made no move to open his eyes or sit up.

I chuckled and walked over behind him. I laid my hands on his shoulders, letting my thumbs push into the muscles in his neck slightly, pulling a happy groan out of him, and leaned down until I was near his ear. "Told you that you'd be a changed man."

I slid my hands from his shoulders reluctantly, but he shot his hand up and grabbed one of mine. He held onto it and turned to look at me with the most relaxed look on his face I'd seen him sport. "That was incredible, Bailey. Thank you."

Now it was my turn to hum my reply, as I was suddenly unable to form words. He let go of my hand and I instantly missed the contact. He sat up, looked in the mirror, just shook his head, and murmured, "Miracle worker," under his breath. "I hate to run on you, but I've got to get to football practice," he said, standing and reaching for his wallet.

I put my hand on his arm, stopping him. "I already told you this one was on me. Aren't you a little old to be playing high school football?" I asked brazenly.

He rewarded me with a boisterous laugh as he walked toward the door, grabbed a few twenties from his wallet and stuffed them into the tip jar on the reception desk, and winked at me. "You can call me coach."

I moaned dramatically. "Oh boy."

He laughed again and put his hand on the doorknob and turned back to look at me.

"I'll see you soon, Bailey."

"I hope so," I replied. And then he was gone.
And I was a fricking puddle on the floor again.
That man! Whew.

Chapter 6 – Walker

I got out of the shower and cleaned the steam off the mirror and looked at myself.

I looked like a pile of dog shit, and I felt even worse. I had a knot the size of Texas in my neck and shoulder, making my arm tingle, and I was hungrier than a grizzly bear.

I'd spent the last week and a half at a summer camp in the mountains with at-risk youths from the area. It was typically a fun time. We did things like hiking, rafting, horseback riding, archery, and all kinds of other outdoor activities, but I was more than ready to get home this time for some reason.

I had gone to the camp as a kid when I started getting out of hand and my parents didn't know what else to do with me, and when I grew older and got my head out of my ass, I started volunteering for a week each summer.

The boys usually started camp cowering away from me, and that was kind of the plan because it taught them there were bigger and worse monsters out there than them and, in turn, it taught them some humility.

I was pretty intimidating to look at, and the camp director Shane loved to use that to his advantage with new campers. I was tall, built, and miserable. Or at least, that was how Shane described me when he wanted to piss me off.

I was tall, over six feet, had dark hair and dark features and tattoos up and down both arms and over my chest and back. I even had one on the back of my right hand and fingers. So when a bunch of fourteen-year-old out-of-control punks showed up to a camp they didn't want to be at and had to face off with me, their bad attitudes typically shrunk a bit in the face of resistance.

Without fail, by the end of the week, most of them had changed their attitudes greatly and I was able to form a bond with them.

The week at camp always left me looking like a caveman thanks to the lack of amenities. I got in late last night and this morning, I needed to get down to town and get some decent food at Thea's before I worried about anything else. I swore camp cooks took pleasure in serving gruel for a whole week when they knew you didn't have any other options.

So, I put off shaving for now in place of hunting down some hashbrowns and bacon with a side of caffeine.

I threw on a T-shirt and jeans and got in my truck and tore off to town. I could almost taste the diner grease as I walked into Thea's and sat at the counter.

She eyed me from her perch at the food window and tsked her tongue at me.

"You're going to scare away my customers," she chided me with her hands on her hips but a smile on her lips.

"I missed you too, Ms. Thea," I replied.

"How do you expect to find a wife to soften your hard side if you go around looking like a wildebeest?"

I snorted as she handed me a cup of coffee. "A wildebeest?"

She raised her eyebrows and smirked. "And that was being polite." She looked out the window and then back to me and a small smile crossed her lips before she bit it back, but I didn't miss it. "Luckily for you, I took the liberty of scheduling you an appointment at the new barber's shop across the street for this morning. I knew you'd need professional help when you got done playing sasquatch in the mountains for a week."

"Barbershop?" I asked and looked out the window. Sure enough, there was a shop open across the street where the old dentist's office had been before Tom remodeled the building.

"Mmh." She hummed. "When you get done eating your meal, head over and see the magic maker."

"You're getting bossy in your elder years,," I grumped but she just leaned over the counter and ruffled my hair.

I looked back out the window and couldn't tell anything about the shop from there. Guessed I'd have to see what kind of magic the man could work on me because to be honest, I felt like a wildebeest.

I ate my meal quickly, as usual, and Thea all but shooed me out the front door for my appointment.

I crossed the street and read the dark gray and gold sign on the front of the building, *Bailey Dunn & Co.* I opened the door and walked into the industrial yet warm atmosphere. Music played softly overhead, a romantic Cody Johnson song I recognized, as I went deeper into the shop.

And then I froze stiff in my tracks.

In more than one way.

At the back wall, a woman I didn't recognize was wearing a white cotton dress and sandals, with a mess of blonde curls pulled up in a bandana tied in a bow on top of her head. She was swaying her hips to the song and singing along with an angelic voice while folding towels.

Desire flowed down my spine and into my limbs from watching her tiny waist move and twist as her wide hips followed the music. I could see the shape of her ass under the fabric, and I could tell instantly that it would fill my hands.

And I had very large hands.

I felt like a pariah watching her while dirty sexual thoughts and images flooded my brain and bloodstream, so I quickly adjusted myself in my pants, to make sure she wouldn't be able to tell how she affected me, then cleared my throat.

She looked over her shoulder, barely even seeing me before her hand knocked something off the counter, making her snap her attention back to catch it before it hit the ground.

"Hey! You know, I was thinking long and hard after you left the other night," she called over her shoulder as she finished folding the towel, and then she turned around with the pile in her hands and looked at me, stopping in her tracks. Her voluptuous lips fell into an "O" shape as she let her eyes travel from my head to my feet and back. "You're not Finn," she said in shock.

I cocked an eyebrow at her and put my hands in my pockets, not offering up anything at the moment.

"Sorry," she stuttered as she started walking toward me again, and she shook her head, smiling in embarrassment. "I just looked quick and I thought you were Finn."

"What were you thinking long and hard about?" I asked, and I watched a slight flush color her chest above the white fabric of her dress.

"Oh, nothing." She shook her head dismissively and then held her hand out. "I'm Bailey."

I looked at her tiny hand with perfectly painted white nails for a second before I reached forward and shook it.

The second her soft skin slid against my weathered palm, I felt electricity shoot through my groin.

I enjoyed watching her suck a tiny breath in between her plump, glossed lips, as if she felt the same thing.

I held her hand for a second longer before I simply said, "Walker."

She nodded in a slight daze and then slid her hand out of mine, and I was surprised at how much I wanted to touch her again as soon as she stepped back.

"I'm assuming you're his brother?" she asked with her eyebrows raised to her hairline.

"Twin," I replied. "Identical twin."

She let her eyes travel down my arms and hands and then looked me in the eye again as she tilted her head and sweetly said, "Well, not identical so much anymore."

I felt my lips pull into a one-sided grin and nodded my head. "Yeah, well, needed something for people to tell us apart by."

She nodded again. "What can I do for you?"

"I'm here for an appointment."

Her eyebrows raised to her hairline again and then came down into a perplexed scowl. "I, uh—" she started then shook her head. "I don't book any appointments yet; I've been so swamped, I can't even answer the phone. It's walk-ins only."

I looked around at the empty shop, confused, and she laughed and walked over to the desk by the door.

"I'm not open yet. I open late on Fridays. I'm just here doing prep stuff. Who told you that you had an appointment?"

I looked past her to the window of the diner and sure enough, the nosey little woman in the window gave herself away.

Bailey watched my gaze fall over her shoulder, and she turned and followed it to the diner.

She looked back with exasperation on her face.

"Thea," we both said together and then laughed.

I couldn't tell you the last time I laughed with a woman. It felt . . . good.

"That woman loves to get involved in everything," she said nicely and chewed her bottom lip.

"Hmm," I grunted. If she only knew.

The pieces were falling into place for me, but that was because I knew about my past, and knowing that she knew Finn, pretty closely apparently, I could follow the breadcrumbs that Thea was leaving.

I would bet my left nut that Bailey couldn't though, or she wouldn't be standing there so innocent and sweet. She'd be scandalized and running for the hills.

"I'm sorry for bothering you. I'll get out of your hair," I said, bowing my head and stepping back.

"No, wait," she argued, stepping forward and holding her hand up.

I stopped and raised my brow at her quizzically.

"I assume you wanted to get your hair and beard . . . tamed," she said sweetly, trying not to tell me how bad I looked currently.

"Thea told me I look like a wildebeest."

She snorted and quickly covered her mouth and shook her head. Curls bounced behind the bandana as she did, and I fought the urge to run the silken hair through my fingers.

How sexy would those blonde locks look wrapped around my inked fist?

Fuck.

"I wouldn't have said wildebeest, but a beast of some sort," she joked and nodded for me to follow her as she walked over to her chair at the side of the room.

"If you only knew," I muttered under my breath, not intending for her to hear me, but she whipped her head back toward me and her eyes rounded.

This poor sweet girl was going to be ruined just by being in my presence.

I followed her over and sat down in her chair, and she flung a cape over my chest and snapped it at my neck.

Her sweet floral scent engulfed me as she worked around me, getting her things out.

"Are you sure it's no bother?" I asked, watching her slip into the role of a master of her trade.

"I actually enjoy corrupting barber virgins," she said, and I choked on my tongue. She watched me in the mirror as a mischievous grin played on her full lips, and she shrugged her shoulder and finished her thought. "If you're like your brother, something tells me you don't get taken care of professionally very often, so I'm going to enjoy showing you what you've been missing."

Oh, honey, if you had any idea what you were doing to me.

She went to work on my hair, clipping away the overgrown mess and shaping it into a fashionable style. I was impressed with her focus on detail and her skills.

"How about this?" she said, lightly scratching my cheek under my bushy beard with her nails.

"Do your worst," I replied.

She paused and smiled down at me with a look almost like affection. "Finn said the same thing," she said and tsked her tongue as she smiled and walked over to get a towel.

I didn't know whether to be annoyed or aroused that she got a certain look in her eye when she talked about my brother. I'd have to talk to him and find out exactly what he had started with this sinfully innocent woman in my absence.

The next fifteen minutes were some of the most sexually arousing of my life, and she didn't even do anything particularly indecent to me. She had her hands on my face, neck, and throat and was standing around the front of me, leaving me nowhere else to look but directly at her, and I didn't mind the view one bit.

When she added some oil to my beard to smooth it out, my toes fucking curled in my boots. I loved having a woman's hands in my beard, and she was no exception to the fetish.

"Can I ask you a question?" she asked as she finished up and pulled the cape off.

"Yeah."

"Does this hurt?" she asked as she ran her fingertips gently over the bulging knot at the top of my right shoulder, near the base of my neck.

I nodded and laughed a bit. "Like a bitch."

"This may sound strange to you," she said as she reddened a bit and pushed a curl out of her eye, "but I can work it out for you if you want." I kept my eyes locked on hers in the mirror and raised my eyebrows in silent question. "Uh—" She started and stopped. "My mom is a massage therapist, or, well, she's a hippie who loves everything touch, so she taught me things like that. If you want, I can see if I can loosen it up for you."

"Do you always go above and beyond for your customers?" I asked and then instantly regretted it. I didn't want to know if she treated every lucky son of a bitch with extra care. Part of me wanted to just think she was doing it especially for me.

"No, I don't. I was just trying to be helpful." I could see a bit of hurt at the rejection in her face and kicked myself.

I leaned back in the chair again and said, "Okay, give it your best shot. God knows I could use some relief."

A shy smile crossed her lips, and she walked over to the cabinet and got a bottle of oil. "C'mon," she said and nodded for me to follow her. She pulled out a table chair with a high back from a desk in the corner and motioned for me to sit straddling it, and I did.

"Take your shirt off unless you want oil all over it." She wouldn't meet my eyes as she said it and instead turned and set the bottle down on the desk and took her rings off.

I tried to hide the shit-eating grin on my face but failed to even disguise it a little. I wasn't going to give her the chance to change her mind and take back the offer of putting her hands on me. I pulled my shirt up and over the back of my head and laid it on my knee, and then I leaned forward, resting my forearms on the back of the chair. She turned around and poured oil into the palm of her hand and walked toward me apprehensively as she let her eyes rove over all of my artwork.

There was hardly any free space on my back at this point. I had started getting work done on my chest more recently.

"Wow," she said softly as she stood behind me and let the oil drip onto my neck and shoulder.

I took a deep breath, trying to steel my nerves and my cock against the fucking light show that was about to happen to my nervous system when she touched me, but it didn't work.

As soon as her soft hands slid over my skin, I was a fucking goner, completely obsessed with a tiny, new blonde girl named Bailey Dunn.

Chapter 7 – Bailey

I didn't know what the hell got into me and made me think offering to massage him was appropriate. As soon as the words were out of my mouth, I knew I wasn't ready to be done touching him.

I felt like a terrible person for it, too, because up until this morning, I hadn't been able to think of anything else besides Finn Camden. Now, I was rubbing his twin brother's naked back and my panties were soaked.

I almost fell over when I realized it wasn't Finn standing in my doorway. They were completely identical in their dark eyes and hair, beards, and muscle mass, but what had given it away first, besides the ink up and down both arms instead of just one, was the mass of messy hair and unkempt beard on his face.

When I found out Thea had told him to come over to me, I knew instantly that she was meddling in my life the way only an older, well-meaning woman could do and get away with. A part of me was confused because I thought I'd caught a few happy smirks pointed Finn's way when we sat together at the diner the other night.

But now, she was dangling his twin brother in front of my face, and I was so confused.

Where Finn was easygoing and charismatic and sociable, Walker was reserved, quiet, and almost brooding.

They were opposites, excellent complements to each other.

I could tell he wasn't one to chat aimlessly or fill easy silences, yet he seemed to want to with me. So I let him.

And then, I had seen and felt the knot in his neck and the giver in me wanted desperately to ease his discomfort.

I just hadn't thought about how much discomfort it would put me in, to have my hands on a man I wasn't supposed to want.

And holy damn did I want this man.

But it was the same way I wanted Finn.

I was so confused and so aroused and so damn screwed.

His back and both arms were covered in incredible tattoos, and as I dripped the oil onto them, I felt like I was playing with a canvas and manipulating the artwork.

He dropped his forehead to his arms and let me start working into the muscles. He groaned and grunted in ways that let me know I was getting into where he needed me, and it excited me to know I was doing a good job for him.

I ran my oiled hands from the hairline at his nape to mid-back, down his shoulder and arm to the elbow and back, and worked the entire area with my palms and fingers.

"Jesus Christ, I've died and gone to heaven." He grunted at one point, and I smiled into the silence behind him, biting my lip to keep from agreeing with him.

I was starting to work up a sweat from the strenuous job so I pushed my darn curls back again and then put my elbow into his back.

"Marry me." He grunted and I laughed out loud.

"If this was all it took . . . ," I rebutted.

"Fuck, that feels good," he said back.

I bit my lip again. The word fuck sounded so sexy coming off his tongue.

After a few more minutes, I could feel the difference I'd made in his muscles and lightened up my touch to bring it to an end.

"All better?" I asked, and he sat up and stretched his arms and rolled his neck.

"Damn," he said and then stood up and swung his leg over the seat of the chair to stand in front of me.

I tried hard not to, but my eyes dropped down his chiseled chest and washboard abs and landed on the deep V that disappeared into his waistband, effectively pointing to his erection.

I snapped my eyes from his crotch and turned quickly, walking over to the sink to wash my hands as he slid his shirt over his head.

He chuckled as I fled, and I knew I'd been caught staring at his dick. I was too mortified to turn around and face him again.

After washing my hands for a ridiculously long time, I had no choice, so I hiked my big-girl panties up, even if they were soaked and useless, and turned around. He stood by the chair with his shirt on and a pensive stare in his eyes.

He was so hard to read, so unlike Finn. It drove me nuts.

"You should put some heat on that a couple of times a day for the next two or three days and that will help keep it from tightening back up," I offered.

"Will do, doc," he joked. And then, just like his brother, he reached for his wallet and pulled out some money, but I stopped him.

"It's on the house." He cocked an eyebrow at me, but I just gave him one back and stood firm. "Really."

He nodded and smirked at me and turned to walk out, slipping the money into the tip jar on the counter exactly as Finn had. I needed to hide that thing when those two were around.

"Thanks for taking care of me today," he called and winked over his shoulder at me. There were so many innuendos in that statement that all I could do was smile and wave to him as he walked out.

Holy shit, these Camden men were going to be the death of me.

And I didn't think I'd complain at all on my way out.

Chapter 8 – Finn

I walked out of the jail after bringing in a guy with warrants and made my way back to my SUV. When I got closer, I saw the hulking dark and miserable frame of Walker leaning on the hood.

"Hey, big bro," I called and slapped him on the shoulder as I threw my stuff on the hood next to him. "I heard you got in last night, but you were still out cold when I left for work. How was camp?"

"Who's Bailey?" he asked, his eyes intense as he stared into mine.

It was then that I noticed the fresh fade of his hairline and beard.

Shit.

"Uh, well, I see you've met her," I answered, grabbing my stuff off the hood and heading for the driver's door, trying to make a break for it. I opened the door and was almost in when he answered.

"Oh, I did more than just meet her," he said, keeping his back to me with his arms across his chest, knowing his words were going to bait me.

I tapped my fingers on the frame of my car as I contemplated my next move here. I tossed my shit in and shut the door and walked back to the hood.

"What did you say to her?" I asked.

He just raised his eyebrows at me and waited for me to come clean.

I sighed and rubbed my hand down my face as I shrunk a bit at the anger in his eyes.

"If you're looking to change things up, just say so," he finally bit out.

"What?" I snapped, stepping forward. "Knock it off, that's not what happened. You and I both know that's not what either of us wants."

"Then why did I get the distinct feeling that something happened between you two, yet she didn't know I even existed." I could see the flare of hurt in his eyes and that hurt me. That was never my intention.

I turned and leaned on the hood with him and crossed my arms across my chest like he did. "I met her a couple of days ago. She just moved here after you left for camp, and I hadn't planned on doing anything past meeting her. But then she needed my help, and Thea got involved, and now I'm—" I paused trying to figure out how to describe what I felt for her. "Now I'm fucking obsessed." I said the last part with a sigh. I was fucked in the head over that girl already and I didn't like it one bit.

He looked over at me and I saw some of the frustration leave his face, but not all of it so I continued on. "I saw her the other night outside of her shop. She was the picture of angelic perfection, and I couldn't get her out of my head. The next day, I was walking by—well, stalking by the front of her shop—and she needed help moving a desk so I offered and we chatted for a few minutes. There was an instant connection between the two of us. Then two nights ago, I was at Thea's, and she said that something happened at Bailey's shop that morning but she didn't know what, just that Mikey was there and came back to the diner upset about something. When Bailey walked into the diner, I saw something pass between her and Clay."

"Mathews?" he asked, and I saw the hate in his eyes at the mention of his name.

"Yeah, he was telling the diner about how they were going out on a date and shit but when she walked in, I figured out pretty quickly that he was making her uncomfortable. So she sat by me, looking for an ally, I think, and then we went across the street after eating and she told me he'd gotten out of line with her at her shop that morning, put his hands on her and shit."

"Son of a bitch."

"Yeah, so I told her I'd take care of him, and then she gave me a cut and shave, and I-I haven't been able to think straight since. I didn't say anything about you to her yet because she's just so fucking pure, and I'm not going to give her half-truths or lies. I want to be straight with her from the start about you and me, but I don't want to send her running for the hills before she gets comfortable first. Please don't think I'm trying to stray out or something."

He nodded again, and I watched as his eyes got a bit glassy as he stared off into the distance. I recognized that look; it was one of desire.

"So what exactly happened between you two?" I asked and tried to keep the humor out of my voice, sensing he was on edge.

"Thea set me up," he said and then shook his head. "I should have seen her meddling brain spinning but I missed it at first, and by then it was too late."

I just waited and let him go on.

"She told me she made me an appointment across the street, which I was in desperate need of so I didn't question it too much. Expect, when I walked in and saw Bailey, damn, I was not expecting that. And I wasn't expecting her to think I was you and start talking about how she was thinking about you after you left the other night." He looked over at me with a question in his eyes but kept on. "Or for her to tell me she didn't take appointments and wasn't even open."

I chuckled. "Fucking Thea."

"Right. So she gave me a cut and shave and then—" He paused again and rubbed the back of his neck and smirked, lost in a memory.

"And then, what?" I asked, pushing off the car to face him head-on.

"And then she made me take my shirt off so she could rub oil over my back and neck and gave me the best damn massage of my fucking life."

"What!" I shot out and pushed his shoulder, playing for the most part.

He laughed and looked down. He didn't laugh very often, and I was shocked stupid to see him do it now, but I knew it was because she had that effect on me, so she obviously had it on him.

"I had a knot in my neck the size of a softball and she asked me if she could work on it, said her mom's into that shit and taught her some stuff. Of course I wasn't going to fucking tell her no. So, I stripped down and nearly came in my pants like a teenager as she got that knot worked out. I think I even asked her to marry me."

"Dude, I'm so fucking jealous right now. Here I am, doing all the leg work, and you swoop in and get her hands on you in the first 10 minutes. Fuck!" I cursed in exaggeration.

We were never really jealous of each other. Envious, sure, but never actually jealousy. That was just how our dynamic worked.

"So now what?" I asked.

"Fuck if I know. My guess is you should go to her and apologize for not telling her you had a twin, and then you should probably be straight with her about us. I'd do it, but I'm afraid she'd pass out on the spot if I do. Man, those green eyes of hers get so big when she gets shocked or scandalized, and it makes me want to do things to her. Dirty fucking things."

"I hear you. As I said, I'm obsessed."

We stood there for a second and let all of the information and questions mull over in our brains.

"Yeah, I have to come clean with her, but I think when I do, we both need to be there."

He nodded and rubbed his hand over his beard in the way he did when he was lost in thought. "Do you really think she'll be down to live our lifestyle? Can she handle it?"

"Honestly, yes. She's pure and good in her soul in a way I haven't seen in anyone before, but there's a connection here and I know she feels it too. I think what we can offer her is exactly what she needs. We should be looking out for her, that's for sure. Way too many people have been overly forward with her already."

"Invite her over for dinner or something. We can feel it out and go from there."

"Yeah, that sounds good. Good idea." I held my hand out and he shook it and pulled me in for a hug like usual, slapping each other on the back.

"Get back to work. Text me when you figure it out."

I headed off and felt nerves settle in my core as I drove toward town. I looked at my watch. It was almost noon, and she opened her shop at twelve.

I hit the gas and closed the distance quickly, parking on Main Street with what I hoped was enough time to convince her to come over tonight.

When I walked in, I was sucked back into the depth of my fixation with her as she looked up at me, until a scowl crossed her brow and her lips pursed.

"Finn?" She tapped her finger to her jaw and stuck her hip out. "Or perhaps a triplet?"

I caught the slightest bit of a smirk on her lips as she tried to hide it.

I held my hands up in front of me and walked forward until I was right in front of her. Her head tipped back as she looked up at me and her scowl relaxed. "I'm sorry," I said.

She chewed on her bottom lip and then looked away. "You don't need to apologize. I just don't understand"—her eyes got big and her hands gestured out at her sides—"so much. I'm so confused."

"What are you confused about?" I said and reached down to take her hand. It was the first time I outwardly touched her because I wanted to, not including the night in the diner when I used her hand in mine to lead her outside.

Her eyes rounded and I was tempted to run my thumb under the long black eyelashes that lay on her full cheeks as she stared at me.

I kept her hand in mine and rubbed my thumb across her knuckles.

"Well, now I'm even more confused than when you walked in here," she said, but she didn't let go of my hand and took an almost unnoticeable step toward me.

"Give me a chance to answer your questions. Maybe tonight over dinner?"

She hesitated and looked down at my chest for a second before nodding her head softly. "I'm here until six though."

"That's fine. Gives me time to get home from work and get cooking."

Her lips parted and formed an "O" that I was learning was a natural mannerism for her. "You want to cook me dinner? At your place?"

"Unless the idea of being at my house makes you uncomfortable," I said firmly, giving her an out if she wanted it.

She groaned and let her eyes flutter closed, "It makes me uncomfortable, alright, but not in a bad way." She bit her lip again, and I understood her reference. It excited her.

Now it was my turn to groan. "You can't say things like that to me, Bailey. Not when there are more than six hours before I get to see you again."

This time, I didn't stop myself from reaching up and cradling the side of her face with my hand before running my thumb across the roundness of her cheek. Her eyes were huge as she looked up at me with her lush lips parted, and I couldn't take my eyes off of them.

The front door to her shop opened, and brand new giant bells hanging from the handle jingled, announcing we weren't alone.

She started to pull back quickly, like she'd been busted doing something she wasn't supposed to be, but I didn't let go of her face right away. My fingers were wrapped around the back of her head and through her curls, and I didn't want to let go.

I eventually gave in and let them slide through my fingers and released her as I kept her stare.

I didn't bother looking over my shoulder to see who was there. They could wait. I reached into my chest pocket and pulled out one of my business cards with my cell numbers on it and handed it to her.

"Text me so I have your number and I'll give you my address. Come over whenever you're free tonight."

"Okay," she whispered and took the card from me.

To make sure I left her thinking of me for the rest of the day, I brought her hand up that was still in mine and kissed the underside of her wrist, never dropping her stare, and then gently let go and walked away.

The intruder was the dad of one of the boys I coached, and he watched with fascination as I walked out, leaving her standing there, staring after me.

The town all knew my past, and therefore they knew my tendencies. I just hoped I had the opportunity to tell her what they were before someone else did.

"See you later," I called from the door, and she gave me a slight wave.

I hoped she gave this whole thing a shot because I couldn't remember a time I ever wanted someone as badly as I wanted her.

Chapter 9 – Bailey

I worked on autopilot all day long, watching the big clock over the windows and praying it would move faster.

I was incredibly nervous to go to Finn's house tonight because I didn't trust myself around him. I was so attracted to that man that if he wanted to, I'd fall into his bed willingly and wouldn't regret it for one second. I would, however, wish that I had waited a bit longer.

I didn't want to get in over my head before I had time to feel things out.

And there was the very giant problem that his brother caused.

I hadn't been able to stop thinking about Walker all day long either. I didn't know what their living arrangements were, but a part of my brain told me there was no way they didn't live together. I could just feel the closeness between them.

I wasn't sure how I was supposed to act if they were both there tonight. Technically, Finn had invited me for dinner, a date so I should treat him like one, but a part of me didn't want to make Walker feel like he was a third wheel either.

I was a ball of nerves by the time the end of the day came around. It was quarter to six and I had just finished my last customer.

I practically ran to the window sign and flipped it over to closed before moving around the shop and cleaning up to have it ready to go Monday morning.

I had my head down when I heard the bells on the door, that I hung up after Walker snuck up on me, jingle. I looked up, half expecting Finn to be there again, but I was instead a bit apprehensive when I saw it was Clay.

"Hi," I said cautiously, unsure of what he wanted.

"Hey," he said with a big smile on his face. He walked into the shop and closed the distance between us rather quickly, leaving me with no chance to put something between us in case I needed space.

"I'm closed up for the day." I tried to sound professional and in charge given the last time he was in here, I'd threatened to kick him out after he touched me.

He ran his hand around the back of his neck and rubbed it. "I wanted to apologize for my actions the other day. I wasn't trying to make you uncomfortable; I promise I'm not that kind of guy."

I nodded at him, unsure what to say to that.

He chuckled a bit and continued, "Honestly, I have to tell you that I've been kind of overwhelmed since that day at Thea's when I saw you for the first time. I felt something pass between us when I shook your hand, and I guess I just let my mind run away with itself after that."

I didn't want to tell him it was okay because I didn't want him to think I agreed that something passed between us. Nothing had happened on my end, not at all like the times I'd touched Finn or Walker. But I didn't think that was appropriate to tell him, so I just went for the polite route. "Apology accepted."

He stepped forward again, putting even less space between us, and I took a step backward, but he acted like he didn't notice. "I was wondering if you'd let me apologize over dinner tonight. We could go to JJ's bar across town. They have a great burger and beer selection and live music on Fridays so we can dance. It'll be fun."

I had to handle this delicately, given my current surroundings. "I appreciate the invite, Clay, but I already have plans tonight." I didn't bother lying and saying maybe another time because that was never going to happen.

The grin slid from his face and something like anger took its place.

"Plans? With who?"

"That's none of your business. I appreciate the invite, like I said, but—"

"Is it Finn?" he barked.

"Clay."

"Or is it Finn and Walker?"

"I think it's time you leave," I rebutted firmly.

He sneered at me. "Who would have thought that you were into getting fucked in your ass and your pussy at the same time, but I guess you just *look* like a good girl."

His words enraged me and before I knew it, my palm stung where I'd slapped him across the face.

Blind fury flashed in his eyes. "You bitch."

"Get out!" Anger and fear burned in my spine, making me fight the urge to run or fight.

"You listen here," he said and stepped forward again, but I stepped to the side and moved around the table, placing it between us.

My front door opened, and I was relieved to see Thea standing there with the teenage football player who worked as a dishwasher at the diner next to her. They saw when Clay lunged for me.

"Clay Mathews, get out of here right now before I have you arrested!" Thea yelled, and the boy walked around her and put himself between Clay and me. He was obviously a linebacker, and he was built for the job. Although he was a teenager, I was glad he was there.

Clay looked at the two of them and then back to me as he worked his jaw opened and closed. "We'll finish this conversation later, Bailey," he said as he walked toward the door, with his eyes locked on me.

"Don't come back here, Clay. I mean it. You aren't welcome," I said firmly, laying down the rules as a business owner even if I was shaking like a leaf on the inside from fear.

He grunted at me, smirking like he was going to challenge me on it, and walked out the door, slamming it closed on his way.

I took a shaky breath, fell backward into the chair I'd been pressed up against, and turned to Thea and her linebacker backup. "Thank you."

"I'm sorry it took us that long to get over here. I looked over and saw him standing in here and knew you were closed so I grabbed Nate and we came running. What happened?"

I shook my head, not wanting to go into details in front of a high schooler, and waved her off. "He just won't take no for an answer. Thank you, guys, again. I'll make sure I'm more vigilant now that I know what he's capable of."

She nodded with a look of speculation in her eyes but gestured for Nate to go back to the diner and followed him out. Before she cleared the doorway, she called over her shoulder, "Make sure you tell Finn and Walker about this. Tonight."

I scowled at her instructions out of confusion and didn't say anything else in reply, and she didn't wait around for one.

I wasted no more time and locked up and got in my car to leave, knowing I'd have to come in early on Monday to finish cleaning up. I didn't want to be here any longer tonight.

I drove home and had to work hard to calm myself down. My hands were still shaking and my blood boiled. What had he meant by that comment about Finn and Walker? Why would he assume I was going out with them?

When I got into my happy little house, I felt some tension ease from my shoulders as I hurried up and changed into a burgundy-colored off-the-shoulder knit sweater and a pair of blue jeans with distressed holes in the knees and a pair of flat sandals.

I forewent a bra, given the off-the-shoulder action, but I made sure my nipples weren't visible through the fabric just to be safe. I took my hair down and added some serum to it to smooth the frizz and let my curls dance around my face and shoulders.

It was a quarter after six before I got back into my car and headed toward the address Finn had given me. It was only ten minutes from my house and as I got closer, my hands started shaking for a whole new reason.

I just wasn't sure if it was with excitement or apprehension about what I was walking into. I did know that I wasn't going to ruin my evening by telling Finn about Clay's visit, even if Thea had told me too. I wanted the night to be drama free and the story would cause the very opposite.

When I got to the address, there was just a narrow driveway in the trees, but I couldn't see the house from the road. When I drove through the tunnel of trees and out the other side, I was struck by the beauty of the area and was even more in awe of the beautiful home nestled in the clearing.

There were two police cruisers in the driveway next to two giant jacked-up pickups.

I guessed that meant that both brothers lived here and they were both home.

This was going to be the most difficult meal of my life if both of them were sitting at the same table as I was. Only because I desperately wanted to fuck them both and that was a problem because there was no situation where that would be appropriate.

Before I could talk myself out of staying, I pushed my door open and slid from my car. When I shut the door, Finn walked out on the front porch and smiled down at me as he wiped his hands on a dish towel.

He wore jeans and a white T-shirt and was barefoot, and I had to swallow a couple of times before I could form words. He was magnificent to look at and I openly let my eyes wander over him.

His smile got bigger as he watched my gaze, and he walked down the stairs toward me and threw the towel over his shoulder.

"Hi," I said. He walked right up to me and let his hand fall to my elbow as he leaned down and kissed my cheek.

He smelled as good as he looked. I was a goner for this man and his brother and utterly fucked. And not at all in the way I wanted to be.

"Well, hello there. You are absolutely stunning, Bailey." The gravel and baritone in his voice sent shivers down my spine. I just looked up at him and smiled sweetly.

"I didn't have time to make anything to bring and to be honest, I didn't know what you liked, so I brought this," I said as I held up a bottle of Jameson awkwardly.

"Jameson is a household favorite, Bailey. This is perfect."

I turned to look at the four vehicles parked in front of the garage and said, "Household, huh?"

A small smile played on his lips and he nodded. "Walker is here. We live together. Are you okay with that?"

"Of course," I answered truthfully.

His small smile grew until it was taking up the entire bottom half of his face, and he slid his hand over my hip to my back and walked toward the house with it resting there.

When we walked in, the house smelled divine. It was a gorgeous home, and I could see so many manly touches to it, but it didn't look like a corny bachelor pad. It was so tasteful and welcoming. "Your home is lovely," I said as he walked me into the kitchen and placed the Jameson on the counter.

"It's loveliness just got at least ten points higher the second you walked in." He hummed as he walked over and pulled three glasses from above the sink and brought them back over.

"Would you like one?" he asked as he opened the bottle and poured two fingers worth into two of the glasses.

"I would love one," I purred, and I meant it. I was going to need it to relax.

He dutifully poured me one and handed it to me as Walker walked into the kitchen from the back porch. I didn't know how it was possible, given he wore just a simple pair of jeans and a green T-shirt, but he looked even sexier than when I'd seen him earlier today.

"Hey, Bailey," he said and walked over to grab a glass that Finn held out to him. I nodded to him and gave what I hoped was a nice-girl smile.

"Bailey brought us Jameson," Finn said.

"Did you know it was our favorite?" Walker asked me.

"No. Lucky guess, I suppose." I shrugged and smiled at them both.

"You look beautiful tonight," Walker said as he lifted the glass and drained it while holding my stare.

I lifted my own glass and drank a large swallow as I tore my gaze away and looked at Finn from under my lashes, expecting to see some jealousy or uncomfortableness on his face. But there was hardly anything besides arousal there when I looked.

I knocked back the rest of my glass and took a deep breath, feeling very out of my depth here.

They both chuckled low in their throats. Finn turned and went back to the stove to stir something on the top, and Walker took my glass, letting his fingers cover mine as he held it in both of our hands to refill it.

He grinned down at me knowingly as I tipped the second one back with him. I tilted the glass back down but left the rim of it at my lips as I watched the muscles in his throat work the fluid down in one shot.

"How's your neck?" I asked, captivated.

"It's quite sore again actually. Maybe you can give me another massage tonight after dinner." There was no sign of joking on his face, and I didn't trust myself to answer him, so I just raised my eyebrows and looked away from his penetrating gaze as I hummed in speculation.

Finn came back over to us and walked behind me, letting his hand fall to my hip as he leaned down to my ear from behind me and asked softly, "Are you running a buy one get one deal on those massages?"

My heart dropped into my belly and my eyes fluttered closed as I bit back a groan. I looked over my shoulder at him as he finished walking around me and winked at me.

"Perhaps." I sighed.

Anything he was going to say back was halted by the phone ringing on the counter, and I was kind of glad because I was sure it was going to make me hotter. Walker stepped over to it and picked it up, looking at the screen, and pressed it to his ear.

"Hey, Ms. Thea."

Ah, shit.

I took his glass where he had abandoned it and tossed it back. Already I could feel the warmth of the liquor filling my veins, but I wanted more if Thea was about to rat me out.

I watched him as he listened to what she had to say, and I noticed how Finn looked from him to me and back as Walker turned to me and stared me down as he listened.

I wasn't sure what the emotion was that burned in his eyes, but he was so intimidating. I kept telling myself in my head that I was an independent woman who didn't owe them an explanation about what happened at my shop earlier so they couldn't be mad at me for staying quiet.

At least, I hoped they wouldn't be. I had seen the protector side in Finn that night at the diner, and I could tell Walker was no different. Finn told me he would take care of Clay, which he hadn't done obviously, but I wasn't mad at him. It wasn't his responsibility. It was mine.

"Well, I appreciate you calling us. She's here now actually so I'll be sure to ask her about it and get to the bottom of it. Thank you for calling us and looking out for her. We both appreciate it."

Finn looked at me and crossed his arms over his chest as he leaned back against the counter, turning the stovetop off and waiting for Walker to hang up.

I couldn't meet Walker's stare once he hung the phone up, set it on the counter, and leaned forward me. I played with the glass in my hands until he took it and set it down by him.

"What's up?" Finn asked.

Walker hesitated for a second and sighed, but I still wouldn't look up. "Thea wanted to make sure Bailey had called us earlier to tell us about a run-in with Clay in her shop this evening," he said.

Walker's eyes glowed with ire and Finn's weren't much calmer as he looked down at me.

I raised my shoulders and sighed. "I just got here," I said.

"Were you going to tell us?" Finn asked.

I bit my lip and sighed again. "No," I answered honestly.

"What happened?" he asked. He was calmer than Walker and I appreciated that right now, but I had no idea why they felt the need to know everything that happened in my life. They hardly knew me.

"He came over and apologized for the other day and then asked me out on a date. I told him I already had plans tonight. He got mad and asked with who, and I told him it was none of his business. He then made some crude statements about his suspicion that it was with you two. And I—" I paused, trying to grasp saying it out loud. "I slapped him and then he went after me."

"He what?" Walker bellowed, leaning off the counter and walking around to my side.

I hurried on to calm him down. "Thea and the football player that washes dishes there busted in and kicked him out. I told him he wasn't welcome in my shop ever again and he left. It wasn't a big deal."

"That's a big fucking deal, Bailey," Walker said as he put his fist on his hip.

"Hang on," Finn said, walking over and putting his hand on his brother's chest to push him back a bit. "Did he touch you?"

"No. I slapped him in the face, and he called me a bitch and lunged for me, but I'd already moved around the table. That's when Thea came in. She said she saw him through the window and grabbed Nate and came over."

He slid his hand through the curls at the side of my face and pushed them back, letting his thumb run over my cheek. I leaned into it a bit.

"Are you okay?" he asked, and I hated how his gentle tone made tears prick the backs of my eyes so I tried to look away, but he wouldn't let me turn my head and saw them pooling in my lash line.

I shook my head no, and he pulled me forward until my forehead was against his wide, muscular chest and his arms wrapped around me, comforting me.

"I'm fine, but it scared me," I finally said, not meeting either of their eyes from my hidden spot against his chest.

I heard Walker take a deep breath, and then I felt Finn's hand slide down my back, his thumb rubbing against my spine lazily.

What warped reality had I walked into where these two amazing, beautiful, strong men bothered to care about me and comfort me when I was unsettled?

Walker sat down on a stool at the counter and pulled me from Finn's arms, and I went willingly, unsure of what any of this was or what any of it meant. I wanted to be in his arms the way I had wanted Finn's, so I stopped myself from thinking and just let myself feel.

I stood between his knees, and he pulled my back against his chest and settled my ass on his thigh, wrapping his arms around my waist. Finn sat on the stool next to us and kept his hands on me as well.

"What did he say about you having a date with Finn and me tonight?" Walker asked. His chest rumbled against my back, and I enjoyed the sensation.

"I didn't understand what he meant when he said it." I paused. "But now, I'm maybe starting to understand some pieces better."

"Pieces of what?" Finn asked.

"He said he thought I was a good girl, but that I must like getting"—I paused and felt the blush shooting up my neck to my face as I tried to say the words out loud to these men—"that I liked getting fucked in both holes at the same time."

"I'll kill him," Walker said, but his hands tightened on my waist and pulled me back into him farther.

"We'll take care of him later. Right now, I want to know what you're starting to understand more of, Bailey," Finn said again.

"Why don't you just tell me what I'm missing here instead of making me guess," I said, feeling bold from having both of their hands on me.

Well, that and the whiskey.

He smiled at me and held my gaze. "You're strong and confident when you want to be, aren't you?"

I raised my eyebrow at him but stayed quiet.

He looked over my shoulder to Walker and I felt him nod back to him before Finn started explaining things to me.

"When I envision what my future looks like, I see myself married to a woman like you, Bailey. I see myself protecting and supporting a woman who allows herself to lean on me for every last one of her wants and needs in life." He paused and reached forward to pull on a curl by my chin and let it bounce back up. "And I see that woman loving me with everything inside of her without hesitation or secrets. And I also see her loving and being loved by my brother in the exact same way at the same time."

I took a deep breath, aware of where Walker's hands were resting on my waist and where Finn's were rubbing up and down the tops of my thighs as I sat there staring at him, at a complete loss for words. "I don't understand."

"We share our women, Bailey. We want to find a woman who can handle that. To be completely honest with you, since the first time we both laid eyes on you, we've been pretty sure that woman may be you," Walker added from behind me as I looked over my shoulder at him.

"Me? What on earth would make either of you want me, let alone both of you?" I asked.

They both chuckled, and Finn added, "We tell you this bombshell about ourselves and you worry about us not finding you worthy? That's exactly why we're drawn to you.

You're unlike any other woman we've met, and your submissive and gentle side calls to both of us in the most animalistic way."

"Animalistic?" I asked and bit my lip to keep it from quaking like the rest of my body wanted to do.

"We can tell you what we mean, but you'll probably run for the hills," Walker rumbled from behind me, letting his hands move on my hips seductively.

I looked over at him and licked my lips, making his eyes fall to them as his nostrils flared. "Tell me anyway," I begged.

"Bailey." Finn groaned, gripping my thighs with his large hands.

"Please," I added, looking at him and smiling softly. "I won't run. I promise."

He answered me truthfully, letting his gaze hold mine. "We want to consume you, own every single one of your thoughts and feelings until we don't exist any longer without you. We want you to be so cared for that you never want for anything ever again. We want to possess your body in every way known to man. I won't lie to you about that part, Bailey. We're both very sexual men, and you make that drive run rampant in both of us. If you want to be with us like we want you to be, there won't be a moment that one of us isn't touching you like we are now or dragging orgasms from your body."

I moaned.

Finn rubbed his thumb across my bottom lip, and I quickly stuck my tongue out, touching the end of it to his thumb by accident.

"How does that work? Do you take turns? Do you get jealous of each other? How do you split time? Have you done this with other women a lot? Had an actual relationship with one woman?" I asked. My mind was running wild!

They wanted me. Both of them. And they wanted me to want the both of them back equally.

Walker answered, "There are no set rules other than neither of us ever pushes you to give more to one than the other. We don't get jealous because we genuinely want the other to be happy and loved as much as ourselves. We love watching the woman we're with being cared for by the other almost as much as we love doing the caring ourselves. We've had a relationship with two other women like what we hope to have with you, but there have been others that we've had casual sex with, both together and separately. There will be times you are with just one of us, and there will be times you're with us both."

"At the same time?" I asked. My voice was a mere whisper, and my chest rose and fell with quick, short gasps as I tried to wrap my head around the idea of having both of these men in my bed at the same time.

Finn answered, "If you want us to take turns, we can. But we both really want to be inside of you at the same time. That's one of our favorite sexual activities, though there are plenty of other combinations to make you feel comfortable."

"Inside of me at the same time. In both—" I couldn't say it. I knew I was as red as a fire engine, but I was trying to get as much information as possible from them at once.

Walker leaned forward until his lips were at my ear. "Yes, Bailey. One cock in your pussy and one cock in your ass. Both fucking you at the same time." He ran the tip of his tongue along the edge of my ear and then asked, "Have you ever been fucked in the ass? Or taken two cocks in your pussy at once?"

I squeezed my thighs together, pinning Finn's hands between them as I rolled my hips in desperate need of pressure on my clit to soothe the ache from the erotic sensations their words and voices were causing me. Finn's nostrils flared as he pushed my thighs apart and slid his thumbs toward the seam of my jeans, and Walker hardened under my ass as he pulled me down into his lap more. This conversation was arousing them as much as it was me.

I shook my head no to the question, but Walker wasn't having that.

"Say it," he demanded.

He was so alpha, but he was right. I was submissive and gentle compared to them. The submissive in me wanted to please him, so I looked over my shoulder and said the words he wanted to hear. "I've never been fucked in the ass before." And then, because I was a crazy woman and desperate for their desires like they were for mine, I added, "I've hardly been fucked in the pussy if I'm being honest."

Finn quickly grabbed me, wrapping his hands around my hips and lifting me from his brother's lap. He pulled me across the space until I was straddling him, his lips mere inches above mine as he pushed his hard erection up into my wet center. I moaned out loud, unashamed of the need I heard in it, and let my eyes close and my head fall back.

"What do you mean your sweet little pussy hasn't been fucked a lot?" he asked.

The delicious dirty talk from their tongues felt so good in my ears, almost as good as their hands and bodies. Walker leaned forward, putting his hands on my ass, and pushed my hips, grinding my pussy down on Finn's hard cock underneath me, making me moan again.

"I've only had casual relationships over the years. Nothing was serious so I haven't had a lot of sex or experimented past the sex you get on a one-night stand, which, honestly, is never that good."

Finn groaned. "We're going to destroy you for any other man in the world with how good we're going to fuck you, baby," he said against my lips. "Tell me you want this. Tell me you want us as badly as we want you.."

I didn't know why, but hearing him say they would destroy me with sex left no question in my imagination about how good it would be with them. I was just so nervous to venture into something like this headfirst.

"I'm scared. I'm intimidated by it all, by you both," I said honestly.

His eyes held understanding and no anger as my words filtered into his brain. He picked me up and set me on the counter between the two stools and then sat back down on his, leaving me completely untouched by either of them as the cold, unforgiving stone cooled my warm crotch.

I also felt like I could breathe for the first time in forever, but a part of me willingly wanted not to if it meant letting them touch me as they had been.

I wanted this so fucking badly. I wanted both of them. I just couldn't bring myself to say that. Not now, not yet.

Chapter 10 – Walker

She sat on the counter between us and panted as we all tried to calm down. The conversation had gotten deep and sexual quickly, thanks to the situation with Clay forcing it to happen before we'd even eaten.

She'd pounded a few glasses of Jameson first thing, and I could see the effects on her. Her eyes were wider, her face flushed, and she was bolder about what she wanted.

But she said she was scared and intimidated by the idea of all of it, and that was ice water to our veins. We didn't want to make her try something she didn't want to do. This had to be her idea; she needed to come to us willingly.

"Then how about we press pause on this for now, eat dinner, and go from there?" I asked, standing up and pouring myself another shot. I didn't offer her another and she didn't ask for one. She had already had enough, and I wanted her clear-headed when she decided.

Finn leaned over her when he stood up and kissed her cheek, but he pulled back and walked away when I knew that was the last thing he really wanted to do. He struggled to keep his hands to himself around her and I did too, which was new for me. Usually, I was only affectionate during times of intimacy, but with Bailey, I wanted to touch her nonstop, even if each one was just innocent and small.

"Can I help at all?" she asked, still sitting on the counter and watching us move around the space.

"No. You're doing everything we want you to right now," Finn said, looking her body up and down.

She blushed but smiled back seductively.

She wanted this. I knew she did. She just had to allow herself to have it.

We got dinner out and placed it on the table. I walked back to the counter and picked her up, sliding her thighs around my waist and holding her up by her ass.

"You feel good in my arms like this," I said, keeping her stare as I walked her over to the table and gently set her down on a chair between us.

"I can walk," she joked, but she never once fought against my hold. Instead, she had slid her hands around my shoulders and let her nails play with the hair at the nape of my neck while I carried her.

"Well, don't expect to do much of that with both of us around." I winked at her and started serving food onto her plate before handing it to her.

We all sat in comfortable silence and ate for a while, stealing glances at each other and smiling. It felt good.

It felt right.

"Where are you from?" I asked after a while, enjoying the way she covered her mouth as she chewed.

"For the most part, Vegas. But I've lived all over the West Coast at one point or another. Have you guys always lived here?"

Finn answered, "Born and raised. Our parents live here half of the year still and then travel around the other time. Where are your parents?"

"My mom lives in Hollywood." She smiled fondly, thinking about her mother. "She's obsessed with the vintage glamour of the area. My dad passed away years ago."

"I'm sorry," I said, putting my fork down, "How did he die?"

She looked up at me and I could see the sadness in her eyes as she thought about it. "He was killed. Uh, a homeless man attacked him when he was walking to his car from work one night."

"Damn. How long ago was it?" Finn asked.

"Almost fourteen years now. Seems like yesterday and another lifetime ago at the same time."

"I'm sorry that happened to you, Bailey."

She shrugged and took another bite of broccoli off her plate. "What about your parents? What are they like?"

Finn looked at me, and I smirked at him. Bailey saw it and watched us closely.

"What?" she asked.

"Our mom and dads are great. We're exact replicas of our dads, and mom's a saint for dealing with all four of us."

"Dads?" she asked, confused.

I chuckled and reached over to take her hand in mine. It'd been almost twenty minutes since the last time I'd touched her, and I needed another fix.

"Our mom is married to two men, brothers actually, like us. It's why we are the way we are today. We saw how much love was in our home growing up and it shaped what we are looking for in life as well."

"Hmm," she said as her brain worked.

Finn took pity on her and changed the subject for the moment.

We talked about our jobs and hers, coaching football, and her love for reading. Soon the meal was over, and we were left at a fork in the road.

"Let's go out on the back porch," I said, standing up and clearing the plates from the table.

Finn walked over and took Bailey's hand, leading her outside behind us. She gasped when she saw it and we both smiled. We had started building this house with our bare hands when we were eighteen, and now at thirty, we were finally enjoying the finished product.

There were lounge chairs and big swings all over the large wraparound porch. We both spent most of our free time out here when the weather was nice.

"It's so pretty," Bailey said, wonder in her voice.

"Well, pretty wasn't what we were aiming for, but we'll take it if you think so," Finn said and pulled her into his side, kissing the top of her head. She smiled, wrapped her arms around his stomach, and laid her head on his chest as they looked out over the expansive large backyard.

I sat on a double swing and watched them get comfortable with each other's touch. After a while, her voice sounded timid as she asked, "What if you don't like me"—she paused and looked over at me—"sexually? You know, in bed?"

"Are you seriously worried about that?" I asked, raising an eyebrow at her in disbelief. "You felt both of our erections under your lush body earlier, Bailey. And you had hardly even touched us."

"That's just letting anticipation key you up, but what if when it comes time, I don't feel good to you or something? Or what if I can't take you both?" She was letting her mind run a mile a minute as her fears were coming to light. "I did feel both of your erections, and they were both"—she bit her lip and looked away from me and up to Finn—"large."

He laughed out boisterously and ran his hand up her back before sliding down to her ass and pulling her in against his body. "We'll work you up to it, Bailey. We're not going to just throw you on the bed and hold you down while we both shove ourselves into your body. We're not cavemen," he said.

I watched as her face flushed and she licked her lips. "Unless you like the idea of being taken roughly."

She snapped her eyes up to mine and contemplated it before smiling seductively. "I don't think there's any other way to describe what you two do to women other than *taking them*."

"You're probably right about it for the most part, but believe it or not, there will be times we let you have control."

She watched me pensively. "There's only one way to know if we work sexually," she said shyly. She took a deep breath and swallowed before tilting her head up to Finn. He looked down into her eyes and let his hands play with her hair. He was as obsessed with that mess of blond curls as I was. "Kiss me," she said with actual backbone to it.

I groaned and Finn smiled down at her lustful grin.

"Our pleasure." He pulled her with him as he sat down on the swing next to me, and she spread her thighs to straddle his hips.

She came willingly, letting her fingers slide around the back of his neck as she adjusted her hips to sit directly in the center of his lap. He slid both hands to the sides of her face and into her hair and fisted it, controlling her motions and pulling her into him, locking his lips over hers.

Her lips were so big and lush against his as they moved over hers a few times. I watched with rapture, almost able to feel her lips on my own from just watching. That was one of those twin perks. I could feel things he did sometimes and could feel his emotions as well, just like he could with me. I watched as he left the kiss light and waited for her to deepen it.

And she eagerly rose to the occasion.

She leaned her head to the side and opened mouth, letting her pink tongue run across his lips as he opened them, and then she pushed it against his tongue, drawing a moan from his throat.

He let go of her head with one hand and dropped it to her hips, and she rolled them for him. I didn't doubt that he was hard and she was using him to rub her clit as she sucked on his tongue and moaned into his mouth.

I was fucking hard just watching and I wanted my turn, but I let them explore more. Almost as if she could sense my need, she reached over and slid her fingers across my stomach right above my belt and gripped my T-shirt, pulling the fabric taut in her fingers as she moaned again.

She leaned back and slowly opened her eyes and sighed as she caught her breath. Finn's eyes were glassy, and his pupils were huge as he caught his breath. "I could do that for days," he said before leaning over and kissing her cheek and then down to her neck and ear. I knew the second he bit the sensitive flesh because she gasped and let her hand slide down farther on my stomach, until she was holding onto my belt like it was keeping her grounded. She didn't have a clue what it was doing to me though.

Finn pulled back far enough to growl into the skin of her neck. "Let Walker taste your sweet mouth, baby."

She didn't hesitate for one second. She climbed off Finn and I lifted her effortlessly onto my lap and groaned the second I felt how hot she was through her jeans. "Your pussy is so hot, Bailey; it's branding me through your jeans."

Her arousal was making her bold, and I loved watching this side of her come out to play. "I've been wet for days because of you two."

I leaned down and roughly took her mouth with mine, pushing my tongue in without preamble, and she welcomed it and bit my lip with her teeth before running her tongue over it to soothe it. I kissed her with everything I had, and she gave it right back. I felt Finn sliding his hand along the exposed skin at her waist where her sweater had ridden up, and I pulled back to watch him push the fabric up, revealing her silky skin to the cool evening air.

Her eyes fluttered closed as he palmed her breast under the sweater, but I couldn't stand to not be a part of it. I pushed her sweater up and she helped me lift it over her head completely, and I dropped it on the porch behind her.

Her tits were fucking gorgeous. They were large, full, and perky, and her nipples were bright pink and so fucking hard, begging to be sucked. I leaned in and flicked my tongue across one, while Finn pinched and pulled the other one. I pulled it into my mouth and sucked on it hard as she dug her nails into my shoulder and Finn's arm as she rode the sensation.

"Please," she begged, pushing her pussy harder against my cock.

"Please what, love?" Finn asked and pulled her head back by her hair, pushing her chest forward and into my mouth farther.

"I'm—that feels so good." She panted.

I knew what she wanted. I could tell she was close, and I wanted to give her an orgasm more than I wanted my next breath. So I pulled off of her nipple and pushed her chest towards Finn, and he leaned down and bit her other one and then sucked it in like I had. I tilted my hips, scooting down in the swing and giving her more pressure against her pussy.

She groaned and panted and begged as we licked, sucked, and rubbed every part of her. Within seconds, her back tensed up and her breath caught, her mouth popped open, and her eyes rolled as she started coming on my lap with her tits in Finn's mouth and hands.

"Yes! Oh god, yes! Please."

"That's it. Come on my cock, baby," I ordered her, and she shuddered as I did. I could feel her orgasm rolling through her body, but we didn't let up any of the pressure.

After a minute, she took a deep breath and sighed as she started going limp in my arms. Finn let go of her breasts and she collapsed against my chest, letting her head fall to my shoulder while she came down from her high.

I ran my hands up and down her naked back and Finn walked inside, adjusting his hard-on as he went. Within a second, he was back with a blanket off the couch. He opened it up and covered her with it and then sat back down next to me, sliding his hand under it to hold hers.

She turned her face to him and offered her lips, which he happily took and kissed passionately before he turned her face and offered her to me. She smiled and leaned up, kissing me with such fervor and attention, it left me shaken—and still rock hard, which she felt because she rocked her hips again and pulled back to look in my eyes.

"Can I help you with that?" she asked shyly and bit her lip as she looked over to Finn's lap to see his hard-on pressing into his denim to match mine.

I kissed her bare shoulder and up her neck to her ear. "No. Not tonight. This was to prove to you that it would be good for you, but we already knew that it would be."

"I want to though," she said as she reached over and palmed Finn's cock, squeezing it and making him moan. He pulled her forward to kiss her deeply again as he reached up and tweaked her bare nipple. "Please let me," she begged, looking between us when he pulled back again.

I could feel my resolve slipping as she reached under her and grabbed my cock through my jeans and worked both of us at the same time. "You guys are so fucking big. I can't even wrap my hands around you," she said in wonder as she continued to explore. "Please let me make you feel good like you did for me."

She was begging and it was doing everything she hoped it would. I wouldn't complain if I wanted to. And I didn't.

"You're topping from the bottom, darling," Finn said, but she smiled sweetly at him as she tentatively pulled on the button of his jeans, and he didn't stop her as it popped open or when she slowly pulled down his zipper. "We're both very dominant men, in case you haven't noticed. You're going to have to be careful trying to take control between us."

"Let me explore your bodies," she said, but we were both already goners. "Please." She begged, tugging on that bottom lip with her teeth again. It was my fucking cat nip, and she was going to be doing it a lot more if I had anything to say about it. It made me imagine other things being played with in her mouth.

"Do your worst," I said, giving up trying to be chivalrous and polite. I was a warm-blooded man, after all, with the sexiest woman I'd ever met topless in my lap, stroking my cock, begging me to let her make me come.

There was no way I could say no to that now.

Chapter 11 – Finn

"Let's go inside where it's warm," I said and stood up, pulling Bailey off Walker's lap. I threw her over my shoulder, eliciting a girly squeal from her as she put her hands on my ass to hold herself up.

"That's a sexy sound," Walker added from behind us as we walked into the house and to the living room.

My pants were undone, and my cock was throbbing in the most painful way possible. I was so hard, it ached with the need to come. I hadn't wanted to let it go this far tonight because I wanted her to be comfortable and not pressured. But she had asked us to kiss her and then she rocked her hips on Walker's lap until she'd orgasmed, and then she had begged us to let her get us off. We weren't going to tell her no when she'd asked so nicely.

I stood her on her feet, holding her while she steadied herself as her world righted, and then sat down on the couch and pulled my shirt up and over my head, tossing it on the floor.

Walker took his off, too, stood in front of her, and leaned down to kiss her. He took both of her hands and placed them flat on his abs and groaned as she let her fingers slide down them to the V leading to his belt and then back up. Her nails teased the skin up and down before she dropped them lower and pulled herself even closer to him by his leather belt.

She quickly undid the buckle and then the button and zipper of his jeans while still kissing him.

She looked up at him as she sexily sank to her knees in front of him and pulled his jeans and boxer briefs down his legs until they sat around his ankles. His cock stood pointing directly at her mouth.

"God, you're huge," she whispered as she helped him step out of his jeans and tossed them to the side, letting him stand there completely naked.

I reached down and palmed my cock as I watched her lick her full lips before she slid her hands up his things and leaned in, letting her tiny pink tongue flick across the slit in the head to taste the bead of precum pooling there.

"Fuck," Walker hissed, wrapping those beautiful curls around his hand and pulling her head up higher as she licked around his head and pulled another groan from him. She let her hands slide towards his cock, wrapping one around the base, the other cupping his heavy balls as she slid her mouth down until he pressed into the back of her throat, causing her to gag a bit and then back out. She slid her tongue around the tip again and then bobbed her head back down, letting her hand chase her lips as her saliva coated his entire cock.

"You taste so good, Walker." She moaned as she bobbed her head up and down on him, letting more of him into her throat with each pass. "Sit down," she ordered and nodded toward the couch next to me as she crawled between my knees. Then for good measure, she added a sweet demure, "Please."

I was all too happy to have her looking at me with that haze of arousal in her eyes as she slid my pants and briefs down my thighs and then off my feet, adding them to the pile of clothes on the floor.

Her eyes flashed as she looked at my cock and leaned in, fisting the base of it like she had his. She locked with me as she ran the flat of her tongue up the entire length of my cock. I groaned and my hips bucked toward the hot wetness of her mouth.

Walker leaned over and fisted her curls again to help guide her mouth over the head of my cock and down the length of me.

I laid my head back on the couch and watched as she stared up at me with her puffy lips wrapped around my cock, Walker's tattooed hand holding her hair back, pushing her and pulling her head.

"You feel so fucking good on my cock, Bailey." I groaned and reached down to palm her breasts as she sucked me with gumption. "You're hands down the most beautiful woman I've ever seen, and with my cock in your mouth, fucking Christ, you're breathtaking."

She was incredible at giving head, and I tried hard not to think about how she obtained these skills. But with each pass, she took more and more into her mouth until her lips brushed against my balls. She paused with me completely down her throat and hummed.

"Shit," I cursed and jerked my hips, pushing the last teeny bit into her throat, and I reveled in the way she gagged but kept me deep inside of her. When she finally pulled up again, she smiled at me and licked up my length and then down to my balls, sucking one into her mouth as she fisted my cock and jerked me off. "You're killing me in the best way possible."

I groaned. I could feel the burning of an orgasm starting at my spine but didn't want it to end just yet, so I pulled her up by her hair until she was standing over me and kissed her deeply. "I want to watch you swallow every last inch of his cock down your throat just like you did mine."

She smiled at me. "Yes, sir," she purred, and I bit her lip hard.

"Don't call me Sir, until you're ready to submit to me," I whispered in her ear, "In every way possible." She shivered but did as she was told as she slid over and knelt between Walker's bare thighs again.

She grabbed his cock and dove down on it, pulling a groan from his lips as she bottomed out on him within a few thrusts. She held him there like she had me and hummed as she ran her nails over his tight balls and thighs. He tossed his head back as she pulled up and then slid back down over and over again. She had one hand wrapped around his sack and the other chasing her mouth, twisting and pulling his cock as she sucked him with everything she had.

She let go of his balls and reached over and took my cock in her hand, stroking it with the same rhythm that she was sucking him. We both cursed and groaned as she worked us toward orgasms.

I could tell Walker was close, just like I was. I wanted her to focus on him and give him every ounce of pleasure she could, so I pulled her hand from my lap and slid off the couch, kneeling behind her and pressing my cock into the tight denim covering her ass.

I reached around and pinched both nipples as she took him deep into her mouth, and she moaned and hummed around him with each pass as I worked her up like she was us.

I slid my hand over the fabric covering her pussy and rubbed my fingers against the hard numb I could feel through her jeans. Within moments, she was bobbing her head with such vigor and using both hands on his cock and balls as he cursed and jerked up into her mouth, his orgasm getting even closer.

"Are you going to swallow his come, baby? He's so close. He's going to explode because you feel so good on his cock," I purred into her ear as I jerked my hips, rubbing my cock between my stomach and her ass.

"Yes. Yes, I want every drop." She panted as she pulled up and off him before biting his thigh as she squeezed him hard with her tiny fist.

"I'm going to come. Fuck, I'm—" He panted, and she took every inch of him back into her mouth as he exploded down her throat. She kept moving her mouth on him and took every single drop just like she'd said she wanted. As he stilled, she slowly licked up the entire length of him, cleaning him up as she went.

He leaned down and kissed her roughly, pushing his tongue into her sweet mouth to taste himself, and he groaned as they both panted. "That was the best blow job I've ever had," he said and smirked as he turned her around to face me.

I lay back on the carpet and she crawled up my legs until she was face down, ass up between my legs, and she wrapped her swollen lips around me. My eyes rolled as she started sucking me again, and I put an arm under my head to watch her as Walker knelt behind her and slid his hand between her legs, rubbing her as she worked.

She was moaning again and swinging her hips as he tortured her. It took nearly no time at all for me to get near my orgasm, and I locked eyes with her as she started pulling the pleasure from my balls.

She hummed and sucked with deep pulls as I shot rope after rope of come down her throat, and she took it all without missing a beat. Walker reached around and pinched her nipple, and she pulled off of my cock, arched her back, and moaned as her orgasm tore through her body. She lay forward and rested her forehead on my thigh as she caught her breath.

"Watching you orgasm with my cock in your mouth was so fucking hot," I said softly, running my thumb over her swollen lips as she looked up at me with a smile in her eyes.

She crawled up my body, straddled my stomach, and kissed me for a moment before climbing off and offering her lips to Walker. He took them and kissed her passionately.

She sighed and sat back on the floor, unashamed at her nudity, but the cool air caused her flesh to pebble, and she wrapped her arms around her waist.

Walker grabbed his T-shirt off the floor, slid it over her head, and helped her get her arms into it.

We each put our pants on and got up onto the oversized sectional to relax and turn a movie on with Bailey between us, lying in both of our arms. It felt natural and easy, and

I was embarrassed at how badly I wanted this to happen. But, I refused to pressure her at all.

Halfway through the movie, she looked up at me and I could see the question in her eyes, so I took the remote and muted the TV.

"What is it?" I asked, running my hand up her thigh and squeezing it.

She hesitated briefly and then went ahead, "Do people know that you share women? Is that why Clay said that about you two? And why Thea has pushed me toward both of you at every turn?"

Walker sat up straighter on the couch and pulled her back against him farther, playing with her hair. This was the hard part about our relationship for most women—the judgment from society—but she deserved to know what she was considering. "Yes, pretty much everyone knows about us because they also know about our parents."

"Do people treat you differently for it?" she asked.

Walker answered, "Some of the older generation give us disapproving looks in public, but honestly, most everyone is just used to it by now, being that we're second-generational polyamorous men. It would be new for everyone to see you in a relationship with us, so there would be stares and comments made toward you, no doubt. I hate that part for you."

She scoffed and dismissed, "I grew up in Sin City. I assure you I can handle stares and whispers. And honestly, the idea of this kind of relationship isn't scandalous to me at all given what I grew up seeing in Vegas and California, so don't think I'm worried about that. I just want to know what we're facing from here on out."

"Does that mean . . . ?" I asked, afraid to be hopeful.

She looked at me and smiled brightly. "Oh, I'm in." She didn't hesitate or question her decision. "You both just gave me two of the biggest orgasms of my life with just your hands. There's no way I'm not going to be selfish and take whatever you're willing to give to me while you're both silly enough to think you want me."

Walker pulled her head back by her hair until she was looking up at him behind her. "Don't talk about us or yourself like that, Bailey. We're not silly to think we want you; we want you in every single way because of how great you are. Nothing less."

She bit her lip and nodded her head slightly, as far as she could because his hands were in her hair still.

"Okay," she said softly.

We spent the rest of the evening watching the movie until it got late and she was getting tired. When I caught her yawning, I leaned over and pushed Walker's T-shirt up that she was still wearing, baring her beautiful breasts to me, lay between her legs, and leisurely started sucking and licking both of her nipples. I drove her wild with my hands and mouth as Walker kissed her senselessly until she was tilting her hips under my stomach and grinding herself on me. I reached down and rubbed her with my fingers, kissing her stomach until she shattered between us again.

She looked at me through hooded eyes, and I crawled up farther and kissed her deeply. "I wanted to make sure you dreamed of us tonight when you slept."

She chuckled and kissed me back before sighing happily. "As if I have any choice in that matter."

I had to work tomorrow night and Walker had to in the morning, so we reluctantly walked her to her car and kissed her goodbye, watching as she drove out of our driveway and went home for the night.

As soon as she left our house, it felt empty and lacking the bright warm sunshine that followed her around, but we knew we had to introduce her into our lives at an easy pace and not rush anything. We let her go home when there was nothing we wanted more than to take her upstairs and bury ourselves inside of her until morning.

But I still went inside and stroked my cock, lying in my bed until I roared as an orgasm ripped from my body from thinking about her soft skin under my lips and how she tasted and smelled as she came in our hands over and over.

I also heard Walker doing the same in the shower before he went to bed and smiled to myself as I felt sleep trying to pull me under.

This girl was exactly what we needed in life and was going to keep us on our toes from here on out.

And we were going to love every single second of it.

Chapter 12 – Bailey

When I got home, I stripped out of my clothes, sank into my comfy new bed, and passed out within minutes. Never in my life had I come as hard and as many times in a row as I had tonight at the hands of Finn and Walker.

The two god-like men had worshiped my body and showed me what it would be like to be theirs. And I was hooked.

I was telling the truth when I told them that I didn't care about people looking at me as the girl shared by two men. I'd been raised around so many other worse things, that one didn't hardly register to me.

If anything, I was looking forward to it being known I was theirs because they were both intimidating officers of the law, so I was sure people would leave me alone.

Or at least, I hoped so.

It was midday by time I woke up. I hardly ever slept in, but this last week had been *hard* and long, and my body was worn out.

When I rolled over and looked at my phone, I saw I had multiple text messages from the two of them.

They were in a group chat, which must be the preferred way to communicate with me, and I didn't mind.

Finn: Good morning, angel, hope you slept well.

Walker: Morning, I hope you dreamed of us all night.

Finn: I hope they were all dirty and absolutely indecent too.

Walker: Uh oh, she's ignoring us. Perhaps we scared her off after all.

Finn: If we did, it was your fault for sure.

Walker: How?

Finn: I'm not sure yet, but I just know it was.

I giggled as I read their banter and decided to make sure they were thinking of me like I was still thinking of them.

I walked over to the full-length mirror at the end of my bed and took a selfie. I was still wearing Walker's green shirt and used my hand to bunch the fabric up over my hip so they could see the bare skin that would be concealed if I were wearing panties while keeping my actual crotch covered. Then, I put my other elbow against the wall and tilted my hips to stick one out, smiled seductively, and snapped a picture.

My curls were everywhere, but I had learned that they were fans of them with as often as one of their hands was tangled into them.

I pressed send in the group chat and added the caption:

Me: Sorry, fellas, you both tired me out so thoroughly, I just woke up.

Their replies came almost instantly.

Finn: Holy shit, you look like a goddess.

Walker: *saves to the spank bank* Good morning, beautiful. You look good enough to eat.

Me: I'm here for the taking.

Finn: Don't tempt me.

Walker: Of course you are because I'm at work until this evening.

I decided to play dirty. I knew Walker was at work but was off later, and Finn was off now but worked tonight. I didn't know the rules for this. I didn't know if I was allowed to be with one of them for the first time or if they would want to do it together like last night. I figured I'd let them decide how it played out and leave the ball in their court.

I took off the T-shirt and set my phone on the top edge of the mirror, set a 3 second timer, and pressed record to take a quick video of me walking away. I was completely naked as I moved toward the open bathroom door, sashayed my hips and pulling my hair up onto the top of my head.

I walked back to it when it was done recording and typed in my address, adding:

Me: I'm not sure how this works, but my front door is unlocked and I'm getting in the shower. You two decide amongst yourselves from here.

I pressed send and laid my phone down on the counter, walked to the front door and unlocked it, and grabbed a cup of coffee, trying to make myself wait a few minutes before jumping in the shower.

After I drank half of the cup, I abandoned it on the counter and then walked back into the bathroom, turning the shower on and opening up the message thread again to read their replies.

Walker: *Go to her, man. Show her just how good we can make her feel. Worship her.*

Finn: *Already in the fucking truck. I hope you're ready for me, baby.*

Walker: *Send me videos. I'll see you tonight, Bailey.*

Hot damn. I squealed and quickly brushed my teeth, jumped into the shower, and tried to calm my erratic breathing. Was I really going to get fucked by Finn right now? And Walker later?

My shower was a big stone walk-in with a five-foot-long bench along the side and a massive rain showerhead. I rinsed my hair and quickly shampooed and conditioned it, so the necessities were done, and then lathered up my loofa and started washing my body.

Part of me was convinced that he wasn't actually coming to me, that he had just been kidding, but as I stood with my back to the door to wash off some of the suds, I heard the telltale sound of boots on the stone floor and looked over my shoulder.

Sure enough, a very worked up Finn stood in my bathroom in jeans and a T-shirt, just like last night, and he was letting his eyes wash over my entire naked back with a need in them I hadn't seen from him yet.

"Hi," I said, almost shyly. Now that he was here, I was nervous.

I kept my back to him and watched as he bent down to untie his boots and then stood back up.

"Good morning, Bailey," he said. His eyes never left my body, but then he flicked them up to meet mine. "You sure you want this right now? Because if I get in there naked with you, I won't be able to stop." His voice was so deep, and I could see the evidence of his arousal growing down the leg of his tight jeans.

I turned around and faced him, letting the water cascade down my chest and stomach as I tipped my head back, closed my eyes, and pushed my hair over my back. When I opened them again, I looked directly at him. "I want you so bad," I purred and dropped my hands to run down over my breasts and stomach.

It took no more convincing. He ripped his shirt off and over his head and undid his jeans, shoving them down and stepping out of them. He was standing directly in front of me in all his naked glory, and I bit my lip and backed up, beckoning him to join me in the hot steam.

He walked in, slid his hands around my wet waist, pulled me against his chest, kissing me roughly. He slid his fingers into my wet hair, fisting it, and pulled back until my lips were aimed directly up in the air for him, and he drank from them for a long, long time. His hands rubbed up and down my back and hips as he explored my mouth.

The coarse hair on his chest and stomach scrapped across my sensitive nipples, and it matched the scratch of his calloused hands on my ass cheeks as he kneaded them.

"You are so beautiful, baby," he said against my lips and then leaned down until his tongue ran down the side of my neck and into the hollow under my clavicle.

I slid my fingers through his wet hair and pulled on the short strands, holding him to my neck as he sucked and bit my flesh.

He knelt on the tile, and that brought his face even with my chest. He used both hands to grab my tits and pull on my nipples.

"Yes." I moaned and pushed them into his expert hands. I leaned down and pulled his head away from my chest to kiss him passionately. I wanted to be consumed by him. I wanted to feel him in my soul.

He pushed me until my back pressed into the wall. "I want to taste you. Hold on to me tight," he said and slid his large hand down behind my knee, lifting it up and over his shoulder, effectively opening me to him. He dipped his head and swiped his tongue out across my clit, and I bowed my back, pressing it farther into his mouth as I gripped the hair on the top of his head and held on.

"Yes. Fuck, that feels so good," I said and rode his face as she licked and sucked on my clit.

He pulled back and watched up my body as he slid his fingers through my folds, using his saliva to lubricate them up, and then he slowly pushed one digit into my pussy.

It felt incredible. His fingers were so big and thick, doing serious damage on my ability to hold off on coming.

He hissed as he pushed it in and pulled it out, and then he sucked on my clit as he crooked his finger inside of me and rubbed against my G-spot. "Finn!" I moaned and rode his hand as he used his palm on my clit and pumped into my body, sliding another finger into me as he pushed me closer to an orgasm.

"You're so fucking tight, Bailey. Walker and I are going to rip you open."

"I told you that you were huge." I moaned as I rode him harder.

He chuckled and sucked on my clit again, drawing more curses and moans from my body. He pulled back and stood up, and I lowered my leg and watched in confusion as he walked over to his jeans on the floor by the shower door and pulled his phone out. "I want to send Walker a video of you coming on my face. Are you okay with that?" he asked, keeping his phone out of the water spray.

"Yes," I said, smiling at him and reaching up to pinch my nipples. The idea of him sending Walker a video of me as he ate me out sent shivers through my entire body. I missed Walker and I wanted him involved in this monumental moment too.

Finn put his phone on the shampoo ledge on the wall next to us and pressed record. I watched the screen as he walked back over and pressed me into the wall, lifting my leg up over his wide shoulder again and diving back in with his mouth.

I moaned and threw my head back as he sucked hard on my clit and pinched my nipple. "Fuck, Finn."

He spat on his fingers and watched up my body as he slid two fingers into my pussy. "So fucking tight." He pumped his hand back and forth, fucking me with his fingers as I rode them. I pinched and pulled on my nipples and pulled at his hair as I got closer to my orgasm. Right before I toppled over the cusp of the climax, he pushed a third thick finger in, and I cursed as my leg gave out, my orgasm plowing through my system. He held me up and didn't stop the vicious thrusts into my pussy or the suction on my clit with his mouth as I moaned over and over again, yelling his and Walker's names.

He slowed his fingers and his mouth as I came down from my ecstasy and kissed his way up my body until he was standing in front of me. He kept my knee in his hand and wrapped it around his hip, pushing his erection against my belly as he kissed me deeply. After a minute of that, he walked over to his phone and hit stop and then tossed it on the bathroom counter.

He was rock hard, and the head of his cock was almost purple. "I want you inside of me, Finn."

His eyes were glowing, and he fisted his cock and stroked it while walking back to me.

"I want you underneath me in your bed when I push into your body for the first time, Bail," he said, biting my lips for emphasis.

"I'm yours. But send that video to Walker first. Then, we can take another one as you fuck me." I felt so brazen and wild from the carnal desires coursing through my body.

He flipped the tap off, stepped out of the shower, and wrapped me in a towel from the rack before tying one of his own around his narrow waist.

It was comical, really, to see his large cock tenting the towel as he tried to dry off in haste. I giggled at him and ran from the bathroom and into my bedroom, but he was quick to catch me and pull my towel off as he picked me up and tossed me down on my bed.

I was in a fit of girly giggles as he followed me, stripping the towel off of him and landing on his side next to me.

He threw something on the end table and then took his phone, opened it up, and pressed play on the video.

We lay there and watched him eating me out in the shower, and I had never felt sexier, knowing he was about to send it to his brother for him to enjoy. I rolled over, kissed his chest, and started moving down his stomach toward his cock.

"Send it so you can fuck me please," I pleaded as I fisted his hard cock in my hand and licked around the tip, tasting his precum on my tongue and moaning.

He put his phone back in front of his face for a minute and sent it. Then, he looked down at me and then behind me and got a wicked grin on his face. "Spread your legs while you suck my cock, Bailey," he said.

I didn't question him, just did as he ordered.

"Put your ass up in the air with those legs pushed wide. I want to see your pretty pussy in that mirror."

"Fuck." I groaned and did it as I continued to bob on his cock. He lay back again and took a picture of me with my ass in the air and exposed in the mirror at the end of the bed, and he sent that to Walker, too, before tossing his phone to the side and fisting my wet curls as I sucked him with everything I had.

"You are so good at that, Bailey. I could spend the rest of my life inside of your mouth and die a happy man."

"Maybe you should wait to make that decision until after you've been inside of my pussy and ass," I whispered seductively.

"Are you going to let me fuck your pretty ass, baby?" He ran his thumb across my lips as I popped them off the head of his cock.

"I want to get there eventually," I answered truthfully. "But I'm intimidated by it."

He smiled down at me and then pulled me up until I was straddling him. "Walker and I will work you up to it. We'll start small and go from there. We'll make sure it feels so good for you before we push our cocks into you, I promise."

He kissed me deeply and then rolled us over until he was on top of me and between my legs. He rubbed the underside of his cock through my wet folds and sucked a groan from both of our lips with the sensation.

"Do you want Walker to send you videos when he's inside of me?" I asked, reaching between us and running the head of his cock through my wet folds and against my clit.

"Fuck yes, I do. I want to watch your body take him deep," he said against my lips and pushed until the tiniest bit of his cock pressed into me.

"Please," I begged, tilting my hips and taking another couple of centimeters of him into me.

"Are you on the pill?" he asked as he reached over for his phone. I noticed then that he had a strip of condoms on the table.

A whole damn strip. Fucking hell, this man was too much.

"I have an IUD. I'm safe." I panted.

"I'm clean. I haven't had sex in months, and I was tested after the last time."

"Me too." I huffed.

"I want to fuck you bare if you'll let me, Bailey. I want to come deep inside of your body too."

"Yes," I purred. "I want you to fill me up."

"Fuck, we don't deserve you, baby," he said, but he didn't waste any more time. He sat up until he was kneeling between my legs, reached down to spread my thighs wide, and looked at my bare, wet pussy like it was his last meal. I reached down and grabbed his cock and ran it against my clit again, letting my wetness coat the head. He spat onto his fingers and pushed them into my pussy and rubbed them around the outer lips, getting me super wet and lubricated for his big cock.

He folded my knees back to my shoulders, lined himself up, and pushed the head of his cock into me. I arched my back and sucked in a breath at the sheer size of him as he stretched me open.

"Fuck. I knew you were tight, but Jesus." He cursed and pulled back until he was out of me completely and then pushed back in, going farther this time.

"Oh my god." I moaned and reached down to rub my clit as he twisted pain and pleasure through my body.

"That's it, play with that sexy pussy, baby." He groaned and pinched my nipple softly as he went farther.

I looked over at the mirror and admired the muscles in his back and the curve of his ass as he thrust in and out of me. I bit my lip and watched him work into me until I couldn't take it anymore and let my eyes close as I grabbed his sides and tilted my hips up to take more of him. "Please, fuck me, Finn. I need all of you inside of me more than I have ever needed anything else."

He pulled out until just the head was inside of me and then thrust forward hard, impaling me completely with his thick, hard cock, pushing all of my breath from my lungs. I reached down and rubbed my clit again as he started pounding into me. The headboard on my bed hit the wall as he punishingly thrust into my welcoming body.

I reached up and ran my nails down the front of his throat where the muscles were bulging with restraint as he tried to control himself.

His eyes fluttered closed, and he clenched his teeth and then leaned down, my knees going around his waist. He started grinding his pelvis into mine with each thrust, sending jolts of lightening through my clit to my entire nervous system.

I was gasping and holding on for dear life as he fucked me with everything he had. I didn't see my orgasm coming; it snuck up on me as he rolled his hips and pinched my clit under his pelvic bone. When it shot through my body, I lit up like a stick of dynamite and screamed his name as I held on for dear life and lost all ability to see or hear as I came in waves around his cock.

He cursed and leaned down to swallow my cries before he bit my neck painfully, causing me to shoot off again and milk his cock deep into my body. He swore a long line of curses as he threw his head back and slammed into me again and again, filling me with his come.

I lay there in euphoria as he slowly and lazily kept thrusting into me, giving me every last drop. It was the first time I ever let someone come inside of me, and feeling the hot liquid fill me up was incredible. I wanted more before we were even done.

I let my hands rub up and down his back as he got his breathing under control, laying his weight heavily on top of me, and I welcomed it because I knew that it was my body that made him fall apart like that.

I did that to this incredible man. He got up, walked into the bathroom, came back with a warm, wet washcloth, and knelt on the bed at my feet.

I watched him lazily as he reached down and spread my legs wide, bending my knees to open me to him. He looked up at me and inspected my eyes as he let the warm, soft fabric wipe up the evidence of his orgasm from between my body.

It was erotic and incredibly intimate and so very Finn.

"Can I be honest with you about something for a second?" he asked as he set the washcloth on the table and crawled back into bed, covering us both up with the sheet. I turned over, and he pulled me into his arms and kissed my nose.

"If you must," I said in response and smiled against his neck.

"That was the most incredible sex I've ever had."

I chuckled and let my fingers play with his light chest hair. "It was the same for me."

"Really?" he asked. I could hear the vulnerability in his voice.

"Yes, really. I told you most of my encounters have been casual with guys I hardly knew. I think I've honestly only ever had an orgasm during sex like three times my whole life. And you gave me three already today."

"I'm an overachiever," he joked as his hands stroked up and down my spine. "Wait until Walker gets here tonight. He's going to have a whole day's worth of pent-up sexual frustration to work out on your sexy little body, baby. I'm so mad I'm going to miss getting to watch in person."

"Hmm, when can I have both of you again, like last night?" I asked.

"We're both off tomorrow and Monday. But after today and tonight, you'll probably be too sore for anything more."

"Good thing my mouth is available," I joked, and his hands squeezed my ass hard, his hips jutting forward, pressing his semi-hard cock into my stomach.

"You're pretty incredible, you know that?" he asked.

"Hmm," I hummed in response, feeling the lazy afternoon trying to pull me under for a nap.

Finn picked up on it right away. "Tired?" he asked.

"I don't want to bore you." I laughed. "But I'm so relaxed and sated, it's getting hard to keep my eyes open."

"Then let's take a nap. I have to go to work tonight, so I could use a snooze."

"Okay," I said, snuggling deeper into his arms and blankets.

Just then, his phone started pinging on the table next to us, and I could hear mine vibrating on the bathroom counter.

He chuckled and leaned over me to grab it. "Sounds like Walker got our video."

He opened the message thread and we both read Walker's replies.

Walker: Well, fuck.

The next one was a video. Finn hit play and I watched in fascination as Walker took a video of him stroking his cock in the front seat of his police cruiser. I could see his gun belt and computer screen with his hand stroking his giant dick as he groaned and cursed. His voice said in the background, "You two are driving me fucking insane. I've never jacked off on the clock before, but here I am. I can't wait to dive into you tonight, Bailey. T-minus four hours."

A shiver of excitement ran through my body and for half a second, I felt guilty for being excited to have Walker when Finn was lying next to me.

"What are you thinking?" Finn asked, sensing my hesitation as he closed his phone.

"I was just thinking about how much I'm looking forward to seeing Walker tonight and I feel guilty because you're here right now in my bed and your come is literally leaking out of my body. It's just, my head says I should feel guilty, but my body says fuck that."

"Your body knows exactly what it should be feeling right now, baby. Your head will catch up. Neither of us will ever get upset about you wanting the other one, even if our come is leaking out of your pussy." He slid his fingers through my sopping wet folds as he said that, pulling a moan from my lips. "Or this sexy, sassy mouth." He brought his fingers up and slid them into my mouth, letting me taste myself and him on them, and I greedily sucked them deep as he did. "Or this perfect, amazing ass." He slid his wet fingers around my back and pushed one against the tight, puckered entrance of my ass, and I fought a moan as he rubbed his slick, calloused finger over my sensitive flesh. "God, I can't wait to dive into your ass for the first time." He swore, rubbing the forbidden area harder, making my hips rock back against the pressure.

"Mmh," I moaned, pushing back against his finger again.

"Do you like that?" he asked, reaching down to rub his thumb over my clit as he kept rubbing his fingertip against my ass.

"Yes, I do. A lot."

"Have you done any anal play? At all?" he asked, putting the same amount of pressure on my clit and my ass at the same time.

"Never. Not even like this."

"That's so hot." He groaned. "Roll over."

I dutifully rolled until I was on my stomach, and he crawled down my back, kissing along my spine. "Do you have any sex toys, Bail?" he asked as he bit one big ass cheek and then licked it.

"Uh—" I said, pausing because that was personal. Even though he was licking my ass cheek, it felt intimate to talk about my sex toys.

He chuckled and bit my cheek again. "Tell me now."

"Yes, I do."

"Where?"

I nodded toward my dresser. "Top drawer."

"Stay exactly like this, okay? Don't move." His voice was deep and sinfully sweet again as arousal poured through his system.

I watched over my shoulder as he went through my panty drawer and pulled out a few pairs of sexy lingerie bottoms and held them up to me. "I can't wait to tear these off of you," he said before putting them back in the drawer and finding what he was looking for.

I had a bullet vibrator and a rabbit vibrating dildo, and he brought them both over to the bed along with the bottle of lube that was with them.

"If you want to stop, just say stop and I will. Do you understand?" he asked, his voice husky, but I could hear the excitement in it too.

"Yes."

He placed his knees between mine on the bed and pushed my legs wide to accommodate him. I wrapped my arms around my pillow and held on in anticipation for what I was hoping was pleasure, but I knew there would be pain too.

"You are so fucking sexy," he said, letting his hands roam over the back of my thighs and ass cheeks. He had a hand on each cheek and pulled them apart to look at my ass and pussy.

He shoved a pillow under my hips, popping my ass into the air.

He lay down again between my legs, leaving his face even with my rear.

"I'm going to eat your ass."

I squeaked with disbelief, but I didn't have time to do anything else because in the next instant, he pulled both my cheeks apart again and ran the flat of his tongue up from my pussy to my asshole and pressed against it.

It wasn't at all unpleasant, and the more he worked his tongue against me, the more I was squirming under him, begging for more.

He slid his arm between the pillow and me, and then I felt the delicious buzz of the bullet vibrator against my clit as he sucked and licked my puckered flesh.

"Finn. Oh yes. Please."

"Do you like that?" he asked as he rubbed the vibrator on my clit.

"Yes. I want more," I begged.

He bit my ass cheek, and then I felt the cold sensation of lube dripping onto my asshole.

I tensed up as his thick finger swirled around my flesh and pushed against my tight muscles.

I was panting as he expertly rubbed the vibrator and his fingers at the same time and with the same rhythm. I circled my hips and pushed against both as I sought my release.

Within moments, I felt electricity jolt up my spine and down to my toes as I exploded under him.

He used the distraction of my orgasm to quickly push his thumb into my ass to his first knuckle.

"Finn!" I screamed and pushed back harder to force more of his thumb into my burning hole.

He kept his finger still inside of me as he switched out the bullet for the rabbit vibrator. I heard him click it on and felt the cold lube he'd prepped it with at some point tingle against my skin before pushing it into my pussy quickly, showing no mercy. The second the ears pressed against my clit, I swung my hips again and spread my legs wider, putting my hips into doggy position, and he fucked me with the vibrator and slowly started moving his thumb in and out of me as he did it.

I was panting and begging and moaning, and he let go of the vibrator and grabbed my hand to hold it.

"Fuck your pussy with this while I fuck your ass with my finger and video it for Walker."

"Yes, Sir." I moaned and started pushing and pulling the dildo in and out of my wet pussy.

I heard the beep of the video starting and pushed back farther again, feeling more of his thick finger press into my body.

"Fuck, your ass is swallowing my finger. You like that, don't you?" He groaned.

"Yes, god, that feels so good. Don't stop! I'm going to come again. It feels so fucking good." I didn't know if any of that was coherent, but that was what I wanted to say.

I arched my back, popping my ass into the air farther, and held the rabbit ears against my clit as he really started fucking my ass with his thumb. He was going in all the way and then back out until just the tip was inside of me.

"I want to feel you milk my finger, baby."

He leaned forward and put the phone against the headboard in front of my face. I locked my eyes with the camera lens as he pushed me over the edge of my orgasm.

"Finn!" I screamed again and started convulsing around his finger and the dildo. He pulled my hair roughly until I was kneeling up in front of him, with my tits and pussy on display for the camera.

"Keep fucking that pussy," he ordered, and I did just what he said. My orgasm made every single muscle in my body tense up and ache as it kept washing over me.

I felt him pull his thumb from my body and then the dildo as he grabbed my hips and slammed his cock deep into me, making me scream again. I kept my legs spread wide and my hands on the bed, holding myself up high as he fucked me like a man possessed. I stared into the camera the entire time as another orgasm sent me into a fit of shivers, and then as I drew his orgasm from his body as he filled me up.

I stayed just like that as he filled me to the brim, pulled out of me, and told me stay put as he cleaned me up. Only when he was done did I collapse onto my bed and drift off to sleep as he got in next to me, kissed my bare shoulder, and fell asleep too.

Chapter 13 – Walker

It was already after seven p.m. I was supposed to have been out of work at six, but I was stuck at the scene of a fatal car accident, taking care of crime scene photos and logging evidence. I took my job seriously and I always wanted to do as much as I could for my victims, but I was having trouble finding the heart for it, knowing that Bailey was waiting for me in my bed currently.

Finn had fucked her throughout the entire day, sending me pictures and videos and keeping my cock in a constant state of pain. I had even jacked off in the front seat of my cruiser at one point, hoping for some relief, but it was short-lived. As soon as I'd come and gotten focused back on work, he sent another one of him eating her virgin ass, and I was rock hard again seconds into the video.

He ate her out and then finger-fucked her while she rode a hot pink vibrator, and then he fucked her brutally, and I was a very envious man. I could have ignored the videos, but I was in no way strong enough to not watch them the second they pinged on my phone screen. Besides, I had told them to send them to me.

Finn reported to work at six and was out on patrol now, but he had taken Bailey to our house before he went to work so that she was there when I got home.

He said her place was nice, but her queen bed just wasn't built for the three of us, and we would all be in the bed together tonight when Finn got home and all day tomorrow.

At least, if I had anything to say about it, we would.

He made sure to give her good aftercare each time they had sex so she wouldn't get sore, but I knew there would be some level of discomfort for her for a while.

But when she called me earlier, she begged me to take her the second I got home, telling me she was sore from emptiness and needed to be filled. I nearly came in my pants like a virgin when she'd purred those sexy words to me through the phone. She had a voice and a body made for sex, so I was going to listen to her and watch her body for cues to make sure I took care of her tonight.

Whenever I fucking got home from this scene, that was.

"Something on your mind tonight, Camden?" my patrol partner Jake asked as he walked up to me from his car. I was sitting in my front seat, doing paperwork, and closed my laptop to look out at him.

"Why do you ask?" I snapped.

He chuckled and held his hands up in surrender. "Because you've bitten the head off anyone who's come near you this evening. Which, in reality, we're all used to when it comes to you, but tonight, you're extra crabby."

"Fuck off," I said, dismissing him but also trying to get my attitude in check.

"He's just mad because his girlfriend is waiting for him at home in bed and he's stuck here," Finn said with a carefree smile on his face as he walked up to my window too.

"His girlfriend, huh? That means your girlfriend too?" Jake asked, shaking hands with Finn. He, like everyone else we worked with, knew we shared women, and they were all a bunch of teenagers about it usually. Most of them were married or settled down and were envious of the fact that we could pull women who were into this sort of thing, but their ball-busting was pretty innocent. "I heard you were sweet on that pretty little bombshell from California or somewhere, Finn. Did you guys lock her down already? She's been in town, like, two weeks, right?"

"Hell yeah, we did. I'm no fucking newbie when it comes to available women in this town, Jake. Every man in the state was chasing after her the second she drove into town. Lucky for us, she's into big, tatted assholes," Finn replied, smirking at him and nudging him with his elbow before putting his hands on my window and leaning down. "I'll take over for you. Get on out of here."

"You sure, man?" I asked.

"Yeah, I'm already over an hour into my eight-hour shift, which means you've got just over six hours of her to yourself before I get home. It'd be a crime to keep you here any longer, especially when you see what she's wearing for you."

"What the fuck is she wearing?" I asked, reaching down, and adjusting my dick for the hundredth time today.

He looked over at Jake, who was leaning in, waiting to hear what our girl was wearing so he could paint a mental picture and wank himself to it later, but Finn just shook his head and winked at me. "You'll find out when you get home."

I stuck my hand out my window and he shook it, and I nodded to him with a shit-eating grin on my face. "I owe you, man."

"I plan on collecting at 2:01 a.m."

I laughed and put my truck in gear and pulled away from the accident scene.

I was about half an hour from the house, and I used the time to call Bailey to let her know I was headed home so I didn't scare her coming in.

Her sweet, angelic voice poured through the car's speakers as she answered. "Well, hello there, handsome."

I smiled. "Hello, beautiful."

"Are you on your way home yet? I miss you," she said easily. It was so tempting to plan a future with this girl from the last thirty-six hours alone. It felt so fucking right.

"I am. I'll be there in about twenty-five minutes. I was told you're wearing something for me."

She chuckled and sighed into the phone; her voice was so sweet and mellifluous, it made my skin tingle with every syllable. "Perhaps what Finn should have said was what I'm not wearing for you."

"Mmm, that sounds just as good, baby." I groaned.

"Yes, it does." She sighed. "What do you want for dinner?"

I was sucked into a rose-colored glasses view of this perfect woman waiting at home for us, cooking us dinner when we were late, and I wanted it so fucking bad.

"You," I answered truthfully.

"I'm your dessert, Walker. What do you want for dinner? You're going to need your strength," she purred, and I could hear her smile in her voice.

"Fuck, I'm not going to last five minutes after walking through the door if you keep talking to me like that."

"Then I better get a move on and get your dinner made so you can scarf it down quickly and then enjoy your sweet treat."

"Bailey," I warned, "You don't need to make me anything. That's not why I wanted you there tonight."

"I know, Walker, but I want to cook for you. Let me take care of you."

I could hear the need in her voice to do this for me, and who was I to tell her no? "Anything you make me will be better than what I was going to have before I knew I could have you; I promise you that. So surprise me. I'll be home shortly."

"I'll see you soon."

"Yes, you will."

I hung up and focused on closing the distance between myself and the woman I was craving. Soon enough, I was pulling up the driveway.

I parked my car, logged out of service, and walked up the side porch steps toward the door to the kitchen.

I paused as soon as I got to the door. Standing in the kitchen in a thin baby-pink cotton robe was Bailey in all of her blonde beauty as she danced around the counters, making dinner for herself and me.

I stood there in awe and watched her as she swayed her hips like she did the first time I saw her in her shop, and she sang sweetly with the Kasey Musgraves song playing.

I needed this woman in every sense of the word, and I'd already had to wait long enough, so without any more hesitation, I opened the screen door and stepped into the kitchen that smelled divine.

She turned when the door shut behind me and a beautiful smile lit up her flawless face. Her curls were pulled up in a messy bun on top of her head, her face was free of makeup, and she was positively breathtaking. I wanted her to know I thought so.

"You are radiant, Bailey. This kitchen looks good on you," I said as I set my bag down on the counter and tossed my keys in the dish.

"You think so?" she asked, propping her hip against the counter as she crossed her arms over her chest. Now that I was closer, I could see that her breasts were bare under the cotton and I desperately wanted to take a bite.

But instead, I slid my hands around her tiny waist above her flared hips and pulled her in for a long, deep, satisfying kiss. By the time I pulled away, we were both panting, and my cock and her nipples were all hard and begging for attention.

I undid my gun belt, walked over to the safe by the living room, and placed it in there. Then, I unbuttoned my shirt and took it and my vest off, and she watched each layer fall away as she chewed on her thumbnail.

"Like what you see?" I asked.

"Oh, do I ever. I don't know if I like you in a uniform or naked more. They're both equally panty-soaking."

I walked back over to her, put my palm on her thigh, and slowly inched it up under the hem of her robe, very happy to feel the bare silky skin of her pussy against my fingers instead of the fabric of a pair of panties. "But, Ms. Dunn, you aren't wearing any panties to soak," I chided and let my fingers lazily stroke through her wet lips. She gasped and spread her legs wider to accommodate my large hand as she stared at my eyes with her beautiful green ones. Her lips fell open when I rolled her clit between my fingers and then slowly pushed my middle finger deep into her incredibly tight pussy. "How is it possible you're still that tight when I know Finn has fucked you a dozen times today?"

"Magic." She moaned and smiled.

I worked my finger in and out of her, enjoying feeling the slickness of Finn's come dripping out around my finger to cover her pussy lips as I worked her up. "I can feel his come dripping out of you and it makes me want to mix my own with it."

"Please do." She panted as she leaned up and offered her lips to me. I leaned down and kissed her soundly as I added another finger. "Fuck, I want to come," she said.

"Let me help you." I dropped to my knees and spread her wide and leaned in to taste her pussy. I'd fantasized about it since the moment I met her, and it was everything I knew it would be. I kept my two fingers thrusting into her as I sucked on her clit. Within seconds, she convulsed on them as she pulled my hair roughly and rode my face.

I pressed sweet kisses to her clit long after her orgasm faded, and then I pulled her robe back down, stood up, and kissed her lips quickly. "I honestly had no intention of attacking you the second I walked in the door, but I couldn't help myself. I'm sorry," I apologized, though I wasn't very upset about the fact that I could taste her on my tongue before I'd even taken a bite of her meal.

"I would be offended if you didn't after how many times you promised you were going to," she jested. Then, she backed me up, walked over to the oven, and opened the door.

I watched with fascination as she bent over, revealing the supple curve of her ass as she pulled a cast iron pan from the oven and place it on the top. There were three steaks in there with potatoes and green beans all seasoned and sizzling, and I realized how famished I actually was.

"That looks almost as good as you do," I said, walking up behind her and kissing her head as I walked over to the bench and sat down to take my boots off.

She grabbed two beers from the fridge and walked them over to the counter, setting them down with plates and silverware and then plating the delicious-smelling meal.

We sat down and ate. I polished mine off quickly and then sat back and watched her eat half of hers. "Is the other one for Finn?" I asked as I slid my hand up and down her inner thigh.

"Yes. I know he won't be home until morning, but I told him I'd leave him a plate in case he was hungry."

"How on earth did we get so fucking lucky to find you?" I asked honestly.

She just shook her head and replied, "It's me who is the lucky one here, Walker." And I could tell she believed that. I wasn't going to get in a pissing match about it right now, but I knew I wanted to change her mind eventually.

I cleaned up the dishes and loaded them in the dishwasher and then turned out the lights in the kitchen, leaving only the stove light on that bathed us in the darkness and locking the door.

"I want you, Bailey. I haven't been able to think about anything else since I tasted your lips last night."

"I'm yours for the taking, Walker. In fact, I insist that you take me. And quickly or I may just combust with need," she said as she ran her hands up my stomach, pushing up the plain white shirt I wore under my uniform up and scratching her nails down my abs.

I leaned down and picked her up, throwing her up over my shoulder, and I spanked her ass forcefully. She gasped and moaned and then giggled as I took the stairs two at a time. I walked into my room and shut the door behind me.

I moved over to the giant Alaskan king bed and gently laid her down in the center of it. She looked from side to side and then back to me. "Holy fuck, this bed is giant. And so comfy."

"We are giant men," I replied as I pulled my shirt off over my head. "And I'm glad you find it comfortable; you're going to be spending a lot of time in it from here on out."

"Hmm, promises, promises." She hummed as she let her hands run up her body and over her breasts and then into her hair.

I pulled at the sash on her waist and then opened her robe like she was a Christmas present, the best one I'd ever gotten in my life. She pushed it over her shoulders and then tossed it to the side, letting me have my fill of her body from my vantage point.

She was so fucking sexy. Her tits were full, over a handful each with the prettiest pink nipples, and her waist was so incredibly tiny, I could touch my fingers together if I put one hand on each side of it. Her hips flared wide to accommodate her large, juicy ass and thick thighs, and there wasn't a single part of her that didn't make my cock throb or my heart ache.

That was a foreign feeling for a guy like me.

I undid my belt and work pants and pushed them to the floor with my underwear and then toed my socks off until I was as naked as she was.

I crawled up the bed and kissed her passionately, and she clawed at my back and shoulders as I did. My cock was rock hard, and I pinned it between her folds and my stomach and rocked forward, letting it grind against her clit.

"You let Finn take you bare," I said. I had nearly come in my pants as I watched him push into her without a condom on. "Do I get to do that too?"

"Of course. I have an IUD in, baby. I'm safe and I'm clean. I don't want anything between any of us."

"Good. The animalistic side of me wants to mark the inside of your pussy with my seed and claim it as ours forever." I growled as I leaned down and kissed her nipples.

"Yes. Yes. Yes. Whatever you want, I'm yours." She panted as her body became desperate.

I rolled us over until she was straddling me. "Get my phone out of my pants pocket. It's time I paid my brother back for torturing me all day long."

She smiled a wicked grin and bounced off the bed to get my phone.

When she came back, I pulled her onto my lap and settled her so her wet lips were parted over top of my cock as she rocked her hips and slid back and forth against it.

I set my phone to record and then placed it on the headboard against the wall and checked to make sure the angle was right to capture everything. It was fucking perfect, and she looked so sexy on top of me from that point of view.

"I want you to fuck your pussy with my cock, Bailey. I want you to do whatever feels good for you, take every single pleasure from my body how you want."

"Hmm." She moaned above my cock that I held upright and watched in awe as she slowly sank her tight, little pussy onto the head of it.

"Shit," I murmured as she rose back up and let the head of my cock fall free from her body completely, and then she sank back down on it, taking just the head again.

I watched her slowly acclimate her body to my size, and I loved how she looked with her legs spread wide, her eyes closed, and her head back as she teased me with her hot, snug pussy.

She slid her hand down to rub her clit as she worked more of me into her body, and I reached up with the hand not holding my cock still for her and pulled her sexy, hard nipple, getting a moan to fall from her lips as her legs quivered and she fell farther down my cock.

"I knew it would feel good to bury my cock in your body, Bailey, but I never imagined it would feel this good," I said, rolling her nipple back and forth through my fingers as she desperately rode my cock.

Finally, when her wet lips brushed against my balls, she dropped to her knees, spread them wide around my hips, and leaned forward. She pressed her tits against my chest, and I grabbed her head and kissed her crudely. It wasn't a pretty kiss; it was all lips and teeth and primal, and she kissed me right back the same way.

She hadn't moved since she took all of me, and I could feel her inner walls tensing and releasing as she adjusted, but I was desperate to feel her slick walls sliding up and down on my cock. I moved both hands around her hips to hold onto her ass cheeks and lifted her until my cock had almost come out again, and then I pushed her down to take it all in one swift move, repeating that action .

She put her hands on my chest and pushed herself up and held on as I worked her pussy on and off my cock.

"I'm so close already." She moaned and pinched her nipple as her hips circled each time my cock was buried balls deep inside of her.

"I want you to look directly at the camera when you come. I want you to stare at Finn while you come on my cock, baby," I ordered her, and she opened her eyes and did exactly as I told her to do.

I stopped moving her on and off of me and let her take over the ride, and she bobbed up and down on me as she chased her orgasm. Her tits were bouncing with each thrust, and I'd never seen anything sexier.

Her pussy clamped down hard on my cock as her orgasm took over. She didn't just experience it in her pussy. It took over her entire body, from her head as she threw it back to her toes as they curled.

It felt so good feeling her come, milking me for everything I had, but I wasn't ready to lose myself in her yet. She felt way too damn good wrapped around me, and I wanted to make it last.

I reached up, turned off the video, and then flipped her on her back, until her head was hanging off the end of the bed, and I thrust deep into her, forcing the air out of her lungs.

Her eyes rolled in her head as she clawed her nails up and down my arms, holding on for dear life as I roughly fucked her into the mattress.

"You feel so goddamn good wrapped around my cock, Bailey. Tell me it feels good for you," I commanded.

"God, yes, it feels so fucking good, Walker."

I loved hearing her curse. The words sounded so taboo falling from her sweet mouth. I reveled in it, knowing I did that to her; I made her so wild with need that she lost control, the same way she made me.

My thrusts were pushing her up the bed, so I slid my hand around her throat to hold her still and her eyes widened and then fluttered closed as I put pressure on her neck.

I was gentle at first, but when I gave her more pressure, her pussy clamped down tighter and tighter on me. I had done my research on breath play over the years, being fond of it myself, and it felt right to use with her, like that.

"Walker." She moaned and pushed her head back and pressed her neck into my hand farther. "Tighter, baby," she begged. "Choke me and make me come. Please." Her eyes were wild when they opened and watched me, and she toppled over another orgasm. She held onto my arm with both of her tiny hands as I squeezed tighter, and she exploded around my cock as her entire body tensed and convulsed. She screamed incoherently, her face reddened from the pressure of my hand on her throat and within seconds, I chased her with my own orgasm.

I yelled out into the silent room, roaring as I filled her tiny body with what felt like gallons of come as I experienced the biggest orgasm of my life. I couldn't stop my hips from thrusting even after I stopped coming and her own body relaxed underneath mine. I just wanted more.

I lazily stroked my still mostly hard cock in and out of her soaking wet and used pussy for minutes longer, and she moaned and gasped as the silky sensation of my come lubricated the motion and continued to keep her aroused.

I watched in wonder as she rolled her hips under me and allowed me to fuck her with my own spent cock, and I kissed her deeply as she orgasmed again under my body.

When I finally pulled out, I knelt between her legs and pushed her knees wide toward her chest, looking down at her swollen pussy as the white evidence of my orgasm dripped down her lips and onto her ass.

"Fuck, that's sexy," I said, running my finger down and spreading the come over her flesh, branding her as mine.

She lay there with an impossibly sexy smile on her lips as she let me play.

I got out of bed eventually, sent the video to my horny brother, walked into my attached bathroom, and grabbed a cloth to clean her with. When I returned to bed, she lay exactly where I'd left her, but her eyes were closed and her breathing was slow and leveled.

I'd fucked her straight into a coma. I chuckled to myself, gently cleaned her up, and then pulled her up to the pillows in the center of the bed and wrapped myself around her underneath the blankets.

She burrowed into my arms and pressed her delicious ass flush against my cock and wiggled.

I reached down and playfully spanked her, and she chuckled sleepily.

"Sleep. You need your rest because I'm far from done with you," I warned her.

"Promises, promises," she chided again and drifted back off to sleep.

I lay there with her in my arms and felt her steady breathing, and before I knew it, I was sleeping with her.

Chapter 14 – Bailey

I woke up in the darkness of an unfamiliar room with an incredibly hot body pressed against my back.

As I went to roll over, I felt a delicious ache in my body and remembered the last 24 hours of events and various sexual positions Walker and Finn Camden had folded me into.

I looked at Walker sleeping next to me, and I couldn't believe that I could call him and Finn mine. I was a lucky fucking bitch.

And I wasn't about to let the last few hours of alone time with Walker go to waste by sleeping when I knew none of us had to work tomorrow.

I slid down under the blankets and kissed my way down his side and then across his hip bones above the smooth skin surrounding his magnificent dick. It made my brain fuzzy, trying to comprehend how these two men were identical in every single way, including the size of their cocks. They fucked like two different men, though, and I loved every single second with each of them and wanted more.

I flicked my tongue across the slit in the head of his cock and tasted the mix of both of us still on his skin. It was my new favorite flavor.

He quickly hardened to stone as I sucked him into my mouth.

His hips jerked and he groaned as I pressed my lips to the base of his shaft and hummed. The blankets flew off of his body, revealing me to the cool air of the bedroom, and I smiled up at him as I let his cock fall from my lips.

"Hi. Hope you don't mind," I said cheekily as I slid both hands up his long shaft and circled the head of his cock, pulling another groan from his lips.

"I don't mind one bit, angel," he said, sleep making his voice even deeper and huskier. He watched me through heavy eyes as I deep-throated him and let my nails tease and torture his inner thighs.

I pushed his thighs wider and tentatively sucked on his balls as I palmed and played with them. Some guys weren't into much oral play south of their actual dick, so I was slow to explore to give him time to tell me no.

He just watched as I lowered my tongue and let my saliva coat both of his balls and the sensitive thin skin beneath them.

"Shit," he cursed and spread his legs wider, giving me more access.

I smiled up at him and fisted his cock as I dropped my tongue again to his taint and swirled it across the bundle of nerves I knew lay right under the skin, reveling as his hips jerked and he cursed again.

He buried his fingers in my hair and pushed and pulled how he wanted as I explored his body.

"This is new for me," he said. I could hear a bit of reservation in his voice as he waited for me to reply.

"I kind of figured, but I'm glad I can claim something that is a first for you." I sucked one of his balls into my mouth hard as I squeezed his cock in a tight grip. "Just tell me to stop if you want me to."

He groaned and threw his head back against the pillow again. I lifted his balls, spit on the skin, and let my fingers spread the saliva over his taint, rubbing him as I deep-throated him over and over again.

"Holy fuck, Bailey." He gasped and I watched in astonishment as he gripped the bed sheet in an iron fist as every single muscle in his body went rigid. "Oh fuck!" he bellowed, and then I tasted the first shot of his orgasm and let my finger dip against his back door lightly, rubbing from there up to his balls and back as I sucked him dry. He continued to convulse in my mouth and under my body as I played and pushed his boundaries, but he never told me to stop.

I gentled my touch as he came down and then laid gentle kisses on his thighs and stomach as he caught his breath.

His big hands grabbed my arms and pulled me up to lie on top of him, and I laid my head on his chest as I let him come back down to earth. I could tell I pushed him past his comfort zone, but I also knew he enjoyed it immensely. He was a strong, virile man, and sometimes those characteristics didn't mesh well with anal play, so I waited to hear what he was thinking without pressuring him.

"How did you learn to do that?" he asked, letting his hand run over my back and down to my ass.

"Do you really want to know?" I asked. I wouldn't want to know how he learned to please me so wildly because I knew it meant he learned it with another woman.

He looked down at me and lifted my chin so that I had to look up at him.

"I want to know every single thing about you," he said.

"I dated an older guy when I was in high school. He was the only long-term relationship I've had, and his idea of romance was me going down on him like that and then fucking me in doggy so he could smoke a blunt at the same time."

"You're kidding me," he said, his face suddenly serious.

I chuckled and shrugged my shoulders. "I wish I were, babe. But that's life, I guess. How's the saying go? You live and learn."

"That's a damn shame, is what it is, Bailey. How old were you and how old is older?"

I shook my head and looked away. "It doesn't matter." I wasn't proud of that point in life.

"Tell me," he ordered, rolling us over until he was on top of me. He pushed my hair back and I could see the intensity in his eyes, even in the dark room.

"I was fifteen," I said quietly.

"And him?"

"Twenty-four."

"That's not older, Bailey. That's predatory assault."

That hurt a bit. I already wore shame from that situation, and I didn't like my nose to be rubbed in it.

"Well, it is what it is at this point, Walker."

"Did your parents know you were fucking someone ten years older than you?"

I pushed him off of me and sat up, pulling the sheet to cover my body. "No, that was kind of the point."

"He should be in jail for preying on you that young, Bailey. I arrest men all the time for sleazy shit, but that's fucked up."

I looked at him and I could feel the shame spreading across my face as I tried hard to push the emotion from my body altogether. I had been at an extremely low point in my life at that time, and the only reason I survived was because that fucked-up relationship distracted me. For it to be thrown back in my face like this, well, it fucking hurt.

I stood up and looked around for my robe, finding it and putting it on.

"Where are you going?" he asked, sitting up. I didn't look over at him as I tied the sash and walked from the room.

My bag and clothes were downstairs in the bathroom, and I just wanted to get them on and leave. Every drop of arousal I'd had in me five minutes ago was gone, and I just wanted to be alone.

"Bailey!" he yelled down the hallway as I ran down the stairs and into the bathroom. I shut the door and locked it behind me. "Hey, talk to me," he said, knocking on the door and jiggling the handle.

I quickly got dressed and made the mistake of looking in the mirror over the sink before leaving the room. My hair screamed bedhead and my skin was flushed from being thoroughly fucked today, but my face was red and blotchy and had tears running down it.

I quickly dashed at them and tried to get them to stop long enough to get out to my car, knowing I had to pass him on the way there. I hated crying period, let alone in front of someone like Walker, who would probably be dumbfounded by the tears as they fell.

Hell, he'd probably make me feel ashamed for crying too.

I took a calming breath and then opened the door without looking up at him.

I slid past him and walked toward the door. He grabbed my arm and pulled me to a stop. "Talk to me here, Bailey. Tell me what went wrong."

I still didn't look up at him. "I just want to go home. Please let go of me."

He sighed. "It's after one in the morning and you haven't slept much. I don't want you driving this late, Bailey. Please just stay."

"Please let go." My voice broke and I swallowed, trying to keep control, but he heard it anyway.

"Just stay here. You can go to Finn's room if that makes you feel more comfortable. I won't bother you and he'll be home in less than an hour."

I shook my head and pulled my arm from his, walked out the door and to my car door without taking another breath.

He came out onto the front porch in all of his naked wonder and watched as I backed up and then drove down the long driveway.

I hated that he made me feel so shitty about myself, but I hated that I let it make me feel like shit even more. He didn't mean anything bad by it, I knew that. My life at that age was hard and I couldn't do anything to change it now. I guessed I still had a lot of regrets about back then that he brought to the surface.

I also hated that Finn was going to come home to this mess instead of the relaxing and orgasmic night and day he had planned on.

But I was in no shape to be good company right now, and I didn't want to just suck it up and stay so they could use my body. I'd done that for too many years of my life already, and I was healthier now and I couldn't fall back down that rabbit hole or I'd never respect myself again.

Chapter 15 – Finn

I pulled into the driveway at ten past two in the morning. I may or may not have moved closer to home the nearer it got to the end of my shift so that when I was out of service, I was just down the road.

I had no shame in my Bailey game.

When I got through the trees, I was surprised to see the lights on in the kitchen and Walker's room upstairs.

I got out of the car and walked up the porch steps and could see Walker sitting at the kitchen counter with his head in his hands.

I walked in and looked around, but when Walker met my eyes, I could see the regret on his face. "What happened?"

I threw my bag down and took my gun belt off and opened the safe to lock it up.

"I honestly don't fucking know, but if I had to guess, I hurt Bailey's feelings. She left about forty-five minutes ago."

"What!" I yelled. "What do you mean you hurt her feelings?" I ripped my shirt off and then tore at the straps of my vest and chucked them to the side as I stood before him.

"We were talking, and I guess I was insensitive and maybe a little bit of a jackass. I don't know. She never told me what was wrong. She just got out of bed, got dressed, and took off. But she had tears on her cheeks when she left so I know I did something fucking stupid."

He hung his head again and I felt for him. Walker was not good with women at all when it came to emotions, and usually, that didn't bother him. But I could physically feel how much it upset him tonight so I couldn't be mad at him.

"Tell me exactly what you said and did, word for word, and we'll figure it out," I said, sitting down across from him and trying to be helpful.

"She woke me up with a blowjob, the best fucking blow job I've ever had. It put the one from the other night to fucking shame. I asked her where she learned, uh, certain things she did during it, and she said she was in a relationship with an older guy when she was in high school that had her blow him like that and then he'd fucked her in doggy so he could get high while he did it. It sounded fucking sad that she let someone use her like that in the name of love. I asked her how old she was, and she tried to avoid the question, but I pressed her on it. Turns out she was 15 and the fucker was 24. I said stupid shit, like he was a predator and a Hebephile and that it was a fucked-up relationship, and then she just got up and left."

He sighed, and I had to fight the urge to punch him out of his stupidity.

"I guess now saying it out loud, I can see why she was upset. I didn't mean that she was wrong for being in a relationship like that. I meant that he was wrong for using such a young, trusting girl, but I guess I didn't articulate it the way I'd hoped. I tried getting her to stay, I told her to go to your room and that I wouldn't fucking bother her, but she left anyway. I don't even know if she got home okay or not. Fuck!" he yelled.

I clapped him on the shoulder and pulled my phone from my pocket and dialed her number. It took her a couple of rings, but she finally answered. I put her on speaker because I knew Walker wanted to make sure she was okay, but I motioned for him to stay quiet.

"Hi," she said tiredly.

"Are you okay?" I asked.

"Yeah, I'm fine. I just needed a moment."

"Come back," I said, hopeful and not ashamed at all for it.

She sighed. "I made a big deal out of nothing and now I feel stupid. Does he hate me?" I could hear the sadness in her voice.

"No, I don't hate you, Bailey. I owe you an apology," Walker jumped in. I rolled my eyes at him and sighed. *Way to be quiet, bro.*

"No, you don't. I just—" She paused. "I guess I have unresolved feelings about that chapter of my life and I let you get in my head. You had no way of knowing, and I'm sorry for taking off like that."

"Then come back," I said again.

She chuckled lightly and then sighed again. "It's so late. I've already embarrassed myself once tonight, and I'd like to avoid doing it again in my sleep-deprived state."

"Please, baby. Please come back. We'll come get you if you want," I offered. "In fact, I insist. I'm still wired from work so I can drive no problem. We can be there in ten minutes."

She paused, not answering right away, so I pushed my luck and pressed on. "That's our girl. We'll see you in ten," I said but still held on the line in case she told me no.

She sighed again and then giggled softly. "Are you sure you *both* want me back there tonight?"

"Yes!" we both answered at the same time, causing her to giggle again.

"We'll be there in eight minutes, Bail. And then I plan on making it all up to you with my tongue for the rest of the night," Walker said as he stood up and headed for the door. I followed after him and grabbed my truck keys.

"Just your tongue? What a shame." She sighed in pretend sadness.

That got us both to laugh and I told her we'd see her in a few and hung up.

"Let's go get our girl, you fuck wad," I said, clapping him on the shoulder and walking out to my truck.

"Let's," he agreed.

I did make it to her house in eight minutes as Walker had promised, and I hardly sped at all. When we pulled into her driveway, she came out her front door with her bag over her shoulder and walked toward the truck.

Walker jumped out and picked her up, hugging her tightly as I flipped up the center console and gave them a moment. I watched as he kissed her deeply and apologized again, which she brushed off and apologized for herself. When Walker helped her climb into my lifted truck, I smiled warmly at her and tossed her bag in the back, pulling her to me.

She snuggled into my side and offered her lips to me, and I drank from her like I was dying of thirst.

"I missed you," I said against her lips.

"I missed you too. I'm sorry for making your night extra dramatic."

I kissed her nose and nudged her back so I could pass her seatbelt to Walker so he could buckle it. "Nonsense. Thank you for coming back."

She giggled as we buckled her in, and then she leaned her head on Walker's shoulder and laid her hand on my thigh as I backed up out of her driveway and headed back toward the house.

As soon as we were on the road again, Walker pulled her into a passionate kiss, and she leaned back and let him drag arousal from her body. She moaned and panted as his hands wandered down her body. I picked her hand up off my thigh and kissed her fingertips and then bit each one lightly when as I saw Walker push her skirt up and slide her panties down. This girl and her fucking sundresses were going to be the death of me.

"Fuck, you two." I groaned and laid her hand on my erection. "It's been nine fucking hours since I've been inside of you, Bailey, and you're making it hard to focus over here."

She snickered at me as Walker pulled back from her lips and looked over at her hand on my crotch.

He winked at me and whispered into her ear. She looked over at me and then back to him and bit her lip as she considered it.

"Are you asking me to break the law, Deputy Camden?" she asked, but she was already unbuckling her seatbelt and turning toward me on her knees.

She started kissing my neck and ran her hands down my chest and purred, "Can I suck your cock while you drive?"

I snorted and pushed my seat back farther, giving her more room between my lap and the steering wheel, and quickly undid my pants. "Only if you let Walker play with your pussy while you do," I answered.

"Mmm," she moaned and popped her ass up into the air as she dropped on her elbows next to my thigh. She made quick work of my pants and soon, her hot wet mouth was wrapped around the head of my cock.

"Shit, your mouth is so warm and wet," I cursed, throwing my arm over the back of the seat and tilting my hips to let her take in more of me. I watched out of the corner of my eye as Walker threw her skirt up and over her ass and leaned down and spit on her pussy before he started rubbing his fingers against her.

I could tell the second he pushed against her clit because she moaned and gasped around my cock. She bobbed eagerly up and down on me, and I focused hard on the road ahead of me. Her moans and the noises her wet mouth were making on my cock mixed with the noises of her wet pussy around Walker's fingers and soon, I was close to blowing down her throat.

Luckily, we were pulling into the driveway, and I parked the truck and laid my seat back the rest of the way. Walker turned and pushed her face farther down into my lap as he roughly licked her pussy.

"Fuck." She moaned and pushed back on his face.

"You like my tongue in your ass, don't you, Bailey?" he ground out as he reached up and smacked her lush ass.

"Shit," I cursed, knowing his tongue was in her ass, and it turned me on so fucking much.

I reached under her body and pinched her nipple. I wanted her to come but I couldn't hold off my orgasm any longer, so I let go, grabbed her head, and held her down on the bottom of my cock as I started coming down her throat. She took it all and massaged my balls as she did.

I let her head up and she gasped as she came off my cock, and I pulled her quickly in for a kiss. Her mouth was wet and silky from my release, and I fucking loved it.

Walker finger-fucked her pussy while he tongued her ass, and she lit up like a firework under his assault. "Yes! Yes! Yes!" she cried as she came.

Walker let her down slowly, massaging her ass and thighs as she came back to earth, and then he pulled her back until she was straddling and kissing him. He popped the door open and jumped down with her in his arms, nodded to me, and called out, "Put your dick away and let's get our girl into bed where we can really drive her crazy."

She smiled like a Cheshire cat as he turned and all but ran up the steps with her wrapped around him. I tucked myself back in my pants and took off after them.

If you insist, big bro.

By the time I locked up and got upstairs, Bailey was kneeling in the middle of Walker's bed, completely naked, and rubbing her pussy as he stripped in front of her.

"What'd I miss?" I asked, tearing my shirt off over my head and pushing my pants down.

"She told me she wanted us in two of her holes tonight," he said and smirked at me.

I knew which two it would be, and the idea had me rock hard again in seconds.

"Eiffel Tower or spit roast?" I asked, joking as I knelt up on the bed and pulled her head toward mine for a deep, soul-sucking kiss.

She ran her hands down my naked chest and then down to my cock and balls and played with both for a moment.

Walker got up on the bed behind her and pulled her against his body, massaging her tits while kissing her neck.

"Whose cock do you want in your pussy And whose do you want in your mouth, baby?" I asked, reaching down and sliding my fingers through her wet pussy lips.

"How about I take one of you in each and then you switch," she purred.

"I like how you think."

"I don't know, man; I'm getting a little territorial here. I've only had her pussy once so far," Walker joked.

"Yeah, you also said you already had the world's best blow job from her tonight too. Yet, I haven't heard what about it made it so earth-shattering."

Bailey looked over her shoulder to Walker and raised her eyebrows, waiting for him to offer up more information. He smirked and kissed her nose.

"We don't keep secrets, Bailey. You can tell him," he answered as he leaned down and bit her neck.

"He likes his ass played with like I do," she answered sweetly, and I snorted in disbelief.

"No way," I said after a second when I realized she wasn't kidding.

Walker just smirked at me and nodded. "She sucked my balls and licked my taint and then rubbed my asshole while I came, and I think I broke the world record for the amount of jizz to empty from a sack in one blow."

I was shocked at how open and relaxed he was about it, and the more I thought about it, the more interested I became.

"And did you enjoy doing that to him?" I asked, looking down at her between us.

"Fuck yes." She moaned, reaching for both of our cocks. "I loved making him lose his mind."

I looked into her eyes and I could tell she was serious, so I kissed her deeply and then threw myself down on the bed on my back and challenged, "Let's see what you're all about."

She bit her lip and crawled toward me as Walker groaned. "Dude, you're going to fucking love it."

"Have you ever done this?" she asked as she took a lick up the underside of my cock.

"Never," I answered truthfully.

Her smile turned sinful as she started sucking on my cock again. Even though I had just filled her stomach with my come five minutes ago, it felt fucking delicious. I ran my hands through her curls and guided her head how I liked, and she hummed her approval as she reached down and started rubbing my sack in her tiny hands.

Walker knelt behind her and ran his cock up through her folds and slowly pushed into her. She moaned as he kept the forward pressure up and pushed all of himself into her in one slow thrust until he was balls deep.

His eyes rolled as he slapped her ass, making it ripple, and then anchored his hands on her hip bones and started fucking her.

She was adding a lot of saliva to my cock and letting it run down my sack and taint, and then she sucked one of my balls into her mouth and swirled her tongue around like she was tying a cherry stem with it and I went cross-eyed.

"So fucking good, baby," I praised, and she dropped farther until her chest was flat on the bed between my legs and her ass was arched straight up into the air. She pushed my thighs wider, and I pulled them open for her as she looked directly into my eyes and let her tongue wander south to my taint.

She flicked the tip of her tongue over the skin and then swirled the flat of it over it, letting the very tip touch my ass with each pass.

Lava poured through my veins as she fisted my cock and licked from my ball sack to my ass and back.

She pulled back and spit on her fingers and then rubbed them against the foreign territory as she went back to deep-throating me.

I was seeing stars and having trouble keeping my hips still as she explored. Walker was fucking her hard, spanking her ass and making it ripple with each thrust, and the visual image with the physical stimulation was so fucking hot.

Walker leaned down, wrapped his hand around her throat, and pushed her down onto my cock deeper, and she cried out as she orgasmed while he pounded into her. As soon as she came down from her high, he grunted. "Switch."

She flipped around and pushed Walker backward off the bed and grinned at me as she lay down on her back and spread her pretty thighs for me. She hung her head off the end of the bed and pulled Walker forward until he was straddling her face, sucking his cock deep into her mouth as she reached down to rub her clit.

I leaned down and pushed her hand out of the way and bit her clit before sucking it into my mouth. Her hips jerked and she screamed around Walker's cock, causing him to groan and curse as she pulled my face in deeper by my hair.

He leaned forward until he was resting his weight on his arms and started thrusting his hips, pushing and pulling his cock to and from her mouth, and she wrapped her hands around his balls.

I grabbed her hips, put a pillow under them, and slammed my cock into her, pushing her knees to each side of her tits and fucking her like a man possessed. And that was exactly what I was.

She pushed Walker out of her mouth and then started fisting him as she leaned back farther and used her tongue behind his balls. His neck tensed, every vein and muscle bunched from the way he was barely holding onto control.

"Just like that, baby. Yes, right there." He groaned and leaned forward to rub her clit as I fucked her.

"Where is she licking?" I asked, goading him, wanting to know exactly what she was doing.

He just groaned and rolled his eyes, unable to speak as he hung his head and rocked his hips.

She pulled back from under him and answered for him. "I'm licking his ass, and his balls are so tight. He's going to come soon, and I want you to come too, Finn," she said and then dived back in to lick him some more. She then pulled off and angled her head off the bed, lining him up with her mouth as she used her fingers on his ass.

"Take it," he roared. "Take all of it." I watched as his hips got jerky and her throat worked to swallow every bit of come that he pushed into her mouth.

It took him a long time to come down, and I leaned down and started pounding harder into her. She pulled him out of her mouth and looked up at me, sliding her hands around my neck and pulling me down to her. Walker rolled and collapsed on the bed next to us and watched as I kept her folded in half and fucked her roughly.

"Yes. Please, Finn, you fuck me so good. I want you to come deep inside of me, baby. Please, give it all to me," she begged and clawed at my back as I did just that.

I emptied into her and kept fucking her through her next orgasm until my come spilled out around my cock and down onto her skin.

I pulled back and looked down at her, and her eyes were glassy and hooded as she caught her breath. She kissed me and then turned to kiss Walker, sighing as if she were the most content person in the entire world.

Walker got some wipes for all of us, and we cleaned up and then crawled into bed and settled in. She lay between us, her head on my chest and her ass in Walker's lap, and we all passed out.

I personally slept the hardest I had in years with our beautiful blonde angel safely tucked between us.

It was then that I decided I didn't want to spend another night without her in one of our beds. She belonged here with us. We just had to be careful handling her because I learned tonight that she was a runner when she was faced with tough situations.

I was going to do everything in my power to keep her happy and protected so she didn't need to run to protect herself.

Chapter 16 – Bailey

I woke up and every muscle ached and protested, and I groaned. I felt a chuckle from behind me and opened my eyes to see Walker sleeping in front of me with his big hand on my hip. I looked over my shoulder and into Finn's eyes as he smiled down at me and then kissed the back of my head.

"Good morning, beautiful," he said. He let his hands run up my chest and palmed both breasts as he pushed his morning wood into my ass cheeks.

"Hmm." I groaned, but not in a good way. "I need Tylenol and caffeine," I grumped.

"Uh oh," Walker added, and I looked back over at him now that he was awake. "What's wrong?" He leaned forward and kissed my forehead.

"Every muscle in my body hurts from the mattress Olympics you boys put me through the last two days."

Finn let go of my breasts and backed up, rubbing my shoulders, and Walker hiked my thigh up over his hip and started letting his hands work out the knots in my leg.

I groaned and tried to not look so miserable, but my body was so sore.

"Let's get you in a bath and then we'll get you some Tylenol, coffee, and breakfast. How does that sound?" Walker asked as he slid backward and sat up on the edge of the bed.

I watched his body move and turn and was mesmerized by the ink on his skin dancing with each movement.

"That sounds wonderful," I purred when he looked back at me, waiting for a reply.

He got up and walked into his bathroom and I heard the water start running. I had yet to go in there, but I was hoping that the tub was a big soaker so I could rest my weary body.

Finn got out of bed and slid his hands under me, lifting me into the air sweetly. I wrapped my arms around his neck and leaned in to kiss him good morning.

He stood strong and tall and kissed me back as the water ran in the other room. When he carried me in, I pulled back and looked around at the beautiful, updated space. The tub was indeed a giant soaker the size of a hot tub with jets, and the shower looked to be three times the size of mine, and I had thought mine was big. There were two sinks with a makeup vanity between them and a private room for the toilet.

"Why do you two bachelors have such a nice bathroom?" I asked as Finn set me down on the edge of the tub.

"Because we built it with the intent of sharing it with a woman someday," Walker answered. "We wanted it to be an oasis for all of us."

"What about your room? Are you stuck in a closet while he has this nice pad?" I asked, poking Finn in the stomach.

He chuckled. "No, my room is almost identical to this, but the bathroom isn't set up as a master. It just has one sink and a giant shower. The guest bathroom in the hallway past my room has a tub and shower combo. The plan is to someday share this room and bathroom and then my room can be another guest room."

The bubbles in the tub smelled like lavender and I ached to crawl into it, so I turned and stuck my toe in tentatively and checked the temperature. It was gloriously hot, and I stepped in and moaned.

The guys watched as I sank into the water and leaned back against the edge. "Well, are you two going to stand there all day or join me?" I asked, holding my hands out to them. I pulled the hair tie off my wrist and tied my curls up on top of my head.

The tub was big enough for all three of us, and I longed to try it out with them.

They both stepped in and turned the water off and the jets on. We sat in silence for a while and let our bodies relax.

"This is the first time either of us has ever gotten in this tub, you should know," Finn said.

"Is that so? Well, I feel lucky," I said and let my foot wander to his lap, poking his stomach with my toe.

He grabbed my foot and started working his thumbs into the arch, causing me to groan and slide farther into the water. Walker chuckled when I started floating away and slid behind me to held me to his chest.

"Were we too rough with you?" he asked, and I could hear the concern in his voice. I reached behind me and patted the side of his bearded face and shook my head.

"No such thing. I'm just out of practice and the orgasms you two give me are whole-body ones, so I'm just a little worn out."

"We'll take it easy on you today. No orgasms or mattress Olympics," he said, kissing the back of my head again.

"Blasphemy!" I gasped and turned in his arms to swat at him. "Those are cruel words, sir."

He exaggeratedly defended himself from my assault and we all ended up laughing.

We soaked in the tub for a while and then made our way downstairs for food.

I wore one of their T-shirts and they both wore just athletic shorts, and they were delicious to look at.

They wouldn't let me help make breakfast. Instead, Walker sat me on the counter of the island and told me to sit there and look pretty.

The independent woman in me wanted to be offended by that statement, but the hopeless romantic decided to let me feel taken care of by these chivalrous men and enjoy it while I could.

Walker turned on music, and it was so nice to enjoy a peaceful Sunday morning with these two men.

Finn was plating eggs and bacon and Walker was pouring another round of coffee for me in a cup when the front door opened.

"Good morning, boys!" a woman's voice called from the foyer. I couldn't see from the kitchen, but a panicked look passed between Finn and Walker before Finn took off in that direction.

He was too late, though, because a second later, a beautiful redhead waltzed into the kitchen wearing a pair of short denim shorts, a silk camisole that was so low-cut, I could almost see her belly button, and a pair of heels that made her tall enough that she didn't have to work at all to lean in and kiss Finn on the lips as she smiled up at him sexily. She rested her hand on his bare abs and licked her lips as she pulled away.

I felt my heart drop to my stomach, yet I couldn't look away from the car wreck happening in the middle of the kitchen.

"You just let yourself into our house now?" Walker asked angrily as he walked over and stood between me and the redhead, resting his hand on my leg. I couldn't tell if he was trying to hide me from her or shelter me from her angry glare as her eyes landed on me sitting on the counter in just a T-shirt.

"I didn't realize you had company so early this morning, Walker. Good morning, I'm Luann," she said as she walked forward and held her hand out to me in greeting.

But all I could see were flashbacks of her lips on Finn's and the fact that he hadn't pushed her off as her three-inch-long bloodred nails hung off her fingers at me, waiting for me to shake them.

I didn't. Instead, I simply raised my eyebrow at her and held her stare.

Her smile slipped and she glared at me again before plastering a fake smile back onto her face and turning toward Finn. "I made you cinnamon rolls, baby. I knew you were off today, and I wanted to make sure you had a good homemade breakfast. I thought we could spend the day together."

I looked past her to Finn, and he looked at me, but I couldn't quite read his expression. "Uh, thanks, Luann," he said, taking the pan from her hands.

Suddenly, I had no appetite for even my coffee. I set my mug down and went to slide off the counter, but Walker stepped between my legs and gave me a pointed look that said to stay put.

"I want to go get dressed," I said through clenched teeth and stared back at him as I pushed him away and jumped down.

Luann looked over at me as I walked away, barefoot and in a T-shirt that wasn't mine that hung to my knees, and I had never felt so inferior compared to someone before. She was done up to the nines, rail thin, and beautiful, and I had twenty extra pounds I hated around my hips, bedhead, and no underwear on.

I was mortified and so uncomfortable.

"Finley," Walker warned from behind me and followed me up the stairs.

My hands were shaking as I grabbed my bag off the floor of Walker's bedroom. The room smelled like sex and the bed beckoned me to crawl into it and fall back asleep in hopes that this was all a bad dream.

"Bailey, calm down," Walker ordered as he shut the bedroom door behind us.

"I am calm," I said as I opened my bag.

He grabbed it and tossed it across the room, and I pushed at him as I tried to get around him to go pick it up.

He blocked my path and lifted my chin to meet his eyes. "Stop. You're not running again."

"I'm not running. I'm trying to get fucking dressed, Walker. There is a woman downstairs probably bent over the counter with Finn inside of her by now and I'm walking around with no underwear. I need some regular fucking clothes on so I can think straight!" I yelled back and moved for my bag.

He stepped in my way again and picked me up, tossing me on the bed. I sat up in a flurry of curse words and flailing limbs, pissed the fuck off, and scrambled to get off the bed.

He was on top of me in a second, though, and pinned both hands up over my head in his.

"I assure you he is not inside of her right now. I also promise you he doesn't want to be inside of anyone but you, the same way I don't. So knock it off."

"Screw you," I bit back. I was jealous and afraid of being made to look like a fool, and it was coming out as anger.

"If you insist," he said as he leaned down and bit my nipple through the thin fabric of my shirt.

"Ah!" I yelled and bucked under him. He held my wrists with one hand and reached down and lifted the shirt up until it was over my face, blinding me, and I couldn't get it off because my arms were held in his hand and my body was pinned under his. "Get off of me, Walker," I yelled.

He just chuckled and leaned down and sucked one of my nipples into his mouth as he rocked his hips and rubbed his cock against my pussy.

He pushed his thighs between mine and spread my legs wide around his hips, and my body responded on its own. I tilted my hips and wrapped my legs around his waist as he kept rocking his cock against my bare pussy while he sucked on my nipples.

"Walker." I hissed and pushed my head back into the bed as I tried to get the shirt off my face. "Fuck." I moaned as he slid his hand down my body and parted my pussy around his fingers, pushing two into me quickly.

"You need to be fucked, Bailey," he said and I felt him push his shorts down until his heavy, bare cock lay against my stomach.

"Don't you dare." I hissed again, but my legs were still wrapped around his waist.

He chuckled and kissed my neck and then pushed the shirt up high enough to bare my lips to him. He kissed me passionately, and I kissed him back with anger and frustration. I bit his lips and he bit mine back as he shoved his tongue in my mouth and dominated me.

He wrapped his hand around my throat and I moaned. I was completely helpless against him; he held my arms above my head and my legs wide around his naked body, and now he had his hand on my throat, immobilizing me more. I felt myself gush against him, and he groaned as he rocked forward again and rubbed it along his cock.

"That's my good girl," he praised.

"Fuck you," I swore again, but he silenced me with a moan as he slid into my body.

"I'll never get over how good you feel when you suck my cock into your tight body, baby girl." He moaned into my ear as he started thrusting into me.

"Well. memorize it well because this is the last time you'll ever get to do it," I threatened, but my voice lacked conviction.

"You lie," he challenged and kept fucking me good. He let go of my throat and slid his hand between us and started rubbing my clit, bringing me to the brink of an orgasm, and then he pulled out of me and sucked on my nipples.

"Son of a bitch," I cursed as he blew on my nipple.

"What's wrong?" he asked, and I could hear the smile in his voice, even if I couldn't see it because of the damn shirt bunched over my face.

He buried himself back inside of me with one brutal thrust, and I screamed and moaned as I rocked my hips forward, trying desperately to rub my clit against him so I could come.

But just as I was getting the friction I needed, he pulled out again and flipped me over quickly.

"Walker!" I hissed and bucked back against him. "If you don't let me come, I swear to god I'll donkey kick you off this bed."

He smacked my ass painfully and then slid the T-shirt off my face and down my arms until it wrapped around my wrists. He twisted it around them until they were effectively stuck together behind my back, and he used them to pull me backward and straight onto his cock.

I moaned and spread my legs wider, arching my ass into the air to take him into my body completely.

"Good girl, Bailey," he commended.

"Go to hell," I challenged, still pissed and desperate for an orgasm. He smacked my ass again, and the burn sent jolts of lightning up my spine.

"Hold on tight, baby girl, and I'll let you enjoy the ride on the way there with me," he gritted out in my ear as he bent forward and bit my shoulder.

"Please." I moaned and pushed back into him as he reached around and played with my clit again.

"Beg me," he ordered.

"Please make me come, Walker." I heard the change in my voice as it went from angry to desperate, and he licked my neck and moaned into my ear.

The bedroom door opened up and in walked Finn. His chest and his face were red, and his eyes were lit with what I thought was anger.

Yeah, well, fuck you too, buddy boy.

I quickly realized he wasn't angry with us, but it didn't help to quell my rage toward him.

"Screw you," I sneered at him and turned my head away as Walker kept fucking me.

Walker chuckled again from behind me but then quickly smacked my ass again, on the same spot the others had landed, and it burned. I could feel the heat radiating off my skin and knew my ass was bright red.

"Our girl here is jealous. Can you believe it? The sexiest woman on the face of the Earth is jealous of Luann Mathews. Speaking of which, did you take care of that infestation?" Walker asked Finn.

"Yeah, she's gone," he said, and I could hear the anger in his voice.

"You should have left with her." I still was not looking at him as Walker kept fucking me.

"You don't mean that," Finn replied as he walked over and crawled up on the bed to sit by my head.

"Come near me and I'll show you just how much I mean that when I bite you," I said.

Walker spanked me again and then spit on my asshole.

"Spank me again and I'm bucking you off, Walker," I sneered but pushed back against his thumb as he started pushing it into my ass.

He pulled his thumb out of me and spanked me three more times in quick succession, and I screamed and turned my face into the bedding and bit down to quiet myself.

He shoved his thumb into my ass again, all the way in, and I exploded catastrophically around him.

"Fuck yes, baby!" he swore and started pounding me as my pussy clamped down on his dick and my ass tried to swallow his thumb.

I was moaning and begging for more, begging him to fuck me deeper, harder, faster, and to fuck my ass. I was desperate for the pain he promised to replace my anger with.

He pulled me up by my hair until I sat reverse cowgirl in his lap, and he started fucking me brutally as he made me stare straight ahead at Finn. He had his cock out in his hand and was stroking it with a glassy-eyed look of arousal on his face.

"You should have fucked her with that thing because you're not coming anywhere near me right now," I said, and his eyes lit with fire.

Walker lifted me, keeping his cock buried deep inside of me, and crawled up the bed until I sat straddling Finn's lap as he fucked my pussy and my ass. My face was half an inch from Finn's, and I moaned and threw my head back as Walker forced another orgasm from my body with his thumb and his cock.

"God, Walker, you feel so fucking good." I moaned and opened my eyes to stare right into Finn's as I complimented his twin brother's dick skills.

Walker's hips faltered and he swirled his thumb as he started pumping me full of his come. Finn reached up and supported my hips, pushing me back and onto Walker's cock as he lost himself inside of me, and I could see his devotion to me in the depth of his irises. That poured ice water on my fury.

I crawled forward as soon as Walker stilled behind me and kissed Finn hard. He lifted my hips and impaled me with this cock in one motion. "That's what I thought, baby," he purred into my ear as he lifted me up and down on him.

"If I'm yours, then you're mine. I won't share," I said as I circled my hips and rolled my clit against his pelvis.

"I don't want anyone else, Bailey. You're all I need."

He undid the shirt at my wrists and flipped me onto my back, slowing the pace down until he was grinding his cock in and out of me painfully slowly and dragging orgasm after orgasm from my clit. I clawed at his back and bit his lips and neck as he drove me into desperation. Walker leaned back against the headboard and watched with a smirk on his face, and I flipped him the bird.

He laughed wildly, got up, and walked into the bathroom and into the shower. "You're so fucking good for us, baby," he said as he walked away.

I looked up at Finn, who was now passionately fucking me in a way that I felt in the depths of my soul, and I kissed him, slowly letting my lips and tongue soothe the wounds I'd left on him with my teeth before.

"You're the only one I want, Bailey. I'm sorry you had to deal with her this morning."

"Shh. Don't talk about other women while your cock is buried deep inside of me, Finn," I said and smiled against his mouth.

"I'm going to fill you up, show you just how badly I want you," he said as he rolled my nipple between his teeth, and I exploded again, milking his cock and forcing his orgasm from his body as I sucked every drop from him.

He stilled and rested his forehead against the bed under my shoulder and caught his breath. "God, I hope that IUD works flawlessly or we're going to knock you up with quintuplets with as much come as we pump into your sexy little body," he joked and kissed my shoulder.

I snorted and pushed him off me. "How romantic."

"Maybe that's what we'll do so you're forced to stay with us forever."

As he said it, I saw the seriousness on his face and I froze. "It's not me I'm worried about getting the itch for someone else, Finn. I've got no others knocking on my door or walking right through it on a Sunday morning with cinnamon rolls in their hands."

He hummed and chuckled again, pulling me into his body, and I went willingly. "I'm sorry she showed up like that. I didn't know that was going to happen. I'm sorry if she made you feel inferior."

"She's gorgeous," I said quietly, "and skinny."

"She can't hold a candle to you in a fucking empty room, baby, and she means positively nothing to me."

I looked at him and tried to understand this emotion in me.

"I've never been a jealous person before. Literally never, not once," I said truthfully. "But she kissed you and you let her."

He sighed and pulled me in closer. "I used to—" He paused and tried to find the right words. In the space, my brain ran wild. "Well, basically, I used to sleep with her. I never wanted anything else from her, and Walker never even entertained the idea of being near her, so it was nothing more than someone to burn some steam off with. It ended months ago, but she still does things randomly like today. I made it explicitly clear to her that I'm with you and want nothing to do with her."

I mulled that information over in my head.

He continued, "My guess is she heard we were together or that I was interested in you and came here to fuck things up for me. I honestly thought she was successful when you went upstairs. Then, we heard you moaning and screaming, and I knew that Walker was fucking the leaving right out of you."

I snorted. "Fucking the leaving out of me, huh?" I asked.

"I've learned in the short time I've had with you, Bailey, that you run when you feel the need to protect yourself. And while both times you've done it have been warranted, I hate that it's your go-to solution. I don't want you taking off and not figuring things out with Walker and me when shit gets tough. I hate that."

I took a deep breath and burrowed into him farther. "That habit goes back many years and isn't something I can just turn off. It's the only reason I've survived this long to be honest with you, Finn."

He thought on that for a while and then added, "Then, we need a code word or something that you say when you need space that we both know has an expiration date to it or something. Like an hour, then we talk."

"You sound so wise and rehearsed in your crazy," I joked.

Walker came back out of the shower and toweled off in front of us. I let my gaze roam his body. "Where do you guys get your ink done?" I asked.

"Why? Are you thinking of getting our names branded on your ass or something?" Walker asked as he walked over and crawled into bed next to me, kissing me soundly.

"Something like that," I joked.

"I can get you his info, though you can't go alone to his studio."

"Why not?" I asked.

"He's not exactly the nicest or most honorable man in the world," Finn said.

"You guys act like I haven't lived in Sin City for the last decade or something. I'm not a virgin farm girl you all are used to out here in Bumfuck, Montana."

"Bumfuck, Montana?" Walker asked, laughing.

"Meh." I shrugged my shoulders and pulled him up against my back. "You two owe me breakfast and a nap."

"I'll go grab the breakfast and we can eat in bed. Then we can nap and order real food later." Finn agreed and kissed my forehead.

"Deal."

When we all woke up later, the afternoon sun was shining in through the large windows across the room from the bed, and I lay in wonder for a few moments, snuggled between my two alpha gods, and started thinking about their comments about me running.

It was true. I had always been a runner, and it had always been my biggest shortcoming in life that I'd give anything to change, especially because it was what had caused my dad to be stolen from me too early. I just didn't know how to just turn off something that had engrained itself in my DNA.

"What are you stressing about?" Finn's voice was deep and thick with sleep, and he didn't even open his eyes as he asked it. I'd thought at first, perhaps he had talked in his sleep, but then he cracked one eye and slid down in the bed until his face was buried in my chest, and he squeezed me tight with his arms around my waist.

"How do you know I'm stressing?" I asked back quietly, running my fingers through his hair and reveling in the way he moaned against my breasts.

"You were scowling, and I recognized the look from the night at the diner on our first date."

I snorted at him, "That was our first date?" I scoffed and feigned shock. "What a terrible first impression of your wooing skills."

He bit my nipple and licked it and then sucked it into his mouth, using arhythmic motion on it like he was trying to get some actual milk from it, and it made my thighs quiver and my brain short-circuit.

"What am I missing out on over here?" Walker slid up against my back and kissed my shoulder, his hand trailing down my side to my thigh and back up, sending goose bumps erupting over my entire body.

Finn let my nipple pop from his mouth, and I moaned and slid my fingers over Walker's hand and pulled it toward my aching center. He chuckled into my ear and then bit the lobe as he lifted my thigh up and over Finn's side, and then he slid his thick, skilled fingers through my wet folds. I was in a constant state of wetness around these two from my arousal and their come and it came in handy in times like this.

"Bailey was just about to tell me what she was thinking about that was stressing her out," Finn answered, sliding back up and kissing my lips, letting his tongue tease the outer edges of them but not actually sinking into my mouth like I so desperately wanted him to.

"Are you trying to distract us from the conversation with sex, Bailey?" Walker's beard teased my skin as he asked.

"Finn started it, and then you joined in," I purred and pushed my ass back into his rock-hard cock that was trying desperately to push its way between my ass cheeks and into my body.

Both Finn and Walker stopped playing with me and sat back, waiting for me to answer the original question.

I sighed and turned so I was propped up on the pillows against the headboard, and I pulled the blankets up to cover my body as I thought about my dark thoughts before Finn woke up.

"I was thinking about how I run away from tough shit." My voice was low and quiet as I looked down at my hands instead of their faces.

"Tell us more about that," Finn said, sitting up next to me as Walker did the same.

"I don't know when I started doing it or why, but it's why my dad died, and I harbor a lot of guilt about that."

"What do you mean, it's why he died? I thought you said he was killed." Walker's large hand slid up my thigh over the blanket, and his fingers drew lazy circles across the fabric as he lent his support.

"We argued that day. I was supposed to be with him at his shop after school, but I'd chosen to—" I paused and felt the shame settle into my heart the way it always did when I thought back to that time in my life. "I did something I wasn't supposed to, and he'd yelled at me over the phone. So, I took off and hid out for a while, but I guess he felt bad for yelling at me and that was why he'd stayed late at work. He was trying to calm down before he came home and faced off with me again. But he never made it home, and that's my fault." Tears burned the back of my eyes as I processed the guilt and shame.

Finn's voice was strong and sure as he looked at me. "You can't blame yourself for someone else's actions, baby."

"I had gone to that guy's house after school, the one who was older than me." Walker sighed and his fingers tightened on my leg. "My dad had suspicions about where I had been spending my time and he'd found out for sure that day when I didn't show up at his shop. He was so upset with me, and it ultimately killed him. My actions directly influenced the order of events that day. That's something I have to live with, and that's why I got upset last night when you brought up how wrong that relationship was."

Walker turned, threaded his fingers through my hair, and pulled me in for a deep kiss.

"I had no idea there was so much depth to that time of your life or I never would have made those comments, Bailey," Walker acknowledged.

"I know that. I'm not mad at you. I regret every second I gave him of my time, but after my dad died, I continued to stay in a relationship with him. Had I not, I probably would have self-destructed and ended my own life out of guilt. By staying with him, he distracted me until the pain and grief were something I could survive."

"You're incredibly tough to have gone through something like that and survived. You're so strong," Finn said and pulled me into a kiss.

"I appreciate it, but just know that I'm aware of my running tendencies and I'm working on it for you two."

They smiled and pulled me into more kisses and embraces as they thanked me for my dedication to them. Then, they showed me how thankful they really were without using words, leaving us all sated and exhausted.

Chapter 17 – Walker

Life with Bailey was becoming so normal and second nature, sometimes I wondered how we managed to survive day in and day out before her. It was incredible having her by our sides, and in our beds.

The sex was something that didn't even compare in this world, yet felt so natural at the same time.

But there was one thing left to take care of before we could truly fall into a happy peace with the three of us.

Clay.

Finn told Bailey when they first met that he would take care of Clay and his improper touching of Bailey that day in her shop. We hadn't had a chance to do it before now, because Clay left on a fly fishing trip with his buddies to his camp up in the mountain range.

But he got back in town yesterday, and Finn and I were both incapable of waiting another second to take care of him and his douche bag self.

"You think he's going to start a fight?" Finn asked from the passenger seat, cracking his knuckles. "I kind of hope he starts a fight."

I chuckled and shook my head at my little brother, never the one to eagerly jump into a fight, but always willing to have my back. Except this time, he was overly eager to crush Clay's face.

"I'd guess not." I said, glancing at him again as his shoulders deflated a bit. "Considering he's at work and already has a couple strikes on his job there."

"Bummer. It could have gotten good with all his buddies there."

I shrugged my shoulders, "Not like they don't all have some ass kicking coming to them either." I hummed. "Who knows, maybe he'll throw a punch and we can lay them all out."

"Well," He unclicked his belt as I parked my truck at the mechanic shop, "Here's to hoping."

We got out of the truck and walked up to the shop, and I noticed how more than one mechanic stopped what they were doing to watch us walk up, nudging buddies and getting their attention too.

We weren't in uniform, we were both off work, but they all knew who we were. Regardless if we were deputies or not, we had a reputation for being badasses long before we joined the police academy.

I had spent much of high school fighting and getting into mischief, and more than a few times, Finn had followed after me and had my back so we'd never lost one, regardless of how many assholes we faced.

"Deputies." Roy the owner walked out of one of the bays, wiping his hands on a red cloth. "What can I do for you, boys?"

"We're here to see Clay." I said, nodding to the bay next to the one we stood outside of, catching sight of his dirty blonde hair as he ducked back down behind a popped hood. "We won't keep him long."

Roy looked over his shoulder, scowling a bit before nodding his head and looking back to us. "I don't want any trouble here—"

I held my hand up, stopping his blabbering. "Then get out of the way so we can have a discussion with Clay and we'll be out of your hair." I commanded, leaving no room for misunderstanding.

"Clay!" Roy yelled, shaking his head. "Get the fuck out here and handle this before I fire your ass for bringing trouble to my door. Again!" He stomped back into the bay, grumbling under his breath as Clay finally popped his head back up.

"Finn." Clay said, slowly walking out toward us. "Walker. What can I do for you?"

I didn't miss the way he kept a hold of the large wrench in his hand as he came to a stop right in front of us.

"We'll keep it quick," Finn nodded to where his boys watched on. "Wouldn't want to keep you from your customer's. We're here to tell you," He glared at Clay, "And tell you only once, to stay away from Bailey Dunn."

Clay tsked his teeth, probably sucking two days worth of unbrushed food off of them as he looked from Finn to me and back. "Where do you get off speaking for Bailey?" He scoffed, "Last I heard she was a big girl—"

"I'm going to stop you right there." I snapped, taking a menacing step forward, and Clay stumbled back one with wide eyes. Chicken shit. "You may not have heard, but Bailey is ours. So that's where we get off speaking for her. Stay the fuck out of her shop, don't fucking talk to her in public, and avoid her at all costs whenever you do come face to face with her, or Finn and I will make your body so unrecognizable, your family will have to use dental impressions to identify your body." I looked down his dirty body and sneered, "Not that you've been to a dentist in a few years, maybe you'll just rot in an unmarked grave as John Doe."

"We mean it, Clay." Finn argued, interrupting Clay as he tried to clap back with some bull shit. "Stay the fuck away from her or you're a dead man."

"You can't tell me what to do!" He yelled, squeezing his hand around the wrench. A couple of his buddies walked outside, like they were going to jump in at his command and I chuckled, glaring at them all in challenge.

"Fucking try us."

"Clay!" Roy bellowed, "Get the fuck back to work, or so help me god, you're fucking fired!"

Clay clenched his teeth as he looked back to his boss in anger. "Got it." He turned back to us and shook his head, giving up. For now. "Whatever. If she wants to be a part of your freak show, I don't want anything to do with her fat ass."

I clenched my fists and took another step toward him in anger but he backed up quickly, retreating to the safety of his work. I wasn't dumb enough to chase him inside private property to beat his ass.

Nah, I'd wait for him to get off work and break his fucking knees if he talked about Bailey like that ever again. "Fuck off Clay. Don't fucking try me on this."

He laughed, shaking his head now that he was surrounded on safe territory and walked away.

"Let's go." Finn pushed me toward the truck, feeling how close I was to following after that scum bag. "Save it for when he really deserves it."

I got in and pulled away, memorizing every single thing about the encounter for later. I wouldn't forget it. I'd just shove it down and wait for a better opportunity to act on the rage inside of me.

No one was going to disrespect Bailey, ever fucking again.

"Let's grab Bail and have her file an order of protection against him. Just to be safe." Finn said, trying to be reasonable and calm headed. At least someone was.

"Yeah." I nodded. Legal paperwork was a good start, but we both knew from personal experience at work, that it didn't stop most people.

It was Friday and our boys had a football game, and Bailey was going to meet us there. We both somehow managed to get the entire weekend off so we were planning on spending it locked away in peace with her. It may have only been a few weeks since we met, but she was our fucking entire world, and being apart from her made an ache inside of me build until she was in my arms again.

I walked into the locker room, where the boys were getting dressed and ready, and loud rock music blared, getting everyone pumped for the game. Finn sat in the office, getting the last of his plays copied over to his charts.

He coached the offense, and I coached the defense. We had two other coaches that we worked with, and we were on track to have a flawless season.

"Hey, man," Finn said as I shut the door behind me and sat down.

"Hey, you got a second?" I asked, making sure the door stayed closed behind me.

He raised his eyebrows at me and leaned back in the chair. "For you, I have two." I flipped him the bird and then leaned forward on the desk with my elbows. "Is this something bad? You never shut the door to chat while we're here," he asked.

"It's just not something a bunch of seventeen-year-old boys should be hearing is all." He shook his head in confusion but let me continue. "I think Bailey's ready for us. I want to spend the weekend taking her to the next level sexually."

His eyebrows shot to his hairline, and he smirked at me. "What are we talking about here?"

"Anal. She's ready but she's fucking scared and won't pull the trigger, so I think we need to pull it for her. It's time to push her over the edge and fuck her ass."

"I agree that she's ready, and I agree that she's scared to ask for it. Do you think she'll go through with it though?"

We had been introducing Bailey to anal for the last few weeks. We used our fingers and tongues in her ass, and it always drove her absolutely crazy. The other night, she had begged for more, but she wouldn't articulate what it was exactly that she wanted more of, so we'd just moved on and didn't come back to it.

"She needs some persuasion. I just want to make sure we're a united front of support for her so she doesn't have to worry about it or stress. She always does best with anything if we take the burden from her shoulders and lead her. I went to the store today and got some things to help her, and I think she's going to enjoy this weekend."

"I'm game," he said, nodding his head. He reached under the desk, and I knew he was adjusting himself. "Fuck, I'm hard just thinking about it."

"Dude, me too. For fucking days now, I've been unable to get it out of my head."

"Well, I had the pleasure of fucking her pussy the first time, so you get her ass first."

"Damn fucking right I do," I scoffed at him.

A knock sounded and we turned to see Nate at the door. "Hey, coaches, it's game time."

We headed out to the field with sinister grins on both of our faces as we thought about what the weekend was going to lead to.

The boys were on the field doing warmups, and I was standing by the fence at the bleachers, shooting the shit with some dads, when I saw the radiant beauty of Bailey walking down the steps toward me.

I ignored what anyone else had to say as I looked at her. She wore a pair of wide-leg blue jeans and cowboy boots with a fitted white T-shirt tied right under her breasts, leaving only an inch or two of her tight stomach showing, and an oversized turquoise cardigan on overtop that fell to mid-thigh, and she looked breathtaking.

Every man and boy in the football park wanted her, but she was going home with us and the thought of that thrilled me.

I held my hand up for her to take as she got to the bottom of the bleachers and then walked down until we were away from everyone else. I climbed up and leaned on the railing, bringing us to the same height, and kissed her deeply.

I wasn't one for a lot of PDA usually, and I also tried to be respectful of her reserved modesty in public by not doing anything to make her uncomfortable, but I needed to put my hands on her or I was going to combust.

"Hi," she purred against my lips as I dropped my hands and let them fall to her hips. "I missed you." She pouted as I kissed her lush lips.

"Did you?" I asked, letting my thumbs rub against her bare stomach between us.

"Yes. I haven't seen you much the last few days and it's killing me. When are you getting some time off?"

I had worked four nights in a row and every single one of them, I ended up getting stuck staying late at an accident or some other scene so I was walking into the house as she was leaving.

This morning, she had been at her place when I got out of work, so I'd grabbed some coffee and met her there as she was running out the door, but I hadn't spent any time with her in days. We both had been desperate with need this morning, though, and I hadn't even been in her house for thirty seconds before she bent over her kitchen table, lifted her skirt, pulled her panties down, and begged me to fuck her.

I happily obliged her, but she deserved more than just a quick and dirty fuck on the kitchen table from me, and I was happy to get the next few days with her.

Thankfully, Finn had been home two of those four nights I was gone, so she hadn't been alone for all of them.

"I have a surprise for you," I whispered, ignoring the looks we were getting from being locked in an intimate embrace in the middle of the bleachers.

"Ooh, I like surprises." She cooed and ran her hands up my stomach, pulling a groan from my lips.

"Finn and I are both off until Monday morning."

"What?" She gasped. "A whole weekend with both of you?" Her eyes were wide, and her lips pulled into a bright smile. "You mean it?"

"Yep, we are all yours from tonight till then. So after the game, we'll meet you at your place and we can go home together. Pack a bag if you want, but don't expect to wear many clothes in the next 48 hours."

She squealed and hopped from one foot to the other. "That's the best surprise ever," she said happily.

"I have one more," I said, pulling back to look into her eyes seriously.

"What?"

I leaned in until my lips were at her ear. "I went to the adult toy store today and bought a few things to use on you this weekend that are going to make you come so hard. We've decided that by Sunday night, both Finn and I are going to be inside of your sexy, tight body at the same time."

She gasped and moaned quietly, pulling back to look into my eyes. There was so much desire in hers as she licked her lips and bit the bottom one. She whispered, "You're going to fuck my ass?"

"Many, many times," I growled.

"God yes." She moaned again and kissed me deeply. I heard a few catcalls but pulled her into me deeper, regardless of the metal railing between our bodies.

"You want that, don't you?"

"Yes. I do. I'm scared but I want you there so badly."

"Good. When we pick you up, I want you in this sexy sweater and boots and absolutely nothing else."

"Yes, sir," she whispered and offered her lips to me once again, and I drank heavily from them.

I groaned. "Go on back to your seat before I throw you over my shoulder and fuck you here on the field in front of everyone."

She chuckled and pulled back. Then, she turned and headed back to her seat but turned and blew a kiss over my shoulder, and I looked to see Finn standing there with an amused look on his face as he watched our interaction.

I had trouble focusing on the game the entire night. Thankfully, the boys knew exactly what they were supposed to do and we ended up victorious. It would have been a difficult situation to explain to the parents and boosters if we lost because I was thinking about my girlfriend's ass swallowing my cock all night.

When we were all back in the locker room, Finn pulled me aside. "What did you say to her that had her looking like she was ready to be ravaged right then and there in the stands?"

I smirked at him and raised my eyebrows.

"You told her?" He gulped and I laughed at him and nodded. "What did she say?"

"She begged us to take her there."

"Fuck!" He groaned and looked at his watch, seeing how much longer it would be before we could get out of there.

"I told her to wear only that blue sweater and her boots when we picked her up tonight."

"I'm going to fuck her so hard in the truck on the way home. I have no choice. None," he muttered.

"That's fair," I chuckled and texted her.

Me: See you in 15. Remember, completely bare.

I showed Finn and he groaned.

In a minute, she replied. It was a picture of her sitting on the end of her bed with her boots and sweater on and nothing else, her legs spread wide and her pretty pink pussy on display.

Bailey: Like this?

I grunted, and Finn asked, "What?"

"Look at your phone," I said, unable to tear my eyes away from the screen.

He pulled his phone out and sucked a deep breath, looking at our girl's wet pussy.

Finn: Just like that. Play with yourself until we get there, but don't let yourself come. Do you understand?

Bailey: Yes, sir.

We shoved our phones in our pockets, finished up what we needed to, relinquishing most of our responsibilities to the other coaches, and all but ran to my truck like our asses were on fire.

When I started it up, our phones pinged again, and this time it was a video.

The camera was on something at the end of the bed, and Bailey lay back in the center of it, working that neon-pink vibrating dildo into her pussy and moaning. I watched in rapture as she reached under her leg, ran her tiny fingers over her asshole, and rubbed it while she fucked herself with her vibrator. Her voice rang out through the video. "Hurry, babes, I'm so close."

I threw the truck in drive and drove the few blocks to her house, laying on the horn when I flew into the driveway.

A second later, her front door opened, and there stood our girl in her pretty blue sweater, cinched together with a large belt in the center, and those fuck-me brown boots, a duffle bag in her arms as she ran over to the passenger side of the truck. Her tits bounced wildly as she ran and they nearly popped out of her sweater, making the fabric work hard to keep them contained.

Finn jumped out and threw her up onto the seat, and she scurried over to me as I tossed her bag in the back.

"I have to come. Please let me come." She moaned as she leaned over and bit my neck painfully.

Finn jumped in behind her and lifted her hips into the air so that she faced me and had her ass toward him. It was so much like the other time in his truck when we'd picked her up after I fucked up and she took off.

The only difference was, we were in different seats tonight and I was about to test my ability to keep my come in my balls as she sucked me dry. She was working my zipper and button open on my jeans while she squealed as Finn licked her pussy.

It was comical to see him folded up in the passenger seat so he could get his mouth on her, but he was as eager as I was.

"Do you want me to suck on your cock, baby?" she purred into my ear as she fisted me.

"Hell yes, I do. And Finn's going to fuck you while you do." I reached over and pushed her sweater open, revealing her big, beautiful breasts to the cold night air and my hungry gaze. "You are so incredibly sexy, Bailey."

She hummed and leaned down until her ass was in the air and her face was buried in my lap as she played with my cock.

I put the truck in reverse and tore out of her driveway toward our house as Finn kicked his pants off completely and sat with his back against the door, his legs toward me.

I watched with quick glances as he pushed his hips up and pulled her down onto his cock. She spread her legs wide and made room for him as he impaled her and caused her to cry out and squeeze my cock tight in her hand.

Finn started fucking her mercilessly, his skin slapping hers as he painfully spanked her and fucked her hard. He was as keyed up as I was and needed to use her body for release.

By the moans and curses she was throwing back at him, she was all too eager to be used.

I slid my fingers into her hair and pushed her face down onto my cock. She spit on it quickly and then opened her throat and let me push all of it up into her in one thrust.

She grabbed my balls and twirled them in her fingers as I raised my hips up to meet her lips and pushed her face down into my lap over and over again.

I was thanking my lucky stars that we lived so close because she was doing her absolute best to drain our cocks and I needed to use all of my focus to come inside of her, and that was hard to do while driving.

"Fuck, that cunt is so wet," Finn cursed and spanked her again.

"Harder," she begged, and he obliged as he peppered her ass with more full-handed slaps.

"That's my dirty girl," I praised as I pulled into our driveway and slammed the truck in park, sending both of them careening into the dash.

They righted themselves, laughing, and then the cab of the truck was filled with slaps and moans and wet sounds as we each filled up her body with our hot come.

The windows were steaming up and she had beads of sweat on her brow when she crawled into my lap and kissed me sweetly.

"I need you, Walker. This wasn't enough." She pouted.

Finn laughed. "I won't take offense to that, minx."

She looked over and winked at him to soothe his wounds. He knew the last few days being apart had been hard on us, and he was all for the reunion, especially knowing what I had in store for her.

"Go upstairs, get naked, and bend over on the bed. I want your face in the blankets and that supple ass in the air, and I want your legs spread so fucking wide that your hips start to hurt. Understood?" I said, wrapping my hand around her throat and pulling her in to kiss her soul from her body.

"Yes, Sir," she said and slid off my lap and out my door, running up the steps to the porch with her sweater flapping around her naked body.

"What exactly did you buy at the store?" he asked, getting out of the truck and walking up the steps with me.

"God, what didn't I buy? I got plugs, lube, beads, vibrators, all kinds of bondage, a spreader bar, and a blindfold."

"Well, that settles it. We should order enough takeout for the next two days because I'm not pulling out of her body until Monday morning."

I laughed, kicked my boots off, and grabbed the bag of toys from the closet in the hallway, starting up the stairs right behind him.

He pushed the bedroom door open and there, bent over and spread open in the middle of the bed, was our beautiful girl. She was exactly like I told her to be, and she watched us from under her body.

I walked over and threw the bag down next to her, watching as her eyes snapped from the bag and up to me and then over to Finn as he took his shirt off and walked up behind her slowly, stalking his prey.

"We're going to play with this pretty little ass tonight, baby," I said as I smoothed my palm over her cheeks and let my fingers dip down over her puckered entrance. "You need a safe word, though, something other than no or stop, in case you need us to stop. It needs to be something you can think of and say even if every cell in your brain is focused somewhere else. Any ideas?"

"Hmm." She pondered as I let my finger slide down over her wet folds and pushed Finn's come up through them and to her asshole, using it to lubricate the flesh. "How about Camden?"

"You want our last name to be your safe word?" Finn asked.

"You said it had to be something I could remember no matter what. I'm not likely to forget your last name, nor am I likely to scream it in ecstasy either."

"She's got a point," I pointed out, letting my finger press against her ass. "Camden it is then."

I reached into the bag and grabbed out the black silk blindfold and showed it to her. "You're going to wear this tonight. It will help you focus on the sensations only and will make it more pleasurable for you."

"Okay." She whispered. I tossed it to Finn, and he leaned down and tied it on her face, checking to make sure she couldn't see anything before pulling her head up to his and kissing her deeply.

"How do you feel?" I asked, pausing to watch her body language for cues she may be trying to hide with her words.

"Excited." She panted. "Nervous too, but excited."

"Good." I praised, "Remember, you're the one in control of the situation here, baby."

"I know." She nodded, taking a deep breath, and calming her body as it nearly vibrated off the bed. I used the distraction to slide over five inches of thick finger all the way in, and she moaned on his tongue and pushed back on me.

"Good girl, darling," I praised her again.

I grabbed the spreader bar from the bag and laid it down on the bed between her ankles. The metal clanked, and she sucked a breath in as she focused on the noise.

Finn locked first one ankle and then the other into the contraption and then opened it farther, pressing her feet out wide and pinning her so she couldn't close her legs at all against it.

"Oh god." She moaned and circled her hips. I kept my middle finger buried deep into her ass, grabbed the lube, and poured it on her skin around my finger, then I started working it in and out. "Yes." She sighed and arched her back more.

It took a second, but the lube started doing what it was designed to do and soon, her ass and inner muscles started tingling, and she gasped and tried to pull forward to dislodge my finger.

But I knew that would be her first reaction, so I grabbed her hips in my hand and pulled her back, slapping her ass. "Stay put."

"It's tingling." She gasped.

"That's the point."

Finn grabbed the bag of restraints, checked out the options, and settled on the waist handles. It was a thick black strap that wrapped around her waist with looped handles all around it to use to push and pull her hips back and forth how we wanted, and it was perfect for the occasion. He slid it around her stomach and tightened it and then leaned down and kissed the base of her spine right under the strap.

"What's your safe word?" he asked.

"Camden."

"Good girl." He awarded her by running his fingers across her clit and then into her pussy.

We stood on each side of her upturned ass and worked our fingers into her body, and before long, she was panting and begging for more.

I took out the medium-sized butt plug from the bag. It was glass and had an emerald jewel on the end that matched her eyes, and I held it up for Finn to see.

"Fuck, that's going to look so pretty buried in her ass," he mused.

"What is?" she asked. I could hear the anticipation in her voice, so I took a bit of pity on her. I placed it against her hand where it rested on the bed next to her head, her fingers tentatively wrapped around it, and she held the cold glass in her palm. "Is that—it's going to go—" She sounded scared and excited at the same time.

"Yes, I'm going to work this into your ass while you sit on Finn's face, and it will make your orgasm so incredibly intense."

"It's big," she said and handed it back to me.

"It's not even half the width of our cocks," I said, leaving her to decide.

"Good point."

"Do you want to sit on my face, darling?" Finn asked as he kicked off the rest of his clothes, climbed up on the bed, and crawled under the spreader bar, settling between her milky thighs.

The bar rested on his stomach and lifted her feet into the air, effectively opening her up even more.

"Yes, yes please," she begged.

He pulled her hips down until he sucked on her clit quickly and she moaned. I felt her clench and unclench around my finger, and I pulled it from her body.

I leaned down and kissed her ass, letting my tongue press into her hole and lapping at her in the way I'd learned drove her wild, as I grabbed the bottle of tingling lube and poured it over the end of the glass plug.

Finn was licking her clit like it was his fucking job. He had his fingers worked into her pussy, and she was swinging her hips wildly and moaning.

I poured some more lube onto her, and worked it around with my fingers before putting the cold glass against her skin. She froze and took a deep breath as I started pushing it into her body for the first time. "Beg me to give this to you."

"Please Walker," She nearly screamed. "Please put it inside of me."

I watched in fascination as the glass started to disappear inside of her tight hole. She tensed up but Finn was all over it. He sucked her clit strongly and within seconds, she started shattering into an orgasm, and I used that time to put more pressure on the end of the plug.

She moaned and panted and pushed back on my hand in the throes of her orgasm, and I watched in wonder as it slid all the way in until only the sexy green jewel was left out, pressing against the insides of both of her luscious ass cheeks.

"God, fuck yes, oh my fucking god." She gasped.

"You look so damn sexy right now, Bailey."

"I want to see," she begged. I took my phone from my pocket and stepped back to take a picture of her sitting on Finn's face, his fingers spreading her pussy lips wide and the green gem sparkling in the light.

I walked up, lay on the bed next to her head, untied the blindfold, helped her lean up, and showed her the picture. Finn sat up from under her and her eyes rolled as she looked at the pretty little sight of her virgin asshole taking a toy for the first time.

Finn knelt behind her and pressed the gem and pulled on it slightly, and she hummed and bucked her hips and looked over her shoulder at him as he spoke. "I'm going to fuck your pussy now while you wear this, sweetheart."

I pushed my jeans down and lay with my head against the headboard, spreading my thighs wide on each side of her shoulders and tugging on her hair until she fell forward again. "And I'm going to fuck this pretty little mouth at the same time."

"I don't know if I'm ready for that," she said as she started to let fear hold her back. But Finn knew what she needed and had already lubed his cock up, sliding both fists through the straps on her hips and pulling her onto his cock forcefully, pushing all of himself into her in one brutal thrust.

"Fuck!" she screamed at the top of her lungs and threw her head back as he pulled back out of her body and then pushed forward once again. As soon as the scream died on her lips, a moan took its place.

"Remember your safe word, love," I said, holding her head still as he started fucking her harder and making her look at me. "Remember."

She took a few deep breaths and then rolled her hips and dropped down to her elbows again, kissing my inner thigh.

"This feels so incredible, Bailey. How does it feel for you?" Finn asked, panting and gasping with each thrust.

"So good, it hurts but it feels so—" She paused and bit her lip and moaned again, her eyes rolling in her head, and she started coming on his cock.

"Oh god." He grunted and pounded into her through her orgasm. "You're so tight right now!" he yelled.

"It feels so good, Finn," she said again and spit on my cock before fisting it and rubbing her saliva down the entire shaft.

She pushed my thighs wide. "Lie down. I want to lick your ass."

I laughed at her but did as she said. "Who am I to tell you no when you're already doing so much for me right now."

"Good boy," she praised and smirked at me before moaning again. I watched up her body as Finn started pushing and pulling on the plug, working it in and out of the tight circle of muscles at her entrance.

She started stroking my cock quickly as she sucked on my ball sack and then spit on my taint and started rubbing it with her fingers.

"You're so good at that," I admired.

"Pull my hair while I get fucked," she challenged and then dove back down to lick my taint and ass.

"Shit." I groaned and did what she asked. I grabbed her hair in both of my hands, held her curls in two pigtails over each ear, and pulled back on her scalp as she sucked me.

Finn was fucking her so hard; she was bobbing on my cock with each of his thrusts until she bottomed out and gagged. Her eyes were watering, and her skin was flushed as she chased another orgasm.

I looked at Finn and nodded. "Our girl is going to come again, brother. I think you should see if you can't make it her biggest orgasm yet," I challenged and tossed him one of the new attachable vibrators.

He caught it and smirked and slowed his thrusts as he turned the little butterfly on high and reached beneath her to insert the flat portion inside of her pussy, hooking it over her clit and letting his cock hold it where it needed to be.

"Oh my god. Oh my fucking god, Finn! What are you doing to me?" she pleaded and braced herself against my thigh with her hand as she swallowed my cock.

"I'm giving you every single thing you deserve, darling. So many incredible orgasms for your incredibly sexy body," he said and started slamming into her again.

She gasped and screamed around my cock with each bob up and down, and she let her small fingers press against my ass and pushed the tip of one inside.

"Holy fuck."

"Safe word, Walker." She smirked at me and then sucked my ball into her mouth as she slid her fingertip in and out.

"I'm coming down your throat. Swallow it all. If you let a single drop fall from your lips, I'm taking Finn's place and fucking your ass right now," I commanded, and her eyes flashed as she took me back into her throat and pressed her lips against my base and hummed, challenging me to come down her throat.

I threw my head back and did just that, filling her stomach with my orgasm. I heard Finn smack her ass loudly and then felt her orgasm shake her entire body as she came on his cock, the plug, the butterfly vibrator, and my cock in her throat all at the same time.

Finn grunted and brutally thrust two more times, shoving my cock into her throat deeper, and then started filling her pussy.

"Take it all, baby. Take all of our come, you good fucking girl," he commended as he orgasmed.

It took us all forever to come down from the explosive orgasms we all gave each other.

"Don't pull out yet," I said and untangled myself from her mouth and arms. "I want to see her stuffed full everywhere."

I crawled to my feet and walked around her ass and ran my hand down her spine. Her ass was so fucking pretty with that twinkling green gem holding it open, and then Finn's cock was buried deep inside of her still with the opaque fluid of his release pushing out around him at her entrance.

"Okay, pull out. Slowly," I said, and he smirked, pulling his cock out painfully slowly until just the head of him remained inside of her. His cock twitched and she sighed and tried to close her legs, but the spreader bar kept her wide open.

When he pulled out the rest of the way, his come spilled out, running down her lips to her clit, and he ran his fingers through it and pushed them into her with it on them again.

The butterfly vibrator still buzzed on her clit, and he pulled his fingers from her and nodded toward me. I took his place and leisurely pushed two of my fingers into her pussy coated with both of their orgasms, and he pushed the vibrator against her clit harder.

"How is it possible that you two can still give me pleasure after everything else you've given me already tonight?" She moaned and looked over her shoulder at us.

"Hold on tight and find out, baby," I said as I scissored my fingers inside of her and pushed against the glass plug through the thin membrane between her ass and pussy. "I'm going to pull the plug out now, okay? Take a deep breath for me."

She did as I told her to and I felt her muscles relax around my fingers, and Finn ground the vibrator into her clit harder still.

I pulled at the gem and slowly twisted and turned it as her tight ass released the widest part. I slid it slowly from her body and sucked in a breath at the way her ass gaped slightly for a moment after it was empty.

I nodded to Finn, and he grabbed the bottle of lube. As I pulled my fingers from her pussy, he poured the cold liquid onto them, and I quickly pushed them into her open ass.

"What are you doing?" she shrieked and bucked her hips forward. I followed her down to the bed as she collapsed onto the mattress and pushed my fingers deep. "Oh fuck."

She moaned and tilted her hips to give me better access. I continued pushing my fingers into her, enjoying the moans and groans she was making along with the wet noises from my actions. She twisted her hips and begged for more, so I added a third finger and took over the pressure on the butterfly vibrator as Finn crawled up to lie next to her and kissed her passionately. I twisted my fingers, occasionally scissoring them and moving them around to stretch her, while also pushing on the muscle between her two holes and putting pressure on her G-spot from the inside.

She held on to Finn as she rode my fingers, and I watched as she twisted her hands in the blanket as every muscle in her body tensed and vibrated when her orgasm rushed through.

It was such an incredible sight to behold, knowing that we did that to her and no one else.

It was such a gift to know that she trusted us with this experience and that she blossomed through it like we knew she would.

I couldn't wait to slide my cock into her body in a way that no one else had ever done before, but it wasn't going to happen tonight. We'd already pushed her to the brink so many times in a row, she needed hydration and rest.

We all crawled back into bed after showering together and eating delicious Chinese takeout, it wasn't long before her supple lips were parted and making sweet, soft noises in her sleep as the exhaustion took her.

I leaned my head down and took a deep breath in her hair and tried to memorize every single detail about her to cherish in my memory bank.

Chapter 18 – Bailey

I stood at the stove and flipped an omelet in the giant pan, somehow managing to catch it without making it flop into a mess. I chuckled and fist-pumped the air at my victory as I set the pan back down and turned to grab the stuff on the counter behind me to make another one.

Finn was leaning on the island, facing me with an amused grin on his face, and I screamed, my hands flying to my heart.

"Finn!" I laughed. "You scared the shit out of me."

He raised his eyebrows at me and sniffed the air. "Are you cooking?" he asked curiously.

I stuck my hip out and tsked my lips at him. "I can cook, believe it or not. You guys just never let me. Besides that one time I made steaks."

"Hmm," he mused and stood up, letting me drink in the sight of him in nothing but tight black boxer briefs. He walked over to me, but I held my spatula up at him.

"No distractions or I'm burning your breakfast," I warned, trying my best to sound authoritative.

"Oh, you're cooking for me too?" he joked, pushing the spatula away from his chest and wrapping his large hands around my waist, pulling me in for a toe-curling good morning kiss.

"A man could get used to having you here every morning," he complimented and kissed my nose.

"A woman could get used to being kissed like that every morning," I joked back. I turned to watch his omelet, and he wrapped his hands around my middle and leaned his chin on top of my head.

I was wearing his long-sleeve shirt from last night, the arms rolled up so my wrists were free from the fabric, and I reveled in how sexy I felt in their clothes.

He watched from behind me as I worked on the stovetop without ever letting his hands slide from my waist or his head move from the top of mine.

I was sure we looked comical, like a marionette and her puppet master, but it made me feel adored that he wanted to be near me enough to do something so mundane with me to get it done.

"I'm falling for you, Bailey," he said quietly, and my hands froze on the pan as I pushed my breakfast onto a plate.

My heart rate sped up, and I could feel it ticking under the skin of my neck as I let his words sink into my brain.

It only took two seconds for the processing to happen, and I turned the stove off and turned in his arms. I could see the vulnerability in his eyes as he looked down into mine, so I slid my hands around his neck and let my fingers dive into the hair at his nape the way I knew drove him mad, leaned up, and offered my lips to him.

He leaned down and kissed them slowly, coaxing mine apart, and then he teased them with his tongue before pushing it into my mouth to play with mine. I moaned and leaned into his strong arms as he held me against him.

He kept the kiss slow and exploratory, and his hands joined the activities by roaming over my body, sliding across the sensitive skin at the back of my thighs and up farther until they were under the oversized shirt and lay flat across my hips.

I pulled back and opened my eyes to look at him. "I'm falling for you too. You make it pretty impossible not to," I said and smiled sweetly at him.

He let a deep breath out when I said it back and then leaned down and deepened the kiss.

He hadn't said I love you and neither had I, but we did say that we were getting there. That was enough for right now.

I didn't know if Walker had strong feelings for me like Finn did, but I wasn't going to worry about it right now. Instead, I was going to show Finn just how much it meant to me that he did have those feelings for me and that he took the chance to tell me.

I slid my fingers into the waistband of his briefs and tormented the nerves right below.

"Your body is so damn sexy," I said and leaned forward and kissed a trail from one of his flat nipples to the other, and then I started kissing down his stomach and over the bulge that had started growing under his briefs.

I dropped to my knees and pulled his shorts to the floor and kissed my way up his thighs until my mouth was at the base of his cock.

He leaned back against the counter and watched as I took him in my hand and swirled my tongue around the head of his cock. I flattened my tongue and pushed my mouth down on him, pressing him against the back of my throat as I twisted my hands up and down everywhere that my lips weren't touching.

"Fuck, that's hot," he said and fisted my hair, pushing and pulling me lightly with each bob.

I wrapped my hands around his back and dug my nails into his ass cheeks as I pushed him down my throat completely and kissed the base of his cock.

When I pulled off him, I looked up and, as sweetly as I could manage, I begged, "Fuck my mouth, Finn. Please."

His nostrils flared and his abs twitched and half a second later, he was doing exactly as I'd asked.

He thrust his cock deep into my mouth and then pulled it out slowly before pushing in again. I palmed his balls and scraped my nails on the sensitive underside of them as he roared and threw his head back.

"I'm close, baby," he warned, and I winked at him and held on as his thrusts got deeper and longer.

Suddenly, Walker knelt behind me and pushed my head forward on Finn's cock. He reached around and pulled me up until I was squatting on my feet and no longer on my knees, my thighs spread wide, opening me to the cool air of the kitchen. I hummed and leaned my weight back into his body. He pulled my shirt up until it was bunched at my shoulders, and then his hands were everywhere. He palmed my breasts and parted my folds and buried his fingers deep into my wet pussy.

"You're so sexy on your knees like this, baby," he said hotly in my ear. He slid his hand up around the base of my throat and held me still while Finn started erratically thrusting into my mouth as closing in on his orgasm pushed him over the edge of sanity.

"Hold her just like that, Walk," he bit out between clenched teeth. His abs were shining with perspiration, and his chest was heaving with exertion. Seconds later, I felt the first shot of his orgasm sliding down my throat against Walker's hand on the outside of it. "Take it, baby."

When Finn finally pulled his long, thick cock from my mouth, I gasped and sagged into Walker's arms as I fought to catch my breath.

"You are the most perfect woman on the face of this earth," Finn praised and knelt in front of me, kissing me deeply. I smiled and leaned into him and then stood to ease the ache in my thighs from the low squat.

"What the fuck did I miss before I got down here?" Walker asked, amused as he palmed the erection straining behind the fabric of his sweatpants.

"Finn was being nice and sweet so I rewarded him," I said and laughed at Walker's dark look.

"Well, nice and sweet aren't in my arsenal, so what do I have to do to get that kind of treatment in the morning?" he asked as he tried to hide a smirk on his lips.

"Hmm, I like you when you're bossy and demanding," I joked.

"Noted."

Finn chuckled and grabbed the omelets and took them to the table as Walker grabbed some juice and glasses.

"Thanks for breakfast, man," Walker said.

Finn snorted into his juice, and I scoffed at him. "Do you two really think I'm incapable of cooking?" I asked, annoyed.

Walker looked from his brother to me, barked a quick laugh, and then held his hands up in surrender as my stare got darker the longer he laughed.

"I guess I just assumed you didn't because you never have any food at your place and we always cook when you're here, other than that first night."

"I hate cooking for one person, so I don't do it often, but I'm actually a damn good cook when I am inspired to be."

"Holy shit, you're not kidding," Finn said as he chewed a bite of his breakfast.

I rested my chin on my steepled fingers and watched in challenge as Walker tentatively took a bite of his meal.

I watched him chew it for a second before his eyes closed and he slid down in his chair a step. "Hot damn," he cursed and nodded in defeat. "Okay, damn, girl, you can cook," he joked and took another bite.

I picked my fork back up and enjoyed my meal and the easy banter between us all in the soft morning light.

Finn got me a cup of coffee, and I sat back into my chair and was admiring the two sexy men on the other sides of the table with their bedheads and sexy bare chests when someone knocked on the front door and then rang the doorbell before walking in.

"I swear to god," Walker bitched, looking at Finn.

I had flashbacks to the time that Luann just walked in the front door and kissed Finn while I sat on the counter, freshly fucked and basically naked.

I felt my eyes go wide as I looked between the two of them before a male voice rang out through the space. "Yo, Walk, Finn, you up?"

"Shit," Walker cursed and shot me an apologetic glance as a man walked around the wall and into the kitchen. He was attractive, almost as tall as my guys, but had shaggy light-blond hair and an easy-going smile on his face until his eyes landed on me sitting between the fellas.

His eyes shot between Walker and Finn, and then he turned around and looked at the wall. "Shit, sorry. I didn't think you'd have company this early. My apologies, ma'am."

"Ma'am?" I asked quizzically to Walker as he stood up and took my hand, pulling me to my feet.

"Go get dressed, baby." Getting dressed was the very last thing I wanted to do because I had planned on being naked and spread out beneath one of my guys in the next few minutes, but I didn't want to be so underdressed in front of another guy either, so I scrunched my nose at him and flipped him the bird as I turned to walk up the stairs.

I was rewarded for my attitude with a loud powerful slap to my bare ass under the hem of the shirt I was wearing.

"Ouch," I squeaked and covered my ass as he went in for another one.

Finn laughed merrily from the table as he took my coffee cup and drained it. "Ass," I muttered at him, and they both laughed at me again, but I went up the stairs like a good little girl.

When I got to Walker's bedroom, I got dressed in a tight black tank top and a pair of maroon skinny jeans. I grabbed a black and white flannel out of Walker's closet and put it on overtop, leaving it open and off the shoulder, and then went into the bathroom to freshen up a bit.

When I walked back downstairs a few minutes later, the guys were out on the porch with their guest, and I wasn't sure how to approach the situation. So instead of dealing with it at all, I started picking up the dishes from breakfast.

Walker saw me through the window and crooked his finger for me to come out to him, but I didn't like being summoned like that, so I rolled my eyes at him and then blew him a kiss in jest as I finished cleaning up.

A moment later, he stepped in the screen door and set his coffee cup down on the counter as he stalked toward me.

"I'm sorry, but what part of that did you think was optional?" he challenged as his eyes glinted with mischief.

I snorted at him and moved toward the pantry, but he stepped around the counter and started to block my path. I froze as his eyes darkened, excitement racing through my veins at the thought of being chased. "Come here," he commanded.

He looked so fucking good in just a pair of gray sweats and bare feet and open desire in his eyes.

"Make me," I dared and shifted quickly, going for the other direction, but he was quicker than I was.

He hurdled the island and landed lightly on his feet in front of me, and I squealed in exhilaration as he wrapped his large arms around me and lifted me effortlessly. I laughed outrageously and swatted at his hands as he threw me over his shoulder and then carried me out the kitchen door to the porch. When the door slammed shut behind us, he slapped my ass powerfully and laughed at my squeak in response.

Finn laughed and I looked around Walker's shoulders to see their visitor watching with an amused smirk on his face, and then I felt a blush creep over me.

"Are you going to behave if I put you down, hellcat?" Walker asked.

"Probably not," I warned and pinched his ass.

"Put her down. I like her wild side," Finn mused, and I winked at him from my upside-down perch.

Walker slid me down the front of his body and held me steady as my brain caught up, and then he kissed me quickly.

I turned around and walked over to sit next to Finn, guessing he was the safer bet for me to be near at the moment since Walker was feeling playful.

Finn wrapped his arm around me and nodded across the porch to the blond man. "This is Jake. He's Walker's partner on the force. Jake, this is Bailey Dunn, our girlfriend."

I tried to keep my schoolgirl smile in check at the title and leaned forward to shake his outstretched hand.

"Finn tells me I may have offended you with the ma'am title earlier. I meant no disrespect by it, I assure you," Jake said lightly and laughed.

"Respectful titles are not something used often where I'm from, so sometimes I forget they're meant kindly here," I said. "But thank you."

"No problem. I also want to apologize for interrupting your morning here unannounced. I have never known the fellas to be busy on a Saturday that they were both home, so I didn't think anything of it until it was too late. I assure you, I'll call ahead next time."

I laughed and waved him off. "It's fine."

"Jake is here to drop off our suits for his wedding in two weeks," Walker said.

"You're getting married? Congratulations!" I said happily. I had loved weddings ever since I was a little girl.

"Yes, in 14 days. And good lord, I cannot wait!" he said excitedly and then laughed.

Walker and Finn made jokes about him tying the knot, but I could tell they were lighthearted.

"I've known Ivy since I was in high school, but I messed stuff up a few too many times over the years, so it took this long to prove to her that I'm worthy. I'm anxious to officially have the title of husband, I guess."

"She sounds lovely," I said. "And don't listen to a single word they say about romance."

My guys scoffed but Jake brushed them off. "She is, and she's going to love having another girl to befriend in you. There aren't many women our age that aren't local girls that have either caused drama over the years or fallen out of touch in life."

"I can't wait to meet her."

"Maybe we can get together for dinner sometime in the next two weeks."

"That would be fun," Finn added, pulling me in closer and kissing my hair.

"Is there any chance you have an opening for me in your shop sometime next week, Bailey? I think Ivy would love it if I surprised her with a fresh haircut for our wedding day," Jake asked as he raked his hands through his long surfer-boy hair.

"Of course, now you're talking my language. I'll get you looking all sorts of spiffy for her if you want. I can do it Saturday morning before the wedding, too, if you want, then she won't know about it until she walks down the aisle. Unless you think she might not like that because I sure as heck don't want to be to blame for pissing off a bride on her special day."

They all laughed. Walker added, "I don't think there's a thing in this world that Jake could do to truly piss Ivy off. You're safe there, babe." His eyes sparkled in the sunlight as he sat in the rocker and looked at me. He seemed so relaxed and at ease, and I let my eyes wander over him, trying to memorize this side of him because he was usually so serious and studious.

This relaxed side of him was refreshing. My eyes traveled the swirls of ink on his hand wrapped around his coffee cup, up his arms, and to his shoulders. I reveled in the way the dark shading across his chest moved and transformed with each breath, down to the lines that ended at the top of his abs and looked like icicles hanging inside of a cave, begging to be touched and broken.

I looked up and noticed that his eyes were locked on me and burned under his arched brows as he studied me. I bit my bottom lip and sucked on it and drank in the way the muscles in his thick neck bulged as I did.

Finn and Jake were talking, oblivious to what was passing between Walker and me, and I was glad for it for a moment.

I brought my hand up to play with a curl at my neck, ran my fingers over the silky lock, and watched as his eyes dropped to the repetitive motion. He constantly had his hands in my hair, sliding the spirals through his rough, tattooed fingers.

Those fingers tightened around his mug in a death grip I itched to have around my neck in a way that drove both him and me mad with need.

I had one knee crossed over the other, and Finn's hand was between my thighs, resting inches from my core. I pressed my thighs together around his hand, gaining both his and Walker's attention to my pressing need.

Walker stood up and let his eyes drip his arousal over me as he tried to politely tell Jake to fuck off, but the intent was clearly there.

"Alright, man, thanks for dropping them off, but we've got plans for the rest of the day that we can't break," he said.

Jake looked over at me and Finn and then smirked and stood up. "Yeah, no problem. You three enjoy yourselves today. I'll see you Monday, man."

"Have a good weekend," Finn said and stood up, pulling me with him, shaking Jake's hand.

When Jake headed down the stairs to his truck, Finn trailed his hand down to cup my ass through my jeans and slid his fingers between my cheeks, letting the rough fabric scrape the sensitive skin.

"Mmm," I moaned and turned to bite his shoulder as he continued.

Jake honked as he got in his truck and took off down the driveway, and within seconds, Finn had my jeans unbuttoned and was pushing me down on the daybed that Jake had just stood up from and pulled them off.

"I owe you an orgasm, pretty lady," he said and kissed my inner thigh before grabbing the strap of my panties and ripping them off of me forcefully.

"I liked those!" I gasped and looked down at him as he spread me wide.

"I'll buy you twenty more because I like nothing more than ripping them off you, baby."

Walker sauntered toward us with his hand on his large erection, palming it through his sweats. He knelt on the cushion next to me and slid both of his large hands up my stomach and under the tank top until it was pushed up to my neck, revealing my aching breasts to them both.

He pinched my nipple and watched my back bow off the bed as Finn slid his fingers through my folds and rolled my clit between his fingers.

"Ah." I moaned and reached for Walker's cock. He pushed down his pants and brought it to my lips, and I swirled my tongue around the head of him, tasting his precum. "I love the way you taste," I said and then started sucking on him like my favorite flavor of the lollipop as I grinded back and forth against Finn's face.

"I love the way you look with your lush lips wrapped around a cock while you fight off an orgasm."

I grabbed the top of Finn's head and held him exactly where I needed him, rolling my hips as he chuckled. "Topping from the bottom again, Bailey?" he asked as he slid two fingers into my pussy and then spit on my ass and slid two fingers in there. He started pumping both into me, scissoring and crooking them to push me over the edge and headfirst into a cataclysmic orgasm that made my eyes roll and my toes curl.

I threw my head back and cursed incoherent words and pleas as he kept fucking me with his thick fingers while sucking on my clit, forcing my orgasm to roll on and on throughout my body.

By the time it stopped, I was breathless and saw stars.

"Oh my god." I moaned, laying my head back on the bed and going mostly limp. My hand was still wrapped around Walker's cock, but to be completely honest, I couldn't focus on stroking him at this moment.

He leaned down and kissed me as Finn worked his fingers out of my body slowly.

"I love the way your sexy ass gapes for a second when we pull things out of there. I can't wait to see it when we pull our cocks out of it."

"Fuck me, please. One of you put your cock in me. I need it," I begged, and Finn leaned down, picked me up, and threw me over his shoulder, carrying me through the house.

"Your wish is our command," he said as he threw me down in the center of the bed and stripped out of his shorts.

Walker followed us into the bedroom and grabbed the black bag of ass-stretching goodies from last night. I squirmed as I got up and knelt on my knees, pulling him into me for a kiss.

He held my head how he wanted and kissed me so deeply, by the time he pulled away, I was panting as quickly as I would have been if he'd been using his tongue on my lower lips instead.

"Fuck me, Walker. I want your cock inside of me," I begged and pushed my hand down into his pants, which he'd tucked himself back into when we came inside.

His cock was still rock hard and wet from my lips, and I wanted him so badly.

Finn had fucked me last night while I had the glass plug in, and I knew Walker craved my ass so badly. I wanted to give it to him, but I'd be lying if I said I wasn't scared of the unknown.

"I trust you," I said against his lips, pulling back to show him exactly how sure I was of that.

His eyes burned and his throat worked as he fought to compose himself. "You don't know what it does to me to hear you say that." He kissed me again and pulled the flannel and tank top off over my head, leaving me naked for his hands to explore.

Finn looked through the bag while Walker kissed me and played with my pussy, leaving me soaked and begging.

Walker pulled back and looked me dead in the eye. "I'm going to fuck your virgin ass today, Bailey. I'm going to put my entire cock deep into your sweet, sexy ass and fuck you until I blow an entire load of come into you for the first time in your life. And I'm going to make sure you orgasm so fucking hard the entire time." His voice was impossibly deep and dark, and I shivered listening to him explain how he was going to fuck me. "But first, we're going to play again and get your ass ready to take my cock."

"Yes please." I smiled at him, leaned over, and pulled Finn in for a kiss as he ran his hands down my back and slapped my ass.

Finn was usually the gentler of the two, but this new experience was pulling the darker side of him out and it drove me mad knowing I could make him slip from his usual poised and relaxed self and turn him into an animal focused on his needs and nothing else.

I loved that I did it to both of these men.

"Stand next to the bed and bend over the edge," Finn said and helped me down. My stomach just barely cleared the top of the tall frame, so when I bent over, my toes were the only thing touching the floor. "Spread your legs wide for me, baby," he said, and I felt his breath on my exposed core a second before his tongue licked from my clit to my ass.

"Hmm," I moaned and spread my legs wide for him, opening myself as far as I could for his talented tongue. "Yes, Finn," I said.

I turned my head and watched as Walker grabbed a vibrating dildo from the bag. It was black and somewhere between the size of my rabbit and Walker's and Finn's cocks.

Finn stood up and grabbed the bottle of tingly lube and then took the dildo from Walker's hands. I turned to face forward, took a shuddering breath, and tried to relax.

I knew it was going to hurt at first, but I also knew the guys were going to pleasure me in other ways that my brain couldn't even comprehend before it happened, so I just relaxed and let them take control.

"What's your safe word?" Finn asked as he poured the lube onto my puckered entrance.

I moaned and bit my lip as he started rubbing his fingers against me.

"Bailey," he commanded, stilling his lovely fingers.

"Camden," I said, gasping.

"Good girl," he praised me and started rubbing against me again. After a moment, he pushed one finger into me slowly. There was no burn at all as he did it, and I enjoyed every second. They had been working their fingers into me for the last few weeks and it felt incredible now. It gave me confidence that getting fucked in the ass on its own would feel good someday too.

Walker stood next to his brother and they both watched as Finn added another finger and then a third into my body.

"Oof," I said and tensed up. Three of their fingers were about two fingers shy of their cocks in terms of thickness and it already burned.

"Relax, Bail, let me make you feel good," Walker said and crawled up to lie on the bed, pulling me until his face was under my pussy.

"Fuck yes." I hissed as he sucked on my clit as Finn rubbed the tip of the dildo against me. He turned it on, the hum vibrating through the noise of my pants and Walker's tongue on my wet pussy. "Fuck me with it, Finn. Please, I need it so badly. I want you to push it in," I pleaded, wanting them to know I wanted this as much as they did.

"Jesus Christ." Finn cursed and Walker's cock bobbed where it lay heavily on his stomach in front of me. "When your pretty pink lips say such dirty words like that, angel, you make men like me desperate to convert you to the dark side," Finn said as he pushed the dildo into me.

He had so much lube on it and me that it slid right in with no resistance. It burned and a cold sweat broke out down my spine, but I couldn't help the way my hips tilted, offering more of my ass to him in response to the pain. He slid it in and out slowly, letting me get used to it, but before long, he was fucking me with it just like he would with his cock.

"It burns," I said and lay my face onto Walker's stomach, kissing the sensitive skin on both sides of his belly button. "But it feels so good too. With Walker playing with me, Jesus, fuck, I'm going—" My back locked up and I pierced my nails into Walker's side as the biggest orgasm of my life ripped my body into pieces. "Fuck!" I screamed. "I'm coming, oh my god. Please, Finn. Harder. Please, I want more," I begged and pushed my thighs wider around Walker's face, lowering my clit deeper into his mouth.

A giant hand slapped my ass, demanding more from my orgasm as it rocked me. Finn pounded my ass with the dildo as Walker spread me open and pushed his fingers into my pussy to match the thrusts of Finn, and I catapulted into a spontaneous second orgasm the second my first was over.

My screams echoed off the walls, and I jerked when I felt Finn's hot release spray my ass and back as I rode Walker's face. I hadn't realized he'd been jacking himself off but as soon as it hit my skin, it burned me like a brand and I craved to taste him.

Walker lifted my leg, pulled himself out from under me, and looked in fascination at the dildo deep inside of me while my ass continued to twitch and spasm around it.

"I want to taste his come," I purred, looked at Walker, and licked my lips.

His jaw went slack, and his eyes closed for a second before he opened them back up and looked at me. "You're so sexy."

Finn cursed, letting his hand rub over my burning ass cheek where he spanked me, and continued to lazily stroke his cock as my words spurred him on deeper into bliss.

Walker ran his fingers over the sticky pools of come on my ass and back and brought them to my lips, and I greedily sucked them into my mouth. When I had licked them clean, he did it again, and I welcomed the taste of Finn's orgasm on my tongue as he spun the dildo in circles inside of me.

This time, when his fingers were clean, Walker leaned down and gripped my jaw in his large hand and kissed me deeply. "I *need* to fuck your ass, Bailey. It's no longer something I want or crave. It's a fucking need inside of me that I've never felt before."

I nodded quickly and licked my lips again. "Please fuck my ass, baby. I need it too. I need to feel you fill me with your come in there and claim me like no one else has." Then,

I turned to Finn and pulled him in to kiss me. When I pulled back, I said, "And then I want you to fuck me too."

His eyes rolled and he laid his forehead on mine. "You have no idea how fucking perfect you are for us. So. Fucking. Perfect," he bit out and then surprised me by pulling the dildo out of me quickly, spanking my ass again.

I moaned and fell forward to the bed, but I should have known better than to think that Walker would let me hide their favorite part from them. He leaned forward and spread my cheeks wide and stared at the gape the toy left before my body relaxed and closed back up.

Finn wiped his release off my skin with a damp cloth and the chill made me shudder. Walker leaned down, licked my hole, and pushed his tongue into me, and I moaned and pushed back.

"On your side," Walker commanded. He pulled back and pushed me up the bed until my head lay on the pillow.

"Whatever you say, baby," I purred, and he smiled at me in a way that took my breath away. I'd never seen him smile like that around anyone else, and I loved that he saved his rare open emotions for me only.

I lay on my side, and he crawled up my body and pushed my hip up so that my knee was toward my chest. He straddled my other leg, which was straight and flat on the bed beneath him.

Finn lay on the pillow next to me, kissed me, and palmed my heavy, aching breasts, rolling my nipples between his fingers.

I watched Walker as he poured lube onto his giant, thick, corded cock and then on his fingers and rubbed them around the skin of my ass.

"Are you ready?" he asked, looking down at me caringly.

"So ready," I said and smiled at him. I watched his eyes as he fisted his cock and leaned forward, pressing the head of himself against me.

I took a deep, calming breath, ran my nails over the wounds I left on his side from my last orgasm, and gasped as the head of his cock pushed into my body.

It burned instantly and I felt like it was ripping me open.

"Breathe," Finn said, turning my head and kissing me, forcing me to focus on just him and the sensation.

"Holy shit," Walker cursed, and I turned back to look at him. I watched as he swallowed and every muscle in his neck, chest, and arms twitched and tensed as he rocked forward, pushing more of his cock into my body. "You feel so incredible, Bailey," he whispered and sighed as he pulled back out, until the widest part of his bulbous head was stretching me open, and then pushed forward again. "Talk to me, baby," he demanded and leaned forward to tilt my chin up to look at him. "Tell me what you're feeling."

I swallowed and laid my head back on the pillow and tentatively pushed my ass up farther into his lap. "It's . . . intense," I said, "but I like it." I smiled at him, and his hips jerked forward quickly.

I sucked in a breath and moaned as he slid back out from me.

"You are so phenomenal." Finn reached his hand down between my legs and rubbed small, light circles over my clit as he sucked on my nipples. I threaded my fingers through his hair and held him to my breast as he teased me.

"Finn! Fuck." I was keyed up and I wanted the intense pain of Walker's cock fucking me completely. Right now, I was getting just the burn of him stretching me without the bite of him bottoming out or slapping my ass or anything else.

I grabbed Walker's arm and pulled him down until he was against my side, his forehead touching mine. "I want you to fuck me how I know you desperately need to, Walker. I need it to hurt and to be intense. I need more. Stop holding back and being gentle." His eyes flared and his hand slid up and wrapped around my throat. I laid my head back and pressed more of my neck into his hand. "Yes. Like that." My eyes rolled as he pushed forward and finally hit bottom with his cock. "Yes." I moaned again.

He sat back up, grabbed my hip in his large hand, and kept his other one wrapped around my throat. "Hold on to me, baby. I'm going to fuck you until you beg me to stop. And you're going to take every single thing I give you."

"Please, Walker. Fuck me hard, own me."

He did just that. He pulled back and viciously forced his cock into my body. I saw stars, and all ability to get air into my lungs ceased. I wrapped both hands around the arm holding my throat and held on as he fucked me like a doll. He squeezed my throat expertly, not cutting off my ability to move air but restricting the blood flow to my brain, and suddenly, I was in a euphoric state of delirium.

Finn kept rubbing my clit, and Walker never let up his assault on my ass as I orgasmed, exploding calamitously, and felt my body suck him deeper into my hole.

He grunted and cursed continuously as he kept thrusting. I felt my head loll and my eyes roll, and incoherent pleas fell from my lips. He waited until my orgasm crashed and ended and then surprised me by pulling out of me completely.

"No." I mewed, but he slapped my ass and chuckled.

He lay down on the bed on his back and pulled me until I was straddling him in reverse cowgirl. "Lean forward," he said, and I placed my hands on the bed between his legs and felt him line himself up again. He pulled me back and slid into my body, forcing more curses and pleas from my lips.

He worked me like that for a while, two more orgasms overtaking me, and I was getting weaker and tired from the total body tremors that he was ripping from me with each one.

But he was so far from done with me. I didn't know where he was getting the restraint from, but he kept fucking me like a madman. He pulled me back, laid me on his chest, and then grabbed my ankles and brought them up, holding them at each side of my pussy and using them as leverage to begin fucking me from beneath.

"No," I begged. "I can't—"

He slapped my pussy, his palm hitting directly on my clit, and continued to fuck me. "Yes, you can. And you will. You're going to take it all, Bailey. That's what you begged for; you pleaded with me to make it hurt."

I was close to orgasm again. His cock was angled deep inside of me and pressed against my G-spot through my body with each thrust, and I felt the overwhelming pressure on my bladder.

"No!" I cried. "I think I have to—oh God, I have to pee," I said, desperate for him to stop so I didn't make a huge embarrassment of myself.

I watched as Finn's eyes widened from where he was playing with my nipples and my pussy, and then he said, "Holy shit." He looked over me to his brother, who picked up his pace, thrusting his hips spastically, forcing his cock into my ass deeper and harder. Finn reached down and slapped my clit again, and I pushed at his hand, trying to get off of Walker's chest, but neither man would let me go.

"Please stop," I pleaded. This was so embarrassing, yet the pressure felt incredible.

Walker's hands tightened painfully on my ankles, and he pulled my legs wider to my sides until I was painfully spread open on top of him, which only made the pressure on my bladder stronger.

All of a sudden, the orgasm that had been lingering at the tip of my spine broke over my body, and what I thought had been the urge to pee burst as Finn rubbed my clit viciously. It was then that I realized it was, in fact, not pee.

I watched in horror as liquid rained out of my body around Finn's hand, and Walker roared from under me.

I was destroyed by the orgasm. My body convulsed on top of Walker, and I came so hard, I felt like I was going to squeeze off his cock completely. Stars danced in my vision, and my entire body jolted like I was being electrocuted as Walker continued to yell and swear from behind me and then pump his hot load deep into my ass.

"That's it, baby. Give us more, that's so hot," Finn praised as he continued to rub my clit and work more liquid from my pussy.

"Don't stop, Bailey, keep squirting. I've never seen anything sexier. You're so tight and hot wrapped around me right now."

Squirting?

Oh, the horror.

Finn put two fingers into my pussy, crooked them toward my belly, and then pressed down on my stomach with his other hand, and I shot off again, moaning and begging. Finn forced more from my body as the orgasm tore me to bits, and I collapsed against Walker's chest in blissful agony.

But soon, the bliss ended and there was only agony.

"Camden!" I screamed and panted.

Walker stopped thrusting instantly, and Finn pulled his hands from my body right away. I tried rolling off Walker to run away and hide in disgust, tears burning at the back of my eyes, but he just let go of my legs and wrapped his arms around my body, holding me still as I fought him.

"Shh. Calm down, Bail. Take a deep breath and focus. It's okay," he soothed, running his hands over my hair and petting me, but I was mortified and I needed a minute away from them.

"Camden." I gasped again. "Let me go."

He reluctantly let go of me and I scurried and crawled off of his lap, effectively pulling his cock from my ass, ran to the bathroom, and shut the door behind me.

I held a hand over my mouth as shock rolled through my used body. My legs were weak and too tired to hold me up, and I collapsed to the floor.

I grabbed a towel off the hook by the shower and wrapped it around my naked body as I lay on the floor, trying to come to terms with what just happened while catching my breath.

Squirted.

Walker said I had squirted.

For some women, they did it all the time and were totally comfortable with it. But for me, a bodily fluid had just shot out of me and I'd had no control of it. It had felt INCREDIBLE when it happened, but I was not okay right now. I was so confused and still so embarrassed. The blanket was soaked and so was I.

My ass ached with a weird sensation of being full of Walker's come. Why was I so embarrassed and upset? They didn't seem to mind what happened, but it had freaked me out and left me shaken.

A gentle knock sounded at the door. "Baby," Finn said. "Can we come in?"

I wanted to say no, to shut them out and run away and hide in shame and embarrassment, but Walker's words played in my head about running when things got uncomfortable for me. I didn't want to be that girl, and I knew they were probably aching to check on me and make sure I was okay. That was part of their love language. Physical care and touch were so important to them.

So I sat up, put my back against the shower wall, and wrapped the towel around me to make sure I was covered. "Yes," I said softly.

The door opened and both men walked in slowly, watching me pensively where I sat on the floor, huddled around myself.

"I'm sorry," I said. I felt my cheeks burn with fire and looked down at my knees.

"Can I touch you?" Walker asked as he knelt next to me.

I felt my eyes widen but forced my head to nod. He wrapped his arms around me, picked me up, and sat down with me in his lap.

"I ran again," I whispered.

"But only to the bathroom. And you let us in when we asked," he said strongly. "That's improvement, baby."

Finn wrapped a towel around his hips and sat down across from us and took my hand in his. "I owe you an apology, Bailey. I didn't discuss that with you first. I forced your body into it. I had no idea you'd never—" He cut off as I groaned and buried my face in my hands.

Walker chuckled and I pinched him to shut him up. "Don't laugh at me," I said, but even I could hear myself giggling.

"You've never squirted before?" Finn asked with shock in his voice.

I looked up and felt my eyebrows pinch and my eyes go wide. "I don't know what kind of sex you two have been having out here in your hay fields, but I assure you, all of my encounters have been terrible compared to what I've had with you. So no, I've never been so overwhelmed or fucked so methodically that my body has decided to become a water hose."

They both laughed again, and I stuck my bottom lip out in a pout and hung my head once more.

Walker threaded his fingers through my hair and brought my lips down on his in the most tender, soft, emotional kiss I've ever had. I didn't even know he was capable of being so gentle. When he finally pulled back, he kissed my forehead and then both of my eyelids.

"Listen to me when I tell you, I have never been so incredibly aroused by any other woman before in my life, Bailey. Feeling you absolutely lose control of your body like that and let the sensations take over, knowing that we did that to you? That you trusted us to do that to you? I'll never be able to describe how good that feels. But I do plan on trying to show you from here on out."

"When did you get so sweet?" I asked and laid my head on his chest.

"The moment I laid eyes on you for the first time."

"Gah!" I said in faux astonishment.

I squeezed Finn's hand, turned to him, and lifted my lips to him. He scooted across the space and kissed me exactly how Walker had. And though it wasn't so shocking to feel the gentleness from Finn,, I made sure to appreciate every emotion and feeling he was trying to show me with the kiss at the moment. I wanted to express them back to him in the same way.

I pulled back and groaned as my aching body protested the movement.

"Are you sore?" Finn asked.

"Deliciously so," I confirmed and chuckled . . . and then winced as I did.

Finn stood up and turned the tap on in the tub and started filling it with hot, steaming water. I stayed in Walker's arms as the tub filled, and Finn poured some bubble bath into it and then helped me stand up. He pulled the towel from my body and rubbed his hands up my spine for a moment and then helped me step into the tub.

I slowly sank down but had to pause as the hot water started to touch my used pussy and ass because it stung. I didn't meet either of their eyes as I finally worked my way deep into the tub and rested against the side.

Walker turned the jets on but made no move to join me.

I raised my eyebrow at him and then at Finn as they stood there and watched me. "Well, are you joining me or not?" I asked.

Finn smirked and shook his head no but leaned down and kissed me before saying, "If I get in that tub with you right now, I'm going to make it my sole mission to get that pussy squirting again. So I'm going to keep my hands off of you and let you rest for a while. I make no promises about the rest of the weekend." He tweaked my nipple under the layer of bubbles at the top of the water and then winked at me and walked out. I watched him go in all of his naked glory and shook my head.

I then looked to Walker and opened my arms.

"Don't tempt me, minx," he said and leaned down to kiss me like Finn had. "Take this time to relax and ease your muscles. I'm going to go make us all some lunch and then we can watch a movie and nap before the evening activities start."

That piqued my interest. "What are the evening activities going to consist of?"

His smile turned predatory, and I watched how his breathing slowed and deepened as he thought about it. He leaned back down to the tub, fisted my hair, pulled it back until my neck was exposed to his teeth, and then bit down on it, drawing a moan and shiver from me. He then brought his lips to my ear and whispered, "You. Tied down. Gagged. Orgasming."

I moaned and pressed my thighs together. "Promise?" I contended.

"I promise that and more," he said and licked the side of my neck and bit my ear. " I can't wait to taste your sweet juice the next time I make you squirt."

And with that, he walked out of the room, and I sank back into the deep bubble bath and panted as I played his words over in my head.

Yes, please.

Chapter 19 – Finn

Bailey was in the tub, and I could hear the hum of the jets from the bedroom as I stripped the sheets and threw them on the floor.

Walker shut the door behind him as he came into the room. I looked at him and just raised my eyebrows and shook my head as a schoolboy grin crossed my face.

"Virgin ass and a virgin squirter," he mused as he rubbed his jaw and pulled on a pair of boxers and jeans. "How the fuck did we get so lucky?"

"I don't have a clue, but I do know that I'm ready to take that girl back to Vegas and go see some man dressed as Elvis in a chapel to make her a Camden legally," I said as I grabbed the bedding and left the room.

He laughed boisterously and followed me downstairs. He started rifling through the kitchen as I started laundry and then took a seat at the counter. I wanted to fill him in on my conversation with Bailey this morning.

"I told Bail this morning that I'm falling for her and that I could get used to seeing her in our kitchen every single morning," I said reflectively.

He turned and looked at me with a scowl on his face. "You didn't think to give me a heads-up on that first?"

"I hadn't planned on saying it, but after what we did last night, she was down here this morning making breakfast, freshly fucked with her sweet curls a mess and her pouty lips all swollen from ours and looking like she fucking belonged here forever, and it just came out."

He thought on it for a second and then sat down across from me, putting his elbows on the cold granite. "What did she say?"

"She said she was falling for me, too, and that she could get used to being kissed in this kitchen every morning."

"And then?" he asked as his mouth twitched.

"And then she dropped to her knees and gave me a world-class blow job for it."

He nodded his head and tried but failed to keep the smirk off his face. "Ah yes, the 'Finn was being sweet and nice' comment. Guess I should have figured that out on my own."

"What are you thinking about her? We've been doing this for a while, but I also know you've never said I love you to a woman before so I'm not expecting anything from you this soon. I do want to know where your head is at though," I said. We didn't hide things from each other ever, so I knew he would tell me, even if he didn't want to actually talk about his feelings.

He sighed and mulled it over in his head for a long time and then said, "I think you're late to the game on the I love you train." He stood up quickly to busy himself at the fridge.

I sat there and processed what that meant and felt my eyes widen and my jaw fall as it hit.

"Are you saying . . . ?" I asked, opened ended.

He looked over his shoulder and glared at me, and his dark deep scowl slid back on his face. "I'm sure as fuck not saying it to you for the first time. But yeah."

"Holy shit," I cursed in shock.

"I don't plan on saying anything about it any time soon either, so keep it to yourself, okay?" he warned.

"Why don't you want to tell her? Even if you don't say it completely, you could tell her you at least have feelings for her."

"She knows I have feelings for her."

"How does she know?" I asked.

He sighed and tried to brush me off.

"Walker, I mean it. If you haven't said it and don't plan to, how is she supposed to know? That's not how it works."

"I don't know, Finn. I'm not a fucking dreamy guy here, okay? I'm figuring this out as I go. All I know right now is I'm fucking stupid over that girl and have been since the first time I kissed her. So there's that. And that's it."

I sat back and watched as he moved, flustered and agitated, around the kitchen, pulling out things to make lunch, and I chuckled to myself.

He turned and glared at me. "I'm happy for you. And her," I said, holding my hands up. "And me," I added.

He held my stare for a minute and then gave me a bit of a one-sided grin but went back to his task. It was quiet for a few minutes more, and then he paused and looked back at me. "It feels right, doesn't it?"

I tried not to note how incredible it was to hear him say something like that about her and our relationship, given that he'd never truly fallen for anyone before. So instead, I got up and walked around the counter and forced him into a big hug and clapped his back. He took a deep breath and held me back as I hugged him. "Yeah, Walk, it does. It feels better than right. We can take this slow if you want to, but I think we both know where it's going to end up."

"Oh yeah?" he asked and pulled back. "And where is that, pray tell, you almighty love guru?" he joked.

"With you and me getting down on one knee and begging her to be our wife. If we have any good karma at all in this world to cash in on, she'll say yes."

"Hmm." He pondered. "Wife."

I didn't comment on it as he worked it over in his head and just winked at him.

I heard the soft padding of Bailey's feet as she walked down the hallway upstairs, and Walker straightened his spine, almost as if he were trying to lock down his emotions once more before she saw them.

It was a shame to see him hide himself from her, but I did not doubt that she was cracking his armor every single day in the way he needed her to. I just kept my hope and faith in this amazing woman who lucked into our lives.

She came down the steps and smiled tentatively at me and then at Walker. "You look lovely," I said, and I meant every word. She wore a long-sleeve dress in a sunny yellow that fell at her ankles and hugged her hips. She had her wet curls piled on top of her head in a messy bun, and she had very minimal makeup on. "Scratch that," I said and shook my head. "You look positively radiant," I mused, and she smiled sweetly and walked over to me.

She laid her hands on my stomach and leaned up on her toes to kiss me where I sat on the stool. "You look scrumptious," she replied cheekily and rested her head in the crook of my neck, letting me hold her to me.

Walker had turned on the radio earlier and a Parker McCollum song hummed romantically. I stood up and slid my hands around her back. "Dance with me?" I asked.

"Yes." She beamed up at me and slid one hand into mine and placed the other over my shoulder.

I pulled her body against mine and gently swayed with her there in the kitchen. She hummed along with the song, and I closed my eyes and breathed her floral scent in, letting her melodic voice soothe my soul. The music changed to another slow country song, and I kept her in my arms. She didn't seem to mind one bit.

I looked up at one point and noticed Walker had left the kitchen to give us this moment, and I hugged her tighter to me. "We don't deserve you," I whispered into her hair.

She chuckled lightly and leaned back to look up at me. "I think you have it backward, but I'll let you think you're the lucky ones for now."

I slid my thumb over her cheek and down to her beautiful kiss-me lips, leaned down, and did just that. I loved the way her lips melted against mine every single time I kissed her. I moved against her and she opened them to me, and I slowly let my tongue explore her minty mouth.

I felt like I was kissing her again for the first time, and it felt like that every time with her. She slid her hands down my chest, letting her nails send trails of shivers down my spine. She hummed along with the new song when I pulled back, and I rested my lips against her forehead and just held on to her.

"You're so gentle and loving with me. I never knew I wanted to feel so worshiped and protected until you did it, and now I can't imagine not feeling it from you every single day," she said and snuggled in closer to me.

"Good because I'm never going to stop."

"Never is a long time." She speculated quietly.

I chuckled and contemplated how I wanted to steer this conversation. I could go left and tell her exactly what I felt and wanted her to know, or I could go right and play it safe and keep Walker's reservations in mind. This was a delicate dynamic; I couldn't push my feelings on her so powerfully when Walker wasn't ready to do the same because I didn't want her to think I felt more for her than he did and set the balance off. But, it was important to me that she knew how wanted she was by us.

I stopped dancing her around and made sure she was looking directly into my eyes as I spoke the truth to her.

"Forever with you would never be long enough for either Walker or me, Bailey." I leaned down until my lips were at her temple. "Even if he doesn't think you're ready to know that yet."

When I pulled back, I could see the wheels spinning in her mind, so I just leaned down, kissed her gently ,and placed her hand on my heart, expressing how true it was without words.

She smiled and shook her head slightly and deepened the kiss until I was hungry for more, my hands pulling her against my quickly hardening body.

"I need to feed you and me and then take you back to bed, Bail. I crave you so much, it makes me crazy."

"Ditto," she said sweetly and pulled back.

I looked around the kitchen and didn't see Walker anywhere. "Yo," I yelled out and pulled Bailey into my side as I waited for him to reappear.

A second later, my phone pinged, and I pulled it out of my pocket and opened a new picture message from my twin. Bailey watched my screen as I opened it, and there was a romantic picture of her and me dancing in the kitchen a moment ago, lost in our feelings.

"And he tries to pretend that he doesn't do sweet or nice," she said and sighed into my neck.

"He does it for you," I said and saved the picture as my lock screen and then slid my phone back into my pocket.

"He does it for both of us," she pointed out, and I couldn't deny it. He did it for me as much as Bailey, whether he wanted us to realize it or not.

Bailey went off to find Walk, and I went about making lunch for all of us with the ingredients that he had pulled out.

I heard Bailey's girly giggle and then a moan from the other room and smiled to myself. It all felt right.

A moment later, they walked back in, Bailey on Walker's back with her legs and arms wrapped around him like a koala bear and smiles on both of their faces.

We all enjoyed our peaceful lunch, and the fact that we weren't interrupted by someone at the front door while we did, didn't hurt either.

Bailey's eyes were getting heavy as we sat on the porch and let the warm fall sunshine soothe us all after our meal. She was snuggled on her side on the daybed between us, with her head on my lap and her feet in Walker's. He had his hand on her hip under her dress, and I was playing with the errant curls that had dried and escaped their confines as her pouty lips parted and a sigh escaped from them.

"If you two keep touching me like this, I'm never going to sleep." She kept her eyes closed but nuzzled her nose into the soft fabric of my shirt at my waist.

"Let's go to bed," Walker said and patted her voluptuous ass under her dress, and she smiled.

She rolled over onto her back and kept her eyes closed but held her arms up straight into the air and asked as sweet as sin, "Carry me please?"

"How on earth could we say no to that?" I asked and kissed her forehead as Walker scooped her into his arms and carried her up the stairs. I was surprised when he didn't toss her over his shoulder but instead held her against his chest nicely, but I wasn't going to point out that I'd noticed.

Walker's bedroom was starting to feel more like home for me than my own, and I knew it was because it was where Bailey had come the first time she was here and where she was most comfortable. He put her on her feet at the end of the bed and slowly slid her dress up and over her head, leaving her in only a tiny pair of black panties and silken skin.

She kissed his chest sweetly and then smiled at me before turning around and crawling up the bed and under the fresh blankets in the center.

Walker and I each stripped down to our boxers, climbed in on either side of her, and snuggled into her.

I pulled her back into my chest and kissed her exposed neck as Walker hiked her hip up and over his and kissed her forehead.

"Go to sleep, little one. When you wake up, you'll be screaming our names as we push you past every limit you never knew you had," I warned into her ear and felt her breath hitch and her body shudder against my chest.

"Promises, promises," she dared with a sultry smile crossing her pouty lips.

"We'll see just how daring those lips looked wrapped around my cock in an hour or two, minx."

We all passed out and honestly, I didn't think I'd ever slept so soundly during a midday nap before I met Bailey. There was just something so calming and comforting about having her here in our arms that made me relax deeper than normal.

It was almost evening time before I woke back up. Walker had flicked me on the forehead to rouse me. I snapped my eyes open and whispered at him, "Rude."

He chuckled at me and then nodded to where Bailey was tucked into my neck, her soft lips against my bare chest and both arms wrapped tight around my waist.

She looked divine. I wanted to encapsulate this moment in my brain for the rest of my life. If in fifty years, I could only keep one mental image of Bailey Dunn in my brain, I wanted it to be this one. She was relaxed and peaceful and so damn sexy, it should be illegal. Her full breasts pressed against my stomach, and I fought the urge to reach down and cup one in my hand to feel the weight of it.

"Wake her up. Slowly. And sweetly," Walker said, overdramatizing the word sweetly in a bitch boy way, and then got up out of bed and went into the closet.

My hands slowly slid down her spine and rubbed back and forth at the top of her perfect ass cheeks. I kissed her forehead, moved my hand between us, and did what I'd wanted to a moment ago—grabbed one of her breasts in my hand and slowly and gently pulled at her puckered nipple before pinching it harder.

She gasped and moaned in her sleep and then arched her hips forward, toward my erection, almost as if she knew it would be there hard and waiting for her.

And of course, it was. She slid her panty-covered pussy on my hard-on and a small smile played on her lips as her eyes fluttered open.

"Good morning," I said, and she tilted her head back and offered her lips to me. I noticed that was something she did the second or third time I kissed her. She didn't ask, and she didn't take one from me, but she presented her lips and did so knowing we would always lean in and take what she offered to us.

It kept us stay in control and let her stay in the role to be led.

It was so fucking hot.

I leaned in and kissed her roughly, waking her up more as I rolled us and ended up on top of her and between her thighs, and then I rocked my cock against her.

"Yes." She moaned and spread her thighs wider around my hips and pressed up into me.

I slid down her body until I was even with her pink, hard nipples and flicked my tongue across one before leaning in and sucking on it powerfully. Her back bowed and she pressed it farther into my mouth. She reached for her other one, to pinch or pull to please herself, but I snatched her hand away and pinned it above her head, gathering her other wrist with it and immobilizing her as I tormented her nipples.

"Perfect. That's just how I want her," Walker chimed in, and her eyes flew open and looked at him and then down at me. I never released her nipple or her wrists and she watched in fascination as Walker attached straps to the four corners of the bed.

"What are those for?" she asked, but he ignored her, giving her only a malevolent grin as he finished tying them to the wood. "Walker?" she tried again. When he didn't answer her, she looked down at me.

I smirked at her as I let her nipple pop from my mouth audibly and then pulled my lip back to show her my teeth as I slowly lowered them to the same nipple and bit down.

"Fuck!" She gasped and jerked. I snickered at her and pressed her restrained wrists down harder above her head, bowing her back and pressing her chest farther into my face.

"That's the plan," I promised.

She licked her lips and took a deep breath. Walker stepped next to the bed, took her wrist from my hands, quickly fastened it in the strap, and then pulled the slack taut and stretched her arm out toward the corner of the bed.

I used my knee to push her leg wide as he snaked his hand under the blanket and tied her ankle to the post in the same fashion.

He made quick work of her other two limbs and when he was finished, I sat back and pulled the blanket off of her to reveal her almost naked body spread far and wide to each corner of the bed, immobilizing her and rendering her helpless.

I leaned down and dropped quick open-mouthed kisses on both of her nipples, down her ribs, over the ticklish flesh at her sides, down her trim waist and wide hips, and then my tongue slid under the top band of her panties.

"I told you I was going to rip every single pair off of your body, and I meant it," I said as I hooked my fingers under the band at her hips and pulled until they tore, and then I dragged them from her body, revealing her bare, pink, wet pussy to our stares.

She moaned and tried to roll her hips but was unable to thanks to how tight Walker had pulled the straps.

"God, I'm going to fucking enjoy this," I said and pulled my rock-hard cock from my briefs.

"You and me both, brother," Walker said as he pushed his own briefs down and then leaned over Bailey's face. "What's your safe word?" he asked.

Her eyes flashed as she looked up into his dark and enigmatic ones. "Tell me what you're going to do to me and then I'll tell you if I remember it or not," she challenged.

I snickered at her as I leaned down and swiped my tongue across her hard clit, making her gasp and bow her back again. "You're not the boss here, Bailey," I warned and sucked it into my mouth, my teeth nipping at it, drawing a scream from her beautiful, soft lips.

"I need to know this time," she said and I sobered. She was talking about the incident earlier where we hadn't discussed forcing her body to squirt in the moment and I nodded at her. She was right.

Walker knew then, too, that she needed the information. "I told you already what we were going to do to you today. We're going to tie you down," he said as he flicked the strap holding her arm above her head. "We're going to gag you." He smirked at her as he pulled the scarf of red from the bag and dangled it in front of her face. "And then we're going to use your body to pleasure ours. If you're a really good girl, we'll give you some pleasure back along the way too."

Her eyes flared and her lips parted to take a deep breath. "Okay," she whispered. "My safe word is Camden."

"Good girl," I said and pulled her tiny pussy lips apart and licked down from her clit to her ass, and then I swirled my tongue around the sensitive flesh where Walker had fucked her this morning. "I can't wait to push my cock into here for the first time," I said, and her eyes rolled as she moaned.

I nodded to Walker, showing him she was ready for more, and he softly tied the gag around her mouth, pressing it between her lips and teeth and pulling it tight. It wasn't to stop noise or words from coming from her mouth but to heighten the sensations by restricting her ability to talk.

"Say your safe word," he ordered.

She tentatively worked at the cloth between her teeth and then said, "Camden." It was muffled but easy to understand, and she relaxed after she heard herself.

"Now for the orgasm part," I said and pushed fingers into her pussy and ass at the same time, like I had earlier today. She tried to press her hips farther into my face and force more of my fingers deeper into her, but she was immobilized by the restraints. I groaned watching her struggle.

Walker stood next to the bed and fisted his cock, watching her fight against the straps to move her body how she so desperately wanted to. "You are so incredibly sexy tied down like this, baby," he said, palming her breasts and rolling her nipples. She watched with rapture as he played with her, and then he slapped one of her large breasts quickly, right on the nipple, and she grunted and moaned as he leaned down and sucked it into his mouth to soothe it.

"Please," she begged around the gag.

"Please what?" he asked, pinching and rolling her nipples between his fingers while I continued to fuck her pussy and ass with my fingers.

"I want more," she said and cursed in frustration as I pulled from her body and bit her thigh lightly. "Bastard," she swore as I stood up off the bed and walked away completely.

"Perhaps we should leave you here like this until you can learn to be nicer," I said.

I looked over my shoulder at how her eyes burned with frustration and then fury when I laughed at her lightly.

I grabbed the sexy butterfly vibrator and walked back over to her. "I don't know what's sexier: you all spread out and open for us like this or you all spread out and open for us like this with this pretty little butterfly kissing your pretty little pussy."

Her beautiful green eyes glowed in the dim room as I laid the butterfly against her clit and slid the small probe into her soaking wet pussy. I turned it on and cranked it to high. Her eyes rolled and her hips bucked up off the bed as I pressed it into her body harder.

"Finn." She moaned. "Yes!" I held it against her, and Walker and I watched her slowly start to fall apart as her orgasm took over.

We played with her like that for quite a while. One or both of us would tease her body, she would chase an orgasm, and when she would crash over the other side of it, we'd switch and do something new.

We had used multiple toys on her, she was sweating and begging for us to finally fuck her, and we were both at the end of our restraint. We wanted nothing more than to sink into her body together for the first time, but we needed to make sure she was good and ready first.

Walker and I undid the restraints on her ankles and wrists and gently massaged the sensitive areas where they had rubbed her skin.

I removed the gag from her mouth, and she worked her jaw back and forth. "Will one of you please fuck me already?" she begged and batted her eyelashes at me sweetly. She knew I was a sucker for her girly seductions, and it worked effortlessly.

"If that's what you want," I said flippantly and laughed at her as her smile slipped.

"Of course, it is, you ass!" she cursed, and Walker grabbed a handful of her hair, pulling her up off the bed and against his chest.

"Are you getting mouthy, little one?" he asked and ran his palm down to rest on her ass, making his intention clear.

She weighed her options and then looked at me and blew me a kiss before looking back at Walker. "And if I am? What are you going to do about it, big guy?" she dared.

The loud crack of his hand slapping her voluptuous ass followed by her gasp and sigh made my cock throb.

"More please," she begged and pressed her ass into his hand harder.

He obliged, bending her over on the bed and peppering her ass with his hand, making her cry out and moan as her skin blossomed into a beautiful pink.

He crawled up onto the bed, lay down on his back, and pulled her up his body. He reached between them and ran the head of his cock through her wet folds, and she pressed herself down onto him, taking half of him into her in one push.

They both moaned, and she bit her lip as she rose back up and sank down again.

"I love how you feel inside of me." She cooed and rolled her hips until he was balls deep.

"I love how it feels to be buried deep inside of you," he replied and flicked her nipple with his tongue. "Ride me, baby. I want to watch these tits bounce in my face as you come on my cock."

She spread her knees on each side of his hips and started riding him, grinding her pussy on his cock with each downward thrust, and I watched from the end of the bed in fascination. Her ass was popped out and the curve of her back made my hands itch to grab ahold of her there and pull her onto my cock as she rode him.

It was like she could read my mind because she looked over her shoulder at me and watched me through hooded eyes as she took his cock deep into her. Her pupils dilated and fluttered closed as she arched even more and threw her head back as she started orgasming.

Walker wrapped his hands around her tiny waist and started fucking her hard from underneath, and she mewed and moaned as he pulled more and more from her body.

I got up on the bed behind her and palmed her breasts as she came down from her orgasm, while Walker kept fucking her brutally.

I wrapped my hand around her neck and pulled her head back to my shoulder, arching her hips forward and letting him hit that spot inside of her that she had discovered this morning.

Walker smirked at me, pressed his big palm to the flat of her belly, and pushed down as he slowed and started fucking her with long, deep thrusts.

"Oh my god," she said and clawed at my arm with her nails. "I need you, Finn." She reached around her to grab my cock.

She brought her hand to her mouth and spit in her palm and then wrapped it around me and started pumping in time with Walker as he slid in and out of her.

I dropped my head to her shoulder as she worked me over so well. I was desperate to be inside of her, but I wanted to make sure she was ready for us.

"I think it's time I got to feel how incredible your ass feels wrapped around my cock. What do you think, baby?"

"Yes, yes, yes!" she begged and pumped me faster.

"God, I can't wait to feel you taking both of us." Walker groaned as he played with her clit.

I pushed her forward, so she was lying on Walker's chest, and he wrapped a fist in her hair, held her close, and kissed her passionately.

I coated myself with lube and then poured some on her skin and worked my fingers into her. She mewed and pushed back against me, begging for more.

"We've turned you into such a little slut," Walker joked and bit her ear. "It's so fucking hot knowing how badly you want us to own you, Bailey. It drives me absolutely mad with need for you."

"Yes. Me too. I can't think of anything else but you two anytime I'm not in your arms."

"Are you ready for me?" I asked as I pressed the head of my cock against her back entrance. I couldn't believe I was about to fuck her ass while Walker was in her pussy. We were a couple of lucky bastards.

"Yes!" she screamed in frustration as she begged me to finally fuck her.

Walker stilled his hips and pulled out so only the tip of his cock was inside of her pussy, leaving me room to enter her.

I pushed forward, and her ass swallowed the head of my cock. "Shit." I hissed and she moaned but tensed up.

"Relax your muscles, baby," Walker ordered and slid his hands over her back and down to her ass cheeks to spread them wide for me.

She hummed and I pushed forward again. "Oh my god," she said and arched her back.

"It's never felt as good to be buried in anyone else as it does with you, Bailey. Your body was made for ours; it's a perfect fit." I pulled back and pushed in again and continued until I was buried balls deep in her ass for the first time.

"Your turn, Walker." She gasped as she adjusted to me inside of her.

He kissed her deeply as he pushed inside of her. All three of us groaned as he buried himself next to me deep inside her body.

He and I started moving together, keeping our in and out drives synced so she didn't get overwhelmed, and within moments, she went off like a stick of dynamite and exploded around us.

"Oh my god!" she screamed, and we picked up our pace and fucked her hard as she milked us both, trying to pull our orgasms from our bodies.

Walker wrapped both arms around her body and held her still as he pounded into her. I had both hands hooked over her hip bones as I fucked her just as brutally.

The sounds of skin slapping, and moans and groans filled the room and soon, Walker's groans turned into loud yells as he climaxed inside of her. It was all it took, and I shot off, filling her ass with my come as he filled her pussy.

She screamed incoherently and had her claw-like nails dug into Walker's chest as we forced ourselves into her body, filling her to the brim.

I fell onto her back and laid my forehead between her shoulder blades as I tried desperately to catch my breath. She reached behind her and ran her nails across my scalp as I kissed her spine and told her over and over again how incredible she was.

Walker never stopped praising her either. We sounded like a mantra of worship for this incredibly beautiful woman who had stolen our hearts and souls and left us reduced to primal needs and grunts.

Walker slid out of her first. She gasped as he did and then he moved out from under her.

She chuckled when she realized why and chided, "You two are so strange."

He laughed and kissed her head as I sat up and waited for him to get a good view of me still buried inside of her.

I slowly pulled out, inch by inch, until the head of my cock was all that was left, and then I watched in captivation as it popped free of her ass.

I held her cheeks wide as we watched her body close back up, and she slid forward and collapsed into the mattress, completely sated and relaxed.

"I don't think I'm moving again for days." She sighed and stretched out her arms.

Walker and I smirked at each other and then high-fived like a couple of teenagers.

"Oh my god, you two are impossible," she said and laughed at us.

And my god, it felt good to feel so young and happy.

Chapter 20 – Bailey

I couldn't figure out why I was so gosh darn nervous, but as I stood in front of the mirror in my bedroom and adjusted my earrings for the tenth time since deciding on my outfit, I couldn't help the butterflies rolling around in my stomach.

Tonight was Jake's wedding, and it was set to be the event of the year for Mayfield.

It was also our first official outing as a throuple, Finn's new favorite word for us.

It was also the first time I would be meeting their parents as well, as they were coming home for Jake and Ivy's wedding.

Their mom and dads were supposed to get into town last night so we could all get together for dinner ahead of time and meet, but their flight got delayed and they hadn't gotten home until this afternoon.

So, I'd be meeting the parents of the most important people in my life in front of three hundred nosey small-town gossipers.

No pressure.

I had decided on a long, Grecian-style, flowing gown that hugged my curves above my waist and somehow made me look taller thanks to the yards of fabric and my killer heels. It was navy blue at the top, and the bottom third of it was covered in soft pink and white flower petals with navy and gold embellishments. It looked like the dress was alive when I moved, and it was breathtaking.

It was V-cut in the bodice with thick straps, and there was a slit to my hip that was hidden wonderfully with the overabundance of fabric in the skirt, so if I wanted to keep my leg covered, I just had to stand straight and it disappeared.

But if I wanted to liven up the dress at all, I simply turned my hips a bit and the tanned silky skin of my leg and strappy gold heels showed and transformed the entire look.

I paired the look with small, diamond, gold hoops and a simple gold pendant necklace that fell to the hollow of my neck. I had taken the two hours and straightened my hair until it was smooth and then tied it up in a timeless chignon with gold clips, leaving only a few tendrils free at my temples and nape.

I felt beautiful, and that wasn't something I ever truly remembered feeling before. Sure, there were times that I'd liked my outfit and felt good in it, but tonight was different, and I knew it was because of the love I felt from my men that truly made me blossom into this confident and powerful woman.

My phone pinged and I picked it up to see a message from Finn. It was a picture of him and Walker standing side by side in their matching gray charcoal suits and pink boutonnieres.

They looked immaculate and I missed them dearly. They both had worked last night to be off tonight and tomorrow for the wedding and because they were in it, they had spent most of the day at the venue with Jake doing last minute tasks.

Me: You two should probably hide behind a tree or you'll distract the whole crowd from the happy couple.

Walker's reply came back quickly.

Walker: Let us see you.

Me: You'll have to wait. Thea is pulling in now. I'll see you two shortly.

Finn: Just one picture. Please.

I laughed and looked out the front door. Thea wasn't here yet, but I knew she would be any second.

Me: Delayed gratification, fellas.

Walker: Everything about you is gratifying for us. See you soon.

Swoon.

Thea honked from the driveway, and I quickly slid my phone into my clutch, grabbed the pink cashmere wrap for my arms later when it got colder, and headed out the door. She had offered to pick me up with her husband, Steve, and Mikey so I could ride home with the guys later.

I ran out to their truck, and Steve jumped down to help me up. "You look very beautiful tonight, Bailey," he said as he slid back into the driver's seat and took Thea's hand on the center console.

"Thank you," I whispered breathlessly, and Thea winked at me.

"Are you nervous to meet Sandra, John, and Grant tonight?" she asked.

"No, not nervous. Terrified is probably more accurate," I joked.

"You'll do great, sweetie. I've spoken to her at length about you over the last few months and I know the boys have as well. She's ecstatic to meet you. John and Grant just want the boys to be happy, so they'll love you as long as you love them."

I smiled at her and nudged Mikey with my elbow. He looked over at me and smiled. "You look very handsome tonight, Mikey. Will you save me a dance?"

His face split in two and he nodded his head quickly. "Yes, Ms. Bailey, but I dance fast, so you'll have to keep up."

We all laughed, and I reached over and put my hand on his and squeezed. "I'll try my best."

Before long, we were at the brewery that the wedding was being held at and the sun was starting to light the sky on fire as it sank toward the tree line. It was incredibly beautiful, and as we walked toward the ceremony area, I looked around and fell in love with the romance here.

Vegas had held more weddings than any other city in the country, but there was hardly ever any romance applied to them. They were mostly booze and bad taste, but Montana had such an ability to write a love story in the clouds and trees, you needed to just look and you could feel the intimacy in the air.

I was looking around when Thea put her hand on my arm and brought me back to the present. I followed her gaze to where we were headed to take a seat and saw Sandra, Grant, and John all standing and talking to some other locals.

I hadn't met them before, but I knew from just looking at them that they were Finn and Walker's parents.

The men were tall and dark, just like my guys, and the air around them crackled with dominance and command. Sandra surprised me, though, because she was a tiny woman, not much bigger than myself, with dark-brown hair that had a bit of salt and pepper in the whisps around her face, but she was so incredibly timeless and elegant.

She was single-handedly the most beautiful woman I'd ever seen, and I felt so much awe being in her presence as we walked closer.

She turned first and saw us approaching and she quickly ended the conversation she was having and walked toward us, embracing Thea affectionately and then turning toward me. I had hoped Finn and Walker would be here to stand by my side for this introduction, but Ms. Thea was the second-best option, so I relied on her confidence.

Her husbands joined us as she pulled back from Thea, and I watched as they both put a hand on her back or arm in silent affection that I recognized so easily as a mannerism Finn and Walker used on me.

"You must be Bailey. My boys told me they had fallen for the most captivating woman in the world, and there is no other word to explain your loveliness and beauty so you must be her," Sandra said as she rested her hand on my arm and smiled affectionately at me.

I was struggling to say something in response, to show her how her kind words affected me, but I was cut short.

"Captivating doesn't even begin to describe how lovely you look tonight, Bailey." I turned when I heard Walker behind me, and he slid his hand down my back. I rested into it and smiled at him as he leaned down and kissed me slowly and sweetly.

"Hi," I whispered and then blushed as I pulled back and saw everyone staring at us. Sandra had stars in her eyes, and her husbands winked at Walker and nodded to us as we turned back.

He leaned down and kissed my hair and then stepped forward to hug his mama and dads. When he came back to stand by me, he introduced us properly and then turned to look over his shoulder. "Finn will be right here. He was handling some drama about flowers and bubbles and who knows what else that had Ivy all freaked out."

"That sounds like Finn. He's probably gentler than Jake in a moment like that," Thea said warmly.

"He's great with women's feelings, that's for sure," Walker agreed and looked down at me and winked.

"Something tells me you're becoming a softer man each day, Walker John," his mother mused and smiled sweetly at me.

"He is," I agreed and leaned into his side. He scoffed and shrugged it off.

"Don't tell anyone. I've got a reputation to keep."

"A reputation for the loudest snorer?" Finn asked as he came up to my other side. He looked down at me and whistled low and long as he stepped back and took my hand to spin me around. "You look exquisite, darling," he said, leaning in and kissing me, sliding his hand around the back of my neck sweetly.

"What have you two done with my rough and tough boys?" Grant asked as Finn leaned in and hugged both him and John and then kissed his mama on the cheek.

"They're exactly where we left them, Grant. They just found the right woman to round out their rough edges, which is exactly what they needed if you ask me," their mom said.

Jake came out to the ceremony area and started rounding the boys up, as it was time to start getting seated.

"We'll see you as soon as we can," Finn said as he kissed me again.

"Stay near our parents or Thea and Steve, okay?" Walker said, and Finn shot him a serious look.

"Is everything okay?" I asked as my eyebrows knitted in the center.

"Everything is fine, and I intend to keep it that way," Walker said mysteriously and then kissed me and walked toward the wedding party. I didn't miss the seriousness in his eyes, though, as he looked back at me before disappearing inside.

"What's that about?" Sandra asked and slid her arm through mine as we turned and headed toward the seats they had chosen.

"I don't have the foggiest," I answered truthfully. But Thea was all knowing, as usual.

"Clay Mathews is here. He's a relative of Ivy's stepdad," she said, patting my other arm as she sat down next to me.

"Oh," I said embarrassedly. I didn't want to approach that with a ten-foot pole in the presence of their parents.

John leaned around Sandra and looked at me and then over to Thea. "What's it matter if one person is here or not? Why would that set our boys on edge?"

Thea leaned forward, looking around me and talking directly to John and Grant, who were both leaning forward now too. "Well, Bailey filed a restraining order against him the first week or two that she was here at the insistence of your boys. From what Walker told me yesterday, he was granted a stay on the order for the event because of the circumstances but was told not to speak to or get near Bailey." She turned to look at me again. "Did they really not tell you any of this?" Steve patted Thea's arm lovingly as she asked, trying to lead her away from the conversation.

"Leave it be, Thea. You're embarrassing the poor girl," he said and winked at me. I tried to smile back but I could feel three sets of eyes on the back of my head and the blush of humiliation crawling up my neck.

"What did he do?" Sandra asked, and I could see a bit of Walker's seriousness in her kind eyes.

I wanted to just get off this topic. "Nothing really." I looked forward as the officiant was starting to walk to the center. "I think the ceremony is about to start."

"Don't change the subject," Sandra said quietly and nudged my shoulder.

Thea answered for me, always looking to be the wealth of knowledge in the group. "He went into her shop one day and got really inappropriate with her by touching her in places not meant for his hands, insisting that she go out with him. A couple of days later, he went back to ask her out again and when he found out that she had plans that night with your boys, he opened his mouth and said very vulgar things to her and then lunged at her after she slapped him for it. Luckily, I'd seen him walk in her shop and grabbed Nate, one of Walker and Finn's football players that works the dishwasher at the diner, and we walked in right when he went after her and kicked him out. Your boys insisted she file the R.O. once they found out and from what I understand, this is the first time he's been in the same area as her since then."

Grant shook his head in a frustrated manner, and John worked his jaw back and forth. I felt shame crawl up my spine at them thinking negatively of me, and I was even more ashamed at the tears that burned the backs of my eyes. This was not the impression I wanted to leave on the parents of the men I was falling in love with, but apparently, Sandra could read me as well as her boys could.

"They aren't mad with you, deary. They're mad because Clay Mathews comes from a long line of jackasses, and it wasn't all that long ago that Clay's daddy tried to push his weight around where I was concerned and two Camden men of my own came to my rescue." I looked from her to her husbands, and they nodded their heads to me and gave me reassuring smiles.

Grant spoke up. "If we'd taken care of him the way we wanted to thirty plus years ago, you wouldn't have been stuck dealing with the same shit our Sandra dealt with. And for that, we're sorry to you, darlin'."

I felt my eyes go wide as my imagination ran wild with what he meant by "taken care of him," and he chuckled at me and winked.

"Oh dear," I said quietly, gaining a giggle from all of them as I turned forward and smiled myself.

"You really are exactly what our boys need in their lives, Bailey. I hope you three find your way through this unconventional lifestyle and prosper in it."

"I'm obviously new to the idea of it and learning every day, but it seems to me that they both had incredible role models in their lives from day one to teach them everything they need to know about it, and they both are incredible men. You three should be so proud of that."

They all beamed, and Sandra leaned into me. "Just wait until you see how they will grow even more with you in their lives," she said and winked.

Just then, the music started playing. Soon, family members of the wedding party were walked down the aisle to be seated, and the groomsmen and groom took their places at the altar.

I couldn't wipe the sweet, sappy smile off my face as I watched Walker and Finn walk down the aisle and stand next to Jake as groomsmen.

They both kept their eyes on me for most of the ceremony, and when Jake and Ivy said their vows, I felt myself start to get emotional listening to them declare their unwavering love for one another.

I tried to swallow down the tears because I hated crying ever, let alone in front of strangers, and happy tears at a wedding were no exception to the case. Nonetheless, as they leaned in to kiss each other for the first time as husband and wife, I felt a couple of errant tears fall from my lashes and tried to quickly wipe them from my cheeks.

I looked at Finn and saw him smile at me sweetly as I smiled and fanned my face to get them to stop, but when I looked at Walker, there was a different emotion in his eyes. He was scowling almost, with an intense stare penetrating me across the distance, and I swallowed quickly, the happy tears drying on my eyelids as worry started to fill my gut.

Was he mad that I cried at weddings? Did he think I was trying to make it about me somehow or push him to acknowledge how happy the idea of weddings made me? I didn't want to make him uncomfortable at all, but I couldn't help the dread that filled my body as Finn nudged him, seeing the change in my demeanor and tracing it back to Walker's scowl.

The newlyweds walked back down the aisle, and I tried to shake the feeling but was faced with a new one as I watched two beautiful bridesmaids wrap their arms around Finn's and Walker's and walk down the aisle with a look of pure, unashamed lust in their eyes.

I got it. Logically, I understood how good looking my men were. But having to sit back here with their parents and watch as other women touched them while I was unsettled left me feeling even more on edge.

To add insult to injury, we had an hour-long cocktail hour to sit and watch the photographer take an array of photos of everyone, including my men with their respective bridesmaids in all sorts of close embraces.

I graciously accepted the glass of wine that John offered me as he handed one to his wife where we stood and chatted outside of the venue. It was warm out, and the chilled wine felt great going into my empty stomach full of nerves and worries.

After my first glass was gone, Steve offered me another one and I eyed him suspiciously. He just winked at me and told me to drink up. Perhaps he could tell I was a bit high-strung.

Sandra and Thea were chatting on and on about all of the wonderful places the Camdens had travelled the last few months, and Steve and the dads were talking about all things fly fishing, so I excused myself to go to the restroom. They were outside and around the edge of the venue, leaving a nice long walk on the beautifully decorated sidewalk to enjoy.

I sat in the stall for a long while and took a few deep breaths, willing my stomach to unravel itself and allow the happy, carefree feeling I'd felt watching the ceremony take it's place, but it wouldn't work.

When I came out of the stall, I walked down the row toward the sinks and froze when my eyes landed on the back of a beautiful redhead with eyes of loathing as they met mine in the mirror. *Luann.* She had applied a fresh layer of bright red lipstick to her flawless lips and puckered up and blew herself a kiss in the mirror before looking back over at me.

"This is his favorite color lipstick on me," she said as she stood back up and slid the tube into her clutch. She adjusted her dress around her fake breasts, the black gown skintight and struggling to hold in her ample cleavage, but something told me that had been the plan. "He loves fucking my mouth with his giant cock and watching it get covered in this color."

I didn't respond to her comment and instead walked to the sink and began to wash my hands.

"I ran into him earlier, and he couldn't tear his eyes away from my lips or my tits while we chatted. Everyone noticed, even his mother. She's so sweet." Her shrill voice made my blood boil, and her words made my teeth clench.

She was lying.

"It was the same way when he stopped into my salon the other day." She paused and turned to look at me as I finished and grabbed some towels to dry my hands. "Did he tell you he came to see me?" She laughed cruelly. "No, I guess he wouldn't tell you he stopped and told me how much he missed me and regretted getting into a relationship with you because he was trapped now that Walker was involved."

I snapped, throwing the towels away and turning to face her. "You're lying, and you're doing it because you're bitter that you didn't get what you wanted. And I get it, but that's not my fault. So aim your anger somewhere else."

"I don't have to lie about Finn, Bailey. What we had was way deeper than anything you think you have with him. He was obsessed with me and still is. That man fucked me raw so many times. He couldn't keep his hands off of me. At one point, we talked about moving in together, but the only thing that held him back was his brother. There wasn't anything about me he didn't like."

"Well, then I guess Walker saved him from a big mistake in the long run." I laughed humorlessly.

"You think you're so much better than all of us, don't you?" she snapped, her sly composure slipping as her anger surfaced. "You waltz into our little town and make everyone think you're just so sweet and perfect. But I know the truth about you, Bailey, and I'm going to tell Finn and Walker both about how you fucked my brother and then cried wolf when they started paying attention to you."

"Fuck you," I sneered at her, my anger rising too. "I've never gone near your brother and they know that, so go fucking try if you want but you'll only be showing your pathetic hand and ending the game for yourself all together."

Her eyes fell to small slits as her anger pulsated through her body. For a moment, I was genuinely afraid she was going to strike me, but she just smiled her fake, perfect smile, tsked her tongue at me, turned, and walked out, leaving me alone in the silence and with my head swimming with everything she had said.

I knew she was lying; I didn't even doubt it for a second. There was no way Finn wanted her over me, but the part of me that always tried to find love and self-worth in men's arms wouldn't let me cast the idea aside completely.

I took a few long calming deep breaths and looked at myself in the mirror.

I was worthy of them, and they cared for me.

I knew they did.

I made my way back outside to go back to the cocktail hour area. When I walked back around the corner, though, I saw most everyone had left. I looked past the makeshift bar that had been set up for the interim time and into the large windows of the venue, and I saw that everyone had gone inside for the start of the reception.

"Shit," I muttered and turned to walk along the sidewalk, around the edge of the bar and to the side door of the venue, to avoid walking across the grass in my tall heels.

I was halfway between the two when someone stepped out from behind one of the large potted plants that lined the sidewalk with white twinkly lights, and I ran square into them, nearly falling backwards onto my ass. I looked down to where my clutch had fallen to the ground and started to pick it up when the person I'd run into chuckled enthusiastically.

"Well, look who we have here."

My heart froze as the familiarity of the voice penetrated my buzzed brain. I looked up and Clay Mathews looked down his crooked nose at me, and I watched in disgust as his eyes traveled from my face to my toes and back, stopping to stare at my breasts and bare leg through the slit in my dress along the way.

I shut my jaw and ground my teeth together as I reached to pick up my clutch again, but when my hand almost landed on it, Clay's foot shot out and kicked it into the grass behind the plants. The aggressive kick opened the clutch and my belongings scattered across the ground in various directions.

"Oopsie," Clay mocked and looked at me with a lewd grin on his face.

"What is your problem?" I asked, but I hated how my voice shook in anger.

He laughed at me openly and then stepped forward to step directly onto my tube of lipstick, and I heard it crunch as he twisted his toe into the ground.

"My problem is you thinking I have one to begin with," he answered, and I backed up a step, putting more space between us, and scoffed at him.

I looked past him to the venue and noticed that the outside bar area had cleared out completely, leaving me alone outside with Clay Mathews. He was apparently in a bad mood, judging by the glassy pinpoints of his pupils and the odor of cheap beer permeating from his skin.

"You must think really highly of yourself to think I was even interested in you enough to be upset that you wanted to go after the circus freaks instead of me. You think I give two shits that you're a whore who likes to be fucked like a prostitute?" He sneered at me, and I could feel the anger vibrate off him.

"Leave me alone, Clay," I said and stepped back again, putting my hand up between us. I didn't know where Finn or Walker were right now, and my phone was on the ground under his feet, leaving me helpless.

"Do you have any idea how much trouble that restraining order got me into with my folks? With my boss?" he asked, stepping forward and eating up the space I'd put between us. "You lied and made people think I wanted you, but you're so damn fat and ugly that I wouldn't touch you with a fucking pole. But that doesn't matter because you got those cops to say I was a threat to you and now I can't go to a public place without worrying about going to fucking jail, you little cunt."

His eyes traveled down to my chest again, and he licked his flat, dry lips obscenely. "Maybe I'll fuck you right here on the grass anyway, treat you like the whore I know you really are. I wonder what your boy toys would think seeing you underneath me, screaming my name."

Bile rose in my throat as I started to panic, and it got worse as he got meaner. "I bet you're not even wearing panties under that dress, are you? You fucking slut." His voice was horrific, and he reached forward and grabbed my bare thigh through the slit at my hip a second before I shoved him away from me. I started to fall backwards as my heel stuck into the sod like a hot knife into butter.

A strong set of hands caught my arms and helped steady me as I stepped back onto the sidewalk, and I looked over my shoulder and shuddered as I saw the dark menacing eyes of Grant as he stared at Clay over my head. John stepped between Clay and me, blocking my view of the threatening man all together.

John spoke to me, never turning around to look at me, but I could feel the intensity of his stare in just his tone. "Go on inside, Bailey. We'll gather your things after we escort Mr. Mathews the hell out of here."

I started to object, not wanting them to get themselves involved in my issues, but Grant gave my arm a reassuring pat and then shooed me toward to door. "Go on now," he added.

I walked wide of Clay, even as John moved and kept himself between us the whole time, and I looked over my shoulder as the two older men formed an unbreakable alliance against the piece of shit who'd tried to intimidate me and probably would have raped me. I scurried inside the venue and took a deep breath as the door closed behind me.

Some guests were seated but most were standing around between the tables and the bar as the newlyweds took to the dance floor to share their first dance.

I was way too jittery to go sit down with Sandra, knowing her men were outside defending me currently, and I didn't see Walker or Finn anywhere, so I walked to the bar and waited for the bartender to come to my end.

I placed my order for another glass of wine and stood there with my hands shaking from it all, trying to figure out what to do now.

"Where the fuck have you been?" I turned and gasped as Walker slid against the bar to my side and scowled down at me angrily.

I stuttered, started, and stopped a few times as I tried to put into words what had happened, but he was riled up and didn't wait for me to compose myself.

"I told you to stay with my parents or Thea, but you just couldn't listen, could you, Bailey? Do you have any idea how exasperating you are when you don't listen to reason?" he snapped, and I stepped backwards in shock. "If Finn had been the one to tell you to stay put, I bet you would have listened to him no problem."

"Why are you mad at me?" I asked, hurt lacing my voice.

"What's going on here?" Finn asked as he stepped up behind me and looked from Walker to me and back.

"Bailey took off alone, even though I explicitly told her to stay near others, and she disappeared for a long time. Apparently, she only gives a shit about what you have to say," Walker said, signaling the bartender who promptly brought him a double whiskey, which he pounded down in one drink.

It was no surprise that the female bartender had yet to get the glass of wine I'd ordered before he showed up, but as soon as the Greek god in front of me snapped his fingers, he got whatever he wanted from her.

"Dude, chill," Finn warned and nudged him back a step, looking down at me. He put his fingers under my chin and tilted it up to look at him. "Where did you go?" he asked.

"To the bathroom," I answered, pulling my chin from his hands. "Where Luann cornered me and told me all sorts of torrid tales of you and her lately."

"I haven't gone near her since that day at our house, Bail—" Finn started, but now wasn't the time. I held my hand up and cut him off.

Walker scoffed and looked around, annoyed.

It didn't matter where I went or why I was held up. He was mad that I'd disobeyed him.

Yeah, well, fuck you too, buddy. Finn's eyes rounded before they lowered to slits as he looked around the room. Probably for his lover.

"Why didn't you listen to me?" Walker snapped again, stepping forward, and I stepped back quickly in shock and put my hand up between us, warning him off. I tried to wipe the fear off my face but it was too late. He had seen it anyway. And so had Finn.

The move surprised him, and I didn't miss the look of hurt that crossed his eyes as I put another step of space between us, looking for an exit. I was too on edge and hurt and embarrassed to be near him right now.

So much for him getting softer every day. Right now, he was all sharp edges and pain.

Just then, Grant and John walked up to us, and Grant handed me my clutch back with a half grimace as the latch flapped uselessly.

"Here are your things, Bailey. I'm sorry, but he broke most of them before I got it all picked up."

I took the clutch from him with shaking hands and tried to smile at him appreciatively. "Thank you both," I said and turned back to the bar as my glass of wine was finally set down in front of me, and I took a large sip.

"Who? What happened?" Finn asked, taking my clutch from me and opening it to pour everything out on the bar. My lipstick, vintage mirrored compact, and cell phone were all cracked and broken. The other things I'd had in there were fine, but they were all inexpensive compared to the others in sentimental value. "What the hell is going on?" Finn asked again, turning to his dads.

I kept my gaze down and blinked back the tears that tried to form on my lashes. Walker was still pissed from whatever happened during the ceremony, and I sure as fuck wasn't going to cry in front of him again and piss him off more. For whatever reason, he got mad when I cried.

I just wanted to go home.

The DJ announced that dinner was served, and tables started getting up to get in line at the buffet.

I could feel John's eyes on me while I stayed silent and drank my wine, and I knew he wanted me to speak up. I just shrugged it off and picked my things up, not looking up to meet any of their gazes. "Nothing. Don't worry about it." I could hear the sadness in my voice and hated it.

"Bailey," Grant warned, but an errant tear broke free from my lashes and hit the bartop as I picked up the compact to put it back into my purse. A piece of glass fell to the floor as I slid it into the clutch. It was a gift that my father had gotten my mom when they first got married. And Clay Mathews had destroyed it without a care in the world.

I leaned down, picked up the piece of glass, and cursed when I cut my finger on it, throwing it into my clutch angrily. "Hey," Finn said, sliding his hand along the side of my face and forcing me to look up at him. I could see his worry and concern, and I closed my eyes as more tears fell.

John stepped in. I could hear the barely restrained fury in his voice as he explained what happened. "Clay ambushed her outside, knocked her purse out of her hands, and then kicked it across the ground and stepped on everything. He threatened her about the R.O. and then he—" He cut off and I shuddered violently, trying to control my emotions.

"Then he what?" Walker asked, anger like John's vibrating through his tone.

John sighed and shook his head and his jaw locked tight. Grant finished for him, placing a gentle hand on my arm as he did. "Then he threatened to rape her and shoved his hand inside her dress."

"Are you kidding me?" Finn burst out and turned toward his dad.

"I'll fucking kill him," Walker said menacingly, and then I could feel his eyes on me as he sighed. "Bail, I'm sorry. I shouldn't have said what I did. I didn't know." He stepped forward and reached for me again, but I didn't want to be touched right now so I evaded it.

"Said what exactly?" Grant asked.

He didn't answer right away, and I sure as fuck wasn't making any of this worse, but Finn didn't agree. "He was yelling at her about disappearing for so long after he told her to stay close. Guess we know why she was held up. Clay violated the order and now he's going to go to jail," Finn said sternly.

"I'll call the station and get an on-duty to file the report," Walker said. "Bailey, why don't you go have a seat with Mom and Thea and we'll be right there?"

I kept my eyes down and drained my glass of wine. "No, thank you."

Finn and Walker both froze, midsentence of talking about what they had to do to get Clay arrested for cornering me, and turned their attention to me. I took a deep breath and squared my shoulders and turned to them. John and Grant watched on from beside us.

"I'm going home," I said firmly.

"Bailey," Walker warned, starting to advise me not to run away from my problems, no doubt, but I waved my hand at him and finally locked gazes with him for the first time since he snapped at me.

"I'm going home, Walker. I was cornered in the bathroom by Luann and told how Finn still visits her and tells her how badly he wants her, and then I was cornered by Clay a minute later and he verbally assaulted me before trying to sexually assault me. Shove your opinion on the matter up your ass. You lost the right to one when you called me names and yelled at me like a child five minutes ago."

John's nostrils flared as he put his hand on his son's shoulder. "You did what, son?"

Finn stepped in, trying to reason with me. "You're not going home, baby. You don't have your car and we can't leave yet."

"I'm going home. I'm in no mood to celebrate, and I won't be a dark cloud on everyone else's day. I'd appreciate if both of you would stop telling me what I can and cannot do."

"Now just wait a sec—" Walker started, but Grant stepped forward and pushed his son back.

"I'll drive you home, Bailey. And while I do, I'll formally apologize for my son's lack of manners and pig-headed tendencies that he clearly gets from John," Grant said.

John scoffed and I tried to smile at their banter, but I was just too raw from everything.

"Please don't leave," Walker begged, and I was taken aback by the emotion in his voice that was finally anything other than anger and looked up at him.

"I can't stay," I said truthfully.

I looked to Finn, and I saw he understood the emotion in my voice. "I'll go with you. Jake can make do without both of us here."

"No. I just want to be alone. I'll go right home and lock the door. I'll be fine."

"You were just almost attacked, and we don't know where he is right now, baby. Please listen to us. We know what we're talking about."

I held my ground, though, and refused to budge. Hurt crossed Finn's face and Walker looked gutted, but finally, I got what I wanted. "I'll have a marked car park at your house until we can get there," Finn said sadly, and I nodded to him.

"Come on, Walk. Let's go find Mathews," Finn said, and Walker stared at me for a moment, intense longing radiating out of his eyes, but he followed after his brother.

Grant stepped forward and offered me his arm, and I slid my hand around it as he turned to John. "Tell Love I'll be back shortly." John nodded and patted my shoulder as we walked by.

Hearing such gruff men talk about their wife in a sweet, endearing way, using the pet name Love, melted my heart. I'd be lying if I said it didn't give me hope that one day my two men would be able to balance both the gruff and the sweet. But right now, I was having trouble having faith.

Grant drove me home, letting me have peace in the silence until we were close to my house. "I do believe he means well," he said.

I turned and looked at him quizzically, so he elaborated, "Walker."

"Oh."

"He's never been gentle, at least not since he was a little kid, to be completely honest. He gets that from John and while it's usually admirable, it's not a trait that makes it easy to love him from a woman's perspective." He sighed and scratched his chin. "It took Sandra a lot longer to fall in love with that side of John than she would like to admit. She was able to eventually because over time, he learned how to soften himself for her. And then when we had the boys, he learned how to soften himself for them. But it's not an overnight change for men like them. So, I guess I'm just asking that you keep that in mind tonight. I know without a doubt that it's killing both of them to be away from you right now."

"I know." I sighed and rubbed my head. "I didn't leave to punish them. I just—" I paused, embarrassed. "I hate feeling weak around Walker, but what I hate more is feeling like me being weak makes him mad. I didn't want to cause any kind of drama tonight. That was never my intention. I hope you three don't think poorly of me after all this."

"Oh, darling," he said and reached over to pat my hand before putting his back on the steering wheel. "I think more of you tonight because of everything, not less."

"How so?" I asked, turning to look at him.

"Because believe it or not, I don't think you're weak at all. I think you're so used to being strong on your own that you don't always know how to let others be strong for you. My boys are the type of men that need to be leaned on, so just keep that in mind."

"I will. Thank you," I said.

His phone rang and he answered it, and I listened to his side of a conversation with one of his sons. I could tell it was news he had hoped to not have to give.

"I'll tell her. I won't leave until he gets there."

When he hung up, he sighed and turned into my driveway. "Clay was gone by time the boys went looking for him. A warrant for his arrest is being processed, so he's about to be a fugitive."

"Fantastic."

"Don't blame yourself for this, Bailey. Had John and I not come along when we did, I have no doubt in my mind that things would have gotten far worse for you than they already were. He is a man unhinged, and nothing is out of the range of possibilities for someone like that. I just wish we wouldn't have let him go so the boys could have him arrested right then and there."

"So what happens now?" I asked.

"Now, they plan on having a marked patrol car parked here with you for the next hour or so until they can leave without causing too many ruffled feathers. And then I'd plan to be smothered by them until Mathews is apprehended because they're not the best at understanding their feelings, let alone displaying them in a healthy way." He chuckled softly, thinking affectionately about his sons. "But they care for you deeply, so know that their crazy antics come from a good place."

"Would it be completely unkind of me to ask you for another favor?" I asked, biting my lip and looking up at him hopefully.

He chuckled and nodded for me to continue.

"Would you be okay if I grabbed my bag quickly and had you drop me off at their house? It's on your way back to the wedding, and I think I'd feel better being there than here."

He smiled sweetly. "I think that sounds like a much better plan. You go on in and grab your bag and I'll call them and tell them to have the officer meet us there instead."

I worked quickly, grabbing the bag I'd already packed for tonight and some new things I'd forgotten, and then ran back out to Grant's truck.

"All set?" he asked.

"All set."

He pulled back out of the driveway and headed toward Walker and Finn's house. We were almost there when he spoke up again. "For what it's worth, I don't know specifics about Luann, but I know my boy isn't two-timing you with her."

I sighed again and groaned awkwardly. "I know. I just hate that she had anything to lie about to begin with. I guess matched with everything Clay did after, I just let all my emotions take over in the moment. I know he wouldn't do that."

When we pulled up, the on-duty cop was there already, and I recognized him as a good friend of Finn's.

He talked with Grant for a moment, walked inside with us, and explained that the judge had already issued the warrant for Clay. He was now wanted for violating the restraining order as well as assault.

I was so tired from the emotional turmoil in my body that I just wanted to go to bed already, and it was hardly even seven p.m.

I sent Grant back to the wedding—I didn't want him missing any more of it than he already had—and then thanked the cop for keeping an eye on the place until the guys got home.

I went upstairs and took the beautiful dress off that I'd put on a few hours earlier with such admiration and excitement. Now, all I was left with was sadness as I hung it on a hanger and put it in the closet.

I slid on a spaghetti-strap silk nightgown I'd bought for tonight in hopes of seducing my men, even though I didn't feel the same hope now. It was white with light pink flowers on it, with a deep V neck landing between my breasts and it was long, flowing around my ankles with a slit up to the hip, baring my leg in the same way that my gown had earlier.

It made me feel sexy, even if my brain didn't want me to right now, so I kept it on. I undid my hair from its updo and brushed it out. It was so much longer when it was straight, and it fell to right above my belly button.

I didn't have a working cell phone, thanks to Clay, so I didn't know when the guys were coming home. I just did what my body wanted and I crawled onto the massive bed that smelled like Walker, Finn, and our love making and took a deep, calming breath.

I closed my eyes, listened to the quiet peacefulness of the house that had started to feel more like home then my carriage house did, and relaxed into the comfy bedding.

I must have dozed off because the next thing I was aware of, a large, warm hand ran down my side and over my hip as delicious kisses pressed against my neck and shoulder.

"Finn." I moaned and pressed my ass into his lap where he lay behind me.

He chuckled. "How'd you know it was me? It's dark and your eyes aren't even open."

I hummed, put my hand over his, wrapped it around me tighter, and took a deep breath. "Because I know you both inside and out. I don't need to see you to know which one of you is touching me."

A loud crash and a slurred curse echoed from the kitchen and Finn sighed.

"What was that?" I asked, opening my eyes finally and turning over.

The hall light was on, bathing the dark room in a soft, warm glow.

"Walker's shit-faced and probably just knocked the fridge over."

"He's drunk?" I asked as I sat up in bed and looked out the door at the other end of the room.

"Yeah." Finn sighed and sat up, pushing my hair back from my face. He put his thumb over my wrinkled forehead, where I scowled, and smoothed out the lines. "Dad ripped him a new one after you left and his guilt over the whole thing, paired with feeling helpless when we realized that Clay was gone, pushed him over the edge I think. Don't worry about him, though, he's a big boy. I'm worried about you. Are you okay?"

I looked at him and leaned up and kissed his lips softly. "I'll be fine."

"I want to talk about what Luann accused me of, and I want to know what happened with Clay exactly before Grant and John got there," he said.

Another loud crash, this time of the glass variety, and a bigger curse came from downstairs, and I didn't hesitate to get out of bed. Finn sighed from behind me but followed me as I ran down the stairs.

I stepped into the kitchen and saw Walker bent over the sink, running water over his hand that was actively bleeding.

"Walker?" I said, walking toward him. He looked at me as I got closer and jumped toward me, alarm on his face.

"Stop, there's glass."

I looked down where he was pointing and saw the glass on the floor a second before my foot stepped down on it. Finn wrapped his arms around my waist and picked me up, swinging me around and setting me on the counter, saving me from a disaster.

"Thank you," I said breathlessly as he pushed my hair back from my face before reaching down to check my bare feet. "I'm okay," I said and turned back to Walker, who was standing there with his hand bleeding all over himself and the tile, staring at me like I was a mirage.

I scooted back and swung my legs over the other side of the island and leaned over to grab his shirt sleeve. "Come here."

He walked over to me, stumbling until he stood in front of me. I grabbed a towel out of the drawer under my feet and wrapped it around his hand. I pushed my nightgown up and over my knees and pulled him into me and looked up into his glazed eyes.

It was then that I saw the starting of a shiner under his left eye and softly touched it. "What happened?"

Walker dropped my gaze and looked away, but he slid his other hand over my hip and held on to me tightly. "Nothing I didn't deserve."

I looked over at Finn, who was standing against the fridge with his arms crossed over his chest, and he raised his eyebrow at me. "I won't say sorry, so don't ask me too."

My eyebrows shot to my hairline, and I looked back to Walker, who still wouldn't look at me, and then back to Finn. "You punched your brother?"

"Sure fucking did. And he deserved even worse than that for his part in tonight," he said straight to me without any remorse.

I felt a smile tug on my lips, and I tilted my head at him and felt the girly parts of me swoon for him. "Thank you."

That surprised him and he leaned up off the fridge and walked closer to us. "Thank you?" he asked. "You're not mad?"

"Why would I be mad?" I asked.

"Hey," Walker complained, offended.

I raised my eyebrow to him in response and dared him to really try to complain, and he shrunk back a bit and hiccupped.

I pulled the towel off of his hand and was happy to see the bleeding had stopped. There was a small cut on the top by his wrist, but it didn't need stitches.

"You'll live," I said, dropping his hand and looking up at him.

"Don't push me away. Not yet," he said softly and squeezed my hip, letting his thumb slide over my stomach under the silky fabric.

Finn sighed, walked over, pulled my head to the side, and kissed me deeply, letting his fingers play with the smooth, long hair at my back. "I'll go get the first-aid kit," he said softly to me and then turned to his twin. "That's all the alone time you get with her tonight, asshole."

He walked away and headed back upstairs.

"You're drunk?" I asked Walker.

"Shit-faced is a better word for it," he slurred. Now that his other hand had stopped bleeding, he slid it around the other side of my waist and pulled me toward the edge of the counter, stepping between my legs and pressing himself to me. He leaned in and put his nose in my hair and took a deep breath.

"I'm so incredibly sorry for tonight, baby," he apologized and kissed my forehead.

"I know you are. And we'll talk about it tomorrow when you're sober."

"I can't lose you," he said, still not pulling back from my forehead, but I could hear the helplessness in his tone. "I didn't realize how jealous I was of your love for my brother until I opened up my damned eyes and saw it firsthand. I can't lose you, baby."

I leaned forward and kissed his throat, where his Adam's apple bobbed when my lips made contact, and he groaned.

"You aren't going to lose me," I said, letting my head rest on his chest, wrapping my arms around his waist.

"Promise me that?" he asked, wrapping his arms around my back and playing with my hair, running his fingers from my scalp to the ends, where they fell above my ass.

"I promise," I said, meaning every word of it. "But you can't treat me like you did tonight. I don't even know what I did to anger you." I leaned back and looked at him, sliding my fingers through his beard and making him look down at me. "I don't know if you noticed or not, but I don't respond well to your mean side."

He took a pained breath in and stepped back. "I've never tried to be mean to you, Bailey," he said and slapped the counter behind him and gripped the edge of the stone. "I'm a fuckup and you deserve better than me. You deserve someone who will never let you know they even have a mean side, let alone aim it at you. Maybe the best thing for everyone would be if I just walk away and leave you to Finn. He can be the man you deserve. I can't."

I slid off the counter and was in his face in a second, and then I slapped him on the cheek, hard. The sound cracked through the house and my hand burned from it. His eyes scorched as he looked at me in shock, and I felt tears spill down my cheeks. "Is that what you want, Walker? Because if you want out, don't you dare throw some bullshit my way about what I deserve in some fake ass way of putting the blame on me. Stupid me has gone and fallen in love with both of you equally, but apparently the jokes on me and I'm just wasting my time playing a game I'm never going to be good enough to win, huh?"

His eyes grew wide at my admission.

"What the fuck?" Finn swore, standing at the bottom of the stairs. "What the fuck is wrong with you, Walker? Get your fucking head out of your ass and stop being a piece of shit. You're right, she deserves better than that. We both do." He threw the first-aid kit on the counter next to his brother. "Sleep down here tonight. You're not fucking welcome upstairs," he said in parting as he picked me up and jogged up the stairs two at a time.

I didn't look back at Walker as Finn carried me away. I was so tired of him hurting my feelings. I just wanted to lose myself in Finn's arms because he never hurt me with his words.

He kicked open the bedroom door and slammed it shut behind him, turning to lock it before he walked me over to the bed and set me down on the edge of it. I didn't realize it before, but I was trembling in his arms.

He ran his hands up and down my arms and pulled the cover up and around my shoulders. "Are you okay?" he asked.

I shook my head no but didn't say anything else.

"I'm sorry he said those things to you. I know he didn't mean any of it and he's just self-destructing in his guilt for how he treated you earlier. The fucking booze isn't helping the situation. Please just have faith in both of us, Bailey. Please," he said and unbuttoned his shirt and pulled it from his slacks.

I watched as he undid the cuffs and then took it off, leaving him standing before me in just his tight dress pants, and he tweaked my nose when he saw me staring.

"I'm not asking for anything right now, Bailey. I just want to get out of these clothes and hold you in my arms in our bed."

He continued stripping, pulling his belt from his pants and then pushing them down, ending up in just his sexy body and black briefs. I reached forward and grabbed his hand and pulled him toward me. He threaded both hands into my hair and took a deep breath before kissing my forehead.

I kissed his chest and then tilted my head and offered my lips to him. He leaned down and kissed me sweetly, keeping it light, but I could feel his desire to turn it into more, so I decided to do it for him.

I pulled him down until he lay on the bed next to me, and I hiked my gown up around my hips, straddled him, and spoke softly against his lips. "I told myself not to say anything yet, that it was too soon. I'm sorry you heard it from me like that for the first time." I paused and looked deep into his eyes. "But I love you. And I don't want you to say it back right now because that's not why I said it. I just want you to know."

He sat up straight into me and wrapped both hands around my head and kissed me so deeply, I wasn't sure where his soul stopped and mine began. I grabbed the hem of my gown and pulled it up and over my head and threw it on the floor. He leaned in, grabbed both breasts, and sucked my nipples deep into his mouth one after the other.

We were frantic with need, and I pushed his briefs down far enough to free him quickly before sinking down on him—without asking for permission. I rolled my hips to accommodate his size.

"That's my girl." He groaned and gripped my hips to thrust up into my body when I rose up on my knees.

He lay back on the bed and pulled me down to lie on his chest as he fucked me deeply from beneath. His hands were everywhere, and his mouth left no part of my face, neck, and chest un-kissed.

"Please, Finn," I begged, "Let me be enough for you."

He grabbed a handful of my hair and pulled it back, exposing my neck to his teeth, and he leaned in and bit me. I screamed as the pain and pleasure mixed and catapulted me into an incredible orgasm.

I held onto him and rode out the onslaught of pleasure he was giving me from beneath, taking every orgasm he gave.

Within minutes of my first, he was chasing me into the bliss of his own and pumping himself into me, filling me as he roared into the darkness.

I laid my forehead onto his shoulder as my heartrate slowed back down to a normal speed and then rolled off of him, lying with my head on his chest as he wrapped both arms around me.

We stayed quiet for a long time, letting the emotions of the night calm in our heads. But after a while, he kissed my forehead and whispered into the night, "Say it again."

It took me only a moment to figure out what he meant, but when I did, I smiled into his chest and quietly breathed, "I love you."

He sucked a deep breath in and smiled into my hair, and then he rolled until I was under him, looking up into his eyes. "I'm glad you're finally willing to tell me because I've been in love with you for quite some time now. I was afraid I'd scare you off if I told you before I was sure you were ready to hear it."

"Liar." I laughed but I knew he was telling the truth. And I loved him more for it.

He settled with his head on my chest, his ear between my breasts, and his body between my legs as silence fell on us again.

I felt bold in the quiet darkness, so I voiced a fear I hadn't given light to yet. "I'm terrified of Clay." He looked up at me and watched my face as I fought for composure, but he let me work it out. "I was so mad at you and Luann when I walked out of the bathroom, I wasn't watching where I was going. I ran right into him, and then I was so scared when I realized there was no one around me and he was saying such terrible things, and then he put his hand—" I paused and swallowed back more tears. "I didn't mean to disobey Walker. I really didn't. But during the ceremony, he looked so angry with me that I was confused, and I needed a minute to myself, so I went to the bathroom. By the time I came back out, everyone was gone except Clay. It was like he was waiting for me. Actually, I think Luann set me up to be left alone with him."

"I promise you we're going to find him, baby. And when we do, he'll face serious jail time for not only violating the order, but for threatening you again and touching you. I owe you the biggest apology for not telling you he would be there and for not protecting you from him today. I won't ever let that happen again, and I'm sorry. I don't know what Luann said to you, but I promise you I've ignored her this whole time. I don't want anything to do with her."

I ran my fingers through his hair and mused quietly, "I don't hold you accountable for anything, Finn. Or Walker. I just don't understand what I did the first few days here to warrant such crazed feelings from Clay. I'm so confused."

"I know, baby. We'll figure it all out. I promise."

With that, he laid his head back down on my chest and I snuggled into his warm embrace as sleep started to pull me back under.

Part of me worried about Walker downstairs by himself. I knew he had heard us having sex and I didn't want him to think I was choosing Finn over him, even though he had said that I should. I recognized him trying to protect me, but I didn't understand what happened between the time he stood by my side and said such wonderful things to me in front of his parents and then as he scowled at me angrily during the ceremony.

A huge part of me wanted to go downstairs and comfort him or call him up to join us in bed, but I forced myself to stay sheltered in Finn's loving arms and resigned myself to face the dark storm in his eyes in the morning, once I'd had a good night's sleep and some caffeine.

Chapter 21 – Walker

I lay on the couch and listened to Bailey moan and scream for hours all night. I had heard them together after they went upstairs originally and then it was quiet, and I thought perhaps they had taken pity on me for the rest of the night. But I wasn't so lucky because an hour later, I heard her sweet, melodic voice cry out in ecstasy, and a couple of hours later, Finn was at it again, drawing pleasure from her body.

I deserved every single second of punishment by having to lie there and listen to her chase orgasm after orgasm from Finn's body for how I acted.

Part of me was happy that she had Finn's gentle arms to comfort her when I was lacking. The other part hated that I had hurt her to even begin with. And I had hurt her so badly.

I could still feel the imprint of her palm on the side of my face to match the shiner under my eye from my brother.

I'd royally fucked everything up today and I had no one to blame but myself for every single second of it.

I had seen Bailey standing there with my parents, looking like a goddess, and knowing she was mine and Finn's had filled my gut with extreme possessiveness. I'd wanted to scream from the pits of my soul that she was mine and let everyone in the world know it, but instead, I'd let my fears and worries come across as anger and disappointment when she needed me the most.

When she cried during the ceremony, I hadn't been able to take my eyes off her. She watched Jake and Ivy so happily and then looked at Finn, and I watched the silent acknowledgment pass between them. They were in love.

For the first time in my life, I was jealous of my brother. I knew he was gentle and sweet with her and deserved every single ounce of love that she gave to him, but I was neither sweet nor gentle most days and I couldn't help but worry that she wouldn't be able to love me because of it.

When I couldn't find her after the ceremony, I walked all around the venue looking for her. When I finally found her, she had been alone and at the bar like she hadn't just made my heart race with worry for ten minutes straight.

But I hadn't read her cues at all to see the fear in her eyes until after both my dads had stepped in and told us what had happened with the fucking predator that just wouldn't leave her alone.

When her tears fell as she looked down at the broken mirror from her purse, I felt my heart ache for her own broken one.

I had seen her use it before, and she'd told me the story of her mom and dad's unconventional wedding and how he had given it to her for their first wedding anniversary in place of a honeymoon.

Now, her dad had been gone for over a decade and Clay fucking Mathews had destroyed one of the most treasured items that she had left of him.

And I'd lost my goddamned mind.

When Dad had taken her home, I'd gone on a mission to find Clay with Finn. We didn't find him anywhere, and the unresolved guilt and anger bubbled up. I'd made an ass of myself in front of my family because of it. Finn knocked me down a few pegs by laying me flat on my ass in the wet grass with a splitting headache for it.

I, of course, tried to numb the pain with liquor, but it didn't help at all.

Dad had come back and told us that Bailey had ended up wanting to come to our house after leaving and that had given me hope, but then I'd let my big fat mouth get the best of me when she had told me that my mean side had hurt her.

I'd never tried to be mean to her, and it fucking gutted me to think that I'd made her feel that way, even once.

So, I'd done what I thought was best in my liquored-up idiocy and told her that she should leave me.

She, in turn, told me that she loved me.

And now, I was even more of a fucking goner for a girl I didn't deserve.

That tore me up.

I had stood up at the altar next to my twin and my best friend and had been afraid that she didn't love me at all. And I had been wrong.

So, I'd lay there on the couch and listened to her moan Finn's name over and over all night long to punish myself for letting her down.

Now that it was morning, I was going to grovel, beg, plead, barter, blackmail, and seduce Bailey in every possible way to get her back to being both mine and my brother's.

And I was going to do all of those things to apologize to Finn too—well, except the seducing part.

I needed her the same way I needed her to need Finn and vice versa, and with me stepping out of bounds, our dynamic was all off and none of us were okay.

It was early still, and I was in desperate need of a shower, but with them sleeping upstairs, I wasn't going to disturb them. Instead, I changed into a pair of shorts and went outside and forced myself to run off my hangover and shortcomings.

I was on mile number six when my phone rang, interrupting the music in my headphones.

It was Bailey's beautiful face that popped up on my screen, so I stopped running and hit accept.

"Hi," I said, trying to catch my breath.

"Where are you?" I could hear the panic in her voice.

"I'm out running. Why? What's wrong?" I asked, turning back toward the house and walking in that direction, even though I was miles away.

"You're not here. That's what's wrong. You didn't leave a note or anything, Walker! I thought—" She paused, and I could feel her emotions through the phone.

"You thought what?"

She whispered her fear, "I thought you left me."

"Baby." I sighed and pinched the bridge of my nose. "I didn't want to wake you. I know you were up all night long, so I wanted to let you sleep in. I went for a run to shake the cobwebs out, that's all. I'm still right here, Bailey."

I could hear her sniffle through my headphones. "Where are you?"

"Uh, by the reservoir."

"I'm coming to get you," she said and hung up.

I shook my head and couldn't help the smile that pulled at my lips. She was worried about me, and that meant she still cared for me. Hopefully, that meant she'd forgive me for last night. I started jogging back home and within a few minutes, I saw my truck roaring down the road.

It was early still, and the road was deserted even on a busy day, but she pulled over on the shoulder and unlocked the doors.

I opened the passenger side door up when she made no move to scoot over and sucked my breath in at the sight of her in the soft morning light.

She still wore that sexy-as-hell nightgown from last night and her hair was still long and straight, though a bit messy from sleep. Her eyes burned with an intensity I'd not seen in them before. Her nipples hardened under the silk as she let her eyes rove over my bare, sweaty chest.

Perhaps there was hope for me after all.

"Good morning," I said huskily, still working on catching my breath. "You look sexy as hell driving my truck."

She kept looking at me for a moment, staying quiet, before she turned to look back out the windshield and bit her lip. "The urge to run you over with it was strong, I won't lie."

I laughed out loud and pulled myself up into the passenger seat and rubbed my jaw. "Yeah, I deserve that."

I clicked my seatbelt, but she didn't make any move to drive back to the house as she kept staring out the windshield. I could tell she was fighting a war in her head, so I gave her a moment.

She finally sighed and huffed. "Do you really not want me anymore?"

I snapped my head in her direction, but she still wouldn't look at me. I flipped the center console up and undid both of our seatbelts, pulling her over until she was straddling me. I put my hand around the front of her throat and forced her to look directly into my eyes.

"I've never not wanted you, for even a second, from the first moment I met you."

"Last night, you said—" she started.

"I know what I fucking said, Bailey. It's been playing on repeat in my head ever since. The same way your moans and screams from last night have. I fucked up, baby. I didn't mean it. I just felt like I was fucking everything up and I wanted to give you an out, not me. I just want you to be happy and protected. That's all I've ever wanted."

"You're the only one that hurts me, Walker," she said sadly. Her giant green eyes looked so sad when she said it and it fucking gutted me.

"Not anymore. Not ever again if you give me another chance. My feelings for you are so strong that I can't control them sometimes and they come out wrong. My love for you gets mixed with my fear and shortcomings and suddenly, I'm being crass and a dick to you, but it's exactly the opposite of what I'm trying to be at the moment. I'm just trying to—" I paused and took a deep breath as she hung on every word I was saying. "I'm just trying to figure out how to be gentle with you when I've never been gentle with anyone else in my entire life."

Her pupils dilated and she put her hands on my chest. "I'm not made of glass, Walker. I don't want you to be gentle with me all the time, but I do need you to be kind." She slid her hand up my arm until it lay on top of mine and squeezed it tighter around her throat. "I like the pain you give me, Walker. Sometimes, I feel the closest to you when you are holding me like this." She dug her nails into my hand and arm and gave me back some of the pain she needed. "I crave the bite of discomfort you give to me when you're the most unrestrained because I know that I did that to you. Me. No one else at that moment. I don't want to change you, Walker. I'd never dream of trying to change you into someone that you're not. I need you just the way you are."

"I love you, Bailey," I said and crushed my lips to hers, sliding my hand from around her throat to the back of her head, wrapping the silky long hair there around my fist, and pulling.

She moaned and rocked her hips into my lap. I pushed both tiny straps off her shoulders and her gown slid down to her stomach, baring her beautiful, full breasts to me.

I leaned down and bit her nipple and then rolled it between my tongue and teeth, and she gasped and slid her hand into my hair and pulled my head in closer. "Hmm, Walker. That feels so good."

She leaned forward and bit and sucked on my ear as she rolled her hips again, rubbing herself against my hard cock straining under my shorts.

"He bit you?" I asked as I noticed the red teeth marks on her neck that weren't there last night.

"Yes, he did." She purred as I licked and sucked on the mark.

"Did you like it?" I asked, massaging her nipples, and rubbing her on my cock as I asked.

She moaned and looked me dead in the eye. "I came like a fucking rocket when he did it."

"Fuck." I groaned and my teeth ached to bite her on the other side of her neck.

"I know what you're thinking," she purred and put her lips back to my ear.

"What am I thinking?" I asked and leaned back to let her play.

"You want to mark me, bite me, and brand me as yours too."

"Those words sound so sexy on your lips. And yes. Yes, I want to mark you so bad right now."

"So do it," she dared me.

I flipped her until she lay down on her back in the driver's seat and pushed her legs wide open. She had no panties on, and I leaned down and sucked on the inside of her inner thigh and watched as her back bowed off the seat and she threw her head back and palmed her breasts.

She pulled and twisted her nipples as I kissed down to her wet pussy lips and then sucked her clit into my mouth and flicked it with my tongue.

"God, you taste so fucking good, Bail." I groaned and dove back in, adding two fingers to her pussy as I ate her.

She was writhing and moaning under me as I gave her everything I had.

She sat up and placed both hands behind her on the seat and tilted her hips into my face as she came. Her tight body clamped down tight on my fingers and spasmed around them. She pulled me up her body until I lay between her thighs and kissed me, tasting herself on my tongue and sucking it into her mouth.

"Make love to me, Walker," she begged. "But do it the way only you can."

I quickly pushed my shorts down far enough to get my cock out and buried it into her body in one punishing thrust.

"Yes!" she screamed. "Just like that." I slid both hands under her shoulders, wrapped them over her collarbone, and held her in place as I pounded into her body.

"You've ruined me for any other woman. I'll never want another woman for as long as I live."

"Good," she bit out.

When she was lost in the sensation of having her pussy pounded, I felt her body start to quicken and chase her orgasm. As she crashed over the top of it and the first waves of bliss blinded her, I let my teeth sink into the skin of her shoulder, opposite of the mark she already wore, bit her, and then sucked on the puckered skin.

She screamed into the air of the truck and her pussy clamped down on me so fucking hard, I saw spots float in front of my eyes as I violently thrust into her tiny, tight body as she held on for dear life.

"You're so sexy when you come on my cock. You make every single one of my brain cells scream for me to fill you up and mark you as ours."

"I am yours; my heart and my body belong to you both, Walker." She gasped as I reached between us and flicked her clit.

"Say the words then," I demanded, and her eyes flew open as she realized what I meant.

"I love you, Walker John Camden. I love you both so much it hurts"

And with that, my balls tightened so badly, they ached and fire shot down my spine as I pumped my DNA into Bailey's body with an animalistic need to possess and own her. I pulled back as I filled her up and looked at her sweet cupid's bow lips parted in ecstasy, the mark of my teeth on the side of her neck, and knew I was forever a changed man.

"I love you, Bailey," I said, pushing her damp hair back from her forehead and kissing her lips softly.

My cock twitched inside of her, and I felt my seed slickening her insides even more than her own arousal. I craved more of her.

"Do you forgive me?" I asked. "Because you should know, I'm prepared to spend the rest of today doing whatever it takes to make it up to you."

"Whatever it takes, huh?" she asked with a small smile teasing her swollen lips.

"Anything. Name it and it's yours."

She mused for a moment and then said, "There are a couple of things I can think of that might soothe my aching wounds."

I chuckled, feeling slightly like I was about to regret my choice of words.

"For one"—she ticked off her finger—"you can tell me that you love me again."

I laughed and kissed her nose. "I love you."

"Good because I love hearing you say that." She laughed and then held up another finger. "When we get back to your house, you can genuinely apologize to Finn for causing strife between the three of us. He's as much a part of this relationship as I am, and he was really upset last night."

"I know. First thing this morning, I knew I owed him and you both an explanation and apology. So consider it done."

"Okay, then I guess the last two things you can do for me to make up for everything is take a hot bubble bath with me and Finn when we get back."

"That sounds incredible." I sighed. It had been too long since we'd had time all together or any time in that tub that she loved so much. "And the last thing?" I asked, still a bit worried.

A mischievous smile turned her lips back seductively. "I want you and Finn to fuck me together again."

My dick jumped where it was still buried inside her pussy. I widened my eyes at her and smirked, trying not to show how much that idea appealed to me when it was supposed to be all about her. "You want us both at the same time? Inside of you at the same time again?"

"Yes!" She moaned, biting her lip. "It's been almost two weeks since both my ass and my pussy have been filled by you two at the same time. I want it again so bad."

"Let's get the fuck home then, baby girl. We're going to soak in that tub until your body is relaxed and limp, and then we're going to fuck you and fill you with our come until it drips from every fucking hole."

She squirmed under me and pushed me, so I had to withdraw from her body. "Promises, promises, big guy."

I pulled my shorts back up, she pulled the straps of her gown back over her shoulders, and then I turned the truck toward home.

Fucking home.

I had known for a while that my home was where Bailey was.

My next step was to do something about that too.

When we pulled into the driveway, I helped her down and then carried her into the house. Her arms were wrapped around my neck and her teeth were wrapped around my ear when we stepped into the kitchen.

Finn sat at the counter with a cup of coffee and watched us walk in with a carefree but skeptical smile on his face.

She walked over to him, and he lifted her onto his lap and kissed her soundly. Seconds later, he pushed her hair back from her neck on one side and then the other and admired our marks.

He looked at me and I shrugged my shoulders. "I felt left out when I saw yours."

He laughed at me and then leaned down and kissed both of them. She giggled and then moaned and sighed as his gentle, sweet kisses turned deeper and darker.

"Wait," she said and pulled back. "You guys need to squash last night between you. I can't handle it if you're out of sync."

I looked at my brother and acknowledged her point. "She's right. I owe you an apology, man," I started, but he shook me off.

"I'm good. If you two are good, then you and I are good," he said.

"No, I personally fucked you over too. It's not just about her, Finn. I'm sorry." She fought against his hold on her and slid from his arms, which did not make him happy at all but he allowed it.

She stood next to him and took a calming breath and pushed her hair from her face. "Let him explain," she chided him as he reached for her again.

He rolled his eyes at her but turned his attention back to me. I rubbed my hand over my face, trying to find the words to describe everything to both of them, and then I just decided to say what I was feeling.

"Last night, during the ceremony, I got jealous of you, man," I said. I watched both of their eyes widen as I said it. "I saw how openly Bailey was in love with you and I didn't think she was ever going to love me like that because I can't love her the same way you do. I'm not kind, gentle, or romantic, and my biggest fear is that I won't have enough to offer her and therefore she won't ever love me the same way."

I looked at Bailey and saw the unshed tears in her eyes as I voiced my fears out loud for the first time. "I've known that I was in love with you since one of the very first days you stayed here with us. I knew then that I was a goner and wanted you to be a part of us forever, but I didn't have it in me to tell you how I felt. I think I was afraid that you'd see I was lacking and call it quits if you knew what was on the line for me."

I worked my jaw back and forth as I felt my own emotions coming to the surface. I never got worked up, but I was now, laying everything on the line for her. "When I watched you crying your sweet, happy tears as two people you barely knew got married, you looked at Finn and I could feel your love from where you sat. I thought that it was only aimed at him."

"Do you still feel that way?" she asked and walked over to me. I leaned down and wiped the tears off her cheeks and kissed both of her eyelids and then her breathtaking lips until she moaned against my mouth.

"No. No, I believe that you love me as much as I love you now. I'm sorry that I ever doubted you."

"Don't let it happen again," she joked.

I looked over her head to Finn. "Forgive me for being a cranky pain in the ass?" I asked, worried about what he was going to say.

"I forgave you the second my fist connected with your face, bro," he joked and stood up and walked over to us. He wrapped his arms around my shoulders and Bailey's and hugged us both. "So, we're in this for the long haul now, huh? No more hiding what we're feeling or pretending to be cool about it all?" he said, laughing and pulling Bailey into his arms fully.

"I'm done pretending not to be in it one hundred percent," I said.

"I never pretended," Bailey said with a stuck-up nose in the air that faded into a fit of giggles as Finn poked her side. "I'm done hiding it though," she added, and he kissed her forehead. "But," she said open-endedly and looked at me pointedly.

"Yes?" I asked.

"You owe me a bubble bath and a ride on the double-trouble train."

I laughed so hard, I snorted and choked, two things I hadn't done in most likely forever. Finn's eyes bugged out of his head when he heard her sweet lips say such things. He quickly recovered, threw her over his shoulder, and ran up the stairs. I heard her sweet girly giggles all the way into the bedroom and just locked the doors and followed after them.

I was in love with that beautiful woman, and she was in love with me and my twin brother, and I had never felt so complete before.

Chapter 22 – Bailey

It was a Monday morning and I stood in the bathroom at the guys' house, putting on my makeup for my workday. Both Walker and Finn had left this morning for their shifts at work, and I'd happily relaxed in bed and watched them dress and prepare for their day.

They both had climbed back into bed more than once to prolong their departure by using my body to pull pleasure from theirs, and I was happy to be used in such a delicious and mutually beneficial way.

I'd be lying if I said their jobs as cops didn't make me worry every time they left to go to work, but I tried my best not to add my own worry to their shoulders. This was their job before I came around. I wasn't going to ask them to quit so there was no point in letting them know I was scared every time they pulled out of the driveway.

Instead, I made sure they thought of me in other moods. Ones like joy, happiness, and all things sexual.

But, trying to help their moods didn't change the dark and serious looks that always passed over their faces when they left me.

Clay Mathews still hadn't been arrested, and that was shocking considering the entire police force was looking for him. The perk to being romantically involved with not one, but two police officers was when someone threatened what was theirs, the entire department rallied behind them regardless of the circumstances.

They had executed search warrants at all the places he was known to stay, and patrols had all been briefed to keep their eyes open for him. While Montana was vast, the population in this area was not, so it was surprising that no one had spotted him in the few weeks since the wedding incident.

I tried not to worry about the fact that he was on the loose and tried to find hope that he had left town and wouldn't be back. But every time the guys left, for a brief second, they would look longingly at me like they didn't want to leave because they didn't want me vulnerable. They would lock it down almost as soon as I would see it, so I hadn't brought it up to either of them yet.

I left the bathroom and went down to the kitchen to fill my mug with coffee and head to my shop when I noticed some papers on the counter. There were two small scraps of paper folded up with my name written on the top of each.

They were numbered one and two, so I opened the first one to start with and felt giddy joy tingle my senses as I read the cute little love letter from Finn.

Good morning,

In your sleep last night, you curled into my side and sighed that you loved me and kissed my chest, never once opening your eyes. I've been unable to think of anything else since those three words crossed your lips in my direction the first time weeks ago.

I love you, Bailey Penelope Dunn. I hope you have a great day today and I can't wait to see you come through our front door tonight after work.

Yours,

Finley.

Literal swoon.

I folded the note back up and slid it into the pocket of my jeans and then opened the second one with Walker's writing on top.

Bailey,

Ditto whatever Finn said.

Love, Walker.

I laughed out loud into the quiet kitchen at the silly simplistic note and then noticed the small arrow at the bottom of it and flipped it over.

You didn't think I'd completely fail to try to woo you, did you?

I love you. I love waking up to you in the morning and seeing your beautiful green eyes flutter open and look at us first thing. I love feeling your soft, curvy body fall into a deep sleep in our arms at night, and I love even more how much you love us.

I'll see you tonight. Have a great day, wonderful.

I love you,

Walker.

I folded up his note and added it to Finn's in my pocket and walked around their kitchen, unable to wipe the smile from my face.

Gosh, I loved these men so much that my heart ached with the need for them.

I tried shaking off my giddiness, locked the door behind me, and headed to my car. I looked up at the sunshine and did a silly twirl as I opened my passenger door and threw my bag on the seat and then turned to walk around to my side.

Something odd caught my eye on the ground, and I backed up and looked down at the front passenger tire.

It was flat.

Like super pancake flat.

"What the hell?" I cursed and kicked it with the toe of my boot softly.

I huffed and went to the back of my SUV to get the jack and tools out to change it, but that was when I noticed the back passenger tire.

It was flat as well.

A chill ran down my spine as I got the sensation that something wasn't right. I walked quickly around to the other side, and both tires on that side were flat as well.

My tires had been slashed.

I quickly turned and looked around the open yard and into the tree line, almost sure I'd see someone standing there, watching me.

There was nothing out here but me and my useless car, but the hair stood up on the back of my neck.

I grabbed my phone and purse and ran back to the house. I locked the door behind me as I stepped into the kitchen and dialed Walker.

He answered almost instantly. "Well, good morning, beautiful. Did you call to tell me how much you loved my note?" he asked. I could hear the smile in his deep, sensual voice, and I took a calming breath as the tone of it settled around me like a cozy blanket.

"Someone slashed my tires," I said. I could hear the tremble in my voice, so I took a deep breath and sat down at the counter.

"Where are you?" Gone was the sensual honey of his loving voice, and in its place was only control and authority.

"Your house. I went out to go to work and all four of my tires are flat. That's not a coincidence, right?" I asked, even though I knew the answer to that.

"Go back inside and lock the door behind you. I'm driving that way."

"I'm already inside. I locked the door."

"Okay. Hold on while I call this in. Stay on the phone with me, baby. Finn might be closer than I am."

"Okay," I said and sniffed and swiped at the stupid tears that fell on my cheeks.

Walker heard the terror in my voice and tried to reassure me over the phone. "It's okay, Bail. You're safe. I'm on my way."

I couldn't respond but he didn't wait for one either. I heard him start his radio transmission and forced myself to let his commanding voice calm me.

"49-01 to dispatch," he said.

A moment later, I could hear the dispatcher answer him, and he carried on.

"49-01 responding to 2698 Old Mill Rd. for a report of vandalism. Possible R.O. violation concerning a wanted fugitive."

I heard dispatch acknowledge and then a second later, Finn's voice filtered through the phone over the radio. "49-02 responding, I'm two minutes from the scene."

"Did you hear that, Bail? Finn's two minutes away, okay?" Walker reassured me on the phone.

"Yeah." My voice cracked. "I heard him."

"Bailey, I want you to go over to the safe and open it."

Dread filled my heart, and I shook my head. "I can't, Walk," I whispered. I looked over at the large imposing steel safe built into the wall and felt my body tremble when I thought about what was inside there.

"Then look out the window. Do you see anyone outside? By your car or in the driveway?"

I stood up and looked out the wall of windows aimed at the driveway and garage. I still didn't see anything out of the ordinary. "No. I looked before I called you and I didn't see anything odd then either."

"Okay. Good. You're doing great, baby. Finn's almost there and so am I, okay? Are you okay?" he asked.

I shook my head no and felt more tears slide down my face but couldn't get my voice to answer him. I could hear sirens coming down the road, and then through the phone, I heard Finn call out, "49-02 on scene."

A second later, his police SUV came barreling up the driveway and skidded to a stop at the front door. I flicked the bolt and ran out onto the porch as he flew out of the car.

"Go back inside," he ordered, pointing back at the house as he looked around the yard.

I paused but Walker talked to me through the phone that was still at my ear. "Go back inside, Bailey. I'm almost there."

I went back in and watched through the window as Finn walked over to my car and checked out at the tires, then he looked around the yard as anger radiated from his body.

Walker's SUV came skidding to a stop next to Finn's a minute later, and he looked through the window at me and nodded and hung the phone up with me and went over to join Finn.

A few more police units showed up and as they started looking around outside, Walker and Finn came up the steps and straight through the front door.

Within seconds, I was in their arms and crying pathetically as they held me.

"It's okay, Bailey. You're safe. It's all okay," Finn said, rubbing my hair and kissing my temple. "Tell us what happened."

I pulled back and wiped at the tears and shook my head. "I don't know. I went to go to work and saw a flat tire, so I went to go get the spare and stuff, and then I noticed the others. I got a really bad, eerie feeling, knowing it wasn't an accident that all four tires were flat, and then I ran back in here and called Walker."

"Okay," Finn said and wiped my tears. "We're going to find him, Bail."

"So you think it's Clay?" I asked, voicing my fear out loud.

They both sighed and Walker pulled me close to him and sat on a stool. "Yeah, we do, baby."

More tears fell from my lashes as I got more frustrated. "Why won't he just leave me alone!" I yelled.

I had told the guys exactly what he had said at the wedding, and they agreed that he was doing these things out of jealousy at first, and then anger at being painted the bad guy after the R.O.

The anger part was what scared me because it was no longer about wanting me but revenge, and revenge was an endless sea of possible forms of retaliation.

A truck pulled up the driveway that wasn't a police vehicle and we watched as John, Grant, and Sandra got out and walked up to the house.

I tried cleaning my face up a bit before they got inside but as soon as Sandra saw me, she pulled me into a sweet, loving embrace and more tears fell.

I missed my mom so much, but I refused to tell her any of this was happening when I spoke to her each week, so having Sandra here to hold me while I cried at least helped bridge that gap.

"I heard you call it in on the scanner and we came right over," John said as he shook his boys' hands.

"Thanks, that means a lot," Walker replied and put his hands on his hips in exasperation.

Time passed, and I stood with a fresh cup of tea as the guys talked to their sheriff and other officers and parents about what could be done and so on, but I was unable to grasp any of it. I just wanted to get away from all of the fear and looking over my shoulder 24/7 for a day or two. That was impossible here in Mayfield with Clay still on the run.

I made the guys go back to work when they were done taking photos and doing what they could with the lack of evidence. They were less than happy about it, but they would have to deal. My car was towed to the garage in town, not the one that Clay had worked for thankfully, and I rode to my shop with their parents as I tried to formulate a plan.

I forced myself to work the day away, doing the cuts and shaves on autopilot but getting them done. I knew if I stayed at home, I'd just go stir-crazy with fear.

It was getting close to the end of my day. Walker and Finn were picking me up when they were off their shift, and I just didn't have anything left to give to anyone else today, so I flipped the closed sign and went into my office.

I picked my phone up and called the one person in the world that could tell me everything would be okay and I'd believe it.

"Hey, baby girl. I was just thinking about you as I watered some new baby spider plants in the den. Do you remember when you were in kindergarten and you all planted baby spider plants in little pink cups for Mother's Day and you were so darn proud to bring it home? I can't believe twenty years later, I'm still nipping babies off that one plant and transplanting them to other people. I bet this one plant has made hundreds of babies for others by now."

I sat back in the chair and listened to my mom's sweet, loving voice as she chatted on and on without a word from me in the usual fashion, knowing exactly what I needed at that moment.

"Mom—" My voice cracked a bit, so I cleared my throat and pushed on, trying to sound normal. "Can I come home for a few days?"

She paused, the background noise of her moving around the room silenced, and I held my breath in anticipation of what she was going to say. "What happened? What's wrong?"

I shook my head and tried to make my voice calm so she wouldn't be alarmed. "I just miss you and could use some time with you. It's been months since I moved and I haven't had time to come back, but I think it's time."

"Why don't I come up there? I'm retired. I can take however much time you need from me to come up and spend it with you. I'd love to see your place and your new shop. I've been dying to, but you always say not right now or not yet."

"No. I want to come there." I did not want my mom put in danger if there was a chance that Clay was going to escalate his fear campaign against me.

"What happened, baby? You sound so sad and defeated." It killed me to hear the sadness in her voice.

"Can I tell you all about it when I'm there? I just want to come home. Please, Mom?" I hated how childish I sounded begging her to let me come home for a break.

"Of course!" She gasped and I heard her start moving around the room again, no doubt already getting a list together in her head of everything she wanted to have ready for me. "When are you coming?"

"Uh, I don't know. I'm going to fly down. I have to see when there are flights available, but maybe tomorrow if I can get on one."

"Tomorrow? Okay. Just send me the info when you get a flight booked and I'll be there to pick you up at the airport. Are you sure you're okay right now?"

"Yeah, right now, I'm okay. I'll tell you everything when I get home. I love you, Mom."

"Aw, baby. I love you too."

I hung up with her and then as my brain started processing what it meant to go home, my heart started to ache. I didn't want to leave Finn and Walker, not even for one day, but I needed a break from this town that had somehow gone from my fresh start to my very own nightmare.

As if on cue, the front door opened, and I watched my two twin deputies walk into my shop, looking for me.

"Hey," I called, and they turned and walked into my office.

"Hi, baby," Finn said and walked around my desk, knelt on the floor, and kissed me deeply. He slid my body to the edge of my chair and pushed my thighs apart and wrapped them around his body as he kissed me so deeply, it felt as if he were trying to consume me.

When he pulled back, I looked deep into his chocolate-brown eyes and felt such emotion emanating from them as he looked into mine. "I love you," he whispered and then kissed my forehead and stepped back.

Walker took his place eagerly, dropping to his knees as well and pulling me in with the same intensity that Finn had moments ago. "I'm right here," I said against his lips as he breathed me in.

"I know," he said but sighed and let his hands slide into my hair and pull it free of the clip holding it on top of my head. He kissed me again and I instantly regretted my decision to go home because I didn't want to leave them when they were struggling with this as much as they were.

"I don't want you guys to get upset but there's something I have to tell you," I said and grabbed Finn's hand and pulled him over to sit on my chair, crawling into his lap in between them.

"What is it?" Walker asked, concern pulling his brows together in the center.

"I'm not running," I started and made sure to look Walker straight in the eye. "But I want to go home for a few days."

"Home?" Finn asked, tightening his hands around my stomach. I looked over my shoulder at him and smiled softly.

"To my mom. I want to just get away from all of this for a few days."

"That's running," Walker said angrily and stood up. I grabbed his arm, but he shook me off and paced the space.

"I'm not running, honey," I tried. "I'm scared." My voice was hollow and quiet as I said it out loud. Aside from the small bits of information they got here and there about Clay, we didn't talk about him much. I didn't say what I was feeling because I tried desperately to not give him that kind of power over my mind.

"We can protect you," Finn said. "We're going to find him. We installed security cameras at our house today and yours and we brought some for here too. He's not going to get near you."

I shook my head and leaned into Finn's strong, reassuring arms. "I trust you." I looked at Walker from where he stood leaning by the door with a scowl on his face. "I trust both of you with my life. But that doesn't mean that I'm still not scared and still don't want to take a break from it for a few days. Besides, I haven't seen my mom in months and a trip is overdue. It just seems like the right time."

"Then let us go with you," Walker said commandingly.

"To Hollywood?" I asked in disbelief. "You guys would hate it there."

"You would be there so we wouldn't hate it for a second," Finn said, and Walker agreed.

"I plan on leaving tomorrow or as soon as I can get a flight. You two have work and—"

"And months' worth of PTO we never touch," Walker cut in.

I looked at him and could see the seriousness in his eyes, and I turned to look at Finn and his eyes matched. "Let us come with you." He kissed my lips, letting his tongue slide across my bottom lip before sucking it into his mouth. "If you need to go see your mom and get away for a few days to feel better, then we support you. But we need you near us for us to feel better, so let us come with you."

"Okay," I whispered.

"Okay?" Walker asked. I looked over at him and a surprised scowl replaced the angry one that had been there.

Oh, my sweet scowl-loving man.

I kissed Finn quickly and then stood up and walked around the desk to Walker and pulled his head down forcefully until his lips were on mine. He chuckled a quick laugh and then his lips pressed against mine hotly, and his anger melted into passion. "I want you guys to meet my mom and see that part of my life. So why not? Let's go on vacation," I said ridiculously and shrugged my shoulders like it was no big deal.

He slid his arms around my body, grabbed two large handfuls of ass, picked me up, and set me down on the desk across the room.

I wrapped my thighs around his and pulled him closer to me, as close as possible with his duty belt and gear on, and kissed him with everything inside of me.

His hands were everywhere, rubbing my back, cradling my face, and sliding up under my shirt until they palmed my breasts through the lace of my bra.

Finn stood up and leaned over the desk, pulled my hair to the side, and kissed my neck before biting it as he reached around and rubbed me through my jeans.

"Damn." I moaned and leaned into him, giving Walker better access to my tits and Finn to my neck.

Finn bit my ear and then instructed, "I'm going to start putting cameras up. You're going to be a good girl and spread these pretty thighs for Walker and let him fuck you until you milk him dry. Then, I'm going to come in and switch with him and fuck you until our come is soaking your jeans the whole way home."

"Yes." I moaned and reached behind me and turned, pulling his lips to mine for a scorching kiss. A couple of orgasms were exactly what I needed to relieve some stress after the shitty day I'd had.

We'd never fucked in the shop before, though it was tempting, but the opportunity never presented itself until now.

Walker flicked open the button of my jeans and pulled them and my panties down roughly without asking and then started removing his gear as he watched me kiss Finn.

Finn reached around my body and ran his fingers through my wet pussy and then pushed two directly into me. I moaned and picked my feet up and placed them on the desk wide, opening myself to his hands and his twin's stare.

"Go before I make you stay and fuck her with me, brother," Walker demanded, and Finn chuckled and pulled away. He walked around the desk, leaving me spread wide and panting, and I watched in fascination as he brought his fingers to his lips and sucked them into his mouth.

"Mmh." He moaned. "So sweet." He winked at me and then walked from the room and left the door open.

I let my gaze fall on Walker as he stripped out of the last of his clothes and then walked forward until his heavy, thick cock pressed against my pussy before any other part of him was even near me.

He pulled my shirt and bra off and left me naked, leaning back on my elbows, panting.

"You look so damn good. I will never get tired of seeing you open and vulnerable for me like this. It's so erotic every single time you trust me with your body."

"I want you so bad. I'm so wet," I said and slowly slid a hand over my stomach and down to my wet and open pussy. I watched his eyes follow the path my hand took and then light on fire when I pushed two fingers into me quickly, gathering more wetness before rubbing it around on my clit and pinching it.

"I'm going to fuck that pussy so hard," he said as he fisted his cock and stroked it as he watched me play with myself.

"What are you waiting for, big guy?" I asked cheekily and blew him a kiss. "I need to be fucked."

That was all the restraint he had, and I heard Finn laugh from the other room as Walker groaned and slammed forward, grabbing under my knees and forcing me onto my back with my legs up high as he bottomed out inside of me.

"Yes!" I screamed and then covered my mouth with the back of my hand as he started thrusting—long, deep drives into my body.

He pulled my hand away from my mouth and kissed me deeply, bending over my body and rubbing his pubic bone on my clit as he brought me closer and closer to a climax.

"Fuck her hard, Walker," Finn chimed in and I moaned.

"Yeah, baby, fuck me hard," I begged, and he groaned and took both of my wrists in one hand, pinning them above my head. He grabbed both of my legs and pushed them forward and to the side, until I lay almost on one hip, my thighs pressed together and my knees against my chest as Walker drove into me madly.

"Your pussy is so hot; it's branding my cock each time I bottom out. I can feel your womb on the other side of my tip and my cock wants to push deep into it," he said dirtily, and I panted as his words ripped an orgasm from my soul.

I moaned over and over and over again as he continued to thrust harshly into my cervix, giving me a bite of pain but so much pleasure.

All of a sudden, I heard the distinct sound of bells jingling on the front door and froze, my eyes tearing open to look at Walker, who stopped thrusting into me. The door to the office was open but whoever came in stopped at the front desk, where Finn quickly met them so they were unable to see us.

"Hey, what's up?" Finn asked, sounding breathless but calm.

"I saw you guys come in a bit ago and figured I'd run over some dinner for you folks. Plus, I wanted to check on Bailey again. I stopped by earlier and she was still really shaken up."

Sweet Thea always had terrible timing. Walker slowly pushed his cock deep into my body again and air left my lungs as he rolled his hips and pressed against my clit. "Stay quiet and I'll keep fucking you. Make a sound and I'll leave you wet and empty," he whispered into my ear and pulled out of me completely and then dove back in.

I bit my lip hard, listening to Finn graciously accept the meal from Thea before he told her that we were busy having a conversation about our plans to go to California and that now wasn't the best time. He assured her that we would stop over for dessert after we got done putting cameras up, and I didn't miss the way he added that we'd add a "sweet dessert" to a meal any day. He was actively trying to spur us on, knowing we were listening and fucking just twenty feet away.

Walker reached under my knees, pinched my nipple roughly, and kissed me to absorb my shriek as he started fucking me harder.

He was close and so was I. His hips were jerking madly, and the veins in his neck and face were bulging with exertion.

I listened as Thea gave Finn instructions on how to help me through the tough times in her overly motherly way, and I was praying in my head for her to leave before Walker forced the next orgasm from my body because I knew it was going to be giant and it would match his, and he'd never come quietly in the hundreds of times he fucked me.

He let go of my wrists and wrapped his hand around my throat and rolled his hips again. I felt the damn break inside of my core and within seconds, I was spasming around his cock.

The bells jingled on the door as a loud roar left his lips and he slammed into me so hard, the desk shook and my lamp fell over and onto the floor as he filled me with his come.

I moaned and whimpered around the restriction on my throat as my pussy milked his cock in tight and long pulses, pulling more and more from his balls.

Finn walked in and slapped his brother on the shoulder and laughed as Walker laid his damp forehead against mine and caught his breath.

"I swear Thea just heard you yell like an ogre as the door shut behind her," Finn said as he started unbuttoning his shirt, staring at us hungrily.

"That's all we need," Walker joked and slowly pulled out of my body. I looked down and spread my legs to watch his thick cock fall from the swollen lips of my pussy and moaned and laid my head back down.

"That was so hot," I mused and stretched.

"You like the excitement of getting caught, sweetheart?" Walker asked and helped me sit up and slide off the desk on shaky legs.

I leaned up and kissed him, sucking on his tongue, raking my nails down his sweaty chest, and pulling a groan from his throat. "Yes, Walker. I do like being naughty from time to time, but only when you or Finn are buried balls deep inside of me like you just were."

He laughed and slid his hand along the side of my face and kissed me. "I think your cervix is permanently dented now," he said and laughed.

"I think you're right," I agreed and then looked over and lost all trace of my next sentence as Finn shoved his pants down and fisted his cock, looking at my naked and flushed body ravenously.

"I think Finn's getting impatient for his turn with your tight, little body, baby. What do you think?" Walker asked leisurely as he let his big hands palm my heavy breasts and pulled on both of my nipples at the same time.

"You can move and let me at her or I can move you. You're running out of time to decide though," Finn said, his voice so serious and needy, and I moaned and licked my lips.

Walker stepped back and pulled his pants and T-shirt back on and then walked out of the room with a pleased smile on his lips.

The fire in Finn's eyes lit me with an insane need to be owned and consumed. And the fresh arousal in my system from being fucked while someone else could hear left me wanting to be brave with him.

"I want to be naughty, Finn," I purred and grabbed his cock in my tiny hand and stroked him from base to tip and back.

He groaned and thrust his cock into my hand deeper as I grabbed his balls and rolled them.

"How?" he asked with his eyes squeezed shut and his nostrils flaring.

"I want you to fuck me out there in my chair."

His eyes opened and a smile pulled at his lips as he thought about it.

"Shut the curtains!" he yelled suddenly and picked me up to throw me over his shoulder.

He walked out into the shop area, both of us completely naked, and a surprised Walker turned where he was perched on a ladder, installing a camera behind a vent cover. "They already are."

"Good." Finn grunted and walked over to my chair and laid a towel on it, and then he sat down and positioned me on his lap. I straddled him and rose until my tits were directly in his face, and he leaned forward and took a bite.

He grabbed his cock and held it up right for me, and I slowly sank down on it. I threw my head back and started riding him. He was pressed forward inside of me at this angle, and he was rubbing on my G-spot with every thrust.

"I feel you rubbing the head of me over your G-spot, baby. You like this position, don't you?" he asked sexily as he put his hands under my ass and started lifting me on and off of him at a sharper angle, forcing more pressure on the bundle of nerves inside of me.

"Oh my god, yes! Holy shit, Finn, you feel so good. Right there—" I gasped as he rocked into me. "Just like that. Please don't stop!" The last syllable dragged on and on as my orgasm took away my ability to think straight.

"Fuck, you're so tightly wrapped around my cock right now. Your sexy little pussy wants all of my come. She's already full from Walker but she wants more." Finn cursed as he fucked me madly through the ecstasy.

"Damn," I heard Walker mutter and looked over my shoulder to see him staring at us in the full-length mirror at the foot of my chair. My entire ass and pussy were on display, and I watched with rapture as Finn's cock slid in and out of me. It was like watching porn, but it was cast with my favorite people in the world.

Finn was wild underneath me; his hands were everywhere, and he was cursing and saying dark and dirty things. I was driving him mad with need and it made me want more.

But Finn was one step ahead of me. "Walker, grab one of those green packets off the shelf," Finn said as his neck and chest started turning red with exertion.

I watched in question as Walker reached up and grabbed one of the small packets Finn had pointed to and looked at it. And then nerves tickled in my belly.

"Anal?" I questioned, looking down at Finn. But there was something different burning in his eye.

"Do you remember the first night you came over for dinner, we asked you if you'd ever taken two cocks at once?"

"Yeah," I nodded, "You asked if I'd been fucked in the ass before."

Walker chuckled from the other side of the room, slowly walking back toward us. "I see where this is going."

"Nah baby," Finn interrupted him, turning my attention back to him. "Two cocks at once." He paused as my mind blanked what he was talking about or how it was different from what I had just said. "In your pussy."

I gasped, letting my lips part as the naughty images of what he was trying to describe started infiltrating my horny brain.

"Double vaginal penetration?" I whispered, like the phrase was so taboo I couldn't speak it out loud.

Finn winked and spanked my ass. "Now you're with me."

I moaned and nodded my head quickly as Walker hummed and walked up to us.

"You want this?" Walker asked, but he was already ripping the packet open and rubbing a drop of it between his fingers.

It was coconut oil that I used in hair masks from time to time. Each packet had about a tablespoon in it, and he rubbed the silky cream between his fingers and gripped his cock in his hand through his work pants.

He was hard just thinking about it.

"Fuck yes." I moaned and kissed Finn wildly. "But do you honestly think it will work?"

"Good girl gone bad," Walker mused and chuckled as he dropped his pants once again and ran his hand up my spine. "Let us take care of you." The chair was the perfect height for him to line himself up as I was bent over Finn's lap. I watched over my shoulder as he rubbed the oil over his entire cock and then down my crack until it coated my entire pussy. The entire time, Finn had been sucking on my tits and slowly thrusting his cock in and out of me leisurely, swirling need so deep inside of me that I was becoming feral.

"Hold still, Bailey," Walker instructed, but I was frantic for another orgasm. Finn was pushing on the nerves inside of me so deliciously that I was desperate to come again. "Bailey," Walker said and grabbed my hips, stilling me.

"Fucking put your cock in me quickly or let go. I need to fuck," I bit out over my shoulder and squinted at him in frustration.

Finn dropped his head back on the headrest and cursed as his hands gripped my hips painfully, trying to keep himself still as well. He pulled out until just the head of his cock was inside of me as Walker pushed against the two of us. There was a sense of being full and I was afraid he wasn't going to be able to physically push his way inside of me.

And then the head of his cock won against the tight muscles of my pussy, and he slid in with just the tip.

I moaned and laid my forehead on Finn's shoulder and pushed back toward Walker, and he happily started filling me up.

He and Finn both cursed and moaned as he slid his cock inside of me and against Finn's. A cold chill broke out across my skin and I shivered in their arms as a crazed need broke free from my core. I was unable to take a deep breath from the overwhelming sense of being filled, but I was so horny and frenzied that I started begging before lifting myself up and dropping back down on both of their cocks madly.

"Holy fucking shit, Bail," Walker cursed as I started fucking them both. I looked in the mirror and watched as he bent his knees to give me full reach of him and held still as I rode both brothers at the same time.

Finn was watching me intently, seeing the crazed need on my face, and his own eyes matched mine as a wicked thought crossed his lips. "We're going to make you squirt. You're going to come so fucking hard on both of our cocks that you're going to soak us. This is your only warning."

I gasped and rolled my hips with both of them buried balls deep in my pussy and felt them press on that same area that Walker had the last time I did it. He reached between our bodies and pressed on the skin of my stomach below my belly button and nodded to Walker who grabbed my hips, halting my movement, and they picked up their own. They were thrusting into me in sync as Finn rubbed my clit and stomach, and I felt the pressure building inside of me.

"That's it, baby. You want to, don't you? You want to let go and let us make you explode so fucking bad, don't you?" Finn ground out through clenched teeth.

Walker leaned forward and I felt his teeth bury themselves into the flesh of my shoulder, and that was the ignition I needed. "You're our dirty little slut."

So many sensations and feelings short-circuited at the same time. I felt the hot liquid pour from my body around their cocks and the electric shock of it to my clit. My orgasm blew my body into bits as I rode wave after wave of ecstasy. They both grunted and cursed and said dirty, naughty things as they shot off and filled my body simultaneously.

I had a death grip on Finn's shoulders and felt the blood pooling under my nails as I came back to earth only to be catapulted into another orgasm when Walker pulled my hair and Finn attacked my tits with his mouth and teeth.

They both continued to thrust into my body as I rode this second orgasm until I was limp and gasping in their arms.

They came simultaneously, filling me in ways I'd never imagined possible before, roaring their release into the silent shop around us.

When they slowly started withdrawing from my body, I protested the feeling of emptiness they left in their wake.

Finn stood up and set me down in the large chair as Walker covered me with a large towel and I curled up into it and felt my eyes close happily as they got dressed and brought me my clothes.

They showed such gentleness as they helped me dress and then cleaned up the chair from our mess, making it sanitary for customers, though I may never look at it again and not blush when I remembered how my guys had fucked me in it.

It was getting late, and the guys finished installing the cameras and setting them up while I booked three tickets for a flight tomorrow first thing, and then we left the shop.

Walker ran across the street to tell Thea that we were headed home because we were leaving tomorrow for California, and she told him that she would keep an eye on the shop while we were gone. He sheepishly came back out with a couple more to-go boxes of pie to add to the dinner already loaded in the back of Finn's truck.

By the time we got to their house, with my packed suitcases, and ate our dinner and dessert, I was thoroughly exhausted, so my guys carried me to bed and held me while I fell asleep in their arms.

They knew exactly what I needed at the moment because we were all so in sync and in love, and it was such an incredible feeling to drift off to sleep feeling so cared for.

Chapter 23 – Finn

Molly Dunn was everything I had expected her to be and so much more. She had picked us up at the airport with cat-eye sunglasses and a silk scarf wrapped around her lush blonde curls that were a bit milder than Bailey's but an obvious family trait.

Watching the way she held onto her daughter in the baggage claim area made me feel bad for keeping Bailey in Montana as long as we had without having her mom up or visiting her. It was obvious that her mom had been missing her, and she had missed her mom just as much.

Walker and I picked up a truck at the car rental spot at the airport, but Bailey wasn't free to leave her mom's embrace for a while, so we decided to let her go with her mom to her place, we went to the hotel to check in, and then met back at Molly's for dinner.

It was stupid, but it was a little over four hours from the time Bailey walked away in her mom's arms until we pulled up outside Molly's small little bungalow and my skin ached to feel Bailey's again. I noticed before we even left the hotel that Walker was keyed up and antsy too.

"Why are we so worked up?" I asked as I put the truck in park outside Molly's.

He sighed and cracked his neck. "You too, huh?"

"I don't get it. We go 24 hours sometimes without seeing her and are fine, but now all of a sudden, it's a couple of hours and we're aching for her like a drug we've craved for years."

"I think it's the Clay shit," he said and looked over at me. "At least for me it is. It's got her rattled, which has me rattled."

"Yeah, I agree." I pocketed the keys and looked at the big picture window of the house and saw Bailey move the curtain aside to look out at us. "We have to find him. She won't feel safe until we do."

"I know. Jake texted me a bit ago and said they had a new lead on a girl's place out in Swanson that they're going to work with the troopers to check into, but I haven't heard from him since."

Bailey opened the front door and stepped out onto the sidewalk and walked toward the truck, looking at us inquisitively. "I'm going to call in the morning and put a request in to go part-time and work opposite of you, so one of us is near her all the time until this can be settled."

He nodded his head as he thought on it for a second. "That's a great idea. I'll do the same. She'll hate our 24/7 presence though."

"Maybe not. She agreed to us coming here without much push," I said and opened the truck door as she scowled at us from the sidewalk. "Don't you know your face could freeze like that, little girl?" I asked and walked around the truck to where she was standing by Walker's door.

She had her hand over her eyes, shielding the sunlight, and pursed her lips at me. "Why are you two just sitting in the truck, talking?"

Walker leaned down to kiss her, but she moved her face at the last second so he only got her cheek.

"Don't ignore my question." She huffed, dropping her hand from her eyes and putting her finger in his chest.

She should have known better. Maybe she hadn't sensed our uptightness yet, but she was about to. Walker grabbed her arm and spun her around until she was pressed against the inside of the passenger door. I opened the back door quickly, creating full coverage against anyone trying to look from the road or the houses, and rested my forearm on the frame of the door over her head as Walker leaned in close.

"You have a problem with my kisses?" he asked, fire igniting in his eyes.

"I asked you a question and you tried to ignore it with a kiss. That's what I have a problem with," she bit back.

"Wrong," I answered, and she looked at me quickly before Walker slid his fingers under her bottom jaw and turned her back to him.

"You asked me a question and I tried to kiss you before I answered it. There's a big difference there."

"So answer it then. What were you two talking about?" she tried again, straightening her spine to stand taller. I admired her for trying, but we were way too needy right now to give her even an inch of leeway.

"Kiss me and then I will," Walker challenged. She didn't respond immediately, which was mistake number two in the last minute.

I tsked my tongue at her and looked around, making sure no one was watching our exchange.

Walker leaned back, letting go of her completely, and stepped away, creating space between their bodies. "Fine," he said, reaching inside the truck and grabbing the bottle of wine we had bought and the bouquet we'd picked up for her mom and handing them to her.

"What are you doing?" Bailey asked, but neither of us answered. Walker shooed her out from between the doors and onto the sidewalk and then climbed back into the truck and shut the door.

Her jaw dropped and she looked at me frantically before juggling the wine and flowers and grabbing for the handle.

"Walker," she started, but he locked the door and full out ignored her. She looked at me again and I hated being in the center of it.

"Ignoring our need to touch you, to reassure ourselves that you are alright, is the worst thing you can do to our relationship right now, Bailey," I said and put my hand on my hip. I was stuck between a beauty and a beast at this moment and didn't have a clue which direction to push against.

"I didn't mean to do that, Finn! I just didn't want you two to distract me with your kisses and touches like you usually do. You try to shelter me and keep things from me, and it's frustrating," she said exasperatedly.

"We try to protect you, Bailey!" I said, raising my voice and shocking her. "It's not sheltering or keeping things from you; we're trying to balance the weight of the world on our shoulders to keep yours tall and upright! There's a difference there. And with everything going on, we're fucking—" I paused and took a deep breath as her face started to crumble. "We're struggling."

She tossed down the flowers and wine into the grass and buried her face in my chest, and I easily wrapped my arms around her tiny shoulders as they shook. Walker watched out the window with a gloomy look in his eyes and opened the door, turning in his seat to put his feet on the running board.

I held her while she cried and tried to soothe her as much as I could. "I didn't mean to yell at you," I said.

"I deserve it," she replied, keeping her face in my chest.

"No, you don't. We're all just on edge. I think we all thought coming here would help with that, but it doesn't make it stop." I kissed her forehead and she pulled back and stood on her tiptoes and offered her lips to me.

I leaned down and sealed mine over hers, letting the warmth of her giant heart warm mine through her kiss. She deepened it, angling her head and sucking on my tongue as she moaned into my mouth, and I groaned.

I pushed her until her back was between Walker's knees on the passenger seat and crowded my body tight against hers. Walker gathered her hair, pushed it to one side, and leaned down to kiss her neck while I continued to ravish her mouth. She slid her hand up and around the back of Walker's head, holding him close as she demanded even more from my body by grabbing my T-shirt and pulling me tighter to her.

"I need you both so bad, my body aches with it." She panted when I let her mouth go and turned her so Walker could take what he wanted from her. She turned to face him, and he kissed her deeply like I had while I pressed my growing cock into her ass and pushed her hips into his.

"You can't say things like that when we're standing on the street outside of your mom's place. You should have come to the hotel with us if you needed to be spread open and fucked," I growled into her ear.

"Fuck!" She gasped and pulled back to rest her forehead on Walker's chest while she caught her breath. He reached down between their bodies and slid his hand under the hem of her dress—I was guessing into her panties because her body trembled and she put one foot up onto the running board to give him better access.

"I'm going to make your pussy come right here on the fucking side of the street to hold you over, Bailey. And then you're going to be a good girl and be patient until we can go back to the hotel. Got it?" he demanded.

"Yes, Sir," she purred and arched her back. I looked around us once again, watching to make sure no one was getting an eyeful of something they didn't deserve, and then turned my attention back to the task at hand. The truck was tall enough that all of Bailey's good parts were hidden by the doors and my body. Walker and I knew her inside and out, so it didn't take long until wet, sexy sounds were coming from her pussy to match the begging pleas falling from her mouth.

I slid my hand under the back of her dress and felt the bare, silky skin of her ass cheeks, and I pressed my fingers between them, down to her wetness and then back up to the puckered entrance of her ass. I slid my wet fingers over the sensitive skin and rubbed in lazy circles, just barely breaching the tight ring of muscles as Walker started fingering her pussy with vigor.

"How do you two do this to me so well?" She pondered as her head fell back to my shoulder and she held onto the handle on the doorframe. She turned her head and kissed my neck as I rubbed her and then bit me as she started orgasming around Walker's fingers.

"Good girl. Come on his fingers like you do on his cock," I ground out into her ear when she released my neck. I knew she left a mark I'd wear in front of her mother, but I didn't care. My girl wanted to play rough, and she would get just that tonight when we had privacy.

When she came down, Walker and I put her dress back in place and helped her settle.

"I'm sorry," she said to Walker and kissed him gently. He put his hands on her face and held her where he wanted as he kissed her back.

"So am I," he replied. "Are you going to be okay for the rest of the afternoon?" he asked with a smirk on his face.

She laughed and blushed as she turned to look at me. "Only if you two promise to be naughty with me later."

"Fuck me running," I cursed and adjusted myself before stepping back and picking up the discarded wine and flowers off the ground.

When we walked in the front door, Molly leaned out of the kitchen with an all-knowing grin and chided us in a sing-song voice, "Hope the neighbors weren't looking."

"Mom!" Bailey gasped and turned twenty-five shades of red from her ears to her toes.

Her mom just chuckled and tossed the dish towel she had been drying her hands on over her shoulder and then winked at us. "If I was your age again, I would have lay in the middle of the grass and put on a show."

"Oh my god, stop," Bailey implored her, but Walker and I laughed. "You are such a hippie, Mom."

She dragged us out back to the patio, and we laughed it off and enjoyed getting to know Molly as the evening went on. She fed us a delicious home-cooked meal of pasta and salad and dessert, and I thoroughly enjoyed watching Bailey be doted on by her mom.

I sat back and looked at Bailey and was struck with an overwhelming sense of pride inside my heart. That girl was ours.

We didn't deserve her, and god knew we hadn't given her any reason to think we did, but she wanted us and gave us a chance when we asked for one and, in turn, fell in love with us.

She had a wine glass in her hand, pressed to her bottom lip where it kept freezing when she'd stop to laugh or rebuke some story that Molly was telling about her childhood. She looked so happy and carefree, and my heart ached to have her in my arms.

Molly was telling Walker about a time that Bailey had snuck out of the house and into Molly's VW bus when she was ten, and Molly and Bailey's dad, Jed, had found her in there an hour later with all kinds of hippie paraphernalia pulled out of all the hiding spots. It was a turning point in her childhood when they stopped parenting her with kid gloves and started treating her as an equal. Bailey had her head tipped back, laughing with tears in her eyes at how scandalized she had been by everything.

She looked over at me and stopped laughing, letting Molly and Walker carry on the conversation, and just looked at me with an intense gleam in her eyes. She stood up and walked around the table, I pushed my chair back to make room for her, and she sat on my lap and wrapped her arms around my neck.

"Hi," she whispered, ignoring the pause in conversation around her. I ignored it as well and wrapped my arms around her waist and held her close.

"Hi, yourself," I replied.

"You alright?" she asked and ran her fingers over the wrinkles on my forehead I hadn't realized were there. "You're scowling like Walker does," she said and looked over at him from under her lashes, and he stuck his tongue out at her insult, causing Molly to laugh out loud and then excuse herself.

"I'm better now," I said and leaned into the crook of her neck and inhaled her heavenly scent. "I love you, Bailey."

She took a large, deep breath and laid her cheek on my forehead and held onto me while I clung to her. "I love you too, Finley." She had taken to using my full first name when expressing deep emotions, and while I hated my full name from anyone else, it falling from her lips was an entirely different experience.

She used her bare toe to poke Walker's arm a few feet away and when he looked over at her, she blew him a kiss. "I love you, Walker."

"I love you back even more, Bailey," he said and took her tiny sole in his hands and started rubbing it, pulling a soft moan from her lips that made my cock harden instantly.

Molly came back outside and saw our moment, and she quickly snuffed out the candle in the center of the table and then picked up our wine glasses. "Well, kids, I think that's all the energy I have left in me to entertain you three. So get out of here." She shooed us and winked as she walked back inside.

"Did you two just get me kicked out of my childhood home?" Bailey asked in mock horror.

"I think you did that all on your own when you rode my fingers on the sidewalk, little girl," Walker chided and pulled her foot to his lips, kissed the inner arch, and then gently set it on the ground before standing up and grabbing the last of the plates from the table and following Molly inside.

"I won't lie, I'm not all that mad to have you to ourselves finally," I said and stood up, letting her lush body slide down mine until she stood with her nose pressed into the bottom of my sternum as she hugged me.

"Don't tell my mom," she whispered, "but neither am I." She chuckled and then slid from my arms.

It took all of ten minutes to clean up and say goodbye before we were jumping in the rental and headed off toward the hotel.

The rental didn't have a bench seat up front, and I offered the front seat to her, but she politely declined with a look of mischief in her eye and climbed into the back seat.

Walker got in the driver's seat, and we drove up the dark streets toward the hotel. A block or two down, he looked in the rearview mirror, choked on his breath, and turned around to look in the back seat. I followed his glance and turned in my own seat and found Bailey with her feet propped up on the backs of both of our seats, playing with her pretty pink, soaking wet pussy with a look of pure unadulterated trouble in her eyes.

"Jesus fuck," I cursed and turned in my seat more, smacking Walker's head around to face forward.

"No fair," he protested but adjusted the rearview mirror to watch the show she was so nicely putting on for us.

"I can't help it. I'm so horny," she whined as her dainty little fingers with their white-tip painted nails rubbed her clit ferociously. I watched with rapture as she played with herself, and she kept her eyes locked on mine and Walker's as she did.

"Let me see your tits," I demanded, and she gasped but quickly unbuttoned the front of her dress and pulled it open, revealing her lush bare tits underneath. "Good girl."

We stopped at a red light and another truck pulled up alongside us. Our windows were tinted, and I knew even if the other driver could see in, they would only be able to see shadows or silhouettes, but it was enough to drive her on madly.

"I need help, Finn," she begged and played with one nipple while she kept rubbing her clit.

"Name it, pretty girl," I said easily.

"I need your fingers inside of me, pretty please." She spread her legs wider and her flesh beckoned me, and I was unable to resist. I reached back and slid two fingers through her wetness, coating my fingers in it, and then pushed them into her tight pussy and started scissoring them and thrusting into her as she gasped and moaned.

"You're such a good girl, asking so nicely to be fucked like that," Walker praised as he gripped his cock.

"Very good girl. I think we'll reward you tonight," I added.

"Oh yeah? How?" she asked as she softly panted as I curled my fingers forward and pressed on her G-spot.

"Hmm. Maybe we'll let you be in charge," Walker surmised.

She chuckled sinfully. "I kind of thought I was already doing that right now."

I used my other hand and slapped her inner thigh quickly and was rewarded with a gasp and the tightening of her pussy on my fingers and a very devilish grin. "She's going to get herself in trouble tonight, Walk. Just wait and see, I'm calling it now." I chuckled and pulled my fingers from her pussy and licked them clean as we pulled up to the hotel parking garage. "Close your legs before someone sees something that isn't theirs to see," I commanded, and she reluctantly obeyed and then buttoned up her dress until her nipples were put away, but not an inch farther.

"You're going to be the death of us." Walker groaned, parking the truck and turning to see her sitting pretty with a flush on her cheeks and the tops of her tits popping out of her dress. "We're going to have to beat men off you on our way to our room."

She giggled and pinched her hard nipples. "I mean, if you're into beating men off, you can do that if you'd like. I'd prefer if you'd fuck me instead, but I guess different strokes for different folks," she said sarcastically. I lunged for her to make her pay for her cheekiness, but for once, she was quicker than I was. She flew out of the truck and bounced on her feet outside my door, and I was left speechless and smiling. She was in a mood alright.

We got out and walked into the hotel with her in between us, and luckily, we made it to our hotel room without any further issues.

As soon as the door was shut, Walker had her arms pinned behind her back and pushed her farther into the room. I locked the door and put the do not disturb sign on the handle and then stripped out of my shoes and shirt as I walked toward them.

With her arms pinned at the small of her back, her tits were pushed out, straining against the fabric of her dress. "Here, let me help you with that," I said, feigning sweetness as I slid both of my big hands into the neck of her dress and ripped it open in one swift pull. Buttons pinged the floor and walls around us as she stood there in the ripped tatters of the dress and nothing else.

She was panting and her eyes were on fire as I leaned in and kissed her neck and then down her chest to each nipple. I sucked on them as Walker held her tight and then pulled back, leaving her frustrated and pleading for release.

I winked at her and walked over to the duffle bag I'd packed my things in and reached in, finding what I'd been looking for, and pulled it out.

I clicked the button and it buzzed to life as I slowly pressed it to the end of one pert nipple.

The hot pink rabbit vibrator that Bailey had owned before us stimulated her nipple aggressively as she panted even deeper. "Oh my god, you didn't." She smirked and then let her eyes roll in the back of her head as I switched to her other nipple.

I nodded toward the bed and Walker leaned her over the mattress until her tits were pressed to the bed and her ass was in the air. "Spread your legs, darling," he told her.

She did so perfectly, arching her back and pointing her toes so her pussy was opened to our hungry gaze.

I slid the pink toy down her spine to her soaked pussy, running it up and down her lips to coat it with her wetness.

"That feels so good." She pulled her head up to look over her shoulder at us.

Walker stripped down to nothing and then stood next to the side of the bed where her face was turned and guided her pretty pink lips to the tip of his cock. "Kiss me," he commanded. She licked her lips and then pressed chaste, quick kisses to the head of his cock and then swirled her tongue around him, pulling a groan from his lips.

I rewarded her for her sweetness by pushing the rabbit into her pussy and pressing the wild ears to her clit and holding it there.

She moaned and threw her hips back as Walker tangled her hair around his fingers and pumped his hips, filling her mouth with his cock as I filled her pussy with the pink one.

I pulled it out and started fucking her with it while she enthusiastically bobbed her head up and down on Walker's cock, deep-throating him each time. His abs were tense as he pushed himself closer to orgasm with her mouth and she could tell.

She shifted her weight and freed one arm, bringing her hand up to cup his balls and play with his taint as he started ferociously pumping into her.

"God yes!" He groaned. "You do that so fucking well, baby."

"Good girl," I added and leaned down to trail kisses across her voluptuous cheeks until my tongue landed against her back entrance and I pushed into her with it.

It opened easily to my tongue, and I buried it inside of her as I fucked her with the rabbit.

"Fuck, I'm going to come deep down your throat. Be a good girl and take it all, every drop," Walker sweet-talked her as his hips jerked and then he stilled, and I knew he was blowing his load deep into her throat and belly.

She tightened around my tongue and the vibrator and started shaking as her orgasm tortured her and I drew it out, letting it roll over her for as long as possible. She pulled off of Walker's cock and then let her head hang to the bed as she came back to earth.

I kissed my way up her spine until I was at her neck. "My turn," I growled into her ear and pulled back and took my clothes off.

She rolled over and lay on her back, scooching until her head hung off the edge of the mattress, letting her soft silky thighs fall open, and showing us her swollen pussy lips. "Fuck my mouth, Finley Grant. I need to taste your come."

Walker chuckled and held his hand out for the toy and then lay on the bed between her thighs. He dove in and sucked on her clit as I fisted my cock and leaned down to feed it into her waiting mouth.

Her lips were puffy and swollen, and they looked so fucking sexy wrapped around my rock-hard cock as it disappeared into her.

"You're so sexy, Bailey. Everything about you makes my cock hard and my balls ache to fill you up."

"Mmh, yes please, baby," she purred and pushed her head back farther to suck on my sack and lick my taint as her hands worked my cock. "I love how manly you taste." Her words were sexy matched with her tongue and teeth nipping at the sensitive skin behind my balls.

I reached forward and grabbed both of her breasts and tormented them as she took me back into her mouth. I used her tits for leverage and started forcedly fucking her mouth, pushing her body into Walker's mouth in rhythm with mine. We were like a well-oiled machine, and all of us were panting and moaning as she pushed me closer to orgasm.

"Come for me, baby," she demanded. "I want to feel your come slide down my throat into my stomach while I come on Walker's face."

"I like that idea," Walker quipped and pushed her thighs up toward her stomach. I grabbed hold of them and the force pulled her ass off the bed and up into Walker's face.

He took the toy from her pussy and spit on it, and I watched as he slowly pushed it into her ass. It was so sexy watching it get swallowed up by the tight ring of muscles at her entrance. She moaned around my cock as he got it in and then started fucking her with it.

"That's so hot," I mused and thrust harder in time with Walker.

She shot off like a rocket, screaming around my cock as her legs locked up and her pussy spasmed as Walker sucked her clit and fucked her ass.

It was so beautiful to watch her orgasm because she did so with her entire body.

It was all the imagery I needed, and I felt the burn in my balls seconds before the first shot of come exploded down her throat followed by a dozen more.

She licked me clean, showing attention to every inch of my cock and balls as I pulled out of her mouth and relaxed from my orgasm.

I collapsed on the bed next to her as Walker crawled up her body and kissed her passionately. I watched as he slid his cock through her wet folds and humped her tiny body with his large one.

"I need your cock deep inside of me, baby," she begged as she tilted her hips and pressed the head of his cock into her entrance. "Please give it to me."

"Ride my cock, take what you want then," he said, so she straddled his hips and worked his thick cock deep inside of her tight pussy. I knew how good it felt to bury myself inside of her from the hundreds of times I'd done it in the last few months, and my cock hardened just watching.

She threw her head back and played with her giant tits as she started bouncing on his cock, switching to grinding back and forth on it, doing everything she loved.

It was such a sight to see. I sat up on my knees and sucked her nipple into my mouth and bit it hard.

"Finley!" she screamed and orgasmed instantly. Walker picked up the pace as she faltered and fucked her hard from beneath, using his iron grip on her hips for leverage.

He reached around her and slapped her ass, and she groaned as her skin pinked and he did it again. The sounds of his hand slapping her skin and her wet pussy taking his cock got me so fucking hard. I wanted to fuck her so bad, but I couldn't force myself to remove my lips from her nipples. Her skin was too delicious.

Walker fucked her like a boss for so long, with help from my mouth and hands, she orgasmed over and over again until she was nearly limp. When he roared his orgasm and pumped her full of his come, I swore three rooms down could hear the two of them and it made me crazy with need.

His cock was barely done spasming when I grabbed her waist and pulled her off of him.

"My turn." I walked over to the chair in the corner and set her on her knees on the seat of it. She laid her head against the headrest and arched her back for me. "Good girl, you're such a good fucking girl," I praised as I lined up my cock against her wet pussy and plunged in.

"Oh my god." She groaned and spread her legs wider for me to have better depth access.

I slapped her ass and fisted her hair, pulling her back onto my cock with each thrust. I was being rough and unforgiving, and she was being a champ and taking it and giving it right back.

"Fuck, I love you!" I groaned as I watched her ass ripple each time my hips hit it.

"I love you so much more, Finn." She moaned and reached under her body to play with her clit.

Walker knelt next to the chair and replaced her hand with his and started rubbing her clit violently and sucking on her nipples as I fucked her into the chair.

It didn't take long for both of us to reach our orgasm, and I loved how her back tensed as she fell over the edge, milking my cock and dragging my release out of me and into her.

I pumped wildly forever, filling her body with every single drop of come I had in me and then pulling out quickly. She protested the abrupt withdrawal, but I dropped to my knees and spread her cheeks wide and kissed them each. "Push it out, Bailey. Let me see our come on your lips."

"God, you're so dirty," she said, but I watched as she started baring down, and the milky white semen we had filled her with started dripping from her body.

"Shit, that's so fucking hot. Why is that so fucking hot?" Walker asked as he looked around her ass with me.

"Because it's us marking her as ours. No denying it when a part of us is inside of her."

"Hmm," he hummed and kissed her deeply. She was exhausted; both of us had fucked her hard and without mercy.

"I'm going to go start the shower and then we're all going to crash and go to bed," I said.

"Yes, Sir," she purred and Walker picked her up so we could do just that.

Chapter 24 – Bailey

We spent a few days in the hot sunshine of California, and by time we boarded the plane to go home, my heart was lighter and my body felt heavier from all the muscle strain the guys had put me through in bed. It was as if they thought if they were on vacation, they needed to be inside of me at every turn.

Finn had even followed me into the bathroom at my mom's house one day and fucked me on the counter with her in the other room. I had no doubt she knew exactly what we were doing, no matter how entertaining Walker had been in our absence. But at least she had stopped commenting on it out loud.

Two days into our vacation, Walker got the call from Jake that Clay Mathews had been found and arrested. He had been barricaded in a basement in York at a friend of a friend's place. When they heard he was wanted, they called the cops and ratted him out. From what the guys told me, it was a pretty messy arrest. He'd fought back and made things worse for himself, adding more charges to his indictment.

I'd be lying if I said it wasn't easier to come home knowing that he was finally behind bars, but a part of me knew this wasn't over yet. We still had his trial and sentencing, if he was found guilty, which I was pretty sure he would be.

Knowing that at any point he could be released from jail due to overcrowding or any other long list of technicalities left me on edge.

And now, I potentially had something so precious to protect from the evils in this world, including Clay Mathews.

I stood at the rack in the pharmacy three towns over from Mayfield and stared at the options in front of me.

"What the hell," I muttered and grabbed four different brands and choices and threw them in the little basket on my arm, already filled with chocolate and tampons.

I checked out, avoiding the eyes of the cashier, and then all but ran to my car and got in.

I drove home with the music off and the windows down, trying desperately to calm the erratic beating of my heart as I thought about my future.

I was madly in love with Walker and Finn, and our relationship had been growing stronger and more intense every single day.

But could it weather this?

Would they *both* be happy if the feeling I had deep in my gut was right?

We had been home from my mom's for three weeks and I was somehow over two months late for my period. I hadn't noticed with everything going on until today when I realized I'd been nauseous for the last week straight.

Every single morning, I woke up feeling like dog crap, on the verge of throwing up until well into the day, and by evening, I was barely able to get home and shower before I was crawling into bed and passing out into a sleep so deep, I didn't move until morning, and then it started it all over again.

Luckily for me, Walker and Finn were away on a tactical training class for the department in Utah and had been gone for the last 6 days. They were due to come home tomorrow morning and I couldn't put off taking a test any longer.

I had talked to them every single day and they were getting worried about me, even though I tried to pretend I was fine. Sandra had shown up on my doorstep yesterday with a dish of chicken noodle soup and some chamomile tea and a sympathetic smile.

She had visited for a while, making sure I ate her soup and drank some tea so she could report to her sons that I was alive and well.

I assured her it was just a bug, but I was pretty sure she didn't buy it for a second. She left nonetheless. I'd been such a wreck last night that I'd ignored both Walker and Finn's calls and texted them this morning apologizing, blaming it on the effects of the relaxing tea from their mom. I had to get my head on straight and figure out what I was going to tell them when they got home tomorrow one way or another.

With my IUD, it wasn't odd for me to be irregular or have super short, light periods, but with my added symptoms, I couldn't rule out the possibility that the abundant amount of sex I had with my guys had led to a baby being made.

I laid the boxes of pregnancy tests out on the bathroom counter and opened all four. I took a test out of each box and then peed in a cup and dipped four different test in it and laid them face down on the counter.

My palms were sweating, and my stomach twisted so violently, I ran to the toilet and threw up for the tenth time today.

I was barely recovered and rinsing my mouth out after brushing my teeth when my doorbell rang.

"Shit," I muttered.

I eyed the tests on the counter and then at my phone and saw that it wasn't time to look, and I contemplated ignoring the bell.

A knock sounded next, and it didn't exactly sound gentle. I turned the light off and shut the bathroom door and made my way toward the front door.

I was wearing a nightgown and a robe, and I tightened the sash around my waist.

I knew logically that Clay was still in jail, but I was apprehensive of opening my door after dark while I was home alone, dressed in so little, so I hesitated with my hand on the handle and listened to the other side.

"Who is it?" I asked when I couldn't hear anything.

"Two hungry wolves looking for our next meal. Open the door up or we'll blow your house down!" Finn's caramel voice rang out through the wood and Walker's deep-timbered laugh followed.

I ripped the door open and stared in shock at my two handsome and sturdy men standing on my doorstep, looking downright delectable and 18 hours early.

I jumped into Finn's arms, climbing him like a tree as he laughed and caught me, walking us into my house as Walker followed, shut and locked the door behind him.

Finn set me down on the counter a few feet from the door and kissed me like a starving man, letting his hands tangle in my hair before sliding down my body to cup my aching breasts and pinch my nipples.

I cried out in ecstasy and threw my head back as his lips landed on my neck and sucked. My nipples were so incredibly sensitive to his rough touch and I nearly orgasmed as he played with them through the silk of my robe.

"What are you two doing home?" I asked, breathless, as I looked over at Walker where he watched hungrily, waiting his turn to have his way with me as his brother devoured me. I let my eyes travel down his sexy body and moaned when I saw his hard-on straining against his jeans.

"We were worried about you, so we left a day early," Finn said, pulling his lips from my neck and kissing me again. "And we missed you like fucking crazy."

"I missed you both so much too. I've been miserable the last few days without you." I clung to him and then laughed when Walker pulled him out of my arms and stepped into me, pulling my legs around his waist as he pressed himself to my bare pussy under my gown.

He groaned and pushed my gown and robe up to look at my naked sex. "You look good enough to fucking eat." He growled before leaning down and kissing me so deeply that my toes curled, and my sex clenched on itself, aching to be filled. I scraped my nails through his beard and sucked on his tongue rhythmically.

His hips jerked and I moaned, throwing my head back.

As I tipped my head back, I opened my eyes the slightest bit and caught Finn moving out of the corner of my eye and balked when he walked toward the bathroom door.

"Wait!" I panicked.

Walker snapped his head back from where he had been biting my neck and Finn turned to look at me, surprised.

"I'll be right back, love. I just have to piss," Finn said and winked at me and then turned back toward the bathroom.

"Stop. Just wait," I said again, looking between Walker and Finn as I tried to process what to do.

"Why?" Finn asked.

"What's wrong?" Walker asked at the same time.

"I just—" I started and then pushed Walker back and slid off the counter. "Just give me a second in there first," I tried.

But Walker slid his hand around my arm and stopped me from moving as his scowl dropped over his face. He looked to the closed bathroom door and back to me and fire ignited in the dark of his eyes.

"Is there someone in the bathroom?" he asked. His voice was low and lethal as he held me still under his intense gaze.

"What?" I asked, and then I realized he thought I was hiding a man in the bathroom. "Are you serious?" I bit back, hurt that he thought I was cheating on him.

"You tell us. We come home a day early, you take forever to open the door, and you're dressed in silk with no panties on and won't let Finn into the bathroom that has the door closed. The door is never closed unless someone is in there, Bailey." His voice was rising the more he spoke and so was my panic. "Are you hiding someone in there?" Logically, I knew he was reacting out of fear. And I tried to remind myself that his fear often looked like anger. But fuck, I was so warped over my own emotions I couldn't handle his right now.

"There's no one—" I said, but he ignored me and nodded to Finn, who had a matching dark look on his face as he took the next few steps to the door. "Finn, wait!" I yelled, but he shoved the door open and flicked on the light. His body was tight, like he was preparing for a physical fight.

My heart seized in my chest as I ripped my arm out of Walker's hand as Finn looked around the empty room quickly before his stare froze on a spot on the counter.

I was so angry right now about them thinking I was cheating on them, ruining my chance of looking at the tests in a peaceful manner. I angrily shoved Walker back with my hands flat on his chest and he stepped back, shock on his face at my violent outburst.

So I shoved him again for good measure. "Fuck you!" I said to him and then to Finn when he turned to look at me with so much confusion on his face.

He looked to Walker and held up a pregnancy test box in his hand in question.

His eyes were round and wide, and it took Walker a second longer than it should have to realize what he was holding and what that meant.

He looked down at me and stepped toward me. There was no longer anger on his face but there was fear.

"Don't touch me right now!" I said angrily and then slapped his hands away as he reached for me.

"Are you . . . ? Walker asked in shock, unable to even say the word, and I shoved him again.

"I don't know! I haven't looked at them yet because you guys rang my doorbell before I could!" I shouted and walked past him to Finn, and I could feel the fire in my eyes as I grabbed the handle on the door and slammed it shut like if the door were closed, I could stop this whole thing from happening.

"Baby, I'm so sorry," Finn started, but my eyes burned with unshed tears.

"Go to hell. How could you two seriously think I'd cheat on you?" I asked with so much hurt in my voice. "I'm sitting here, peeing on a half a dozen pregnancy tests alone and terrified!" I screamed. "And you two think I'm fucking around?"

He dropped the box and grabbed me, and I fought him off, but he held on as I tried to get out of his arms.

My fear was bubbling up as anger and hurt right now and I was raw. The tears fell from my lashes as he wrapped his strong arms around me and held me as I started crying.

I fought against him momentarily and then fell into a mess of tears and tremors as my emotions took over. "I'm so scared and I don't even know if I am pregnant or not yet," I said when I calmed down enough to talk.

He kissed the top of my head, and I leaned into his chest, taking a deep breath of his scent and letting it calm me.

"Talk to us, baby," Finn said, sliding his fingers through my hair.

I pulled back, wiping at my face, and leaned against the wall, separating myself from his arms. Walker stood rooted where he had been at the kitchen counter with his scowl still intact.

"My period's late, which isn't abnormal for me, but I'm also nauseous and exhausted and my tits are so fucking sensitive and the longer it went on, the more I couldn't deny those sounded like pregnancy symptoms. So, I forced myself to buy tests today in York so no one would recognize me doing it, and I was going to find out so I knew how to approach it when you got home tomorrow. But then you came a day early."

Finn sighed and ran his hand over his face. "You don't think you should have waited for us to come home to find out? Why do you insist on handling everything on your own, Bailey?"

I felt my eyebrows shoot to my hairline as I looked between the two of them, and I threw my hands out at them wildly. "Uh, I don't know, maybe because since you two found out I even took a test, you both look positively green in the gills. Believe it or not, that actually physically pains me. You two don't understand how it feels to possibly be holding a ticking time bomb inside of me that could destroy us."

"No," Finn said. "We're just shocked, baby. It's not going to destroy us. We're just"—he paused and leaned against the other wall—"processing it all."

"Maybe you should tell that to your brother. He looks like he's ready to bolt out the front door the first chance he gets," I said accusingly as I shot my chin out toward Walker. He looked as though I'd slapped him, marched forward until he was toe to toe with me, wrapped his hand under my jaw, and held me still as he kissed me roughly.

I grabbed onto his arm to steady myself as I lost my balance from the intensity in which he kissed me, and I kissed him back.

I hadn't realized how scared I'd been of him rejecting me in this moment until he did the opposite. I sobbed against his lips, and he absorbed them all and held me.

"Sometimes, it's so hard to understand your emotions and how you react to things," I said as I pulled my lips away, but his grip got tighter around my throat, and he laid his forehead on mine.

"Marry us," he said against my lips and pulled back far enough to look into my eyes.

"What?" I whispered in shock.

"Smooth move, dipshit." Finn chuckled and cleared his throat. "Do I get to be a part of this marriage or is it just between you two?"

I pulled back and looked at him in confusion. "We don't even know what the tests say yet," I said.

Walker looked over at Finn and smiled. "You were thinking the same thing, Finley. I could feel it."

Finn agreed, "I know but still, man, that was a shit ass grand gesture. I know you're not big on hearts and flowers, but you could have at least gotten down on one knee."

"Stop it, you two," I said loudly. "Stop joking about all this!"

"We're not joking, baby. I mean it. Regardless of what those tests say behind that door, we want you to marry us," Finn replied, kissing me while I still stood in Walker's arms. "We talked about it this week at length, and we're ready to take this step with you. And now, with the possibility of you carrying our baby, damn—" He shook his head with a goofy smile on his face. "It makes even more sense now."

He kissed me again and let his knuckles slide down my chest until they ran over a hard nipple under my robe, and I moaned into his mouth.

Walker joked and leaned down to kiss my neck while his brother bit my lips. "You weren't kidding about how sensitive these are." He palmed my aching breasts in his strong hands and rolled my nipples between his fingers, causing my knees to go weak and a moan to rip from my throat.

"Stop it, you two!" I pleaded half-heartedly. "I need to know what the tests say. I'm going crazy here."

"Then say yes to us and we'll all look together," Walker said, and I could hear a note of begging in his voice.

I pulled back, putting a hand on both of their chests and stepping back to look at them. My brows creased as I saw the need in his eyes. "We hardly know each other; we've only been together a little over six months! You're trying to take care of me, and I love you both for that, but—"

"Bullshit!" Finn cursed, surprising both Walker and me. "We talked on our trip about wanting you to move in with us and marrying us. We planned on asking you as soon as we got back. Neither of us care about what amount of time we've been together, and sure, maybe if you didn't have to worry about this right now, you wouldn't be doubting us, but it's what we want." He pushed my hand off his chest and stepped into my space again, pressing my back against the wall and kicking my feet apart so he could put his thigh between mine as he leaned down to be eye level with me. "And to be completely honest with you right now, Bailey, I want that test to be positive."

I sucked in a quick breath at his admission and shook my head. "I don't understand how you're so sure about this so quickly! I'm freaking out and I've had days to think about it!"

Walker leaned against the wall next to me and smiled his dark, brooding smile at me. "You're a natural-born worrier, baby. And we're natural-born protectors and providers. Finn's right, there's a part of me that's hoping that you're carrying our baby right now. And that part is getting bigger with every single second that passes because you call to the animals in both of us as well as the primal need to breed you with our babies."

I groaned and closed my eyes. His words were making me pant with need and my thighs were getting slick. Hearing them both say they wanted this before we even knew helped calm the worst of my fears.

I opened my eyes and looked at each of them, letting my eyes bore into theirs, looking for any hint of a lie, but I didn't see one.

"Are you both sure?" I hated how scared my voice sounded as I asked them to confirm that they wanted me.

"We're sure," Finn said.

I bit my lip, but I couldn't come up with any reason to say no. Instead, I nodded my head and gave them a tentative smile. "Then yes."

Both of them moved on me at the same time. They kissed me and promised me the world as we clung to each other in the hallway of my rental. I wasn't able to wait any longer, though, and I pushed them back and reached for the bathroom door handle.

I walked in and looked at the tests lying facedown on the counter as they walked in behind me and stood at my sides. Walker put his hand on the back of my neck, and Finn held my hand as I flipped over the first test.

Pregnant.

In plain letters across the screen, it said what I already knew.

"Oh my god," I whispered as Finn flipped over the test in front of him and Walker followed suit with the other two.

All of them were positive.

"Fuck yes," Finn said and kissed me deeply. "You're going to be a mom, Bailey. You're going to be the best mama in the entire world."

I groaned and wiped at the tears that fell from my eyes and smiled at him.

Walker pulled my head around and kissed me. "You guys are going to be dads," I whispered and turned into his arms and pulled Finn against my back. Walker dropped his hand to my stomach and splayed it across the soft flesh under my gown.

"I can't wait to watch your belly grow with our baby; god, that makes me fucking crazy with need, just thinking about how beautiful you're going to be with that glow."

"You have to stop; you're making me so hot talking like that," I joked.

Finn turned me in his arms, picked me up, wrapped my legs around his waist, and turned so my back pressed into Walker's chest.

"Please," I begged as both of their lips started teasing me. Walker untied my robe and slid it off my body and pushed the straps of my nightgown down to bare my breasts to Finn's mouth. "Oh my god." I bucked in his arms as he sucked on one nipple while Walker played with the other one.

"I can tell you're pregnant by just looking at your tits. I'm not sure how we missed it before now," Finn said as he licked my nipple and ground his denim-covered cock into my wet pussy.

"How can I be so horny and so scared at the same time?" My voice was shaky, and my breathing was rapid as I clung to them.

Finn carried me into my room and set me on the bed in the center. Walker took his shirt off as he stalked toward me. His abs rippled and tensed under his tattoos as he flexed to tease me.

I panted and my legs spread of their own accord as I arched my back, pressing my breast into the air, offering them up to them in desperation.

Finn took pity on me and tore his shirt off over his head and then shucked off his pants until he was naked and crawling down my body, settling on his stomach with his face only inches from my bare pussy. "God, I love the way you smell," he said, leaning in and kissing my inner thigh. I groaned and grabbed my breasts.

"Fuck me, please, somebody put their cock in me now or I'm going to fucking cry!" I begged and covered my face as tears actually burned the backs of my eyes.

Finn lowered his mouth to my pussy and sucked on my clit, Walker leaned down and sucked on my nipple powerfully, and I spontaneously orgasmed, shooting off of the bed with my back bowed as they held me down and took more from my body.

I screamed as Finn put two fingers into my clenching pussy and fucked me roughly with them. Walker covered my mouth with his hand and bit my ear. "Your screams make my cock so hard, Bail. I'm rock fucking hard for you right now." He moaned as I reached over and slid my nails over the tight denim over his cock.

"Fuck my mouth, Walker." I licked my lips as he cursed, shoving down his pants and as he knelt next to my head. Finn pulled me down on the pillow farther until Walker was poised over my face, and he bent over my head and pushed his cock into my wet and waiting mouth.

I relaxed and took his entire cock as he thrust wildly, cursing madly as he bottomed out over and over.

Finn sat up, kneeling between my legs and pulling my hips wide and up until they rested on his thighs, and he plunged his cock into my body.

I screamed around the head of Walker's cock before he buried it back into my mouth, cutting off the noise, and held it there momentarily as he moaned.

He pulled out of my mouth and wiped his brow with the back of his hand before lifting me to sit up on Finn's lap fully. I started riding him, griding my hips front and back and losing myself to the pleasure of his cock and body on mine.

"I need to come again." I panted and palmed my breasts as Finn smirked at me.

"Your wish is my command, beautiful." He grabbed a fistful of my hair, bent me backwards with my knees still on the bed around his, and slammed into my body. The angle was magnificent for my G-spot, and I saw the intent in his eyes milliseconds before he reached down with the palm of his hand and ground it in small circles on the top of my pubic bone, rubbing the bundle of nerves from inside and outside at the same time.

"Fuck." I groaned and tried to climb up his body. "It's too much."

"No way, baby," Walker said and slid under my back to support me so Finn could angle his hips even more. "Take that cock like a good little girl and give us what we want."

I panted as Finn pressed harder on my pelvis and bolts of electricity started shooting into my clit and spine.

"Good girl. Fucking squirt all over me." Finn's teeth were clenched tight as he fucked me maniacally.

Walker wrapped his big, tattooed hand around my throat and forced my head back and kissed me, pushing me into euphoric bliss as he restricted the blood flow to my brain. I orgasmed involuntarily and then moaned as the hot liquid poured out of my body around Finn's cock.

He roared and cursed and demanded more from me as he bottomed out and exploded inside of me. I could feel his own hot release coat my insides as he poured on and on.

"How do you make that feel so good?" I panted as he slid out of my body and leaned down to lick my stomach and inner thighs. "Mother of—" I cursed and fell back onto my back in the center of the bed and panted as he moaned and feasted on me.

"Should we be gentler with you? Because of the baby?" Walker asked with caution in his eyes.

I shook my head and cupped the side of his face sweetly. "I've had plenty of friends who have been pregnant, and they all said their OB said sex was completely safe the entire pregnancy."

"Promise?" Finn asked, looking a little nervous given he'd just fucked me hard and rough without much thought for the new factor in our lives.

"I promise, baby. I'm okay. In fact, Walker, I demand that you fuck me like that. Don't hold back."

His scowl lightened and turned into an alpha, challenging look as he scooped my body up and flipped me over onto my knees. He grabbed the bottle of lube from my nightstand, and I moaned as I watched him coat his cock with it and then rub his silky fingers over my ass and push two into me quickly.

"Ahh." I sucked in a quick breath at the burn and then moaned and pushed back against him. I'd told him to fuck me hard and he was game to play, and so was I.

He withdrew his fingers and his thick cock started pushing into my ass. When the bulbous head pushed through the ring of muscles, the delicious burn I'd grown to welcome hit and I rolled my hips, sucking more of him inside of me.

He spanked my ass, and I moaned his name and reached up to play with my tits.

"Holy hot damn." I groaned. Finn sat down on the bed next to me and I grabbed his hands and pushed my breasts into them as he chuckled. "Play with them please. I'll do whatever you want for the rest of my life, just play with them right now please," I begged and moaned as Walker bottomed out into my tight ass. "You're so deep in my ass, Walk," I said, looking over my shoulder at him.

"You're feeling naughty tonight, aren't you? You never talk this dirty."

Finn agreed, "It's so fucking hot too." He lay down and sucked my nipple into his mouth like he was trying to actually get milk out of it, and I begged for more before biting my lip and bracing myself as Walker started fucking me roughly.

He reached down under my body, tweaked my clit, and I started coming again, feeling Walker start moving madly, jerking his hips to combat the pull of my ass around his cock. He lost the battle and with a giant roar, he filled me up, coating my ass in his seed.

I was in so much trouble with these two, my fiancés now and the fathers of my unborn child.

Holy fuck.

The guys took one look at me after fucking me ruthlessly and started working in sync around my apartment without any actual words passing between them.

Freaky twin talk.

I lay in bed with my eyes drooping heavily as Walker went into my closet and started packing all of my clothes up and Finn went around the bathroom, gathering all of my toiletries and personal belongings from the living room.

"Care to divulge what you're doing?" I asked.

Finn looked at me and licked his lips, letting his gaze fall to my breasts where they spilled out of the top of my nightgown. "Taking you home for good."

"For good?"

"Yes, you're our fiancée and are carrying our baby. Don't you think we should all live together?"

"Well, yes, when you put it that way, I suppose that makes sense." I smiled at him sweetly. "But can't we do it tomorrow? I'm so tired," I whined.

"You go ahead and sleep. Whatever we can fit in Walker's truck and your car goes tonight. The rest we'll come back for tomorrow or this week."

"Hmm," I mused and relaxed into the pillow. My eyes closed as I listened to the noises they made as they worked around the space, but I must have fallen asleep.

"Honey, wake up." I curled into the pillow more and shook my head, refusing to open my eyes. Walker chuckled where he bent his face to mine. "Wake up so we can go home and then you can sleep till noon tomorrow."

"Hmm. Or I can just sleep here till noon," I contemplated, still not opening my eyes.

"Or I can spank you and take you home with us anyway."

"Now there's an idea." I stretched my arms above my head and felt both of my breasts slip from my nightgown, smiling as he groaned seconds before his tongue flicked one nipple back and forth and his fingers pinched the other one. I moaned and tried pulling him into bed with me, but he popped my nipple out of his mouth and sat back, just out of my reach.

I cracked one eye and looked at him. He was dressed, and I looked around my bedroom and every surface was empty. I could see into the bathroom, and it was empty as well. "Did you guys pack everything?"

"Just about, mostly furniture left, and we can discuss what you want to bring and what we replace. But we can do all that tomorrow. Let's just get you home and in bed."

"I like that idea." I slid my legs from the bed, fixing my gown the best I could, and he picked me up into his arms and held me against his chest. "Hmm. You smell so good." I sighed against his neck as his strong arms carried me out into the cold night and into the front seat of his truck.

Finn walked out after us, locking my door, and came over to me. He leaned in the truck and kissed me sweetly. "See you in a few, baby mama."

I swatted at him, and he laughed wildly and got in my car and started it up as Walker climbed in the front seat of the truck and pulled me over to him.

"I love you," he said softly into my hair as Finn pulled out and he followed.

"I love you."

"I'm really excited to have you and the little peanut with us all the time."

I put my hand on my stomach and could feel the slight pudge under my skin that hadn't been there before. "It's so crazy."

"Are you scared?"

"Terrified," I answered truthfully. "But I know you two are going to make great dads and you seem to love me endlessly, so that part calms the worst of it."

"We do love you endlessly. More than that and then some." He kissed the top of my head and kept his arm wrapped around me. "When do you want to tell our parents?"

"About the wedding or the baby?" I joked.

"About all of it."

"Hmm, how does seven months from now sound?"

"Well, I doubt our mom is going to let us go that long before she drops hints that she thinks you're pregnant, so—"

"What? What do you mean?" I asked, sitting up. "Did she say something to you?"

He laughed and tucked me back into his side. "No. But she has some freaky baby radar and can always tell when someone is pregnant before they tell anyone. I know she came over yesterday to see you, so I have no doubt she's already told our dads that she thinks you're knocked up."

I groaned and buried my face in his chest. "Then, I guess we should tell them soon. Maybe after we get a doctor's appointment and find out for sure how far along I am and when the due date is."

"Okay. And your mom?"

"The same time maybe. She's been wanting to come up to visit, so maybe we double duty it."

"We could always have the wedding then too."

"Oh, geez."

"Do you not want to get married right away?" he asked, playing with the hair at the base of my neck.

"I don't know what I want past sleep and sex at this point in my life. I've seriously never been so horny and tired."

He took his arm off my shoulders and dropped his palm to my stomach again and winked at me. "If that little one is anything like Finn and me, there's two in there and they're probably going to be giving us all a run for our money for the rest of our lives."

I snapped my head back in shock and looked at him with my jaw open. "Don't you dare wish twins on me, Walker John Camden! Do you want me to be bigger than a whale for the rest of my life?"

He laughed hysterically at me as he parked the truck in their driveway, drawing a confused look from Finn. I dramatically refused Walker's help and instead got out of the truck on the passenger side and fell into Finn's waiting arms. "What did I miss?" he asked, kissing my hair.

"Your brother just cursed me with twins! Twins! Of you!" I pointed at him frantically. "You two are giants and you're terribly snarky and he's an asshole most of the time and—" That sent Walker off into a fit of laughter worse than the first time, and I picked up a rock from the ground and threw it at him in frustration. It soared past him three feet wide, but I felt better for trying. "Ugh!" I yelled into the stars and walked up the front steps, stomping my feet like a toddler.

I heard a slap, a grunt, and a warning, but I didn't turn around to watch Finn punch Walker for being a turd, though it would have been nice. I was too manic and needed to go to sleep before I let the joking we'd been doing bubble up into a rage of emotions I couldn't turn off. I could feel them pushing at the lid of my patience and it felt like PMS times a hundred.

I walked in the door, dropped my purse on the entryway bench, walked straight upstairs, and crawled into bed. An idea struck me, and I grabbed the other pillows off the bed and hid them under it and then lay diagonal across the mattress, covered myself up, and fell asleep.

An hour later, the bed dipped behind me, and I was pulled across the sheets to a cold part and I protested, "Brr, now I'm cold."

"I'll warm you up." Walker breathed into my neck and lined his body up behind mine. "But only if you share your pillow."

I couldn't help the grin that crossed my face, though I tried by biting my lips, but it was useless.

"I told you she hid them," Finn added as he crawled in on the other side of me. "Tell me where my pillow is, sweetheart. I didn't say anything mean to you. Or snarky because apparently, I do that a lot too."

"You do, dude. She's right."

"Yeah, well, you're an asshole."

"You're not telling me anything I don't already know, fucker."

They were leaned up on their elbows, talking over me in hushed tones, arguing like it wasn't going to disturb me if they did it that way.

"If you two girls don't stop bickering and warm me up, I'm going to kick you out of bed."

Finn chuckled and leaned down to kiss forehead. "I'm sorry, baby."

"Thank you," I said and bumped my ass backwards into Walker's lap, and then I waited.

A long pause of silence hung with no answer, so I turned and looked over my shoulder. "Hello?"

Walker winked at me. "I'm sorry too. And I'm sorry for making you worry about how many Camden spawns are growing inside of your belly currently."

"Jesus fuck, Walker!" Finn cursed and laughed.

I just shook my head and rolled back over. I looked at Finn and smiled at him, "Your pillows are under the bed."

"Thank you!" he said and jumped out to grab them and then got back in, pulling me close to him and warming me up.

"I'm really not a fan of these Montana winters," I said as Walker rubbed his hands up and down my arms to sooth the goose bumps there.

"We'll keep you warm, darling," he whispered, but I was already falling back to sleep in the safe and warm cocoon of their arms.

The next morning, I started working on getting an OB doctor and an appointment scheduled and was lucky enough to get one in just a few days' time.

I was nervous but so excited to see proof and have a professional confirm that I was pregnant.

Finn and Walker had a few days off once they got home from their training sessions, and we spent those days curled up around the fireplace in our living room and making plans.

Yes, I said it. Our living room.

It had been odd at first to see all of my belongings moved into their home, even if I had spent almost every night there for months. It was different to not have anywhere else to go.

Finn had taken to the idea of being a dad exactly like I thought he would. He embraced it with open arms and did hours and hours of research about baby items and pregnancy cravings and was doting and supportive. He made it feel all too good to be true.

Walker had also taken to it exactly like I expected him too.

He spent ninety percent of his time scowling and looking at me. At first, I'd been worried that he regretted his hasty decision to propose and move me in and to be happy about us expecting. He had quickly squashed that when he'd seen the worry in my eyes.

He, instead, confided in both Finn and me that he was terrified of something bad happening. Walker had such protector tendencies, and something happening to me that he couldn't physically do anything about to help with drove him absolutely nuts.

So, he would just sit there and imagine every worst-case scenario in the world and stress himself out until he was physically unable to keep his hands off of me, and then he would nearly smother me with his need to have me close.

And fuck me.

That part, I was more than happy to deal with, and they were insatiable lately. In fact, over the three days that they were home and off work, I'd basically walked around naked. There was no point in getting dressed when I'd just be ripping any clothing off ten minutes later when I'd offer myself to one of them again and beg them to fuck me.

That was where having two strapping, virile young men in my life had its benefits. But, life had a way of taking all the fun out of things, and we all soon headed back to work.

Today was baby doctor day, and I was so giddy I could hardly contain my excitement as I finished up my last client for the day.

It was only noon, but I was ducking out early, leaving the salon in the capable hands of my new barber Stephanie, and going to find out how far along I actually was.

None of us dared to breathe a word of this pregnancy to anyone outside of our relationship. The way the rumor mill worked in this town, word would get around to his family quicker than a wildfire and we wanted to be the ones to tell them the news.

The bells on the door jingled, and I looked over at Finn as he walked in with a bouquet of lilies and roses in his hand and a huge smile on his face. He didn't work until later tonight, so he wore a pair of light-wash jeans, boots, and a black zip-up jacket paired with red baseball cap. He made my knees weak with how good he looked.

"Be still my heart," Stephanie, my new barber, quipped from her station as she turned to watch him come in.

I smiled like a full-blown freak and all but ran to him and kissed him like I hadn't seen him in days, instead of five hours ago.

"I thought I was meeting you two at home?" I asked when he finally pulled back and gave me back my lips. It seemed he was as hungry as I was today.

"I couldn't wait any longer. We'll take my truck and pick Walker up at the station and go from there."

"Okay." I smiled and ran to the office for my things. He held my hand as we walked down Main Street, toward his truck, and he helped me up, pausing before shutting the door to kiss me deeply. "I love you," I whispered to him.

"I love you so much more, darling. Now, let's get Walk and go see our baby."

"Let's."

When we pulled into the police department parking lot, Walker stood at the back of his truck looking downright delectable. He had changed out of his uniform and wore dark jeans with a white and teal flannel and a black flat-billed baseball cap. I was as desperate for him as I was for Finn.

Walker opened my door and I scooted over toward Finn, and he jumped in, burying his hands into my hair and kissing me deeply, pushing me back into Finn's side as he devoured me.

"I need you." He groaned against my lips and let his hands trail down my body. "But first, how's our baby?" he asked, putting his hand flat on my stomach.

"Baby is mean and made me throw up my oatmeal this morning," I said dramatically and stuck my lower lip out.

He scowled at me, and I saw him switch from sexual to worried in a second flat.

"What was the last thing you ate that you were able to keep down?"

I shooed him off and turned in my seat as Finn chuckled and put the truck in drive, heading toward the hospital for our appointment.

"Your come last night? Or rather yet, Finn's this morning?" I joked and winked at both of them as they laid their hands on my thighs.

"You were a damn good girl, taking it all so nicely too," Finn quipped.

"Hmm." I leaned into Walker's side, trying to calm him down a bit. "I'm fine, baby."

He just grunted at me but kissed my forehead.

The drive was short to the doctor's and when we walked in, both guys took a seat in the crowded waiting room and I checked in.

The receptionist was a young woman I recognized from Thea's diner a few times, but she was incredibly professional while going through my information with me.

When she asked what the father's name was for the visitor passes for my appointments, I froze for a second. She looked past me to where my guys sat and she just smiled warmly at me.

"I can put them both down if you'd like," she said softly.

"That would be great," I replied.

"No problem. Don't worry about anything, okay? Dr. Talbot is incredible, and she's totally open to any kind of relationship with or without titles."

"Thank you so much," I said and took a deep breath and then went to sit down with my guys to wait for our turn.

I tried not to notice the way the other women in the room stared at both Finn and Walker, who, of course, were oblivious to it. They ignored everyone else and, instead, focused on me only. Walker got me a cup of water from the cooler, and Finn handed me a magazine to read while we waited.

I was glad when my name was called after only a few minutes and we all got to leave the small, uncomfortable room.

The nurse took us back to an exam room with an ultrasound machine in it, and I felt butterflies in my stomach as I looked at the different types of tools and machines for baby stuff.

"This is so surreal," I said quietly.

The nurse smiled at me, handed me a paper blanket, and told me to pee in a cup and strip from the waist down and then wait for the doctor.

Walker and Finn sat in matching chairs along the wall, and I almost laughed at the fear in their eyes underneath the excitement. We probably all looked like a group of deer in headlights as we sat there.

There was a knock at the door and then an older woman popped her head in. "All set?" she asked, and I nodded to her.

She wore a blue dress with butterflies all over it under a white lab coat and a pair of medical clogs. She had long gray hair that she had twisted up from her face elegantly and a sweet smile. I knew instantly that I liked her.

She shook my hand and then walked over to both Finn and Walker and shook theirs.

"Well, hello, Mama and Daddies. How are we doing today?" she asked as she stood next to me on the table.

"Nervous," I answered truthfully.

She chuckled and patted my arm. "That's understandable. So, this is your first pregnancy and you don't know exactly how far along you are, correct?"

"Correct."

"And you have an IUD in still?"

"Yes."

"Can that hurt the baby? Or Bailey?" Walker asked, and she looked over at him and smiled.

"There's a potential risk if left in there, so we'll remove it today after the ultrasound."

"Will that hurt her?" Finn asked.

I smiled over at my men and then to the doctor and gave her an apologetic smile. "You'll have to forgive them. Finding out about this baby has turned both of these rough and tough men into nervous nellies."

"That's a very common side effect for new dads, believe it or not. I've found that they feel like they have no control over certain parts of pregnancy, so they try to make up for it mentally. But don't you two worry, I'm going to take great care of your two precious ones here."

They both relaxed into their seats a bit and I could tell they liked her too.

She turned to her computer and pulled up my chart. "Well, good news is, you are in fact pregnant. Very pregnant by the looks of your urine levels, so let's start with an ultrasound and see how far along our little one is, shall we?"

She helped me lie down on the table, and Walker and Finn both came to stand by my side, holding my hands and touching me in some way while the doctor poured gel on my belly and put a small wand on it.

We all watched the big screen at the end of the bed in wonder, as there instantly was a picture of a teeny tiny little baby on the screen.

"Wow," Walker whispered; his hand held mine in a death grip.

Tears burned the back of my eyes as I watched with fascination as the little one moved on the screen.

"Let's listen to the heartbeat," Dr. Talbot said. There was a whooshing sound in the room as she moved the wand around and then the soft steady fast beating of our baby's heart.

Finn leaned down and kissed my forehead and wiped at the tears that slid down to my hair as I looked at up at him. "I love you," I said to him and squeezed Walker's hand quickly before looking back at the screen.

"This little flutter right here," she said, pointing to the screen where something flickered. "Is your babies heart. It's small but you can clearly see it beating."

She printed out some pictures and then went about measuring the baby, explaining along the way what we were looking at, and I fell so deeply in love with the little one inside of me.

Both guys were staring so intently at the screen with looks of wonder on their faces, and I fell in love with them even more in that moment too.

"When was your last period?" Dr. Talbot asked.

"Uh, three months ago."

"Was it heavy or light?"

I was starting to get worried about why she was asking but tried to remain calm. Walker ran his thumb over my hand, soothing me as he picked up on my anxiety. "It was light."

"Okay, nothing to worry about. I'm just reading your numbers here and you're actually pretty far along. Let me finish putting them in and it will tell us how far exactly."

I looked at Finn and Walker and bit my lip while we waited. Walker winked at me, and Finn kissed me softly. "Deep breaths, baby," he said and chuckled when blew out my held breath.Dr. Talbot smiled and chuckled at me. "Okay, you're over fifteen weeks along already."

"Fifteen?" I snapped in shock. "That's like—" my brain fried as I tried to do basic math in my head. "Four months!"

"Holy shit," Walker cursed and then apologized and smiled at the doctor guiltily. She laughed and smiled at him knowingly as she went back to taking more pictures.

"Normally, we don't scan for the sex of the baby until the twenty-week anatomy scan because it can be difficult to see before then, but I could easily tell what this little one is when I was measuring it, if you'd like to know today. Or we can wait and give you time to digest everything if you'd like."

I snapped my eyes to the guys and held my breath. We hadn't really discussed finding out because we thought I was closer to eight weeks pregnant, not fifteen.

Finn answered first. "I know you're dying to know, and I'd love to find out too. What about you, Walk?" he asked, putting his hand on his brother's shoulder.

Walker looked at him and then at me with a huge smile on his face. "I have to know."

I laughed and wiped at more tears as they fell. "Let's find out!" I practically bounced off the table with excitement.

She aimed the wand down by the babies legs and took a still shot and pointed her arrow at the screen. "Congratulations, guys, you're having a beautiful baby girl!"

A girl!

My heart swelled. I instantly imagined a tiny baby wrapped in pink with a bow on her head, cradled in the arms of these giant, beautiful men, and more tears came out.

I looked and saw the awe on both of their faces. Walker's was mixed with fear, and I could only imagine how scared he was to be responsible for a little girl in this world, but I knew without a doubt that he would figure it out along the way.

Finn was shaking his head back and forth as he looked down at me. "A girl," he said in wonder and kissed me. "I hope she looks just like her mama."

I closed my eyes and cried, covering my face as it all sunk in. Finn held me as I calmed down, and I tried to reassure them I was happy, just overwhelmed.

Dr. Talbot got ready to take my IUD out, and I wanted to tell Walker and Finn to sit down so they didn't see anything down there but then thought better of it. They were going to watch the birth of their baby girl someday soon, so this was good practice.

She started the exam, and I did what every woman did at the gyno: I crossed my arms over my chest and took a deep breath as I stared at the ceiling and tried to relax. There was a bit of discomfort when she pulled it out, and I tried not to flinch or gasp but I wasn't successful.

Finn looked worried as he watched, and Walker looked like he was crawling out of his skin from having to just sit by and let someone hurt me.

"I'm okay," I said as she took her gloves off and cleaned up the utensils from the exam.

Neither of them looked like they believed me, but they helped me sit up and I kissed each of them sincerely.

Dr. Talbot took the next half hour to explain everything I needed to know about what to do, what not to do, and what to expect in the next few weeks. We'd come back in a few weeks for an anatomy scan, but other than that, I'd be fine to just live my life with a few more naps involved.

Walker interrogated her extensively about the morning sickness and fatigue I'd been hit with the last two weeks, and she assured him that it should be ending any day now.

I loved how concerned he was, and when we made our way outside and to Finn's truck, none of us could wipe the smiles off our faces.

"We have to tell our parents soon. You're already four months along and that means there's only six left, which is practically no time at all."

"I know. We won't be able to wait for my mom to come up to tell her, so we'll call her and you guys can let me know how you want to tell your parents."

Later that night, Sandra called to invite us all over for dinner the following Friday night and we made plans to tell them then.

Finn joked that there was no denying that she knew now, hence the random invite to dinner.

Only time would tell if she did, in fact, know or not.

Chapter 25 – Walker

I walked into our childhood home, holding Bailey's hand and a pie that Bailey had spent all day making for tonight. Finn also had a pocket full of baby sonogram pictures to show Mom, and none of us could keep a straight face.

Bailey had been so nervous today before we got ready to come over for dinner. She put all sorts of love and care into the pie and her appearance. She'd been so anxious, I had to give her a dozen orgasms between the time we got out of bed and when Finn got home from work at three just to keep her from climbing the walls.

Which, of course, was no hardship on me, but even after my balls had been effectively emptied, she'd still been keyed up. Finn worked this morning and when he walked in the door after his shift, I pointed her in his direction and let him loose.

He'd fucked her in the shower, in the bedroom, on the kitchen counter, and again in the truck on the side of the road on the way here. I may or may not have lent a helping hand with that one and blew another load I didn't think I was even capable of making in the process. There was seriously nothing sexier than Bailey on any given day, but now, with her body changing and glowing from our baby growing inside of her, I couldn't seem to keep my cock or tongue out of her.

She was even worse than Finn and me put together. She had taken to walking around the house half naked altogether, blaming it on her constant state of arousal and the fact that her pants were getting too snug on her belly and none of her shirts fit properly anymore because her tits had grown as well.

And man, I was a sucker for those fucking tits. The fact that they were so damn sensitive was a bonus. I'd laid her out on the kitchen counter this morning and feasted on her luscious breasts and she'd orgasmed twice from just that stimulation alone.

She was so fucking sexy, and Finn and I were desperate for her all the time.

He looked at me over her head as we walked up the front steps and I could see it on his face too. He fucking wanted her again. "We're keeping this dinner short," he said.

Bailey looked up at him and then over at me, and she could see what we were thinking without us having to say anything else.

"You two are terrible," she muttered and bit her lip to hide her smile.

"It's your fault," I said and slid my hand up the back of her thigh and under the hem of her sweaterdress. I pushed my fingers inside of her panties and through her wetness quickly before she swatted my hand away and scolded me. I winked at her and brought my fingers to my mouth for a taste. "Mmh." I groaned and she blushed terribly.

She looked fucking gorgeous. She wore a sage-green sweaterdress that ended right at mid-thigh and black zip-up boots that came up to right above her knee, leaving only a couple of inches of skin showing above them, but I knew every inch of skin under both of them like the back of my hand. Her baby bump was visible to all of us now that we knew to look for it, and it drove me wild with desire.

When Finn and I were near her, there wasn't much time that passed when one of us wasn't resting our hand on her bump or buried deep inside of her.

Her hair was straight and smooth, and it fell to almost her ass, making my hands itch to wrap it around my fist. But I needed to be a good boy, so I stopped messing with her, committed to being on my best behavior considering how important this was and how anxious she was about it.

Mom opened the door when we got to the top of the porch. She hugged us all but held on to Bailey a little longer and then welcomed us in where it was warm.

We headed into the kitchen and found our dads sitting at the island, reading the paper and shooting the shit. They both stood and hugged Bailey and then shook our hands when we walked in.

We had discussed how we wanted to do this and decided to rip the Band-Aid off quickly, especially because Finn and I had gone and picked out a ring for her the day after we asked her to marry us. That rock was hard to miss on her left hand, which was exactly what we had wanted.

She had wanted to leave it off until after we told everyone, but Finn and I forbade her from taking it off at all ever again, so we had to tell them before Mom noticed it.

"It was convenient of you to invite us over tonight because we have some news to share," Finn said, sitting down on a stool and pulling Bailey down onto his lap.

"Oh yeah?" Mom asked, wiping her hands on a towel and looking at all of us excitedly. I noticed how both of our dads shook their heads and smirked at her excitement.

"We asked Bailey to marry us and she said yes," Finn said and held up Bailey's hand to show them all the ring on it.

"Oh my goodness!" Mom shrieked and ran over to hug Bailey again before pulling each of us into her arms as well. "I'm so happy for you three! Oh my gosh! This just is the best news I've ever gotten." She gushed on and on as she wiped away a tear in the corner of her eye. "Have you guys set a date yet or have any idea of when you want to do it?"

"Well, hold on a second, Mom. That can't be the best news ever when you haven't even gotten all the news yet," I said and stared her down as she raised an eyebrow at me and then at Finn.

"What could be better than a wedding?"

I shrugged my shoulders and looked at Bailey, who was beaming at me with Finn nuzzled into her neck to hide his shit-eating grin.

"I don't know, how about the birth of your first grandchild?"

"WHAT?!" she screamed and put her hands on her face in shock. She looked back and forth between us all and then ran around the counter for another round of hugs and congratulations.

Our dads hugged us and congratulated us both and after a minute, I pulled Bailey out of Mom's arms and into mine.

"How far along are you?" Mom asked, wiping at the tears and cuddling into my dad's side as he held her to keep her from bombarding Bailey again.

"Already sixteen weeks, but we just found out last week," Bailey said, and Finn pulled the ultrasound pictures from his pocket and handed them to Mom.

"You'd better get ready, Mama," Finn said, "because this babe is a little girl and she's going to need to be spoiled."

"A girl!" Mom gasped and I thought perhaps she was going to faint from all of the good news at once, but she handled it well. "Oh my god, I can't wait to snuggle a beautiful little girl. Oh my god! Oh my god!" she yelled, jumped around, and turned to our dads. "We're going to be grandparents!"

That was how much of the evening went. Everything would be calm and easygoing and then all of a sudden, Mom would gasp and ooh and ahh over something from the wedding or pregnancy and start on a tangent again.

We stayed for hours, thoroughly enjoying our evening, but I could see the fatigue setting into Bailey's shoulders as it got later.

"Okay, it's time for us to get our girls home for the evening," I said, standing up and taking our dishes to the sink.

"Our girls." Mom swooned and everyone laughed at her, but she followed me to the sink and put her hand on my arm. "Those two girls are exactly what you were born to have in your life, Walker. You're going to protect them from every harm in the world and make them feel so safe and loved. And you make sure you do everything Bailey needs from you these next few months. Pregnancy is not easy on a woman, though we're told to embrace it and love it like we're not allowed to complain about it along the way."

"I hear you loud and clear, Mama," I said, leaning down to kiss her on the cheek and pulling her into a bear hug that I knew she secretly loved, even if she did gripe we were breaking her bones when we did it.

We took Bailey home and put her straight to bed, even though she tried to entice us to join her with her lush, naked body sprawled out between the sheets. We both knew she was exhausted and needed to sleep more than fuck.

It settled a part of my soul to know she was being taken care of, which meant so was our daughter.

Those were my only priorities in life.

Chapter 26 – Bailey

"God yes." I arched my back and spread my thighs wide. The tongue flicking my clit was working hard at pushing me over the edge of my orgasm. I reached up and slid my nails over the tight skin of my breasts, teasing my nipples before pinching them as I started falling over the top of my climax. "Yes!" I groaned and grabbed an entire handful of Finn's hair where his face was buried between my legs. "Fuck yes, Finn!"

He hummed and bit my clit before pumping two fingers into my body.

The cold marble countertop bit into my hips and my shoulder blades underneath me, but it felt great on my flushed skin.

"More, please, I need more," I begged.

"As you wish, darling," he said and stood up, pushing his sweats down and freeing his giant cock.

"Your cock is so sexy," I purred as he fisted it and lined it up with my soaking wet pussy and pounded into me.

"Your pretty pussy is so sexy. And so are your massive tits. And your gorgeous face. And your—"

"Don't you dare say my belly!" I warned, pointing my finger at him angrily before dropping my head back down to the counter and moaning as he circled his hips and rubbed my clit.

"I wouldn't dream of saying something so insensitive in a moment like this," he said with a smile on his face but leaned forward and whispered in my ear as he kept thrusting. "Your stomach, swelling with my baby girl growing in it, is by far the sexiest thing I've ever seen in my entire fucking life. It makes me want to fucking blow load after load of come deep into your body and get you pregnant over and over again."

"Oh god." I bit my lip and started orgasming on his cock. His dirty words pushed me over the edge, and I dug my nails into his back and I held on for dear life as he fucked me into the unforgiving stone.

"Fuck!" he roared and threw his head back as he thrust his hips one last time, impaling me with his long cock.

"That's exactly what that was," I purred and kissed his neck and ear and jaw as he settled.

It was at that moment that our daughter got tired of being squished by her daddy, though, and kicked him hard.

"Oof." He groaned dramatically, like it actually hurt him, and stood up, sliding out of my body, putting two hands on my giant stomach, and leaning down to talk to his daughter. "I'm sorry, baby girl. Blame your mommy for being so desirable."

I grunted and pushed him away and then held my hands out for him to help me sit up. It was ridiculous how hard it was on my own with this beach ball in front of me.

Okay, I was being dramatic. I was only 24 weeks along, but my belly had "popped" a couple of weeks ago and I felt ginormous, though I was measuring perfectly with my doctor.

My guys couldn't seem to get enough of me, even with my carry-on suitcase in front of me.

I slid off the counter and put my arms around Finn's stomach as he held me close in the bright sunshine of our kitchen.

"I love you, Bailey Penelope Dunn, future Bailey Penelope Camden."

"Hmm," I hummed. "I haven't even thought about that yet."

"Changing your name?"

"Yeah."

"Do you want to?"

"Yes, I do." I leaned back and looked up at him. "But I just thought about the fact that I won't have the same last name as our baby at first."

The idea of that broke my heart.

"Hey," he said, lifting my chin to make me look back at him. "The courthouse is just down the road, or we can have a small wedding in a week if you'd prefer. It doesn't matter to us how we do it, baby, you know that. But we do want you as our wife and I agree, I want you to have Camden as your legal name when our girl is born."

"Let's talk to Walker tonight. Let's get married, even if I look like a whale during it."

"We can have a vow renewal after she's born, and you can have every single thing you've ever dreamed about during it, okay?"

"You three are the only things I've ever dreamed of wanting, Finn," I said as I held my stomach and our girl did flips.

"Right back at you, baby," he said, kissing me deeply and then picking me up and carrying me into the living room to cuddle on the couch and watch a movie.

I'd cut back my hours at the shop a bit. I had Stephanie and a new barber, Roger, there with Sammy, my assistant, most afternoons, and Sandra's friend Margo worked most mornings in her place, helping with scheduling and upkeep.

We all worked together like a well-oiled machine, so I felt comfortable switching my schedule to four-day weeks.

Perks of being the boss, Finn always told me.

We lay on the couch and watched movies all day, and hours of cuddling were starting to take their toll on me and my libido.

I got up off the couch and kissed him. "Where are you going?"

He looked so damn good lying on the couch in only a pair of sweatpants and ink and my mouth watered. "Upstairs for a minute. I'll be right back."

"Okay." He eyed me suspiciously but let me go.

I ran upstairs into our bedroom and locked the door behind me. I knew he wasn't going to let me disappear for long before he came to investigate, so I had to work fast.

I slipped out of my lounge pants and sweater and ran to the closet to dig through my clothes to find the outfit I'd hidden from my guys for this exact purpose.

It was a black and lace, sheer and practically see-through, but that was the point. It was deep V cut and tied behind my neck and hugged my body and opened up at the crotch, completely open with lace straps over the ass. I slid on a pair of thigh highs and a garter belt and clipped them to the tops of the stockings.

As soon as I slid it all on my body, I felt sexy. I went into the bathroom and ran some product through my hair, calming the curls and defining them, and then added some dark eye makeup and a bright red lip.

I looked at the clock. Walker was due to get off work in fifteen minutes and I knew he'd be home in twenty if everything went how he wanted. He always tried to end his shift close to home to cut down on the time away. They had lessened their schedules the same time I had, being that we were three adults with full-time incomes so we lived very comfortably. Therefore, working four days a week instead of five or six didn't hurt us financially and helped make it so we could all spend time together like we loved.

I grabbed my phone, walked from the bathroom, set it on the dresser across from the bed, and pressed record as I walked back toward the bed, letting my ankles cross seductively with each step on my toes and then grabbing the post on one corner and running my hands up it seductively as I looked over my shoulder to the camera and blew it a kiss.

I walked back to the end of the bed and knelt on the bench there then crawled up onto the giant comforter, letting my legs spread as I bent at the waist and showed my bare core. I turned around and sat on the edge with my feet on the bench and spread my legs, keeping my toes pointed, and looked at the camera as I leaned my head back and played with my hair, letting my hands slide down my body and to my breasts. I played with them through the lace before pushing it aside and baring my breasts to the air and playing with them for the camera.

I moaned as my fingertips pleasured my sensitive flesh. Then, I lay back on the bed and put my heels up, opening my thighs, letting my hands travel down my body, and then pushing my fingertips through my wet folds.

I moaned again and then pushed two fingers into my body and started pumping them with one hand and rubbing my clit with the other. I knew it wouldn't take long. Cuddling in Finn's arms the last few hours and my little show had gotten me worked up, and before I knew it, I was orgasming on my fingers and moaning loudly as I rode my hand.

After a few seconds of deep breaths after, I stood up and walked to my phone and blew a kiss up close, and then I stopped recording.

I watched the video and liked it, so I opened the group chat between me and my baby daddies and typed out a quick message.

Me: I want to have my pussy and my ass filled with your cocks as soon as you get home, Walk. I'll be on my knees with Finn's cock in my mouth waiting for you, baby.

I pressed send and then put my tits back into the outfit and quickly walked downstairs as quietly as I could.

When I got to the bottom of the stairs, I could hear my moans coming through Finn's phone from where he sat on the couch, watching it with his hand on the hard outline of his cock.

I watched from around the corner as he watched me bring myself to orgasm in our bed and bit my lip to suppress my moan when he pulled his cock out of his pants and started leisurely stroking it as the video cut off.

I walked out into the room and his burning eyes snapped over to me and drank in the sight of me in the outfit.

He threw his phone down on the couch and leaned back, stroking his cock. "You'd better be wet because I'm not going to be gentle."

I licked my lips and walked toward him, sinking to my knees between his thighs.

"I'm soaked, baby, but I'll make sure your cock is nice and wet too, just to be safe."

"Good girl," he purred and ran his fingers through my hair, gathering it into one fist as I started stroking his cock. I loved how my hands didn't even reach around it as I fisted it and leaned forward to lick the bead of precum that leaked from the top.

"Hmm." I moaned and then dropped my mouth over the head of him and took him deep.

"Yes." He hissed.

His phone pinged from next to him and he smirked at me. "Shall we see what big brother Walker has to say about your video, minx?"

I popped my mouth off of his cock. "Yes, please."

He opened it and read it, smiling, and then showed it to me. "He liked."

Walker: I swear to god, if your pussy isn't wet and open for me to bury myself in the second I walk in the door, I'm going to blow in my pants. I'm two minutes out.

Finn: It might be wet with my come but it'll be wet.

Walker: Fuck.

I kept bobbing up and down, taking him all the way to the back of my throat and humming against his sensitive head.

He tossed his phone and scooted down on the couch cushion, giving me better access to his balls, and I smiled around his cock.

I popped off of him again and used my tight fists to stroke him as my tongue pulled one ball into my mouth and I sucked on it before lifting them and licking his taint.

He groaned and pushed my head lower, and I spit and rubbed my lips and tongue all across the nerves under the thin skin there.

He pulled my head off of him altogether and then slid down until he was on the floor with his back against the couch. "Get that fucking ass straight up in the air so Walker has something to aim for."

"Yes, sir," I said and put a pillow under my knees and dropped my head to lick at his balls again. I spread my thighs wide and reached back to play with myself as I added the fingers of my other hand into the mix, and he started rolling his hips and rubbing my lips on his taint and ass. "You're so goddamned good at that, baby. Shit, that feels good."

I pushed my wet fingers against his ass, and he groaned and threw his head back against the couch cushion and jerked his hips, pushing his cock through my hand.

I heard the kitchen door slam and heavy boots practically run across the floor to the stairs. "Where are you guys?" Walker yelled.

"In here," Finn yelled back over another moan. I didn't look over my shoulder, but I knew the instant Walker saw us because the heavy stomp of his boots stopped short and he cursed. I heard metal clanking and leather sliding through hoops as he stripped out of his gear.

"I'd planned on coming home and taking you into the bathtub with candles and making slow, sweet love to you and you send me a filthy fucking video like that, and I come home to you bare and wet for me, Jesus fucking Christ, Bailey. You're going to be the death of me, and I'm going to go to hell with a fucking smile on my face."

I finally pulled out of Finn's lap and looked at him. He was in a white shirt and his work pants before he shoved them down and ripped his shirt off over his head.

I bit my lip as all of the black ink on his arms and chest was revealed to my hungry eyes. "Pick a hole, Walker. I don't care which one, just pick one and shove your cock inside of me."

"You're going to feel so good wrapped around us, baby," Finn said, pulling my face back down to his cock and thrusting up to push it all into my mouth roughly. I moaned and bobbed quickly up and back down.

Walker growled loudly and knelt behind me, running his hands over my ass and spreading my cheeks. "I'm not going to be gentle with you right now, Bailey."

"That's what I want, Walker. I want the pain you both give me."

He spat on my ass and pushed two fingers into it and two into my pussy at the same time.

"Walker!" I moaned and circled my hips, taking more of him into me greedily.

"Suck on my balls again, baby," Finn commanded. I dug my nails into his thighs and bit his stomach before leaning back down, pushing my tongue directly against his ass, licking from there up to his balls, sucking them both into my mouth, and flicking my tongue against them.

"Good girl," Walker praised, pushing me forward and against Finn's ass deeper.

He pulled his fingers from my body and spit on my ass again, and then I felt the hot brand of his fat cock pressing against my entrance. "Push back on me, Bail."

I did as he said and felt the head of his cock press into me and groaned as he pulled back out quickly and then pushed back in.

Finn reached under my body and took two large handfuls of tits and pinched my nipples, pulling them toward him and making me gasp and moan.

"I want to watch you fucking come with his cock in your ass," Finn said, his voice tense and his balls tight.

Walker chose that moment to bottom out in my ass and smack it painfully.

I screamed and moaned as he started fiercely fucking me, giving me all the pain I'd asked for as he tore my ass apart with his monster cock.

"Yes!" I moaned as my body exploded and convulsed around him. Finn pulled my head back by my hair to watch my face as his brother fucked my ass into an orgasm. He leaned forward and kissed me, shoving his tongue into my mouth and sucking on mine, prolonging my orgasm with intense sensations.

"That's so hot." Walker grunted as his hands grabbed ahold of my ass and held onto the cheeks using them as leverage to pull me on and off of his cock.

"I want you in my pussy, Finn." I panted against his lips. "Please, baby, fill me up."

He nodded to Walker. "Lie back, hold her open for me."

"Fuck yes, man."

Walker wrapped his arms around my waist, careful of my growing belly, and slowly sank onto his ass and lay back, flat under me, pulling me with him so my back was to his chest, never letting his cock pull out of my ass.

"Oh god," I said as he slid his large hands under my knees and pulled them up toward my shoulders, opening my pussy up wide for Finn. I let my head fall back on Walker's shoulder as Finn straddled his legs and pushed the head of his cock into my pussy.

Walker didn't pull out like they normally would do when fucking me together to leave room. Instead, he stayed buried and Finn pushed into me alongside him and stretched me to the max.

They both groaned and cursed as Finn bottomed out. He reached forward and grabbed my breasts and played with them as they both started fucking me, sending bolts of electricity through my body and up my spine.

"I'm going to come; fuck I'm going to come so hard." I panted and Walker rubbed my clit as Finn leaned down to suck my nipples into his mouth with so much pressure. "Fuck me, fuck me, fuck me!" I screamed

That was it.

I exploded, headfirst into outer space, and both guys followed after me, pounding into me with no reservations for anything else but their own orgasms.

"I'm the luckiest girl in the world." I lay there on Walker's chest and was completely unable to move or care for modesty, or anything else in the world, in my spread-open position.

They put extra into the aftercare when we were getting cleaned up, and we spent the rest of the day relaxing and cuddling.

We were sitting at the table, enjoying dinner, when I broke the silence. "I want to get married."

Walker looked up at me and raised an eyebrow before looking over at his brother, who didn't offer anything up.

He put his fork down and took a pull off his beer. "I thought that was the plan all along?"

I laughed and smiled sweetly at him., "I mean before she's here. I want to be married to you when I give birth."

He got a look in his eye and slid down from his seat until he was on his knees next to mine. He put his hands on my stomach and leaned in to press his lips to my belly and said softly, "Do you hear that, baby girl? Your mama wants to marry us. How did we get so lucky to have you both in our lives?" He kissed my belly and then looked up at me.

I couldn't help it. Tears were running down my cheeks when he did, and he rolled his eyes at me. "You are getting so soft in your old age, babe." He crooned and I kissed him, letting my tongue explore his mouth, and before too long, my hands were joining in on the fun.

He groaned and pulled back to rest his forehead on mine and took a deep breath. "Eat," he commanded and pushed my plate back in front of me, kissing my pouty lips. "Then play."

I bit my lip and rolled my hips, pressing my thighs together as I looked over at Finn and could see the desire in his eyes as well.

"So when do you want to do it then?" Walker asked, and I shrugged and answered, trying to keep a straight face.

"Well, my mom could be here tomorrow. How long does it take to get a marriage license?"

"A week, I think," Finn said, taking a drink from his beer.

"A week then," I said like it was no big deal.

"Are you sure this is how you want to do it?" Walker asked, reaching over to let his fingers cover mine.

"Are you having second thoughts about marrying me?" I asked, afraid he wasn't ready after all.

"Fuck no, I'm not, and you know it. Don't fucking say that again, Bailey."

"Then you shouldn't worry about me either. I want to marry you both before she's born, and I want to have the Camden name when she arrives," I said, leaning back and putting both hands on my belly. She kicked and squirmed, and I watched as both men saw it and leaned forward to put their hands on her to feel her too.

"Next week then," Walker said softly, lost in the wonder of our daughter existing inside of my womb.

Finn leaned up and kissed me. "I can't wait to watch you walk down the aisle to us."

The plans started to have a small, intimate family wedding. My mom flew in the next day to be with us and help with arrangements.

She had refused Walker and Finn's offer to stay with us, not wanting to impose, and, instead, stayed in the hotel in town.

I wasn't overly upset by that because I didn't want to be restricted sexually in my own home with my men during such a peak time of libido.

The soft music wafted through the doors as I stood, waiting for my cue.

"Are you ready?" My mom asked, brushing back a curl that framed my face. "Just say the word and I'll whisk you away back to Hollywood where you can live with me forever."

"Mom." I smiled sweetly, shaking my head. "I've never been more sure about anything in this world."

"I know that, baby. I just wanted to let you know you had options." She winked and then held her hand out for me. "Let's get you down that aisle then."

The music shifted to the planned piano piece that would be played as I walked down the aisle, and I took a deep breath. "I'm ready."

When I cleared the doorway everything else melted away. The restored barn that John, Grant and Sandra decorated with white fairy lights and white linen drapery disappeared. The few family and friends we had invited to our impromptu nuptials faded into the darkness. The soft piano music drifted off to neverland as I walked down the aisle toward the two men who stole every piece of me the first time I looked into their eyes.

Walker stood on the right, with his dark brooding features zeroed in on me as I gracefully walked down the candle lined aisle. His black tux fit his body to perfection, hugging every muscle and inch of him. It matched the one that Finley wore to his left, smiling at me with love and adoration shining from his eyes.

My men.

Twins who were identical in looks alone, and complete opposites in disposition and personality, somehow complimenting each other completely.

Mine.

"Bail." Fin sighed, taking my hand from my mom as she handed it off, kissing my cheek before taking her place behind us.

"Hi." I whispered, smiling at him and fighting off the urge to lean in and kiss his perfect face. I turned to my right, sliding my other hand into Walker's calloused one as he squeezed it, like he was fighting for grounding. "Hi." I said to him, squeezing it back and reveling in the way he took a deep breath and relaxed his shoulders. "I love you both." I whispered, looking back and forth between them as the officiant took her place behind them.

She started the planned speech we had discussed in length two days ago when we finalized everything, yet I heard nothing. I had no attention to give to anyone beside the two lovely men standing before me, ready to commit themselves to me and our daughter equally.

"Bailey?" Norma, the officiant said, "Are you with me?" She smirked.

"Yes!" I gasped, shaking off the distraction as everyone chuckled, "Sorry."

"No worries, this is a big moment for you three. It's normal to be a bit distracted by it all. But I was asking if you were ready to recite the vows."

"Yes." I blushed, dipping my head as Finn smirked and Walker squeezed my hand again. "I'm ready."

She spoke the vows for each of us to recite, and we did, staring into each other's eyes the entire time, committing, and promising ourselves through good and bad, sickness and health.

"I want to kiss you both so bad." I whispered, as she finished up, shifting from foot to foot in anticipation. My guys chuckled and waited anxiously as well until we were given the all clear.

"Walker, Finn, you may kiss your beautiful bride. I now pronounce you married." Norma said.

Walker leaned in first, pushing Finn's shoulder out of the way in jest before sliding his warm hands on each side of my face and kissing me with such passion my toes curled in my silk heels. He didn't care who watched or where we were, Walker always used his actions and touches to express his emotions. And I could feel his love with the passion burning in his lips as he took mine.

"I love you so much, Bailey Camden." He whispered against my lips, pressing his forehead against mine and breathing me in. "You're more than we deserve, but I will spend my entire life trying to earn you."

"I'm yours." I cried, dashing away the tears that fell over my lashes. "I'm yours."

"And mine too I hope." Finn winked, when I pulled back, pulling me from his brother's embrace. "I'm pretty sure that's how this works."

I giggled and let him slide his hand into my hair and around my waist, hitching me against his front. "I'm yours too, whole heartedly Finley Grant."

"Hmm." He hummed, leaning down and finally pressing his lips against mine. He teased my lips with his tongue and I opened for him eagerly, offering him whatever he wanted from me. The kiss was heated and passionate and soon I found myself wanting to flex my hips against his and stroke the hardness I could feel building in his suit pants, but thought better of it at the last second. "I can't wait to make you scream my full name tonight, Mrs. Camden."

"God, that's hot." Walker added, leaning down to kiss my cheek and join the embrace. "Let's enjoy this dinner everyone prepared to celebrate us, then we can bail out and go home."

"That sounds heavenly." I moaned, smiling up at them both. "A whole week, uninterrupted with you two." I shook my head and let my eyelids flutter closed. "I can't wait."

Chapter 27– Walker

It had been two months since our wedding, and I'd never imagined married life could feel so good. I'd never been one to think about the future over the years and imagine being married to anyone in particular, but when things started getting serious with Bailey, those images started rolling around in my head far more frequently.

We'd honeymooned at home, locking ourselves away for a week in our slice of paradise because it was where Bailey was most comfortable. And Finn and I would do anything to make her happy.

We planned on vacationing with our daughter when she was born, so we enjoyed a relaxing time for now.

Since Clay's arrest, Finn and I continued working part-time. We each only worked two nights a week max and two days a week and never at the same time. We never left Bailey home alone at night unless there was an emergency or something that called off-duty officers in. And, we made sure we had every Sunday off.

Neither of us liked the idea of our girl being alone at night, and we tried hard to not smother her with our overprotective craziness.

Her shop was so incredibly busy, she had Stephanie and another barber, Roger, there full-time. Her assistant Sammy was the girlfriend of Nate, the dishwasher at Thea's diner who had helped protect her from Clay at the beginning of our relationship.

They wanted to get an apartment after graduating in the summer so she worked every second that Bailey would let her, and she took so much burden off of our girl's shoulders by doing it. She was worth her weight in gold really.

Bailey was thirty-two weeks pregnant now and got more radiant every single day. She was the most beautiful woman in the world with her baby belly and her luminous glow.

We hadn't decided on a name yet, but we had narrowed it down to two and decided to wait until we saw her to know which way, we wanted it to go.

It helped that Jake and Ivy were also expecting, and Ivy and Bailey had become best friends quickly and were bonding over their pregnancies as well.

Life was starting to feel normal and right. And peaceful.

So damn peaceful.

Except for the fact that Luann was still a problem in our lives.

Luann Mathews, Clay's sister, owned Lu's Beauty Parlor down on Front Street and had lost quite a large portion, if not all, of her male clients when Bailey had opened. That was enough to piss in her oatmeal, if you would.

And then, when word got around that Bailey was dating not only me, but Finn too, that had sent Luann off the deep end and caused her to show up at our house. She had made a scene a few different times with Finn in public, trying to make it seem like he either cheated on her with Bailey or was cheating on Bailey with her.

Of course, none of that held a candle to the stunt she pulled the night she cornered Bailey at Jake's wedding and told her all sorts of tales and lies to upset her.

I also genuinely believed that she had held Bailey up in the bathroom that night so that Clay was able to get her alone outside the venue on her way back to the party.

Finn and I couldn't prove it, though, so she was still walking around Mayfield like she was queen shit herself.

It was all in terrible fashion, and even Ms. Mabel Thompson, the town's most notorious gossip at the beauty parlor, had had enough of her and told her in no uncertain terms that she needed to grow up and stop acting like an idiot.

Things had been quiet the last few weeks on that front. I guessed perhaps Luann had given up, but I was still uneasy given the fact that she was Clay Mathew's sister and Bailey had sent Clay to jail. At least in the eyes of Luann, that was how it happened.

The whole town knew that dick was no good. When news had broken that he had not only touched her against her will but then verbally assaulted her in her shop after she turned him down for a date and tried to attack her at Jake's wedding, everyone was all irate and nearly ran the boy from the town once and for all, had he not already been on his way to jail.

Now, he was awaiting sentencing for his charges and Bailey was able to breathe a little easier, knowing he was behind bars.

While that piece of shit still walked the face of this earth, I wouldn't breathe easy knowing he could hurt Bailey or our daughter at any given time.

It was Wednesday, and I was working the day shift and Finn worked last night and was off until tomorrow morning, so we were meeting Bail at Thea's for dinner tonight and then taking her home for dessert. Or rather, we were taking her home because she was our dessert.

It was only three in the afternoon and she had three more hours until she closed, but I couldn't seem to get her off my mind today.

I had woken up with her in my arms this morning, naked and pressed against me from nose to toes, and I had lay there and watched her sleep peacefully, unable to shake a sense of dread that had settled into my bones since she fell asleep the night before.

I couldn't put my finger on it, but something was off. She didn't act like anything was bothering her, but I was still catching vibes from the universe all night and day and I was seriously off-kilter because of it.

So, as I parked my cruiser on Main Street, I took a deep breath and tried to get my head on straight before I walked into her shop. I needed to see her, to kiss her and tell her I missed her and loved her and couldn't wait to see her later, but I didn't want her to think anything else was up with me.

She was so in tune with both Finn and me that she could read us easier than we could each other, and we had the *Freaky Friday* twin thing going. Sometimes, it was wicked to see how quickly she honed in on something out of the ordinary, but it was because she was as hung up on us as we were on her.

I opened up the door and let the bells jingle as I stepped in. Sammy sat at the front desk and hung up the phone when she saw me.

"Hey, coach!" She smiled brightly at me, and I nodded to her.

"Hey, Sammy. How's it going today?" I stopped and leaned on the desk, but I let my eyes travel around the shop, looking for my wife. She was at the back wall, washing a client's hair and laughing at something he said over the noise of the sprayer. She hadn't seen me come in yet, so I just stood there and watched her as she talked and laughed some more.

She wore a pair of black distressed jeans with holes in the knees, a white shirt that hugged her sexy belly, and a pair of white heeled boots with fringe on them. She, like always, looked divine. Her hair was down, and she wore a red bandana tied in a bow at the top of her head, holding her curls back; she looked like she did the first day I had seen her.

I realized then that Sammy hadn't said anything so I looked back down at her, and she just sat back in her chair with her arms crossed over her chest and smirked at me as she watched me watch Bailey. She raised her eyebrows at me, and I stuck my tongue out at her in a very manly and mature way.

"Hush," I told her, and she went off into a fit of girly giggles.

"You three are the cutest," she gushed, and I scowled at her and tried my best to be menacing. But in reality, it was impossible to be anything but lovesick when I was thinking about Bailey.

"Stop harassing my assistant, officer. Good help is hard to find around here," Bailey chided as her client walked over to her chair and she walked over to me.

I turned and watched her long legs bring her closer to me and loved how they crossed slightly at the ankle with each step, like she was walking down a catwalk. I kissed her deeply when she stepped into my arms and took a deep, calming breath of her scent into my system to help settle me. I laid my hands on her belly and felt around for my baby to kick and right on cue, as if she could sense me, she kicked my hand and squirmed around.

A couple of the men in the shop catcalled and I glared at them, silencing them all.

Sammy and Bailey just giggled at me though.

"I missed you," Bailey said, taking my hand and leading me to the back where her office was. "Sammy, will you go ahead and get a hot towel on Mr. Jenks please?" Bailey asked, and her mini-me lit up at the task.

"Of course."

Bailey pulled me into her office and shut the door and climbed me like a tree. I slid my hands around her waist, sat her down on her desk, pulled her knees apart, dragged her body against mine.

"Mmh." She moaned and wrapped her ankles around my legs.

"Mrs. Camden, are you trying to seduce me in your office with your customers right outside the door?"

"Is it working?" she asked and kissed my neck and jaw, the best she could around my bulletproof vest and radio.

"Very much so." I chuckled.

I kissed her deeply and something passed between us. The kiss turned from feverish and sexual to something deeper. Our lips slowed down, and our hands stopped clawing, and I pulled back, afraid that I'd said the words out loud that had been swimming in my brain for hours.

Something wasn't right.

Her eyes were hooded and her lips swollen when she finally looked at me and I swore, I heard her tell me she loved me with just the green glow in her eyes. And then she whispered the words I longed to hear every second of every day. "I love you, Walker."

"Not anywhere near as much as I love you, sweetheart," I said back and softly kissed her supple lips and then the apple of each cheek and around to the side of her face and up her ear. "I can't wait to have dinner with you and then take you home and spend the next twelve hours inside of your body."

"Hmm, that's the most romantic thing you've said to me in days."

"I clearly need to step up my romance game then," I joked and kissed her one more time. "I have to get back on patrol. I just needed to feel you in my arms for a moment."

"I'm always available to be felt up—" She winked. "I mean in your arms." Something changed on her face, a flicker of something as she chewed on her lip like she wanted to say something.

"What is it?" That foreboding feeling in my spine came back as she looked almost scared and nervous for a second. But she smiled up at me and shook her head.

"I just love you both so much. You make me so happy. I never want to lose this."

I leaned down and kissed her slowly, letting my lips coax hers open again, and then I possessed her sensually as I tangled my tongue with hers.

I watched her as I walked backward out of her office and across the shop with a love-drunk smile on my face and a burning in my soul. "I'll see you at six."

"I'll be there with bells on." She smiled with a silly, girly smile and then shooed me away.

God, I fucking loved that girl.

I was going to do something about it tonight, to ease this worry in my heart.

I had hardly made it out of town again when I got radioed to a barn fire on the outskirts of town and my heart dropped.

It was Mr. and Mrs. Thompson's place and it sounded bad. I took off and when I got on the scene, two of their five cattle barns were fully engulfed.

"Holy fuck," I cursed as I ran from my car toward the fire. There were workers and neighbors everywhere, pulling gates and cutting fences to get any animal they could away from the fires. We would round up any of them that got loose later, but at least they would be alive to round back up.

Mr. Thompson was pushing seventy years old, but he was still out here with us working his ass off to save his livelihood. His wife Mabel Thompson stood at the edge of the yard and clutched at her pearls as she watched hundreds of years of family history burn to the ground.

We all worked tirelessly to save as many animals and pieces of equipment as we could while the fire department worked to try to contain the fires in the two barns and save the others.

Finn and other off-duty officers and firemen responded along with hundreds of community members. They set up water and food stations for first responders, who had been called in from three counties wide, and the family who was losing everything. It was a picture of a small town during a tragedy.

When I saw Finn show up in street clothes and a police vest, I stopped for a moment and hugged my brother amidst all the chaos. He pulled back and recognition lit in his eyes as he clapped me on the shoulder and turned to run in the other direction to help. He felt the change in the air like I did. I needed to get us both out of here and get Bailey and lock ourselves away for the night to settle whatever was fucking with the universe.

It was almost six now, and there was no way either Finn or I was going to make it to Thea's for dinner. I wasn't sure the diner was even open given that Thea herself was here serving meals to anyone in need of one.

I shot Bailey a text, telling her we wouldn't be making it and why and that I'd call her when I could.

She texted back right away and said she'd head up when she closed down to see if she could help anywhere, and I went back to work.

At one point, I was taking a break against my squad car and drinking from a bottle of water when Finn came up and sat next to me.

"This is terrible," he said, watching as the smoke billowed up into the air as the fire finally started getting knocked down.

"Mr. Thompson said it was arson."

"What?" Finn asked, shocked.

"Said one of his boys saw a man running from the back pasture toward a truck and when he started to go after him, he saw the smoke rising from the back barn."

"Who the fuck would want to kill hundreds of heads of cattle from nice folks like them? It makes no sense. Did he get a description of the guy?"

"Said the only thing he saw was he had on a black hoodie and was bald. The sheriff plans on working with him after things settle down here and maybe get a sketch artist in from York, and then we can start looking for him."

"That's so fucked."

"Yeah, and we're missing dinner with Bailey because of it. That pisses me off," I added, taking another pull from my water.

"I know. I was planning on stopping over earlier to see her but then got called in. I miss her, man. How was she this morning?"

"Good, tired but good. I stopped in for five minutes right before I took the call here to see her. I have this—" I paused, unsure how to describe the feeling.

"Bad feeling?" Finn asked, all-knowing.

"Yeah, man, and I can't fucking shake it either. So I stopped in and checked on her and she was absolutely perfect and horny." I laughed and so did he.

"Sounds like our wife."

"Sure does. I just want to get home and hold her so fucking bad. Baby girl was kicking like a pro today when I stopped, and I just want to turn off the world and hold on to them both for a bit to ease this fucking feeling."

"I hear you, man. I can't wait to get home either, though I doubt she'll let either of us near her smelling like smoke and manure."

I tipped my head back and laughed. He was right. She would hate how bad we had stunk right now.

"Walker!" our Sheriff called out and waved me over to him, so I stood up and shook Finn's hand. "Tonight, whenever we get done with this, we'll pick her up if she's not here or home and we'll—fuck, I don't know." I shrugged my shoulders. "We'll keep her hostage until the baby is born if we need to."

"Fuck yes, we will." He laughed and then I took off, focusing back on work and anxious to get out of here and get to Bailey.

Chapter 28 – Bailey

Walker texted me that they were going to miss dinner. They were both at a bad fire up at a farm on the way out of town and they didn't know how long they would be.

I had heard the chatter about the fire the last hour or so as most of the town headed up to help out where they could or, more than likely, stand around and watch it in good-hearted curiosity.

It was after six, my last client had left as had Stephanie, and I was cleaning up before I was going to head up and see if there was anything I could do to help. Sammy had texted me earlier and told me she was going to help out Nate and Thea since she had the evening off here and asked if I was coming since the guys were there. I told her yes, that I planned on stopping home and changing and grabbing some food for my guys in case they were hungry.

Which, let's be honest, my guys were always hungry for two things.

Food.

And me.

And I was happy to feed their appetites as often as possible.

I looked out the window and noticed that there wasn't another car parked on Main Street in either direction. Normally at dinner time around here, Thea's was bustling and there wasn't an open spot on the street, but everyone had headed home or on up to the fire given that Thea had closed down to go help out as well.

I turned off the lights and walked toward the front door with my purse over my shoulder after shutting the curtains on the front window and turning off all of my equipment.

When I opened the door, a man stepped in at the same second with a large box in his hands.

"Oh!" I gasped, startled as we nearly ran each other over.

"I'm sorry!" he stuttered as the box started teetering out of his hands. "I'm so, so sorry. I have a delivery for this address and I'm so late, so I was rushing and wasn't looking where I was going and—" He huffed and then smiled at me. "I'm sorry."

I laughed and stepped back. "It's okay. Who's it for?"

He looked down at the label on the top. "Uh, says Bailey Dunn. Is that you?" he asked hopefully. "This thing is so darn heavy."

I laughed and said, "Yes, that's me, come on in. Do you mind setting it down right here?" I walked back into the shop and motioned to the desk by the door, and he hurried forward and set it down.

Something rattled around inside, and he made an apologetic grimace. "Thank you so much, I was so afraid I was going to drop that thing."

"No problem." I grabbed my purse and hiked it up on my shoulder as I stepped toward him. "Is there something I have to sign or is that it?" I asked.

"Yes, I have a form for you right here, let me just find it." He started rifling through his pockets and I looked down at the top of the box to see who it was from. As I read it, though, I was confused because it didn't say my name on the top. It said a name I had never heard of, and the address was for a business in York, which was the city about forty-five minutes away.

"Are you sure this is for me? It says—" I started and looked up at the gentleman.

He cut me off. "Oh, yes, I'm sure it's for you. In fact, here's the form."

He pulled his hand out of his pocket and I watched as his facial features morphed from friendly to menacing. Instead of handing me a form, he pulled a closed fist from his pocket, and the next thing I knew, he slammed it directly into my face.

I screamed in agony as my head snapped back and pain exploded behind my eyes. I stumbled backward and fell to the floor as my feet tangled under me. My ears rang and my vision was blurry as I held my hands to my face and blood poured from my nose and mouth.

I was disoriented and unable to think straight but I tried sitting up as shock started pumping through my veins. However, I couldn't make my head and my body communicate.

I lay there and watched in horror as he grinned down at me and cracked his knuckles. The skin at the edges of his eyes crinkled into laugh lines as he looked at me like he was a cheerful person normally and not a psychopath who had just punched me in the face for no reason.

He walked slowly over to the front door, flicked the lock, pulled the shade down over the glass, and turned back to me. "Oh, Mrs. Camden. It seems you've been a very naughty girl and I've been paid greatly to teach you a lesson."

"Oh my god."

I started to scramble away and then turned onto my knees to crawl as my legs were slow to catch up with me. I made it a few feet before he stepped next to me and kicked me square in the side of my ribs with his booted foot.

Any ounce of air I had in my lungs got trapped as they seized from the pain. I was unable to breathe in or out as I curled in on myself and wrapped my arms around my belly to protect my baby.

NO! I screamed in my head as fear and adrenaline rushed through my body.

I looked around for something to use to protect myself but there was nothing around to help me against this man who was large and strong.

He wore black jeans and a black zip-up sweater with a red logo on the chest, but I couldn't make it out through my blurry eyes. His boots were the kind you'd see on a guy riding a motorcycle with a silver buckle at the side, and they jingled with each menacing step that he took around me.

My purse lay back where I'd dropped it with the first hit, and inside of it was my cell phone. There was the office phone on the desk where he'd set the box, but he was between me and both of them now.

I forced my chest to move some air through my lungs and made the effort to lunge forward and try to run to my office.

My office door had a lock on it and a window to the back parking lot if I could make it in there, so I could run out back and scream for help.

Someone had to be around to hear me scream.

I made a break for it, running full speed to my office. I had my hand on the doorknob when his meaty hands tangled in my hair, pulling me backward and throwing me to the floor in a heap.

"Help!" I screamed, but he was quick to land on top of me after he threw me down and put his hand over my mouth. I hit him with my fists and gouged at his eyes as he pulled back and hit me again in the face.

I sobbed as I tried to protect myself.

I had to survive. I had to fight back and endure.

I was pregnant but he didn't care.

He laughed in my face as he pinned my arms at my sides and headbutted me in the chin. My body went limp as stars danced in front of my eyes. His shaved head started to perspire as he lay on top of me like he was working up a sweat by attacking me, though he made it seem so effortless.

I felt like I was thrown into a half-conscious, half-asleep state and just lay there as he stood up off of me and then spit on the ground next to me and wiped his head off with the sleeve of his shirt.

"God, you're fucking sexy, even with that tumor on your waist. He said you were a looker, but she said you were fat and ugly. Guess she was just jealous." He grabbed his crotch and adjusted himself as I tried to roll over and away from him.

I watched, stuck on the floor, unable to make my limbs coordinate with each other, as he walked over to the box and ripped the tape open.

My heart sank into my stomach as I watched him pull out a small red gas can, a large hunting knife, and a metal baseball bat.

"No," I begged in horror and sat up, putting my back against the wall and holding my sides in agony.

God, please no.

He smirked at me and set the can on the floor as he shouldered the bat and put the knife in his waistband and started walking around my shop.

"Do you have any idea how pissed off you've made people around here?" he asked.

He swung the bat aggressively and shattered the mirror over my workstation, sending shards of glass raining down on me and the floor. My skin burned where the sharp edges sliced it open on my arms and chest.

"Hmm?" he asked again as he walked over to an empty station and did the same. "I'll tell you, sweetheart." He smashed the glass table that held magazines in the waiting area and more shards exploded around us.

"Twenty-five thousand dollars' worth of pissed off to kill you."

I had to get out of here. "Please don't."

He ignored my pleas. "Of course, they each paid me five grand more for separate add-ons. Can you guess what they were?" He turned back to me and started walking toward me as I pulled myself across the floor, trying to get to the door.

He lifted the bat and swung it down against my knee, and the sickening sound of it against my bone reverberated in my ears.

I screamed again but this time, he just laughed sinisterly at me.

"I'll tell you because it's going to make it more fun for me. She paid me five grand more if I made sure to cut your baby out of you first so you could watch it die before you did. And he paid me five grand more to make sure I raped your sexy little body before you were dead."

My stomach lurched and I vomited on the floor next to me as pain and fear overtook my entire body.

"You must have really pissed him off. He wanted to pay me more to make sure I mutilated your pussy and your ass while you were still very conscious. But I told him I didn't need more money to do that. I'd throw that part in for free." He leaned down and grabbed my hair, pulling my face up to his. He was panting and his eyes were crazed as I sobbed and fought against the pain in my scalp.

"So tell me, Bailey Camden. Is your pussy worth the extra cash? Hmm?" he asked. He leaned down and licked the side of my face and I swung at him, pushing him away while trying to inflict pain on him, but he just threw me back against the wall. "I think I'll find out in just a minute."

He reached down and grabbed his dick again and then looked around the space as if an idea struck him.

"Perhaps when I'm done with you, I'll string you up in the front window, naked and cut to pieces, and that way the entire town can see your body before you're nothing but a pile of ash and bones on the floor. What do you say?"

He laughed as I crawled across the floor again. My knee was throbbing and so were my sides. I was fairly certain I would never breathe again, but I had to keep fighting either way.

"Help! Please help me!" I screamed at the top of my lungs.

God, Finn and Walker could not find me the way this man was describing. It would kill them to know I had been attacked when I was supposed to be with them. They could not lose their daughter because of me either.

I had to survive this for the three of them.

He was walking around the shop and destroying every single thing he could get his hands on. He cut the leather of every chair and table, and he broke anything that was glass or metal with the bat. He knocked everything over and spilled anything liquid.

I watched closely and started moving toward my office again, trying not to attract his attention. I made it almost to the office door when he caught me. I thought he had been so distracted with the destruction that I was going to make it, but he lifted me by my hair once again and slammed me against the wall. My face left a giant red smear from the blood pouring from my head and face, and he pressed himself against my back and ripped my head to the side at a painful angle.

"Hmm, you smell good, Mrs. Camden." He leaned in and smelled my neck and hair and licked me again as he pushed his hand down the front of my jeans and into my underwear. I revolted against his touch and pushed back off the wall, trying to dislodge him from my body.

But he was so much bigger than me.

"Please stop! Please!" I screamed as I bit down and pushed harder. "I didn't do anything to you! Please!"

He pushed his fingers into my body and ground his erection into my ass as he painfully fingered me.

"Hmm. Your cunt is so fucking tight. Damn, maybe I won't kill you at all. Maybe I'll just take you with me and make you my fucking cum slut for a while first." Another wave of nausea rolled through me as he roughly continued to violate me. "At least until that spawn rips you open on the way out and ruins everything."

I elbowed him, stomped on his feet, and tried headbutting him with the back of my head. I tried every single thing I could think of to get free, but it was all in vain. Tears poured down my face, mixing with the blood as they fell to my body.

He pulled his fingers from me and wrapped his arm around my throat as he brought them to his face and smelled them. He groaned and then stuck them in his mouth and sucked on them noisily while my stomach flipped violently. "You taste as good as you smell, baby."

"They'll kill you," I sneered, changing tactics. "They'll find you and kill you in ways that make whatever you do to me look like kid's work." I felt a sense of calm settle over me as I thought of Finn and Walker enacting revenge on this man for everything he was doing to me before killing me.

If I had no hope of surviving, then I would endure it knowing that they would make him pay.

He laughed again and grabbed me by my hair and turned me to face him. "Are you talking about your husbands? The deputies?" I spit in his face and then sneered at the red stain it left as he wiped it away, but it was short-lived because his eyes turned violent again and he smashed the back of my head off the wall and I went limp.

He wrapped both hands around my throat, lifted me off of my feet, and held me in the air with my back against the wall as he cut off all of my air supply.

I kicked and scratched and hit him over and over again, but nothing fazed him. I could feel blood vessels in my neck, face, and eyes start to explode as the pressure in my head became unbearable.

I felt everything start to fade to black as I lost my ability to see completely. I was almost unconscious when I heard a cell phone ring on the man and then a second later, he cursed.

"Son of a bitch."

He dropped me to the ground, and I landed in a heap as I gasped for breath, clawing at my neck, trying to pull the skin and muscles back out to their normal shape to make way for my airway beneath them, but it was slow to regain function.

The man pulled his phone from his pocket and then started looking around wildly and back down at me.

"I guess it's your lucky day today, bitch. It seems I'm out of time, so you'll have to settle for a quick death after all. But don't worry, I'll still manage to make it painful for you and your baby."

He turned his back to go to his box of tricks and I made my move. I heaved myself up off the floor and lunged for the office door.

"Bitch!" he yelled, but I threw myself into the office and slammed the door shut as he ran into it. I flipped the lock and then grabbed the phone off the desk and dialed 911.

The wood was cracking, and the lock protested as he tried kicking the door in. I held the phone to my ear as I pulled the heavy desk across the room with strength I didn't know I had and jammed it under the door handle.

"911, what is your emergency?"

I screamed for help and then tried to force myself to speak slowly. "155 Main St., Mayfield. My name is Bailey Camden." My voice was hoarse and cracked. "I've been attacked, and he's still here. He has gasoline. He's going to light the building on fire! I'm thirty-two weeks pregnant. " He screamed through the door and tried to break it down still. "Please help me," I begged.

I ran to the window and shoved it open and screamed into the parking lot that all of the other buildings in Mayfield backed into. "Help me! Please! Somebody help me!"

I couldn't get out the window. It sat too high off the ground, and with my knee, I'd never land safely.

"Where are you now?" the dispatcher asked.

"I'm in the back of my shop, in my office. I locked the door, but I can't get out the window. It's too high." I was sobbing and praying as the door rattled more and more with each kick.

"Help is on the way, Bailey. Stay on the phone with me. Do you have anything in the office to use as a weapon if he gets through the door?"

I looked around, but there was nothing. "No!" I cried. "I have nothing and he's huge! He has a metal bat that he's hit me with and a giant knife. He said he was going to cut my baby out."

"Does he have any other weapons?" Her voice was urgent but calm and I tried to take strength from her.

"I don't know. I don't think so. I didn't see any, but I don't know."

"Okay. You're doing great. Stay on the phone with me, okay? Help is so close, you should be hearing their sirens soon. They're on their way."

I screamed as the door broke, and a deafening crack sounded through the room as his foot flew through the wood.

"Bailey? What happened? Talk to me?" she yelled through the phone as I watched in horror as the man's face appeared through the hole he'd made.

He slid his hand through the wood shards and started reaching for the knob to unlock the door.

"Bailey!" the dispatcher yelled again, but I was in shock.

What the fuck did I do?

His fingers were almost touching the doorknob as he laughed from the other side of the wood, taunting me. "I'm coming for you, Bailey." He swore as his fingers touched the lock.

I didn't tell my body to act, but the next thing I knew, I grabbed a pair of scissors out of the cup on my desk, ran to the door, and stabbed them into his hand over and over again as I screamed.

His blood splattered the door and me and he screamed from the other side. "You fucking bitch. I'm going to fucking kill you, cut that baby from your stomach, and cut it into pieces, you fucking cunt!"

I backed away from the door and held the scissors to my chest as I panted and shook.

"Bailey, are you with me?" the dispatcher asked.

"I'm here," I whispered in shock at what I'd just done.

"Bailey, your husbands are on their way to you. They're coming, I promise, okay? Hold on for me."

All of a sudden, the door exploded into a million pieces as he threw himself through it and landed on top of the desk in my office.

I screamed and backed into the wall, clutching the scissors to my chest as I watched in horror as he stood up and started moving toward me.

"I'm going to make you beg for death," he said menacingly as he stepped toward me. Blood poured down his arm and his eyes were cold and psychotic as he looked at me with sick calmness. I couldn't back up any farther, and I looked out the window, contemplating throwing myself out it as a last-ditch effort to survive.

I didn't think I'd be able to land without hurting the baby, though, if I did. But if I let him get to me, I was dead and so was she regardless.

I held the scissors up in my hand, pointing at him, and prayed to God that it would be enough.

He lunged for me, and I closed my eyes as I braced to feel his body collide with mine and begged God to save my baby, even though he couldn't spare me.

Chapter 29 – Finn

I was bone weary from running around this damn farm for the last six hours after working all last night. I smelled like smoke and was covered in it, and I just wanted to go home to our girl.

Walker and I had talked in the few minutes of break we had a couple of hours ago and both agreed we needed to get to Bailey and get home, and now time was dragging at a snail's pace.

Most of the fire was out at this point. The damage had been contained to two of the barns. They estimated that over two hundred head of cattle had been lost in the fire, but almost five hundred more had been saved.

I walked over to Ms. Thea where she, Steve, and Nate had set up a tent with food and drinks for anyone here that needed a refueling, and she happily handed me a giant sandwich.

"Eat up, boy, you look positively drained," she said, grabbing another sandwich and handing it to Walker as he walked up next to me. "You too, Walker."

"Yes, ma'am," we replied and started eating her delicious meal.

"Have you heard from Bailey?" Walker asked me and Thea between bites. "She said she was going to come up after work, but I haven't had a chance to look for her."

I shook my head no and then looked around. I noticed a lot of people had started clearing out. It was a little before seven now and almost everything left to do needed daylight, so everyone would be back in the morning to help start the cleanup.

Thea shook her head., "No I haven't seen her. I've run back to the diner a couple of times and her car was still at the shop. Maybe she got wrapped up in doing something there. You know how she is; she's probably installing something fancy to make everyone love her place even more. That shop is so nice already, but she keeps coming up with new ways to make it even better every day."

"She's so damn dedicated, it's admirable really," I added.

"Sammy is headed back home now; I'll ask her to swing by and check on her," Nate added and grabbed his phone to call Sammy.

"Thanks, man."

"No problem." He walked away and talked to Sammy for a second and then came back over.

I tried to place the unease in my stomach, unsure of where it came back from all of a sudden. The sandwich in my mouth turned to sawdust as I got a bad feeling deep in my bones.

I looked over at Walker and he was staring at me with a confused look on his face as he watched me mulling it over in my head. "What's up?" he asked, setting his half-eaten meal down.

"I don't know." I shook my head and looked around the group of people left. "Something's not right though. I've got that same feeling out of nowhere but it's worse all of a sudden, and I can't shake it." I took a deep breath and tried to process it.

"You think it's Bail?" Walker asked.

I nodded my head, unable to say the words out loud. I didn't want to will something into the universe, but I was getting more and more of a bad feeling in my gut the longer it went on.

Just then, every police radio on the scene squawked with the emergency tone that blocked all other radio transmissions while dispatch called out a priority message.

"911 center to all available units, respond to 155 Main Street, Mayfield, the Bailey Dunn & Co. Barbershop."

My heart exploded and I took off at a dead run next to Walker to his cruiser parked across the field. My legs ran on instinct only as I tried to process what I was hearing from Walker's radio.

"Armed assault in progress. The caller is barricaded in the back office of the shop in the northwest corner of the building, but the assailant is breaking down the door. She's been attacked with a bat and knife and states the man has gasoline and is planning to burn the building down."

We threw ourselves into the cruiser and Walker shot out of the field, kicking stone and mud up as he tore off toward town.

"No!" I screamed as the transmission cut off.

Walker was in a trance as he drove at breakneck speed toward town. I hung on to the handle and mentally walked through her shop, planning how to enter tactically to get to her in the office.

Dispatch started another transmission. "911 to EMS and LifeAir, the caller is thirty-two weeks pregnant and has been attacked, respond priority one. Squad 91, set up a landing zone for LifeAir."

"Please let her be okay." Walker gasped finally as we got nearer to town. They were calling the helicopter in, which meant it was bad.

There were a dozen cruisers behind us as we tore into the town square. Walker turned off his sirens, and so did the cars behind us as we made it to the front of the shop.

Walker looked at me and a silent agreement passed through our brains.

She survives, no matter what.

Even if we don't.

We tore out of the car and drew our guns and ran to the front door. I pushed on the door, but it was locked. I stepped back and kicked it, breaking the lock, and we rushed into the shop.

I heard Bailey's screams from her office as we rounded the corner and watched as a man threw himself through the hole he'd kicked into the door.

The man's cold voice called out, silencing Bailey, "I'm going to make you beg for death."

Walker grabbed my arm and pointed directions and he rounded wide around the door. I took the near side, and as we cleared it to see into the hole, the man lunged forward toward Bailey where she clung to the wall in the corner to get away from him.

Walker and I each fired our guns in succession and hit the man multiple times, stopping him in midair and causing him to fall to the ground at Bailey's feet.

I shoved my shoulder into the door, Walker shoved with me, and we opened it and pushed the desk away that was against it and ran into the room.

"Bailey!" I screamed, but her eyes were locked on the man bleeding out a foot from her where she huddled on the floor.

She clung to the phone and a pair of bloody scissors, was shaking like crazy, and bled from multiple places on her face, arms, and legs.

Walker jumped over the man and holstered his gun as I grabbed the man's leg and pulled him away from our wife and baby.

"Bailey, look at me. Baby, please look at me. You're okay. We're right here." Walker was pleading with her, but she was in shock and was completely unresponsive as he blocked her view of the man. I quickly checked for a pulse and didn't find one.

He was dead. And I wanted to kill him all over again.

"We need to get her to the hospital, Finn!" Walker yelled as he started scooping her up into his arms.

She started flailing her arms and legs as he wrapped his around her, screaming with her eyes closed as she sobbed.

She was in shock and couldn't even see us standing in front of her.

"Baby, it's me. It's Walker," he said, putting her hands on his face, forcing her to look at him and not through him anymore.

She stilled and stopped screaming after a moment and I could see that she was focusing on him finally.

Her body crumbled as she threw her arms around his neck and sobbed. My heart was breaking in my chest as I looked at her broken and beaten body. I put myself between her and her attacker as Walker picked her up, and she gasped and cried out in pain as they left the room.

She reached for me when he passed, and I linked my fingers through hers, held on, and followed after them.

Jake cleared a path for us to the front door as more police arrived and when we got her to the sidewalk, the ambulance was pulling up.

I swung the doors open wide and Walker carried her up the steps and into the back of the ambulance as the EMTs climbed up and started working on her.

They pushed us out of the ambulance to stand on the ground as they started examining her and called out medical terms that made my stomach sick.

Decreased breath sounds.

Blunt force trauma.

Collapsed right lung.

Low O2 stats.

Deep lacerations.

Brain injury.

I watched in horror as they cut her clothes from her body, revealing open wounds and broken ribs visible under her skin.

"Finn! Walker!" she begged, pushing away their hands as they tried to stop the bleeding on her head and arms. "My baby! Is my baby okay?"

Her voice gutted me, and I couldn't stay still anymore. I pushed my way into the ambulance and knelt at her head, holding the gauze the EMT was trying to wrap onto her forehead as she swung at him in fear.

"Bailey, it's me. It's Finley. I'm right here. Stop fighting, Bailey. They're the EMTs. They're trying to help you, okay? You have to relax and let them help you and the baby. Do you hear me?"

She went still and looked up at me, one of her eyes swollen shut and the one that was still open completely bloodshot, and purple veins spider-webbed out away from it across her cheek.

"Finn?" she asked as she tried to look at me better, but she was in a neck brace and the EMTs were holding down her arms as they tried getting an IV line into her.

"I'm here, baby. I'm right here. Walker's right outside the door too. We're here, baby. I love you. I love you so fucking much."

She cried silently as the shock of it all wore off and everything started hitting her.

The EMT that we'd worked with constantly over the years looked at me from where he was administering medications into her IV. "I'm sedating her. It's the best thing for her right now."

I nodded to him and leaned farther over her face. "I love you. We're going to be right here when you wake up."

She watched me closely, but I saw as the medicine started affecting her and her eye started to close and roll. "Save her," she said before she slipped into unconsciousness.

I looked at Walker standing at her feet and grimaced at the look of unapologetic rage in his eyes as we watched the love of our life suffer because of one man's actions.

"We're going to the trauma center in York," the EMT said, nodding to the first responders around him to get rolling. "We can't wait for the helicopter."

"Ride with her, stay by her side. I'll follow behind you," Walker said and started to turn away.

"Walker!" I yelled, waiting for him to turn back to me and look into my eyes. "Don't drive."

He was in no shape to drive right now, and it gutted me to have him alone when he needed to be with Bailey and me to settle the anger in his veins. There was simply no room in the ambulance, though, and I wasn't going to leave Bailey without one of us to protect her until we figured out why this happened.

"I won't," he said and nodded to me. "I'll have Jake drive." He paused and a pained expression passed his face as he looked down at Bailey before he looked back to me. His voice was eerie and disturbed but he gave me a command. "Save Bailey."

I knew how much that destroyed him to say that, but I understood why he did.

I nodded back to him in understanding. "See you in a few."

The ride to York was the longest ride of my life as Bailey lay unconscious and her belly remained still.

Our daughter usually squirmed constantly this time of night, and the fact that she wasn't moving scared the life out of me.

"Can you tell if the baby is alive?" I asked. My voice cracked as the EMT looked at me and shook his head.

"I don't have the equipment to know for sure. I'm so sorry. They'll check as soon as we get to the center."

As soon as we pulled in at the trauma center, she was whisked away into the emergency room immediately, and I was left standing in the corridor with her blood covering my arms, shirt, and face and an empty ache in my chest.

"Finn?"

I turned and recognized the nurse manager from the ER as she walked toward me. We came here so frequently for work, that I saw her all the time, but I couldn't think of her name right now. Everything in my brain was blank.

"Amy," she answered for me as I came up blank.

"Sorry." I sighed and went to run my hands through my hair but stopped short as the dried blood cracked between my fingers.

"Please don't apologize," she said, her face full of empathy. "Would you like to use an on-call room to clean up?"

I nodded and looked around the waiting area. There were people in all sorts of shock at my appearance and I grimaced. "I can't leave her."

"She's in the best hands possible right now. They're not going to know anything right away, as they have to run tests on her first. I'll stay posted outside her room and come get you with any updates as soon as they have them," she said, and I looked longingly at the double doors blocking me from the room she was in.

I turned back to her and nodded, letting her lead the way to a provider on-call room that was empty. "The woman you brought in?" she asked as she grabbed some towels and a pair of scrubs out of the closet.

"Uh, Bailey. Bailey Camden. She's my wife," I answered and took the items from her.

She nodded and then grabbed some toiletries from the sink. "She is with Dr. Peters. He's the best trauma surgeon in the state. As soon as a doctor comes out with an update, I'll come to find you, okay? You can wait here or I can show you to a private waiting room. This time of night, it will be quieter than the ER waiting room."

"I appreciate it," I replied, looking down at the items in my hands and feeling lost. "My brother, Walker," I started, and my voice cracked, so I cleared my throat and tried again as she waited patiently. "Walker and I are both married to Bailey, and he's on his way in a cruiser. He should be here shortly. He's as big of a mess as I am."

She nodded and looked sympathetically at me. "As soon as he gets here, I'll bring him here and he can get cleaned up as well."

"Thank you, Amy."

"Of course, Finn. I'm so sorry that this happened to her and you both."

"Thanks," I said, still unable to look in her nice eyes. I was a hair trigger from breaking down and crying like a baby as I worried about the love of our lives.

Amy left and I stripped out of the smoke and blood-covered clothes and stepped into the shower in the small, attached bathroom. I placed my palm on the tile wall and let my head fall forward under the spray, the tears falling in the silence of the room.

Who the fuck was that guy?

Why the fuck did he do it?

Then, the reality of everything else hit me.

I killed a man today.

Clay was in jail, and I didn't think any of his friends would have done something so severe for him as a favor.

I wracked my brain for answers before I pulled myself together and started washing away the dirt, grime, and blood. I was almost done when there was a knock on the door and Walker stepped in.

He looked at me, and I could feel the pain in his body as though it were my own. I grabbed a towel and wrapped it around my waist and stepped out of the shower, leaving the water running, and nodded for him to get in.

"I grabbed a bag of clothes for us from the house and some things I thought Bail—" His voice broke, and he coughed and rubbed his hands down his face as he regained his composure. "Some things I thought she would want when she wakes up."

"That was smart. Thank you." I slid my hand around the back of his head and pulled it toward mine, resting our foreheads together for a moment as we both caught our breath.

"She's going to live. She's going to be fine and so is our baby," I said. I'd been repeating the mantra in my head for the last hour, and saying it out loud felt necessary.

He pulled back and nodded and then clapped my arm as he started taking off his bloody and dirty uniform. I left the bathroom, giving him some time as I got dressed in the clothes he brought me.

I saw the laptop bag from Bailey's office next to the duffle bag and grabbed it.

The cameras were linked to it.

I was getting the program loaded up when he came out dressed and fresh.

"Did you watch it yet?" he asked, sitting next to me on the bed.

"No, just got it pulled up."

My finger hovered over the touchpad as I took a deep breath and looked at him. "Whatever happened to her, she will survive. So we need to watch this and process it and get over it so that we can help her through it when she wakes up."

"I don't know if I'm strong enough to fucking watch it," he whispered. "But I have to at the same time. I have to know what happened."

"I know. It's going to hurt like hell," I said but took a deep breath and pressed the button before I could waste any more time.

The video started this morning, and we fast-forwarded it to the evening, slowing down to watch as the clients and Stephanie left the shop and pressed play on it as Bailey started closing up.

"She was almost out of there," Walker whispered.

She had her purse on her arm and was at the front door when the man appeared. We watched in silence as she chatted with him and then walked him over to the desk as he smiled at her, and she leaned back to laugh at his jokes.

My heart was racing in my chest and my palms were sweating as I looked at the man. "Do you recognize him?" I asked.

"No. I've never seen him before," Walker answered, leaning forward to get a better look.

She caught on that the box wasn't for her after all, and then I watched in horror as the man punched her in the face and knocked her flat onto her back, a scream ripping from her lips.

My fists clenched around the laptop as I watched this man that was twice her size punch and kick and stomp on her tiny body as she huddled into the fetal position and begged for her life and the life of our baby.

As he continued to attack her, she fought back. She punched, kicked, scratched, gouged, begged, ran, and did every single thing she could to get away and stop the attack, but none of it worked.

Walker cursed and covered his mouth, struggling to sit still as the man explained in detail what he was going to do to her and how he'd been paid to do so much worse.

"Who is he talking about?" Walker asked.

"I don't know. Clay is my first bet, but he doesn't have that kind of money, and who the fuck would be the woman that went along with—"

Cold dread spilled down my spine as I realized exactly what woman would have told the hit man that Bailey was fat and ugly and paid him more to kill her painfully.

"Luann," Walker whispered through clenched teeth, and I nodded in agreement.

"Fuck."

The man took a bat and smashed Bailey's leg in, leaving her unable to run away. The scream and cries that ripped from her body as she fought to survive would haunt me for the rest of my life.

He pushed her face against the wall. The camera was across the room so we couldn't see what he was doing, but we could fill in the blanks with his words and her pleas.

He was violating her.

"I'm going to be sick." I cursed but forced myself to watch as he continued to abuse her.

They're going to kill you. They'll find you and kill you in ways that make whatever you do to me look like kid's work.

She was talking about us. Her sweet, pained voice strained against the pain she was in as she told this man that Walker and I would murder him for what he did to her.

And she was right.

It didn't matter if we were deputies of the law or not.

"He tried to kill our wife and our baby," Walker said, his voice full of pure violence and malice, and I nodded my head in agreement.

"And we killed him for it," I added. "Her stomach wasn't moving at all in the ambulance. Baby girl wasn't moving around that I could see from where I sat."

Walker's knuckles cracked as he clenched them so tightly.

"She has to survive. Bailey won't survive if our baby doesn't."

We watched as she fought back again, and something snapped in the man. He slammed her into the wall and wrapped his hands around her throat and choked her. She swung at him and kicked but his arms were longer than hers, and she was helplessly pressed against the wall as her face turned purple and then blue. I felt tears burn the back of my eyes as she started going limp in his arms.

His phone rang and he dropped her to the ground, where she gasped and coughed but didn't move. He looked at the screen and then cursed, saying he was out of time.

I wouldn't have believed it was possible, but it was then that Bailey got fierce.

She ran and made it into the office and slid the desk in front of the door.

He kicked and shoved at the door endlessly, trying to get in, and it gave her the time she needed to call 911 and get us there to save her.

"Clay is a dead man." I locked eyes with my twin and understood exactly what needed to be done.

"We'll make him and Luann pay."

I saved the file and sent off an email to Tom, the sheriff, and then closed the computer, unable to watch Bailey suffer for a second longer.

"We should go to the waiting room in case there's an update," I finally said and stood up.

Walker nodded, grabbed his gear from the bathroom, put it in his bag, and we walked out.

Amy was coming down the hall toward us. "Your parents are here," she said, placing her hand on my arm, leading us toward a private waiting room off of the larger ER one.

Our mom and dads were in the waiting room and as soon as she saw us, Mom started crying and ran toward us. Walker and I stood there and let her hold onto us as she cried for Bailey, but we were unable to offer her much more support at the moment. Both of us were too broken and raw to do anything but hold on.

John pulled her back as she sobbed, and he held on to her while Grant hugged us tightly.

Walker had called Molly on his way to the hospital, and she booked a ticket on the first flight here. She'd be arriving at five in the morning and the sheriff's office had an officer scheduled to pick her up and bring her directly to the hospital.

An hour passed by in a blur. People came to wait with us until the room was overflowing and staff had to move some to another room down the hall. Deputies and townsfolk alike held vigil with us while we waited for any word on Bailey's condition.

And if our daughter had survived the attack.

Our sheriff, Tom, came into the waiting room with a solemn face. A quiet hush fell over the room as everyone waited to hear what he found out.

"No word yet," Walker answered Tom's unspoken question.

Tom nodded and then started with technicalities.

"I need your gun, Finn."

I paused for a moment and couldn't register in my head why he needed my gun. And then it hit me.

Because I had used it to kill her attacker. It was then that I noticed Walker didn't have his service gun in his belt when he showed up either.

I took it off my hip and handed it to him and watched as he cleared it and emptied the magazine into an evidence bag. Seven of my bullets were gone. I'd fired seven times into the fucker as he lunged for Bailey.

"He had a ten-inch hunting knife in his hand when you shot him," Tom said, reading my thoughts as I struggled with it. "If you hadn't shot when you did, he would have plunged it into Bailey a moment later. You saved her life. You both did," he said as he slapped Walker on the shoulder.

My dad laid his hand on my shoulder and offered his silent support to me.

"Any idea who the man and woman in the video are?" Dad asked. We'd filled our parents in on a few pieces of the attack.

Tom shook his head no, and Walker cut in.

"We think it's Clay and Luann."

Mom gasped and held her hand to her chest, and Thea shook her head angrily.

"We can't prove it from the video, but we do have a lead though," Tom answered back.

He took his hat off and held it in front of him as he spoke to Walker and me, family and friends hovering around.

"What is it?" Walker asked.

"We don't know who he is, but according to Thompson's son, the man that attacked Bailey in her shop is the same man that he saw running from the pasture when the fire started. The black truck left on Main Street matches the description too."

The world around me narrowed down to pinpoint vision. "He set the fire to get her alone."

Tom nodded. "But I don't think the Thompson farm was hit randomly. I think there was a vendetta against them as well."

Walker chimed in, "Mabel called out Luann in the middle of her shop, made a big stink about Luann needing to grow up and move on when she started going at Finn in public to make a scene. Mabel hadn't been back to the salon since."

Mom chimed in, "He's right. I spoke with Mabel a few weeks ago and she said that Luann had cornered her after that at a football game about it." She turned to us. "Do you really think Luann and Clay hired someone to kill Bailey and set the Thompson farm on fire to get back at them?"

"I think Clay did, and I'm sure he was able to talk Luann into it if he wanted to. He probably got the money from her in the first place," I added. "Can you look at all of Clay's phone call recordings and see if anything was said about money or anything else related to this?"

Tom nodded. "I've got units inbound to pick up Luann now for questioning, and a judge is issuing a warrant for Clay's logs and visitor records. If there is anything at all connecting either of them to this hit man, they're both going down. They'll turn on each other quick as shit once we throw out what we already know at them. I'm guessing they didn't know about the cameras in the shop. It's not typical around here for a business to use security cameras, and they were also planning on the building burning down and destroying any evidence."

Sharp, shooting pain exploded in my chest at his words. "They planned on destroying any evidence of Bailey." Anger followed the words as I reached up to rub the spot in my chest that ached.

Walker put his hand on my shoulder and squeezed. "Keep your head calm, little brother."

I shook my head but kept my mouth shut. It wasn't every day that he was the one telling me to calm down.

The doors to the room opened and two doctors walked in, looking around the room, with Amy. She led them over to us and I held my breath as I tried to read their faces.

"Finn and Walker, this is Dr. Peters and Dr. Wellington," Amy said, and the two male doctors shook our hands.

Dr. Peters looked around the room and then at us. "Would it be okay with you if we went somewhere more private to have this conversation?"

My heart sank and Walker stopped breathing completely next to me as the doctor looked between us.

"Is she alive?" I asked. I couldn't move from this spot until I knew that much at least.

"She is alive," the doctor confirmed but then stepped back and motioned for the door.

Walker looked at me and then took the lead from the doctors and followed them to a consult room down the hall. Our parents came with us and when the eight of us were in the room, the trauma doctor started the hardest conversation of my life.

"Bailey is alive. We have sedated her for the time being so her body can recover some. Her injuries are extensive, but we are hopeful that in forty-eight hours or so, if everything goes to plan, we can try to lessen the sedation and wake her up if she hasn't already done so on her own. She has a bleed on her brain that we are going to monitor, and the best-case scenario is that it does not get any bigger. If it does, we will need to open up her skull to relieve pressure and fix it." He pulled out his tablet and opened it up to read down the list of more injuries. "She has 3 broken ribs, and her lung is partially collapsed. Her left knee was dislocated, but other than that, it's mostly just contusions and superficial lacerations."

"And our baby?" I asked, forcing my voice to stay strong and even.

He sighed. "Your daughter is alive and well. However, Bailey's blood loss and extensive trauma did cause her to start contracting while we were doing tests, so we called in a high-risk OB to monitor her. She is still contracting but the OB is starting her on a cocktail of medications to try to get them to stop."

"And if they don't?"

He looked between Walker and me. "If the contractions don't stop, Bailey will go into labor and your daughter will be born eight weeks early."

The air was sucked straight out of my lungs, and I fell back into the chair behind me as my head swarmed with all the terrible things that would mean for Bailey and our baby.

Chapter 30 – Walker

"What did you just say?" I asked in a voice I didn't recognize. My mom gasped from behind me, and I felt one of my dads grab my arm as the other one went to Finn.

Dr. Peters looked from Finn to me and back and then adjusted his glasses.

"Don't stress about that just now. There's still a good chance that the OB will be able to get them to stop, and even if she can't, your daughter's heart is strong and there is a good chance of survival with the help of our NICU."

"Chance of survival," I said bitterly.

"Bailey has a very long road to recovery in front of her, and the next 48 hours are the most crucial in that journey. I suggest you two take some time to process everything because she's going to need your support when she wakes up," Dr. Peters said.

"Can we see her?" Finn asked, wiping his face with his hands.

"She's in the ICU, so for tonight, only the two of you will be allowed to stay with her. Amy has arranged for a cot to be placed in her room for you two to sleep on as a favor to the department for all that you do for the community."

The two doctors excused themselves and Amy told us she would give us a few minutes and be back to take us to her.

When the door shut behind them, Finn held his head in his hands.

My parents stayed silent, but my dad Grant grabbed me and hugged me to him, and it wasn't until that moment that I realized I was crying.

I wrapped my arms around his wide torso and held onto him as I broke down in pain for what Bailey survived and the fear of losing our baby.

"We need to get over the shock of all of this and be strong or Bailey will crumble under our fear and worry," Finn said from behind me. I pulled out of my dad's embrace and pulled my little brother into one. We stood there and just absorbed everything for a moment as we tried to accept it.

After we were able to compose ourselves, Amy came back to take us to see Bailey.

Our parents went to the waiting room to pass on the information we'd been given as we went to our girl.

When Amy slid open the glass door to her ICU room, my body seized up painfully as I looked at our tiny, beautiful love lying in the bed, attached to tubes and machines and looking so near death.

She had IV lines in her neck and arms, and I was so scared to touch her for fear of hurting her.

Finn went to one side of her bed and I went to the other, and we both stood there and stared in horror at what our girl had survived.

Finn leaned down, let his lips hover above her ear, and cried as he told her how much we loved her and begged her to fight for us.

I sat down in the chair and picked up her hand in mine softly and kissed it as I prayed for her to wake up.

She had monitors on her belly, and our daughter's strong heartbeat echoed out into the room rhythmically. A nurse came in at one point and offered to mute the noise for us, and I snapped at her and told her not to dare touch it.

I needed to hear it to know she was alive inside of her mama. I had to hear that steady drum to keep me sane or I'd lose all grip on reality as everything else slipped through my fingers.

We sat there all night and long into the morning, even after Molly had gotten into town and come to sit with us. She stayed with us at her daughter's side. She was destroyed by what happened to Bailey, and I could see the age it put on her heart and soul to feel so helpless here while we waited for Bailey's body to have time to heal some.

Jake had been the lead deputy on the arrest of Luann Mathews and when he had interrogated her, she had admitted to giving Clay money to hire the hit man to kill Bailey. She was offering up information on the entire situation in exchange for a deal from the DA. The judge granted access to Clay's phone records and they had identified the man hired as Kent Skellington.

When Jake and Tom came to us with the information early this morning, I felt a sense of relief knowing who had done it and that we'd been right, but grief that all of this was done to our sweet girl because of us wouldn't leave me. The love of my life had been tortured and our baby's life was in peril because a man and woman were mad that they didn't get what they felt they deserved from us.

Finn was handling it far worse than I was, too, because of his involvement with Luann. I saw him withdrawing into himself more and more the longer Bailey lay in this bed, unmoving. He needed her to wake up or he'd never forgive himself. The guilt of it all would eat him alive.

I sat in the chair at the side of her bed, holding her hand, and Finn sat on the cot at the edge of the window as we waited. Molly had gone with Thea for a break to the cafeteria and it was just us, which hadn't happened often over the last eighteen hours.

When I looked over at Finn at one point, he was staring at me in a trance. "What?" I asked, leaning forward to hold Bailey's hand in both of mine and kiss it.

He shook his head and sighed.

"Tell me, man," I said, giving him my full attention.

He watched me with her for a moment as he worked it out in his head and then walked over to sit on the bed next to her other hand where it lay. "What if she never forgives me for my part in this?"

"You didn't have a part in this, Finley," I answered sharply. "You are not to blame for the actions of a couple of whack jobs. If I thought for one second that Luann was capable of this, I would have done something about it myself, but I didn't know either, just like you. All we can do at this point is help her through all of this however she needs."

I watched him try to process it as he leaned down and kissed Bailey's forehead for the hundredth time, but this time, her eyes opened.

"Oh my god." I inhaled and stood up to look directly into her eyes. She looked from Finn to me and back and then down to her belly. Her hand slid from the bed to her baby bump and she delicately touched it.

She looked at me with tears in her eyes, and her grip on my hand was unbelievably tight as I smoothed my other one over her hair, trying to calm her as she started to grasp everything that had happened.

"Shh, baby. You're okay. Everything is okay," Finn said and covered her hand with his on her belly. "She's alive."

She gasped and closed her eyes as she started crying hard, and I pulled her hand to my face for a kiss. "I love you, Bailey. I love you so fucking much," I said, leaning down to kiss her face gently.

Finn was reserved and hung back on the edge of the bed, but she wasn't having that and pulled him down to her and offered her lips to him to kiss gently.

"You—" She started and cleared her throat and then tried again as more tears swam in her eyes. "You killed him?" she asked, looking from Finn to me and back. "He's dead, right?"

"Yes," Finn answered forcefully. "He's dead."

She started sobbing again and we held her as she held her stomach and cried for all the pain she'd been put through.

As the day progressed, her hospital room filled up with visitors and flowers alike. Her doctors kept a close eye on her and her OB monitored our daughter as Bailey's contractions slowed and then stopped as she spent more time awake.

"We need to name her," Bailey said when the room was quiet for a moment, and I looked over at her from my spot in the chair next to her bed. Finn lay in the bed with her, holding her close to him, and she held my gaze. "She needs a name, now. I don't want to wait any longer."

"Okay," I said and leaned forward to hold her hand. I laid my head on the side of her belly to listen to our baby, careful not to push on any of her broken ribs, and looked up at her from my perch. I pretended to be listening to what our daughter was saying and then nodded my head. "She said she wants her name to be Bailey, Junior. Because there's never been anyone better to be named after."

Bailey snorted and then held her side and scowled at me. "We are not naming our daughter something that can be shortened to BJ."

Molly laughed from her seat at the window and my mom agreed vehemently.

Finn was quiet, the same way he had been since we discovered the attack had been orchestrated by Luann and Clay. I looked at him. "What's your vote?"

"Whatever Bailey and you want, I'm fine with," he said and kissed Bail's forehead.

She looked up at him with a scowl, her cute eyebrows knitted in the center, and she looked at me before aiming her attention over to our family in the room. "Will you all give us a minute?" she asked nicely, but I knew exactly what kind of ass whooping was about to ensue when we were alone, and I turned my lips to her belly and stage-whispered to our baby.

"Your daddy is about to get yelled at," I said dramatically and kissed her belly.

Bailey flicked my ear and shot me a smirk before she kicked Finn off the bed so she could look at him as our family left us alone.

"Alright, that's enough," she said, raising the bed to sit taller. "Whatever is going on in your head, you need to spill right now."

Finn dropped her gaze and took a seat at the end of the bed, rubbing his hand over her ankle. We both couldn't stand not touching her since everything happened. "I'm fine."

"Bullshit, Finley Grant Camden. Don't lie to me." Her voice was firm and I sat back in my chair to let her chastise him. He didn't need me in on it, adding to the shame he already felt.

"I'm just dealing with everything, okay?"

"Stop lying to me, Finn!" she said exasperatedly. "You've been beating yourself up since I woke up and now you dare to sit there and say you don't care what we name our daughter? What the fuck is with that?"

She was getting angry, and I turned and watched the monitor on the wall start keying up, indicating her heart rate was rising.

"Bailey, take a deep breath and calm down," I said, and she started to light into me for mothering her, but I pointed to the screen and she saw her numbers rise and she put her hands on her belly instinctively. "Just take a deep breath and have a calm conversation," I tried reasoning with her again.

She looked me square in the eyes and took a few deep breaths and watched the monitor as it slowed back down.

Finn just looked even more guilty as the whole situation got worse.

When she was finally calm again, she took a different tactic and turned to Finn. "You're hurting me."

His eyes widened and his mouth fell open in disbelief, but he didn't say anything.

"You think I can't feel you punishing yourself?" she asked him, tears in her eyes. "Do you think I can't feel that and feel your pain? I can, Finley. I can feel your guilt over dating a psychopath that did this to me, and by doing that, you're physically hurting me."

"I'm not—" he started and then stopped. I watched quietly as I tried to give her support, but I also ached to support him too. I could feel both of their pain and it sucked.

His eyes grew dark and he looked away, but not before I recognized the tears in them.

"Finley, please!" she begged, reached for him, grabbed a fist full of his shirt, and pulled. She had no strength in her tiny body thanks to her injuries, but he came willingly, and she pulled him in until his lips were against hers. He buried his hands in her hair and kissed her back, giving her everything she gave to him. She pulled back and rested her forehead against his. "It is not your fault. And this baby"—she took his hand and put it on her belly—"and I and Walker all deserve for you to believe that and love us the same way you did the other morning before any of this happened. You trying to punish yourself for what you feel responsible for distances you from us. We need you!" she begged again, and he kissed her tears away and held her tight.

"I'm sorry, love. I'm so, so, so, so sorry." He breathed her in, and I watched as our daughter kicked his hand on her belly, and we all let a good-hearted smile and laugh out at her addition to the conversation.

"She's right, Finn. We need you 100%, now more than ever," I added and stood up and walked over to him, pulling him from her arms and hugging him tightly.

He held me back and took a deep breath, trying to let it all melt off his shoulders.

"Our girls are still here. Let's not waste any time at all and give them everything in the world that we can."

He nodded and sat back down on the bed next to Bailey and pulled her back into his embrace. She held her hand out for me and I walked around the bed to her other side.

She tilted her head back and offered her lips to me, and I hungrily kissed them and then just breathed her in. "Let's name our baby," I finally said, pulling away and forcing myself to sit in the chair next to her.

"Okay, I know we had it narrowed down to two names—" She paused and looked at us both. "But I had a sort of dream."

"A dream?" Finn asked.

"The night before the attack, I dreamt of our baby." Her eyes were whimsical, and a small smile kissed her face as she thought about her dream. "She was so beautiful. She was about three at the time and she had dark-brown curly hair and green eyes and your scowl," she said as she reached over and ran her thumb over my forehead between my eyebrows. I laughed at her and kissed her hand. She turned to Finn. "And she had your laugh and overwhelming ability to make everyone she came in contact with happy." She groaned and leaned back as she laughed. "And, oh my god, she had John and Grant wrapped around her tiny little toddler fingers. It was so incredible to see. I heard them call her by her name and I remember being so in awe of it."

She wiped away a tear as she fought to keep her composure. "And I was so scared that I was going to lose her the next day and never get to see who she turns out to be. You guys are going to think I'm crazy when I say this, but when he choked me—" She hiccupped on a sob that tried to rip through her chest, but she just squeezed our hands and pushed on. "Right before everything started going black, I saw my dad."

She took a shuddering breath. "He told me to run. He said I had to get up and try again or I was going to die. And that's why I got up and tried again. I couldn't breathe or move but all of a sudden, I got a jolt of electricity in my spine and took off. And I got to my office because of it. Without him there in that moment, I would have died and so would she."

I slid my hand over her belly and felt our peanut move around under her skin, looking for more room in her cramped confines. "What was her name?"

She smiled and wiped away the tears and looked at us both before she spoke to her belly. "Eloise Jade Camden."

"Jade for your dad, Jed," Finn mused with a look of adoration on his face. He added his hand to Bailey's tummy and Eloise started flipping around even more at the added weight on her. "It's perfect."

"Yeah?" she asked, trying to gauge our reactions.

"I love it," I answered, confirming that our girl finally had a name. "Eloise Jade Camden."

She sighed happily, relieved to have us love the name as much as her and that she was finally able to call our baby something other than a peanut.

"I can't wait to meet her," I mused. "But not for another eight weeks."

She chuckled and added her small hand to her belly with our large ones. "At least!"

"Then we can get started on number two," Finn added and ducked to avoid her swat.

We were all going to be alright.

Epilogue – Bailey

"EJ! Don't you dare—" I yelled out the kitchen window as my three-year-old daredevil daughter jumped off the railing of the deck onto the daybed and into a pile of pillows that suspiciously grunted when she made contact with her knees. "Ooh, that girl!" I groaned and scrubbed the pan in the sink with a bit more vigor.

"I don't have a clue where she gets it from." Warm breath rumbled into my ear as my husband's large body pressed into my back.

"Hmm. No clue at all," I mused.

Finn chuckled into my ear and let his hands slide around my waist and land on my growing belly. "Have I told you yet today how sexy you are when you're growing my babies?" He kissed my neck and licked my sensitive skin. I groaned and laid my head back on his shoulder. "Or how fucking incredible your tits look when your pregnancy hormones make them grow even bigger than normal?" He guided his two large hands up under both breasts, taking the weight of them into his hands and tweaking my nipples between his thumb and finger, making me moan.

I dropped the pan back into the sink and wiped my hands on the towel on the counter as Finn played with my breasts through the thin fabric of my dress. "Yes, that feels so good. I need more."

I begged and ground my ass into his hard-on pressed into me.

Pregnancy hormones had hit me hard again, making me crazy for sex as they did with my pregnancy with Eloise Jade, but this time was even worse. I suspected it was because I was carrying identical twin boys.

Fucking male Camden twins. I hadn't talked to either Walker or Finn for three days after we found out we were having twins, frustrated about how outnumbered I was about to be.

EJ shrieked and peals of laughter carried out into the sunshine as Walker grabbed her from underneath the mountain of pillows and tickled her until she threatened to pee on him.

That's my girl.

"Finn." I gasped as he continued working me over.

"Shh, darling. They'll never know if you're quiet," he purred into my ear.

"I haven't had a single quiet orgasm since the day I met you, Finley Grant." But I bit back a moan as his hands dropped past my pregnant belly and snaked under the hem of my dress and pulled my panties to the side.

"Be a good girl and spread your legs for me," he whispered, and I dutifully opened my thighs for him, and he slid his fingers into my wet body and rolled my clit between his expert fingers.

I moaned and it was loud enough to grab Walker's attention. He sat up off the cushions and looked in through the window, and I winked at him before letting my fingers pull on one of my aching nipples and moaning again.

"Nap time!" he yelled, and Finn laughed into my hair.

Walker grabbed EJ and carried her under his arm like a football, and she giggled and shrieked the whole way into the kitchen and up the stairs to her bedroom, yelling out, "I love you," and, "Goodnight," to her other daddy and me.

"Take me out on the porch or she'll never go to sleep," I begged and turned in Finn's arms.

He picked me up and carried me out onto the porch and laid me down on the bed of pillows and cushions they had left on the day bed, his body on top of mine.

"I love you so much." He worshiped my lips and my neck before dropping down to unbutton the top of my dress and pushing my large breasts out and over the fabric, revealing them to the warm summer air.

He sucked on them and flicked his tongue over one sensitive nipple before moving to the other and back, working me into a frenzy.

"I need more!" I begged, scratching his arms and shoulders as I ripped his T-shirt off over his head.

He had worked himself into a crazed need right along with me, and he was quickly shoving down his shorts and ripping my panties off completely before lining himself up with me and plunging into my body.

"Fuck yes!" I moaned and held on as he wildly fucked me into the cushion.

I heard a car drive down the road on the other side of the full trees and moaned at how amazing it was to be able to have sex on our porch without anyone being able to see us.

"Your pussy is so hot, baby. God, it feels so fucking good." Finn sat up and pushed my thighs wide as he slowed down and pulled his cock out of me and slowly pushed it back in from tip to base over and over again.

"Look at how sexy you are, damn," Walker mused as he walked out onto the porch with a video monitor in his hand. He set the monitor down on the table by the door and stripped his shirt off over his head as he leaned down to slide his tattooed hand around my neck, turning my lips to him and taking what he wanted from me. "You take cock like such a good girl."

"Oh my god." I pulled my lips back, baring my teeth, and bit his lower lip as an orgasm ripped through my body. "Holy—oh yes! Don't stop!" I dug my nails into Finn's stomach as he leaned forward again and picked up his pace and fucked me straight through the orgasm and into a spontaneous second one.

Walker covered my lips with his hand as I lost the ability to keep my voice down when his fingers found my clit and added to the pleasure and torture Finn was already giving to me.

"Fuck!" Finn groaned. "Take it all like a good girl, baby. I never want to pull out of you ever again for the rest of my life." He started fucking like a madman and chased his orgasm before stilling and filling me full with his come. I could feel the hot brand of it on my inner walls as his cock spasmed and jerked wildly inside of me.

When he stilled, Walker helped me sit up and took my spot on the bed, sitting with his back against the wall and shoving his shorts down to bare his sexy cock. I straddled his hips, and he fisted his cock, lined himself up, and thrust up into me without waiting.

Finn's come made the invasion smooth, and I threw my head back and begged for more as my nails dug into Walker's shoulders.

I rode him like a damn cowgirl while he played with my tits and rubbed my clit, forcing orgasms from my body over and over.

Finn knelt next to me, pulled my lips to his, and kissed me so sensually as Walker continued to thrust into me.

"I love you so much," I said to Finn and turned to Walker. "I love you too, so fucking much."

"We love you more." Walker grunted as he sucked on my nipple powerfully, causing me to orgasm so painfully that my back arched, my toes curled, and my legs cramped as he bellowed out into the forest and then stilled, adding to Finn's come deep inside of me with his own.

I fell forward and laid my head on his shoulder as I fought to catch my breath. Finn ran his hands up and down my spine, and Walker kissed my temple as we all came back to earth.

We ended up laid out on the bed, snuggled together in our naked wonder in the warm afternoon sunshine.

Walker slid his hands over my belly affectionately from behind me. "How are my boys?"

"Ornery," I chided, and right on cue, one of them kicked his hand and shoved himself down onto my bladder. I was only 20 weeks pregnant but with twins, it was a totally different ball game. I had no idea how I was going to carry these acrobatic hooligans to term.

"That's how we expect them to be," Finn added, kissing my nose.

"Hmm." I was unable to pretend to be too upset about them. I loved these teeny tiny babies more than my own life already and had since the lines on the pregnancy test had turned pink a few months ago.

I knew our lives were going to change with our second pregnancy, adding to our perfect little family of four, but what a change it was going to be with twin boys running around.

I didn't fear or regret any part of this life for a single second. I was so incredibly blessed to be wife to Walker and Finley Camden and mama to Eloise and soon to be two more.

The silence stretched on around us as I started slipping into a peaceful slumber, when Walker's voice rumbled in my ear from behind me. "So, would now be a good time to tell you that I got EJ a dog for your birthday tomorrow?"

"Walker John, you did not!" I cursed and shoved him backward with my hips, pushing him straight off the side of the bed.

My life was apparently going to get even more hectic. God bless these Camden men.

The End.

Made in the USA
Middletown, DE
17 June 2024